Revive

SARA BROWNE Series Book 2

Tricia T. LaRochelle

FLAMING HEART
PRESS

Manufactured in the United States of America

ISBN: 979-8-9861756-2-1 (ebook)

ISBN: 979-8-9861756-3-8 (print)

Published by Flaming Heart Press, United States of America

Distributed by Ingram Book Group

Cover design by 17 Studio Book Design

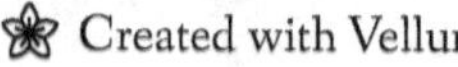 Created with Vellum

What people are saying about the SARA BROWNE Series ...

2022 Incipere Award Honorable Mention for Romance.

LaRochelle keeps a tight rein on her winding plot, and the lengths that her vulnerable but strong heroine goes to in order to leave her traumatic past behind make for satisfyingly moving reading. This is as much a novel of suspense as it's an exploration of grief, trauma, personal choices, and courage in the face of difficulties. A solid sequel with authentic characters and a gratifyingly knotty plot.
 —The Prairies Book Review

Be prepared to consume this book in one sitting – it's a fairly quick read, and fast-moving enough to be difficult to put down.
 —IndieReader

Tricia LaRochelle understands what makes an effective romance story work. She doesn't just offer a girl-meets-boy setup. What she assembles is an interesting pair of characters with flaws that make them distinct, relatable, and utterly human. She handles Sara's traumatic past with sensitivity and keen attention to its emotional and psychological components, which makes Sara a convincing and fascinating case study in PTSD.
 —Readers' Favorite

I love when you are so hooked on a book you can't read it fast enough. I couldn't stop reading this one. It is those intense and emotional moments that have you really connecting to the characters. I loved it and would recommend it. It is an amazing new series that I can't wait to read more.

    —Swoon Worthy Books

This was a fast-paced read with a lot going on. The story was extremely layered, and the characters had great depth. There were several subjects that were handled with great sensitivity. I can't wait to read what will happen next in this amazing new series.

    —Reading in the Red Room

Tricia LaRochelle has established an excellent beginning to this series, which will certainly continue to delve into these deeper mysteries of our hearts and what it takes to heal them.

    —Craig Allen Heath, author of *Where You Will Die*

I dedicate this book to the victims of sexual abuse and the struggles and courage it takes to overcome, and to my friend Shelley and her beautiful son, Ryan, may he Rest In Peace.

Revive

Prologue

Past an oak tree and through the tall grass, a mound of dirt stretched over six feet long. The berm was somewhat old, though a new layer of grass, left behind from the previous summer, now sat brown and dormant for the winter. A few twigs and leaves decorated this earthly blanket, providing an obstacle course for bugs and worms and a perch for the seasonal birds that snacked on them. Snow fell from the sky, lending the berm a new layer of camouflage, especially to one section that had been disturbed to confirm that a backpack —*her* backpack—was still there, precisely where she would remain ... forever.

Chapter One

An ear-piercing scream ...

Someone grabbed my shoulders and shook me, lifting my torso off the mattress.

What is happening?

A voice rang out. "Sara. Wake up!"

I startled as light filtered in through my eyelids. I couldn't fathom where I was or when. Then the nightmare resurfaced. *Oh, God. Is it him?* My mind was locked in another world, one where l was running down hallways, trying to hide, a shadowy figure always close. Too close. Danger lurked around every corner ...

Scott's voice broke through the haze. His hands were warm and embracing, his tone frantic. "Wake up, babe."

I forced my eyes open and focused on the face in front of me. My heart raced, sending perspiration to my chest, my body encased in an uncomfortable sweat. I took a few long blinks, allowing Scott's distressed blue eyes to come into full view. I tried to swallow, but my mouth was beyond parched. That dream—that horrible dream still plagued my mind. Even though I was awake, the trauma still felt very real.

Painted bloodshot red, Scott's eyes were wide with worry, his brow creased. "You were having a bad dream. Are you okay?"

He smoothed my hair back, his breath coming in short pants, like one does when startled awake.

"Was I talking in my sleep?" Then I remembered the scream. *Did that come from me?* My gaze traveled around Scott's fraternity room, orienting myself with the soccer player and sports car posters that decorated his walls, his bookcase full of loose papers and notebooks, his dresser, and his futon. Everything was in its place. Even his PlayStation, which sat atop a beat-up old coffee table, brought me an unexpected feeling of comfort. I wasn't in an old decrepit *dream* house full of cobwebs, mold, and terrifying darkness, and *he* wasn't coming after me. *It wasn't real.* For a moment, I felt like Dorothy in *The Wizard of Oz*—Scott was my Auntie Em—my beacon back to safety.

"You were screaming." Scott slid a hand down his unshaven face.

So it *was* me. My scratchy throat confirmed it.

"It was just a dream. You're okay, now." A lingering doubt played at the edges of his words. He pulled me into his arms and held me there. The stubble growing on his cheeks bristled against my neck as I inhaled a hint of musk that had collected in his soft golden curls from his late-night shower. God, I had missed that smell just as much as I had missed those strong arms that always made me feel so safe.

I glanced at the clock, realizing we had only been asleep for a few hours. The dark circles shadowing Scott's eyes were a testament to that. We had spent most of the night wrapped in each other's arms, fully clothed and grateful. Whenever I dozed off, I'd startle myself awake, fearing he was gone ... again.

Scott pulled away, his gaze roaming over my face. He placed his hands on my upper arms leveling his eyes with mine. "Are you feeling any better?"

I took a moment to appreciate the man in front of me. I never wanted to lose him again.

"Yes, I'm fine." My trembling lip and wavering tone told a different story.

Scott kept his gaze locked on mine for a moment longer. He stroked my cheek with his thumb and then exhaled as though he'd been holding his breath. "I'll get you some water." He swung his feet over the side of the bed and then winced, reminding my tired brain of the knife wound on his side—the injury—a remnant from Scott's altercation with my rapist and the two men Rick brought with him to the water tower. Two nights ago, I almost lost Scott, right along with myself.

"Does it hurt?" I had examined and then re-examined Scott's side so many times I'd lost count. Every time I looked at the droplets of dried blood speckling the bandage or the sutures holding the damaged skin together, I was reminded of how severe the situation had gotten. I held back my tears. I'd done so much crying already. After the rape, I'd fallen to pieces, nearly losing myself entirely. My inner core ordered me to be strong. If not for me, then for Scott.

"I've felt worse. I'm just stiff from sleeping on my side." Scott looked away, his face pale and his mouth crimping downward.

Moving slowly, he walked toward the bathroom, returning a moment later with a small plastic cup in his hands. Inscribed on the cup, the letters "CU"—short for Commonwealth University—sat over an image of two dog paws with the word "Foxhounds" below it, all of it a medley of orange, black, and white to match the school colors. Scott had all sorts of school paraphernalia: pennants, clothing, car window clings, shot glasses—even a keychain. A gifted soccer player for the school, he spent every summer on campus, and they rewarded him with all sorts of stuff.

He lowered himself onto the mattress, making the bedsprings squeak under his sinewy body. "Here you go, babe." He handed me the cup and then ran a warm hand down my back.

I took one small sip and then another. The water helped loosen the clump of anxiety that had gathered in my throat. Unfortunately, it hadn't stopped the nightmarish images that coiled around me like a python.

Just as I was lifting the cup to my mouth for another sip, a loud knock barged through the door like a freight train. My body jolted, causing the cup of water to fly from my grip. I put my hand to my chest to catch my breath while Scott glared at the door.

"*Not*. Now." When his gaze returned to me, his brow relaxed. "Do you have a headache? I've got some pain relievers …"

"No, thanks. The water helped."

Another round of knocking blasted into the room, even louder than the last. My body tensed. I wondered if it was the police, which brought my mind back to something that had happened last night: after Amy, Luke, Jason, and Heather left us at the police precinct—soon after Scott had been released—several cops came storming out the building. I counted three men in uniform and two women. At first, I thought they'd changed their mind and were going to arrest Scott again for beating Rick to a pulp, but then they split off into three cruisers and squealed out of the parking lot.

"What's going on?" I had asked.

From his exhausted six-foot-three tower of a frame, Scott glanced down at me, trying to blink the fatigue away. "I overheard them talking. You remember that girl who went missing last year?" He rubbed my back as he spoke.

I *had* remembered. She was a student who left class one January night, not to be seen again. To this day, they hadn't found her. I also recalled dreading what was coming next. "Did they find her body?" I trembled thinking about this girl lying in a ditch or in some remote location.

Did she have a family?

"Someone found the backpack that they believe she had with her on the night she disappeared. I heard something about a monogram, I think," Scott had said.

My first thought was that Rick must've done it. He was certainly evil enough. Like me, maybe this girl had turned him down, and he was angry about it. But if that were true, then why did he let *me* go? Especially since I could have accused him of rape, which was exactly what I did—though only to his father and only because he was set on keeping Scott behind bars for a very long time. We'd made a deal: I wouldn't accuse Rick, and Senator Sweet wouldn't put Scott in jail for nearly killing his son. *Did they find the girl?*

More knocking persisted, interrupting my thoughts, and causing my heart to leap from my chest.

Scott released a heavy breath, carrying the words, "What the fuck?" on his tongue.

He looked ready to blow. Why wasn't he answering the door? Did *he* know who was behind it?

Before he started shouting, I put my hand over his mouth. "It's okay. I'm fine. You better go see who it is."

Maybe it *was* the police after all. With Rick in the hospital and Rick's father on the warpath, the tide could have turned against us. If Senator Sweet had broken our deal, I would be forced to expose his son for the rapist he was. And I wouldn't stop until—

The next bout of knocking made the door rattle, or maybe that was my nerves. I wanted to scream.

Scott did instead. "Jesus Christ." He flew to his feet. A grimace flitted across his face as he rushed toward the door and swung it open with such force, I expected it to fly from its hinges.

"What?!" With his back to me, Scott stood as tall as a human mountain, his shoulders up around his ears. He could be quite intimidating when he wanted to be.

Curious about who felt the need to nearly break the door down, I leaned to one side to find Christian, the fraternity president standing in the doorway. He was the last person I expected to see. Preppy, clean-cut, and flawless russet skin, Christian wore a gray-and-blue football shirt that hugged his muscular arms and chest. A pair of navy sweatpants stretched across two powerful-looking thighs. If there was a person who seemed to excel at most anything he tried, Scott would say it was Christian. Athletics, academics, he had what Scott referred to as the Midas touch. But Scott didn't play football, he played soccer, so why was Christian here? Was it frat business?

Christian opened his mouth to say something when two more fraternity brothers appeared. After a round of fist pumps and greetings, they stopped to chat.

What was he going to say? By now, everyone in this frat house had to know that their brother, Rick, was in the hospital. It was even on the news.

"Who was screaming?" Christian's voice yanked me back into the moment. The fraternity brothers had gone, leaving him glaring at Scott. "What in the hell is going on?" His eyes narrowing, Christian leaned sideways and peered over at me, the basket case sitting on Scott's bed hugging his blue-and-white-striped comforter for dear life.

Scott glanced over his shoulder; his brow raised. He forced a slight smile and blinked in an "It's okay, babe," sort of way before he turned back to Christian. "It was Sara. She was having a bad dream." His speech was rushed, his posture stiff.

"That must've been quite a dream." Christian's gaze shot back to Scott. "Is she all right?"

I was mortified. How loud did I scream? Once again, my scratchy throat told me the answer.

Scott put his hands on his hips, his shoulders rising and falling with each breath. "Yeah." He exhaled loudly. "It was." The impatience in his tone was hard to miss. Scott grabbed the high end of the door as though preparing to close it. "Look, Christian, this isn't a good—"

"We need to talk." Christian squared his formidable shoulders.

Gripping the door tighter, Scott said, "Can't it wait? I—"

"No." Christian crossed his bulky arms. Being the quarterback for the college football team, he was used to dealing with men who were much taller and bigger than himself. "We need to talk … now." He eyeballed me again. "Are you *sure* you're okay?"

Cringing inwardly, I wondered if he thought Scott was hurting me. Nothing could be further from the truth.

I nodded as definitively as I could while keeping my head attached to my body. "Yes. I'm fine."

Christian lifted his chin toward Scott, his eyes unfriendly. "Jesus, Scott, what the hell is going on with you, dude? I told you that temper of yours was going to get you into trouble." The muscles in his jaw tightened. "I just found out about *Rick*."

Like a lightning bolt, that awful name came crashing through my airspace. I was right, people knew.

"Be in my room in five." The inflection in Christian's voice didn't leave any space for negotiation.

Normally Scott would have protested such a direct order—especially from one of his peers—but given the circumstances, I figured he wasn't in the mood for more fighting. In less than twenty-four hours, he'd battled three men on a hilltop who were set on causing him major harm. Thank God Scott knew how to defend himself. And from what he'd told me, Rick's thugs, who Scott had referred to as "the Sasquatches" given their mangy appearance, didn't need much convincing to flee the scene and leave Rick to deal with Scott by himself.

Scott paused before offering a ghost of a nod. He closed the door and stood with both hands braced against the jamb as though trying to shut out the world. If only that were possible. If only I could erase the last few days. Maybe my life—our lives—could get back to normal.

I knew that wasn't possible, no matter how much I wished it were.

Scott turned to face me. "Sorry about that." He crossed the room, carrying with him a dark and distant look in his eyes. He took the empty cup lying on his bed and walked back into his bathroom. A squeak of the faucet preceded running water. By the time Scott had returned, an assuring smile played on his lips that didn't agree with the wrinkle forged across his forehead or the deep lines fighting for dominance at the corners of his beautiful blue eyes. Nonetheless, he tried.

"Here you go, babe." He perched himself next to me and handed the cup over.

"I'm so sorry, Scott. We should have stayed in my room." I took several small sips, trying to hide my remorse.

Scott tilted his head, his brows pinched. "Sorry? For what? A bad dream?"

"No, for—"

"*That* isn't on you."

"I just don't want to make things harder for you. Eventually, everyone is going to blame *you* for what happened to Rick."

Tightening his lips, Scott shook his head. "I don't care. That piece of shit deserved what he got." He met my gaze and leaned closer, and then, as though he'd been struck by a cattle prod, he pulled away and shifted his body weight. He visibly swallowed, his Adam's apple bobbing up and down.

When I asked if he was okay again, he blamed a muscle spasm this time.

"You should go talk to Christian. He sounded upset." If Scott waited too long, I feared Christian would return. I hated that people would blame Scott for what happened to Rick, but there was nothing I could do about it. I couldn't tell people that Scott was retaliating on my behalf.

I stared down at my cup, picking at some loose plastic fraying the rim, my thoughts heavy, my heart beyond sad.

Scott placed his fingers underneath my chin, lifting my face toward the light in his eyes. "He can wait. I'm more concerned about you."

Staring into Scott's intense eyes, I let the refreshing warm pools of his irises wash over me, wishing I could take a swim in them and never leave.

For a brief time, neither one of us spoke.

Finally, Scott inched closer to me. He reached his hand out to touch the back of my neck, where he massaged the muscles with those strong yet tender fingers of his. I remembered how much I used to love his touch. I wanted to enjoy the gentle massage now, and I tried, but the nightmare brought flashbacks that rattled like thunder throughout my nervous system.

"I'm okay," I said, even though I wasn't.

Needing to do something—anything—I scooted to the edge of his bed and placed my cup on his nightstand. "I may take a shower." As I stood, a dizzy feeling effervesced through my head as if it was made of soda pop and someone had just dropped two ice cubes into it.

Scott rose slowly and approached me, his hand reaching out to take my shoulder. "You haven't gotten much sleep, babe. Why don't you lie back down, and I'll stay with you?" His tone was soothing, serenading my body toward rest. "I'll rub your back until you doze off."

He knew how much I loved that.

I wanted so badly to curl into his arms and fall into a deep slumber, but I couldn't risk the possibility of another nightmare. If it happened again, I wasn't sure I could hold it together. Even in my sleep, Rick was tormenting me.

I shook my head and forced another lie. "No. I've had enough sleep."

Shoulders slumped and eyes puffy and red, Scott exhaled through his nose. He leaned closer and kissed the top of my head through my rumpled and messy hair.

"Are you sure?" He ran his hands through my tangles so softly, I fought the urge to melt into his arms. When my body started to sway, he pulled me closer, wrapping his arms around me, his heart pounding and his hands sliding up and down my back, ready to comfort and soothe.

"I love you so much." It came out in a whisper, the love in his voice unquestionable, like a song that urged my heart to soften and my muscles to unclench.

Relax, I told myself. I was in the arms of the man I loved. My soulmate.

"I love you, too." I sighed and rested my head against his chest while trying to block out a monsoon of uncertainty and fear. My hands seemed to have a mind of their own as they traveled up the sides of Scott's torso. I reacquainted myself with the feel of him, the solidness of his body, and the scent of his musky skin. I thought about his chiseled abdomen, hiding beneath his white T-shirt. Suddenly, images of Scott's naked body danced through my mind. It brought me back to a time when love and sensuality topped my priority list—right up there with water, food, and oxygen.

I was starting to enjoy the sensations embracing my insides when a pair of dark, foreboding eyes flared like a torch inside the cavern of my brain, his voice cruel and unrelenting. "Don't be so dramatic, you may enjoy your-self." *Enjoy myself?* What kind of person could rape someone and expect them to enjoy it? The echo of Rick's voice ordered my organs to constrict like a drill sergeant. *You can't have him. I won't let you.* I tried to force Rick out, but he wouldn't leave. I was remembering too much and it was flooding my brain with distress. I couldn't take much more.

As if he sensed my internal battle, Scott's protective arms formed a cocoon around me.

I wished he could help, but he couldn't. Instead, he made me feel pinned, claustrophobic. The more Scott's hands roamed over my back, the more my body stiffened, my legs pulling together. Could he feel the perspiration seeping through my shirt? I wanted to tell him to stop, but he was trying to comfort me, and I didn't want to worry him—or worse, push him away.

Another horrible image exploded from my brain cells: Rick bearing down on me in a most gruesome way, devouring, feast-ing. *Oh God, make it stop.* While trying not to panic, I did what

I had been trying to avoid, I pushed Scott away as forcefully as I could. It was that or a total meltdown.

Scott's breath caught in his throat, and then he winced.

I looked down and released my grip from his waist—from the bandage—from the wound!

How can I be so careless?

I thrust my hand to my mouth. "I'm so sorry. Did I hurt you?"

Last night, everything felt like it was going to be okay. Scott and I were together again, it was a miracle. Today, however, nothing seemed to be going right.

Scott waved me off, giving his head a subtle shake. "I'm fine, babe." Lips pursed, he softened his expression that had tightened against the pain. "It's just a cut."

Just a cut? I wanted to say. The knife could've killed him had the blade sunk any deeper. I rubbed at my chest trying to loosen a knot of heartburn. If I didn't do something to calm myself down, I was going to be sick or faint.

"I'm gonna go clean up now." Trying not to run, I turned and walked toward his futon, where my overnight bag sat waiting. While Scott followed me visually, I swung the bag over my shoulder and headed for the bathroom.

When I had the doorknob firmly in my grasp, I looked back at him, forcing a smile for support. "Go see Christian. Try to work things out. I'll be here waiting when you get back." *That, I can do.*

With the door closed, I found my way over to the shower, where I rotated the handle to hot. A few minutes later, the room filled with steam. I dropped my bag on the floor, where I pulled out a pair of jeans and a loose full-sleeve T-shirt to wear, along with my undergarments and socks. I laid my clothes out on the edge of the sink, undressed, and stepped into the scalding hot water, which I quickly adjusted. I lowered my head and allowed the water to cascade over my hair and face. The warmth from the water felt amazing. So tranquil. My mind drifted for several minutes from the white noise and the balmy spray, until I eventually reached for the shampoo bottle. My clumsy fingers managed to knock it off its shelf, causing it to plummet to the tub's floor with a thud.

I gulped; grateful the bottle had spared my toes.

A moment later, the door creaked open, and a cold draft entered the room. "Everything all right, babe? I heard a noise." The door opened wider, Scott's silhouette forming on the other side of the flimsy shower curtain. His tone more urgent, the shadow of his hand reached out to me. "Sara, are you okay?"

Not even close.

"Yeah. I dropped the shampoo bottle, that's all." I pulled the edge of the curtain tight against the wall, my teeth clamping down on my lower lip. I didn't want him to see me naked, not after what Rick had done to me. What was worse: I wasn't sure I ever would.

Silence filled the room, along with puffs of steam emanating from the showerhead. For several uncomfortable seconds, Scott stood on one side of the curtain while I stood on the other, water dripping off my nose and chin. We were inches away from each other, yet worlds apart.

"I thought you were going to see Christian?" Self-protection told me to cover my private parts. My heart said otherwise. The rest of me stood frozen, not sure what to do.

"I am, but I ..." His voice was low, more like a murmur. "I just wanted to make sure you were okay."

"I'm fine." The lies were piling. "You better go." I didn't want him to. I put my other hand over my mouth to stop a sob that was rumbling up my throat like a whistling teakettle.

"Okay." After a few moments of silence, Scott's hazy image shrunk and whittled as he drifted out of the room, leaving me with the realization of how damaged I truly was.

Chapter Two

I spent the next several minutes in the shower, where I did a lot of thinking, especially about that dream that continued to batter my mind.

I had read an article once that claimed it wasn't the events in your dreams that was significant, but more the feeling that you experienced *while* you were dreaming. What I remembered most from my recent nightmare was a feeling of vulnerability and helplessness ... and, of course, insurmountable danger. Whatever was about to happen to me in my subconscious was going to happen whether I liked it or not. I couldn't stop it. Not so different from reality.

I still felt dirty. It was as if Rick had tattooed invisible fingerprints onto my skin. My body didn't feel like mine anymore. At times, I wanted to crawl out of it.

I was drugged when Rick had raped me but not enough to spare me the memories. "I only gave you half. I want you to remember this experience," he'd said. Even with half a dose, it took days for the fogginess to subside, the sourness to leave my tongue. All I remembered was sharing a glass of wine with Rick one moment, and the next, I was struggling to hold my head up. I could hardly speak. I was at Rick's mercy, and he had none. Some of the images were so unbearable, I forced them out before they did further damage to my fractured soul. Most of the time, my heart whimpered as it was doing right now. My silent cry. In these moments, I just wanted to be alone, keep the burden away from Scott. I could feel in his heart his longing to make it all go away.

Once I got dressed and brushed my teeth, I pulled out a blow dryer from my bag and tried to tame the knot that had made a nest on the top of my head. I had gone to bed with wet hair—not a good idea when you have long waves like mine. It took so much effort to unsnarl the tangles, I started to sweat from the exertion.

I turned off the blow dryer and opened the door to prompt a burst of cooler air into the room. No movement came from the adjacent room—no Scott. According to the clock on his cable box, I had been in the shower for close to twenty minutes. The meeting had gone longer than I had expected. What was Christian saying to him? Or rather, what was he accusing him of? I imagined Scott sitting in a chair; a spotlight aimed at him—fraternity brothers swarming, all of them devout to their *other* brother, Rick, the guy who paid for their parties and anything else they needed. How much money had Rick and his father put into this fraternity? Or the school, for that matter?

A few minutes later, my periphery picked up movement. I unplugged the blow dryer, set it on the edge of the sink, and rushed in to find out what happened.

"Did it go okay? What did Christian want?" I remained hopeful.

Scott rolled his shoulders back as though trying to release some tension. "Not much. I just need to find another place to live."

"They kicked you out of the fraternity?"

I suddenly felt like one of those wavy inflatable tube men that I'd seen standing outside of a car dealership. Only *my* balloon had just been unplugged.

When he noticed his deflating girlfriend, Scott crossed the room in two long strides. "Look. I'm not worried about it. I didn't want to be in this lame fraternity anymore. Most of the guys here are assholes, anyway. Jason was the only reason I hung around."

Jason was Scott's childhood friend who was more like a brother to him.

It was hard for me to look at him. I didn't want to see his life fall apart. "Yeah, but I thought you liked being here. Did you tell him the truth?" I tugged at a fold of Scott's T-shirt hoping he'd say no but ready to understand if he had.

He rested his hands on my upper arms. "No, I didn't tell him anything. It's none of their business. I'm leaving on my own terms." He maneuvered his head to catch my gaze. "This fraternity was only worth my time when I had nothing else in my life. You're all that matters to me now."

I opened my mouth to speak, but he cut me off.

"Do you think years from now I'm going to look back on my life and wish that I had had another year and a half with my stupid fraternity? No. I won't give a shit. I have more important things to think about."

I gazed up at him, forcing a nod. My logical side knew what had happened to Scott wasn't my fault. I hadn't asked him to find Rick and beat him to within an inch of his life. Scott's impulsive behavior had catapulted him into that situation. It was *his* actions that had almost caused him to spend the better part of his life behind bars, not mine. So why did I still feel so guilty? It took only a second for my heart to answer. As irrational as his actions were—and they were irrational—he did what I wasn't able to do for myself: he made Rick pay for what he had done to me. How many people would go to such lengths for someone they loved?

The ding of a cell phone distracted me.

Our heads turned in the direction of Scott's dresser, where *my* phone sat. I stepped out of Scott's loving hands and grabbed it.

It was a text from Amy: "How are you doing? Are you going to your first class? I'm sure it's fine if you miss another day, but if you are going, want to meet me for breakfast?"

Her text was a stark reminder that it was Wednesday, and the world was still functioning. How was that possible? How did the sun come up this morning? Searching my memory bank for my class schedule, Child Development came to mind, which started at ten o'clock. While I processed that information, the time on my phone flashed eight thirty. If I could muster up the energy, I still had time for breakfast and for class. My stomach rumbled its approval. When had I last eaten? The hollowness in my abdomen said a year ago.

Last night you couldn't have pried Scott and me apart with a crowbar. Today, however, I wondered if a little distance might help us both. All morning I'd been floundering, not sure what to do or say. Plus, it would be good to talk to Amy. I could tell her things I couldn't tell Scott. She didn't need to be shielded. He did.

I typed, "Sure. Give me fifteen minutes, and I'll meet you outside of our dorm."

Scott, hands on his hips, stood there watching me, his brow furrowed.

I set my phone down on his dresser and approached him. "I'm going to meet Amy for breakfast, and then I'm going to class."

It seemed having a goal in mind helped me to focus. Before

Scott could argue the point, which judging by his tight expression he was about to do, I hustled into the bathroom, where I threw on just enough makeup to hide the distress underneath.

When I was finished, I grabbed my overnight bag and then my hair dryer, which I carried back into Scott's room. I set the bag on the futon and then stuffed my hairdryer inside of it.

Scott made a grumbling sound in his throat. "Are you sure you're ready for that? So soon?"

If I was being honest, my answer would be no, absolutely not. I didn't want to be at this school anymore. I'd suffered the worst moments of my life here. If only I could lose myself on some tropical island, where I could meditate to the sounds of the surf—or maybe a mountainous retreat would suit me better, where the birds could sing me back to health and wellness. The one person anchoring me to this purgatory was Scott. I couldn't leave him now. Even if I tried to get away, I knew he would insist on going with me. His academic career would suffer, and his family would want to know why. I thought about his father and how unforgiving Scott had told me he was about Scott's grades. According to Scott, his father was a tough man to please. If Mr. Williams found out what his son had done to a fellow classmate, I wasn't sure what he'd do about it. Not to mention how Abigail would react.

I had to stay, which meant I had to get back into a routine as soon as possible. Either that, or crawl under my bed and stay there—not an option.

"Sara?" Scott's voice sent a zigzag of electricity down my spine.

How long was I gone?

I tried to appear unfazed as I grabbed my backpack off the floor and sifted through the contents. "Well, I've missed two full days already, and I don't want to get too far behind. Three unexcused absences and you're on probation, right?" Without waiting for his reply, I made sure I had the essentials for class: a laptop, a notebook, and plenty of pens and pencils. A laptop charger was crucial since my battery *had* to be dead by now, right along with my optimism.

Scott stood a few feet away, staring. "It depends on the teacher. You have a valid excuse." He clamped his mouth shut and looked away as he rubbed his chin, the chords in his neck protruding.

You have a valid excuse? Did he really just say that?

I gave him a sideways glance, doing my best not to scowl. He knew that I couldn't tell anyone what had happened to me —nor did I want to. Ever. Plus, Scott had his own secrets to keep tucked away in a safe place.

With his cheeks turning pink, he raked a hand through his hair and scratched at his head, his eyes cast downward. "So much has happened over the past few days, and I wonder if ..."

I pulled my backpack zipper closed and then paused to look at him. "What?"

Scott rubbed at his ear next, clearly uncomfortable with his thoughts.

Whatever he was laboring to say, I wasn't sure I wanted to know. I crossed the room to grab my boots by the door. I plunked myself into Scott's desk chair and shoved a foot into each boot with painful precision.

"Well, shouldn't we call Abigail?"

I had just snagged my coat and was shouldering my arms into the sleeves when his question hit my eardrums like a fog horn.

"No!" I practically screamed it at him, and he flinched.

The thought of telling my adopted mother, Abigail, what had happened to me caused that vice to unleash a bucket of acid into my chest. After my parents had died, Abigail was all I had left.

Calm down. He didn't mean any harm. I took a breath. "I mean, not right now." I clutched my backpack and flung it over my shoulder, pulling out a few loose strands of hair from its grip. All I could envision was Abigail jumping into her car and driving here like a madwoman. The ten-hour-plus journey wouldn't deter her, nor would the winter roads. At the age of forty-four she was pregnant with her first child—a girl—my little sister. The last thing I wanted to do was cause her any unnecessary stress or risk. If anything happened to her or that baby ...

While I followed that logic to its end, my feet drifted toward the door.

As though he were standing on a turntable, Scott swiveled his body in my direction. "Wait!"

I peered over my shoulder at his fallen expression.

"I'll go with you." This tower of a man looked so depleted. So drained. If he were a plant, his leaves would be brown and brittle. He needed rest, just like I did. And even though *I* couldn't sleep, I was sure he could, which I used to justify my reason for leaving—to myself, anyway.

"But Amy's waiting." My gaze darted between Scott and the door, when something occurred to me—something we used to do whenever we had to leave each other—*something* that may just ease his mind a bit.

I turned and approached him, stretching up on my tiptoes to give him a kiss goodbye.

At least my lips still work.

He touched my cheeks with delicate fingers, his mouth moving lightly over mine, his breath, sweet and welcoming on my skin. It always amazed me how a man so masculine, so packed with solid muscle, could have such soft lips. When he pulled me closer, my confidence waned, right along with my toes as they lowered to the floor.

Scott cupped his hands around my cheeks, tethering me in place. "Goddamn it, please let me be here for you. You don't have to go through this shit alone." Emotion glistened in his eyes, his voice cracking. "You don't always have to be so strong."

I wanted to laugh. *Strong?* I was anything but. My nervous system rattled like a rickety set of stairs. Scott didn't need to know just how *weak* I really was—how fragile I had become.

Tightening my jaw and swallowing hard, I chose my words carefully. "I know, and I love you for saying that. Maybe getting back into a routine will be good for me ... and for you, too. You should rest. You look exhausted."

That was all I had left. If I didn't leave soon, I was going to fall apart like a house of cards. My foundation was already wavering.

One last glance, and I turned and shot out the door.

Chapter Three

"I'm almost there," I said to Amy before hanging up my cell phone and returning it to my coat pocket.

A cold front had sailed through and the temperatures plummeted. After yesterday's thaw, the variation in temperature amplified the morning's chill as I walked across campus. Virginia winters were like that: warm one day and brutal the next. On top of that, it was snowing. The only thing my brown riding boots were good for was keeping the cold off my shins.

I thought about Rick again. I didn't want to, but the memory of him was involuntary, like a case of hiccups you couldn't rid your body of. If I was able to ask him one question, it would be why? He had privilege and immense opportunities that 99 percent of the population would die for. What made a person who had so much so willing to torment and abuse others?

I may never know the answer to that question, and I guess it didn't matter. It wasn't as if knowing what made an evil person like Rick tick would change anything.

I sighed. Thank God I still had Scott and Amy. At least, he hadn't taken *them* from me.

Wearing her typical black skinny jeans and combat boots, the best friend I had ever known stood waiting in front of our dorm. Spiking in all directions, her short raven hair fought valiantly against the wind, her makeup thick and expressive. If not for Amy, I wouldn't have made it through the past few hours, much less the past few days. She had faith in me when I had lost faith in myself. Grateful didn't begin to cover it.

Her moist breath collided with the cold as she examined her phone at close range. Her smoky eye makeup allowed her eyes, a vibrant shade of green, to pop. She looked like the same old Amy I so loved and adored. My sister.

She glanced up as I approached. "Hey, Al," she said, using the nickname she had branded me with at the beginning of the school year. Amy had nicknames for everyone. Al was short for Alice of *Alice in Wonderland*, a character who was out of her element in the fairy tale—and so was I when I had arrived at this school. As much as I had tried to hide my insecurities and fear back then, she saw right through me. Not to mention, she had my back when I really needed her.

I forced a smile. "Hey. You look rested."

"Yeah, I got a few solid hours of shut-eye." After putting her cell phone in her coat pocket, she gave me an appraising stare. "How about you? Did *you* get any rest?" She cupped her hands around her mouth while blowing warm air on them. "Jesus, could it be any colder?" She stuffed her hands into her faded-green army jacket, which was far too thin for the current temperature. Neither one of us was dressed well.

Once again, Virginia winters.

"I'm okay. And no, I didn't sleep well." I took a step forward, hoping she'd keep pace with me. We needed to move to avoid freezing to death.

As Amy walked alongside me, she closed one eye and fiddled with a piercing in her right eyebrow. I wondered if the cold had made the metal freeze against her skin. She removed it and put it in her front pants pocket. She didn't touch the stud in her nose nor the small ring in her lower lip. Of course, those areas had the benefit of her warm breath. While I thought about that, Amy glanced over as though ready to resume our conversation.

"Well, you've been through a lot ... like a fucking Armageddon." Fog danced around her lips, the color of a black coal, as she spoke.

Although Amy's choice of words always made me cringe, I appreciated her ability to get right to the point.

"I had a horrible dream." The images were still swirling around in my head like a dust devil, dragging my mood down.

"Yeah? Do you want to talk about it?"

My face fell into a frown. "It was awful, Amy. All I remember was running into these strange-looking rooms, trying to find a place to hide. It was like I was in a horror movie." Goose bumps crawled up my already chilled arms. "And then I was trapped inside this wall and you-know-who's fingers were touching me ... all over. They were like tentacles." As I explained the dream, I could almost feel his morbid touch all over again. The revelation made me quiver. "I kept swatting them away, but there were too many of them."

Amy nodded slowly but stayed silent as though waiting to hear more.

"If that wasn't bad enough, then I realized I was naked." I blew out my lips, which were starting to go numb, right along with the rest of my face. "I guess I had been screaming in my sleep, and Scott had to wake me up. His fraternity president heard me out in the hallway and came to our door. That's how loud I was." I shook my head, exasperated. "I think he thought

Scott was hurting me." Tears ran through my nose and mouth. "It was awful."

I looked around at all the students littering the walkways, hoping no one would overhear. Collars up high and with rosy cheeks and noses, everyone walked quickly, not giving us a second glance. I could thank the weather for that.

Amy stopped walking. She put her hand on my arm and pulled me off the path and under a covering by one of the side entrances to a nearby dorm. Swirls of dried snow curled up into the wind leaving coats of white powder against the brick.

"You know, you should talk to someone about all of this. Someone who's trained with—" She paused, her lips pressing into a thin line.

By now I was shivering, but only partly due to the weather. Scott had suggested that I talk to Abigail and now Amy wanted me to speak with a professional? Sharing the absolute worst moments of my life was not high on my list. Where would I start? How could I relive that experience all over again? I wanted to cast those ugly images out of my head forever, not invite them back in.

"I can't. I mean, not right now. I have other things to worry about, first."

Amy leaned in, her brow bearing down. "Like what?" she said in a what-could-possibly-be-more-important sort of way.

"They kicked Scott out of the fraternity." I shook my head and rolled my eyes. "He said he didn't care, but I think he only said that to spare my feelings."

Amy's face paused, her expression hard to read. *Confusion?*

"Now he's got to find new housing. What if his parents find out? You should have seen how angry his fraternity president was. He brought up Rick's injuries as though he knew Scott had caused them. It didn't help matters that Scott punched Rick even before this mess all started before break. What if everyone blames Scott for what happened to Rick? What if the news *really* gets out and then the school does an investigation?" My mind had already left the gate and was racing all over again, the knot in my chest tightening. "Or what if the school contacts his parents?" I braced one hand against the brick wall, trying to stabilize myself from the cataclysm that was playing out in my mind's eye.

Amy's entire face seemed to take one long blink, her mouth forming an "O." When I stopped ranting, she placed her hand on my shoulder. Just as it had been for the past several days, her voice was slow and steady. "Let's take it one step at a time. Colleges don't contact the parents, they contact the students. This isn't high school. Plus, didn't you say that the senator wasn't going to press charges? Don't forget, you have his son by the balls."

I nodded but wasn't entirely sure I agreed with her. Not only had I put my faith in a man who I didn't know, but I had to rely on someone who I knew hated Scott with a vengeance for almost killing his son and in a most brutal way. I could still see Rick's battered face as he lay there on the ground at the water tower. The ghastly thought made my gut wrench.

Amy watched me as though she could hear my thoughts. "Sara. He's not going to change his mind. You can still accuse Rick, and you have the evidence that Derek-the-traitor gave you. You can make life very uncomfortable for the senator and his family. The media would have a field day."

Out of everything she'd just said, three words stuck out to me: *Derek the traitor.*

Coming here from a life on the farm and with very limited means, Derek was my friend before Rick stole him away, and even though I was grateful that he came to his senses and stole some damning evidence from Rick, I hated that he waited so long to tell me what a monster Rick was. The rape had brought

Derek to his senses. Now Derek was back at home, back to his life on the farm, and I was struggling to pick up the pieces of my life.

Amy shuddered. "Come on. Let's make tracks before my fucking ears freeze off my head."

On that, we agreed.

* * *

We continued through the center of campus, our shoulders hunched to combat the cold. The thought of a hot, steaming cup of tea pushed my frozen legs forward. By the time we had reached our destination, my toes were throbbing, and my cheeks chafed.

We pushed through a set of heavy glass doors and into the Student Union Building, where a large crowd had gathered near the entrance. I weaved through several people, most of them too old to be students, intrigued. Was it a study abroad or job fair? Maybe there was a guest speaker. The size of the Student Union Building, with its spacious lobby, three-story atrium, and marbled floors, allowed for many events. I searched for posters that might offer clues but saw none.

Several men and women clad in casual attire stood with large cameras hoisted on their shoulders, their prospective TV news stations scrolled across their equipment. Outfitted in more formal wear and with perfect hair and makeup, reporters were doing sound bites while others touched their ears and mumbled like secret service agents.

The crowd shifted, allowing a platform on the opposite end of the lobby to appear. A wood podium with two microphones sprouting through the top like a water fountain, took center stage. A news conference? About what?

And then it occurred to me. How could I be so dense? I

knew exactly what this news conference was about. Only hours ago, a senator's son had been brutally beaten. All at once, the room spun around me like a cyclone, the words *you're going to lose him again*, whooshing past my ears.

This can't be happening. And then I realized, of course it could.

Chapter Four

I looked over at Amy, squeezing the words from my throat: "This is about Rick, isn't it?"

Amy's head panned back and forth, her gaze scanning the area. "I'll find out." She dashed off.

While she was gone, I stepped away from the crowd until my back slammed hard against a nearby wall. I clenched my fists trying to stay calm. If the story had made the national news, then it was only a matter of time before everyone found out the truth. Or had they found out already? Maybe the cops were searching for Scott right now. I shouldn't have left him. What was I going to do if they threw Scott back in jail? While my intestines twisted into unbearable knots, my pulse battering my heart, Amy emerged from the crowd.

She waved one palm out in front of her. "It's the one-year anniversary of that chick who went missing."

The missing girl. My mind shifted, my entire body taking one long exhale. "I forgot to tell you," I said. "Right after you and Luke left the precinct last night, several cops came running out of the building and drove off. Scott told me he overheard them saying they may have found her backpack." *Could this press conference be good news?*

Just then a reporter within earshot said, "Carrie Stevens," which I correlated with the missing girl's name.

"Do you think they found her?" I asked Amy.

She had taken off her coat and was shaking the snow from it. "I have no idea."

"Do you think Rick had anything to do with her disappearance?"

Amy's expression hardened. "Nothing would surprise me about that asshole. If he did, I hope they nail him for it."

I stretched my body upward to observe a man with short brown hair and a woman with shoulder-length, wavy blonde hair, standing near the podium. Both had small pieces of paper clutched in their palms. *Notes for a speech?* Of average height and build, both the man and the woman wore glasses and looked to be in their mid-to-late forties. Abigail's age. While the woman straightened her gray knit dress, a man wearing a Commonwealth University polo shirt walked behind the podium to place a poster, of generous size, on an easel. As he did so, the man and the woman turned and stared at what appeared to be a high school graduation picture of a girl, who I *assumed*, was their daughter, Carrie. The woman reached over and took the man's hand as they stood in silent vigil.

Carrie's photogenic eyes and bright smile shined back at her parents, like most students ready to venture out into the world. I knew what it felt like to lose your family, and my heart went out to them. The not knowing must be agony. *Do they have other children?*

Interrupting my observations, a frigid gust of winter air rode through the entrance door on the coattails of a tall man with broad shoulders and wide sideburns. A dark leather coat and a pair of tan pants with a brown stripe down the side clothed the formidable-looking man.

I watched as he navigated long strides toward the couple, who turned away from the poster as he drew near. The man spoke to Carrie's parents, shaking both of their hands, and then stood back and dusted the snow from his collar made of sheepskin. As he removed his coat and his broad-brimmed hat, which he draped over a nearby chair, I recognized him right away. Sheriff Murphy's commanding presence was difficult to forget.

The last time I saw the sheriff, I was at the precinct with the senator negotiating Scott's release. It had just happened.

Beneath a pair of bushy eyebrows, Sheriff Murphy examined the crowd with his steely gray eyes. I shrunk against the wall, hoping he wouldn't recognize me. I didn't need the judgment.

A moment later, Carrie's mother stepped up to the podium, positioning herself in full view of the crowd. She cleared her throat, the noise amplified by the intrusive microphones pointed directly at her, waiting to deliver her message. Her verbal prompt caused all the reporters to swarm around her like bees to honey, their attention rapt.

Looking like a pillar of strength, Carrie's father stood next to his wife.

The sheriff positioned himself behind them, his hands to his sides.

"Thank you all for coming." As she blinked in rapid motion, the woman's voice wavered, while the cameras clicked away. "First of all, I'd like to thank my family, my friends, and the public for the outpouring of support my husband and I have received this past year. All your letters and gestures of kindness will not be forgotten. I'd also like to thank law enforcement." She pivoted her body toward the sheriff, fanning one hand out. "And the media for keeping our daughter's disappearance circulating." She put a soft fist to her mouth as though trying to gather strength. "I wish we had better news to report." Carrie's mother sniffed, staring past the crowd in front of her. "The backpack they recently discovered was *not* my daughter's. It was the same color and style of my daughter's backpack, but it wasn't hers." She sighed. "Some say that finding no body and no evidence is good news ..." She stared off, words falling short of her mouth.

That poor woman. She was obviously too upset to speak.

After a few uncomfortable seconds, the sheriff walked up to Carrie's mom and whispered something in her ear, causing her to step back, her husband taking her hand.

"That will be all, folks. We need to give the Stevens family some time to deal with this recent development."

The sheriff's request sparked a cacophony of questions from various reporters, which echoed off the marble walls. They were relentless. To me, it sounded like a flock of geese with their honks, cackles, and clucks.

My stomach rumbled just as Amy tugged on my arm. "Let's go," she said. "I need food *and* lots of caffeine."

* * *

"You good here?" Standing on the third floor of Lexington Hall outside of my Child Development class, Amy looked at me and then back at her cell phone for the fourth time. I knew she was worried about how I would handle myself being on my own. We'd had a quick breakfast, which did wonders for my stomach and my mood. We didn't say much of anything new to each other, which was kind of nice, too. It gave me a short reprieve.

I nodded and waved her away. "I'll be fine. You better get going." I took a step away from her, trying to ease her mind. Somehow, the exchange reminded me of my first official day of grade school when I had to leave my mom. "Just remember that on the first day of school, sweetie, everyone is new. You are not alone." If only Amy would make me homemade chocolate chip cookies at the end of the day as my mom had.

When she hesitated, I looked at the time on my cell phone. "Amy, you're going to be late. Go." I made a shooing motion with my hand.

Amy waited for another second before she spun on her heels and darted off. Her words, "You got this, Al," followed behind her. No chance for freshly baked cookies at the end of the day, but at least I had a friend, one that could move mountains for me if she wanted to.

Al. There was that nickname again. I shook my head. She called her boyfriend, Luke, "Sky" since he reminded her of Luke Skywalker. Even Scott had a nickname: "Big Guy."

Derek was "Shag," short for Shaggy Rogers from Scooby-Doo, which matched his unkempt hair, scruffy beard, and lanky body. That was before Rick had changed him.

Rick had changed all of us.

Enough.

It seemed like a decade ago when my life was filled with eating pizza in my pjs, watching movies, talking about music, boys, and life in general, with Amy. Only a few short months ago, I was consumed with my hotter-than-hot boyfriend. Normal stuff. I hoped that someday we would all get back to laughing again—when our biggest fear would be passing our courses. It seemed I didn't experienced that calm for very long.

A petite girl strode past with two long, blonde braids draping down her back like ropes. I turned and followed her into the lecture hall feeling as though the roof was about to collapse or maybe the ground would open up and swallow me whole. My gaze flitted around the room, catching all the students who were pulling out their laptops or checking their phones. No Rachael, no Mindy or Charlene—three women who had refused to accept my relationship with Scott and who went out of their way to destroy what we had. I hated them all.

From what I could see, it was a regular school day. And to my surprise, no one leapt to their feet and screamed, "It's all her fault! She's the whore who *claimed* she was raped and the reason Rick Sweet was nearly killed."

Amy had told me once that most rape victims blamed themselves. I could see why—it was the shame of it all, the humiliation. I had told Rick on numerous occasions that I only wanted to be friends, and I had thought he had gotten the message—or at least that was what he had told me. He was a liar and a good one.

I sat in the closest seat to the aisle and pulled out my laptop, trying to focus. I'd already missed the first class, so there was no slacking off. Inside of my head, a constant traffic jam of unpleasant thoughts, worries, and fears prevented me from being present no matter where I was.

"Good morning, class," said a heavyset woman with shoulder-length frizzy gray hair. Her colorful boho maxi shirt that reached all the way to her feet, supported by Birkenstock sandals, and her loose-fitted off-white peasant blouse emitted an easygoing vibe. My nose picked up the scent of patchouli in the air.

She clapped her hands together, her smile wide. "Now that we have our introductory class behind us, I hope you're ready to get down to business ..."

* * *

Even though I liked the professor, my Child Development class droned on, as did the class following it: Environmental Science. Because of my absence, both professors had assumed that I had dropped their course. "I was late returning from break due to a family emergency," became my go-to excuse. I had only missed a couple of days, but that didn't stop them from loading me down with work. In all honesty, it provided me with something to think about, other than my pathetic life.

I walked from one building to another, keeping my chin down to protect my neck from the bitter blasts. Had it gotten colder? Passing by the library, I decided to stop and grab a hot tea in the lobby cafe.

Once I had finished paying for my beverage and I could feel my fingers again, I headed toward the exit, spotting a familiar face along the way. Wearing dark-gray coveralls and work boots, a man named Henry was busy mopping up a layer of dirty water, which used to be snow, from the floor tiles. I had met his wife, Ethel, at the hospital yesterday, when I was checking on Scott.

While sitting on a bench outside the hospital, trying to figure out how to prevent Scott from being charged with attempted murder, a volunteer had wheeled Ethel out from the side entrance. Eyes clouded with compassion and cataracts, the silver-haired woman sat next to me while waiting for her husband, Henry, to arrive. Her skin tone sallow, Ethel looked so frail I could almost hear her bones creaking as she moved. No matter, she brimmed with kindness. "Find your strength," she'd told me after I had broken down in front of her, blubbering like an idiot. "It's in you. It's in all of us. Sometimes we just have to delve down deep to find it." She patted my arm while a gentle smile stretched her beautifully wrinkled lips. For a moment, it felt as though a pair of guardian angels had tasked her with delivering that inspirational message: specifically, my parents. She was right. I did find my strength, however temporary.

Before I could thank her properly for her support and wisdom, Henry had arrived in his beat-up old truck. It occurred to me now that I had never even asked her why she was there. *Not cool of me*, I thought, ashamedly.

I glanced over at Henry again. My dad was a custodian at a local Vermont college, giving Henry and me something else in common. *Small world.*

"Hi, Henry," I said walking closer. "I didn't know you worked here."

Henry made one more swipe with his mop, and then he looked up at me. He paused and went back to work muttering, what sounded like, nasty comments under his breath. *Did I get his name wrong? Does he not recognize me?*

I contemplated walking away, but being the doofus that I was, I cleared my throat and tried again. "I don't know if you remember me, but I met Ethel at the hospital yesterday. How is she, by the way?"

That caused a completely different reaction. This time, Henry stood straight as an arrow, his eyes shooting daggers.

I gulped.

"You have a lot of nerve, asking about her." His already red neck and cheeks darkened to a deeper shade, exposing broken capillaries that weaved through his skin like a spider web. The man wasn't well, evident by his coloring and his gnarled fingers that stuffed the mop into the bucket of water with such force it caused some of the murky water to splash out onto the tiled floor. A waft of dirty ashtray floated off his clothing, amplifying his frightening appearance.

What was happening? Knocked off my axis, I jumped to all sorts of conclusions: Did he know about the rape? Was he a friend of Rick's family? Mental fatigue was drumming all sorts of weird scenarios.

"Could I help you with that?" I asked, though I wasn't sure why. Nervous tick, I guess, and I had a lot of those. *Just walk away.*

"I don't need your help. You brats have done enough damage already. Get away from me if you know what's good for you." He bared his teeth, yellow and uneven. "I-said-GIT."

They say that the mind has what's referred to as muscle memory: a mental cognizance that helps people become very good, or at least better, at something through repetition. Runners run farther, swimmers swim faster, weightlifters lift heavier. If that were true, then I had what was called stress memory. And I had gotten good at it. Acidy stomach, tightness in the chest, sweaty palms, and a racing heart, my body knew the drill. If I ever had a real heart attack, I'd be hard-pressed to know the difference.

"Sorry," I said, barely able to squeeze the words from my windpipe.

I was sure Henry didn't hear me, anyway. He was too busy walking away, using his mop like a rudder to steer his rolling bucket.

I felt like a building on the verge of collapse, and Henry was my wrecking ball. One more hit and a full-blown panic attack was imminent.

Chapter Five

"Don't let Henry get to you. He's been going through some tough times."

Tough times? I spun around to find my favorite member of the Commonwealth University staff standing right behind me. My gaze traveled over his standard tweed blazer, corduroy pants, and loafers (no socks) with a feeling of familiarity. The color of Dr. Adams's clothes rarely changed, nor did the style. A lustrous crop of wavy brown hair, shoulder-length, and a full beard framed the welcome sign spread across his face.

His arms loaded down with two good-sized banker boxes; he moved his head to the side as if pointing. "Are you on your way to my class?"

Amy and I had taken Professor Adams's art class last semester and had loved it so much, we signed up for another— 2D Design—my next class of the day. With a slight squint in his eyes and a crooked smile, Dr. Adams always kept our class entertained, reminding me of a younger version of Jeff Bridges.

In fact, *The Big Lebowski* was one of his favorite movies, judging by the quotes he often wrote on his whiteboard at the front of his art room.

Consumed by Henry and his "tough times," I had completely lost track of real time. "Yes. I'm going there now."

"Good. We can walk together." Dr. Adams glanced around the vicinity. "So, where's your other half?"

"Who?" I swiped a hand across my cheek. I glanced at my cell phone, hoping for an encouraging text from Scott but found none. Maybe he did fall asleep after all, but then again, that was hours ago. I tried not to stress about it. He wasn't my keeper, and it wasn't his job to cheer me up, a task that was impossible, anyway.

Dr. Adams cleared his throat. "Um ... Amy?" His tone held a smidge of who-else-would-it-be judgment. I couldn't blame him. Around him, Amy and I were joined at the hip.

"Oh. Yeah." I swallowed a quick sip of tea, hoping to calm my restless stomach. "She's probably just getting out of her last class now. I'm sure she's on her way."

Dr. Adams shifted his entire body, which adjusted the boxes he was carrying. "Well, we'd better get going."

"Let me help you with that." I reached my hands out to take one of the boxes. They looked heavy.

"That's okay. I got it." Dr. Adams made his way toward the door, leaving no room for negotiation. He was a man on a mission.

Outside, the sky was an iron gray, the clouds filled with an arsenal of freezing rain or hail, I wasn't sure which, that poked at my skin like tiny needles. At least the library was halfway across campus, which meant Madison Hall wasn't far off. We continued east past the chapel, our pace accelerating with each step.

Once again, I offered to help Dr. Adams carry his load, but

he refused to let me. If he was trying to be a gentleman, there was no need, I wanted to help. And this *was* the twenty-first century.

Maybe he was old school about that sort of thing.

"Yesterday was so warm. It's hard to believe the weather could change so quickly."

I nodded, my gaze skipping over the heads of students in search of Scott like a small rock on a pond. We'd only been back together for a few hours, and I had no idea what his schedule was. I wondered what it would be like when I saw him again. Would the apprehension I'd been struggling with lift?

As we weaved through hordes of people and I obsessed over Scott, Dr. Adams continued a one-sided conversation. "I should've worn my gloves ... I bet the temperature has dropped forty degrees ... Yesterday, I had my office windows open ... Of course, my office is always too hot ... my heater doesn't work right."

When I grew silent, Dr. Adams released a light cough that sounded more like *ahem*, as if to say, "Hello, anyone home?" Then he asked a real question: "So, are you feeling any better?"

I stared over at him, my mind blank. "Huh?"

"You know, your stomach bug?" The left side of his face crinkled. "Are you feeling any better?"

I was acting like an imbecile.

I took another sip of tea, now tepid, to clear my throat and my thoughts, and then I threw the cup away in a nearby trash can. "Oh. Yeah. I forgot about that." I hadn't missed *all* of my classes thus far. On Monday morning, I had made it to one, and it was Dr. Adams's class. He sent me home when I told him I was sick. A stomach bug was the first thing that came to mind. I was sure I had looked bad enough for it to ring true.

The professor chuckled. "You forgot about your stomach bug?"

His confusion was completely understandable. He must've thought I was nuts. The reason I'd forgotten was because a stomach bug would have been a vast improvement over what I was really dealing with.

"I guess. I've had a lot going on." I swallowed, the understatement sparking through my mind like a plasma ball—the kind at science museums that when touched, would make your hair stand on end. "So why was Henry so upset?" I asked, hoping to shift our conversation in another direction.

"Well, to be honest, I don't really know him all that well. The custodian from my building, Chuck, is good friends with him. What I *do* know is that his wife was the victim of a hit and run a couple of years ago—it happened near campus."

"Oh my gosh, that's awful." I thought about Ethel and how fragile she looked at the hospital.

The professor nodded as best he could around his boxes. "Yeah, well, Henry and his wife live just a couple of miles from here, and I guess they were walking their dog that night. I think Henry had stopped to pick up some trash when his wife was hit by a car—the driver didn't even stop."

Trying to imagine the tragic scene, I wished I had paid closer attention to Ethel when I had the chance. I guess I could forgive Henry for scaring me and being so rude.

"Chuck told me that Henry swore he saw a female student driving the car. He said he saw her campus parking sticker in the rear window—which made sense since we're required to put them there. Henry worked with the police, put up flyers all over campus, and asked around if anyone knew anything about it."

"Did they find the person?" I asked as we met our reflections in front of the glass door to Madison Hall, the home of our next class and every other creative course on campus.

I opened the door, allowing a gust of warm air to blow my hair back from a heater stationed near the entrance. The sudden warmth was welcoming, although it did wiggle the lid on Dr. Adams's highest box, which he held down with his chin.

We continued inside where a small population of students and faculty milled about.

"As far as I know, no arrests were made." The professor's voice rose above the racket of conversations in our vicinity. He greeted a fellow staffer with a half nod. "I guess Henry's wife has had to undergo several surgeries from the accident. If I remember correctly, her kidneys were damaged so badly she had to go through dialysis." He looked over at me. "Like I said, it's been a couple of years, so she might be doing much better now."

What I saw at the hospital told me that Ethel hadn't improved much. She appeared shaky, hunched over, and her coloring was bad—not to mention, her ankles were swollen.

"Unfortunately, the experience seems to have soured Henry's attitude toward college students." Professor Adams smirked in a sympathetic sort of way. "Especially, the ladies."

I nodded, my thoughts absorbed with Ethel and her health issues. Life was a challenge for most, but for others, downright brutal. I hoped Ethel's condition would improve, although, given her age, the odds weren't in her favor.

We crossed a white marbled floor, adorned with an orange-and-black compass rose, also made of marble. The words "Start Your Journey at Commonwealth University" inspired students from its center. We proceeded down a hallway and past several artist nooks that housed small sculptures and artwork tagged by students. No sign of Amy yet. And no text from Scott.

Just as the elevator doors sprang open, a cluster of college students burst forth and scattered in various directions like ants in search of a morsel. That was when the professor turned to face me. "It was nice chatting with you, Sara, but I'm going to take the stairs."

Really? His face was growing visibly red, his knuckles white, and the way he kept adjusting the weight of the boxes he carried, I could tell they were heavy.

I glanced over at the elevator, which sat open. "Wouldn't the elevator be much easier?"

The professor paused. "I'm sure it would, but unfortunately, I've never been good with tight spaces." He smiled in a bashful sort of way. "It's been a problem for me since I was a kid."

I was about to insist on taking one of his boxes, when a sign taped to the door at the stairwell about fifty feet away, warned, "Wet paint. Do not enter. Use stairwell on opposite end of building."

Madison Hall included five stories of classrooms, a dance hall, and a full-scale theater the likes of Broadway. The other end of the building was quite a hike.

"It looks like the stairwell is closed." I pointed. "Do you want to take the other one?" I looked up and down the hallway, wondering which way would be faster and trying to estimate the distance.

Dr. Adams released a deep and measured breath, his boxes shifting with the synchronicity of his lungs. He hesitated for a moment as though weighing his options. "No. If I try to reach the other stairwell, my arms are going to give out." He frowned, something I hadn't seen him do often.

I was relieved he had chosen the easier route, although I wasn't sure he was.

"Here, let me take one of those." I reached my hands out, prepared to *not* take no for an answer.

Finally, he handed over a box as we loaded into the elevator. "Thank you, Sara," he said with a deep sigh.

I was right, the box *was* heavy. Professor Adams was stronger than he looked.

Inside the elevator, the professor took several loud, rhythmic breaths. He was nervous for sure. I was grateful we were the only passengers for this trip. It was also fortunate that our classroom was on the third floor and not the fourth or the fifth. Tension rippled over my teacher's body like a stiff breeze through a field of tall grass. He even smelled stressed, with a pungent odor emanating from his side of our metal transport. I tried not to stare but couldn't help it. He zeroed in on the display as though he was counting the seconds from one floor to the next, which seemed to take forever. In support, I mentally counted with him. It was between the first and the second floor when Dr. Adams's body swayed in place. *Crap.* If he fainted, I wasn't sure what to do. I knew of a few people who were plagued with claustrophobia, and I always pitied them. I had my own issues. Like being in constant fear of getting into an accident, every time I rode in a car.

The number "2" illuminated on the display when the professor's gaze locked on the doors, his breathing shallow.

Trying to appear casual, I glanced over, taking mental notes of his condition, especially the sheen of sweat glossing his brow. No longer red, his cheeks were as pasty as a bowl of oatmeal.

"Are you all right, professor?"

He nodded but in a subtle way. "It's only one more floor, right?" he said as though to convince himself.

I nodded. "Yes. We're almost there."

This was intense.

For the remainder of our ride, Dr. Adams kept his head down, his eyes closed. He tightened his grip on the handles of his box—a bracing mechanism. I could hear him breathe in and then out. He was doing his best to stay calm; I could tell.

All I could think was, *please don't break down*. If that happened, we were screwed.

When the elevator *did* finally stop on the third floor and the doors dinged open, the professor practically knocked over a male student on his way out.

"Jeeeesus." The student said, with a glare as the professor hustled down the hallway.

Poor man. Witnessing this new side of my teacher was just another reminder of life's struggles. In an odd sort of way, it brought me comfort to know that I wasn't the only one plagued by fear.

I walked down a long hallway and around a corner before I entered the art room, where Amy sat staring at her phone at the back of the room. Dr. Adams was hustling off to his private bathroom. I imagined him splashing water on his face, trying to collect himself before class.

I unburdened myself of the heavy box, placing it next to the other one, which sat on the floor by Dr. Adams's desk. Then I hurried over and took the seat next to Amy.

Amy lifted her eyes and smiled. "Hey, Al, how ya doin'?" She placed her cell phone on the table, her voice soft and supportive.

Without sharing my experience about Henry or Dr. Adams's near breakdown, I smiled back. "I'm okay, actually ... and you?"

"You won't believe my luck." Amy didn't waste a minute before unloading about a new professor who had already earned the nickname "She-bitch."

"The first words out of her flapping jaw were 'I like to give pop quizzes.'" Amy said in her snarky voice, "'And if you start asking questions about the reading, it only tells me that you didn't take the time to understand the content or do the exercises.'" She elevated her pitch as she pantomimed her new teacher. "'You are adults now, not teenagers. Whatever cakewalk you had in high school is over.'" She made an angry noise in her throat. "Damn right we're not teenagers. We're adults who are paying *her* salary."

While Amy went on about her strict new teacher, Dr. Adams had materialized and was now busy at the front of the classroom, clearing student artwork from his desk, which he transferred to a nearby cabinet and some adjacent shelves. His coloring was better and his brow, dry. After closing the cabinet, he went to his desk, where he straightened a stack of papers, tapping the side of the pile like a deck of cards.

Still no word from Scott. I was starting to worry.

" ... She includes all her office hours and then tells us that she's rarely ever there. Total bullshit, if you ask me. The school should fire her ass."

I stared at my distraught friend, amused. "You seem to always get the worst professors, Amy."

For the first time in a long time, I actually had something to giggle about.

She exhaled heavily. "Yeah, I've got shit luck." She dropped her forehead on the table. "I'm going to check my course schedule to see if I can switch to another class."

At that moment, a hand placed an assignment sheet on the table in front of me.

I stared up at Dr. Adams as Amy raised her head.

"Sorry, Sara. Didn't mean to put you through all that. And thanks for the help." He grinned, but it didn't coordinate well with his dismal eyes. "Here are the next three assignments. I'll go over them with the class as soon as I have them all handed out."

I glanced at the paperwork, which included some portraits

of famous people, and then up at my teacher. "Okay. And no worries, Professor. I understand. It's totally fine."

Amy's posture straightened, her ears pricked. "What are you talking about? Putting who through what?"

"Oh, nothing," I said with a short wave of my hand. It wasn't my place to say anything.

Amy turned her entire body my way, her brow raised. She hated to be left out of anything. She leaned in, her eyes probing. "What the fuck are you two talking about?" After she waved her fingers inward, in a tell-me-more fashion, she looked at Dr. Adams, who was still standing there.

I cringed inwardly at her choice of words. Dr. Adams was our teacher, and she was using F-bombs? *Geez, Amy.*

He cleared his throat. "I'm a bit claustrophobic, that's all. Poor Sara had to endure a stressful ride up here in the elevator." He moved behind Amy and placed her class assignment in front of her. "You would've known that if you had walked with us to class." He winked. "I missed seeing you at the coffee bar this morning. And you were right about that dark roast." He scrunched his face and subtly wiggled his head. "Nasty. I'll have to bring you some of my special blend to try sometime."

Dr. Adams continued his stroll around the classroom, dropping papers on prospective tables.

"How often do you see Dr. Adams?" I asked.

Amy unzipped her backpack and pulled out a dark-blue folder. "I see him a lot in the morning. We caught an independent movie at the Shenandoah Playhouse the other day."

Now it was my turn to probe. "Wait, what?"

Amy froze and stared me down. "I'm not screwing him, Sara." She gave me a disapproving glare. "Not that I wouldn't consider it ... if I was single, that is. If you get past the dorky clothes, he's not too shabby." She smirked. "Probably not a bad lay."

It appeared that my friend and my professor were ... friends? How was that possible? Everything seemed so bizarro lately. The press conference reminding me about the missing girl, my encounter with the curmudgeon also known as Henry, and my stressful elevator ride with Dr. Adams, made me wonder if I *was* Alice and this *was* my alternate reality.

I looked at my phone again. Why hadn't Scott texted me?

Chapter Six

The rest of my afternoon was uneventful and chilly ... until Scott finally called me back, which warmed my insides like a bowl of hot soup. He said his phone had died and he had to run back to his room to grab his charger.

Given recent events, it was understandable, if not expected.

He insisted I meet him for a late lunch, and I was excited at first, until he admitted he'd be missing a leadership class to make it happen.

"There is no need to miss a class for me. I'm okay. We'll meet up afterward." I kept my voice firm, yet perky, trying to convince him that things weren't as bad as he probably feared they were.

"I just need a minute with you. I want to see for myself." His voice sounded wobbly over the phone, heavy. "When my phone died, I almost skipped all of my classes to wait for you at your dorm."

I'd heard leadership classes were challenging, and he'd already missed one. I was sure *all* his upper-level classes weren't easy. Then there was his father's expectations. I didn't want to be selfish. Just hearing from him was enough for me.

"I'm fine. Stop worrying. I'll come by your room later. All right?"

The phone went silent, then a loud exhale carried his response. "Okay. Promise?"

"Cross my heart." I actually crossed my heart and then rolled my eyes. *What a dork I am.*

After I ended the call, I spent an hour in my room, trying to fall asleep. Every time I'd come close to dozing off, a disturbing image would slap my mind awake like an evil stepmother. To be this tired and not be able to sleep was torture.

Frustrated and getting nowhere, sleep-wise, I gave up and ventured outside to visit the registration office in the Student Union Building. The school had sent me an email with the words "Second Notice" about a pending invoice, so I had to find out what was going on. I'd tried to call them, but it seemed the person I needed to speak with was never available.

Once inside the Student Union Building, I swerved past several students and their trusty backpacks. A group of women were busy setting up tables for a "study abroad" fair. The gift shop was crowded, as usual, with students taking advantage of a recent sale on school apparel (last year's selection). I passed by one of the smaller snack bars where a male student was wiping down tables. Even though Derek didn't work at this particular snack bar—he worked at Campus Creations—it made me think of him anyway. An image of him wiping down tables brought another rush of sadness to my heart. Amy used to pick on him about that funny-looking paper hat which he was required to wear and his thin plastic apron. I could almost see her ripping the hat off his head and wagging it in front of his face, Derek's cheeks the color of a tomato.

I sighed.

With my head hanging low, I visited the registration office next and was able to solve the problem within minutes: I had clicked the wrong screen and funded the wrong account.

* * *

At the end of the day, and at ease knowing Scott was finished with his classes, I changed into a button-down blouse and some jeans and walked across campus toward the Kappa house. My heart was leaping at the chance to see him again, although my pessimistic gut wasn't quite sure *how* to feel. Wild parties, alcohol binges, not to mention, the vulgar language and the putrid smells; the misogynistic environment of the frat house was not a place I had ever enjoyed. Given recent events, I had grown to despise it. Every time I walked beneath those bold Greek letters, I never knew what I would find. Since Scott had been "told" to find another place to live, I hated it even more. *Not much longer.* I'd be rid of the frat house soon.

When I arrived, the crowd was somewhat subdued. Several fraternity brothers were lounging on the sofa and recliners. Some were watching TV while others engaged with their laptops or cell phones. As I strolled past, a few of them looked up and then did a double take. What rumors were circulating? Their brother, Rick Sweet, was in the hospital with serious injuries, and at least one person, Christian, had blamed *my* boyfriend for it. At least, it seemed that way to me.

I proceeded past the tiki bar in the adjacent room, where Rick's ghostly image stood waiting, ready to mix poisonous concoctions for anyone who would consume them. I imagined Rick's sardonic smile, much like the bartender in the movie *The Shining.* As I approached the kitchen, I swore someone mentioned Scott's name. Kevin, Owen and a few other Kappa men turned and stared at me as I entered the room, all of them going mute.

Owen was the only one who acknowledged me. "Oh, hey, Sara."

I offered a half wave as my stride lengthened down the hallway toward Scott's door, which I found cracked open when I got there. I didn't have a key, and he must've remembered.

I took a breath before I went inside, trying to center myself. I thought about our relationship *before* everything fell apart. At the point when we'd started getting all hot and heavy, we had a few pitfalls sexually. He was ready and willing, but I was cautious. Our first big argument was about that very issue. Somehow, we had come full circle. How was sex going to work between us now? He was still ready and willing, and I was ... well, that was the problem—I wasn't sure what I was. As I stood there, my inner critic offered her two cents.

He loves you, you idiot. Stop worrying. Get in there already.

I entered his room and found him sprawled out over his comforter, his breathing deep.

The light from his desk lamp cast eerie shadows over a pile of his things stacked in the corner. My eye caught something, and I gasped. At first glance, it looked like a person, hunched over and creepy. I realized it wasn't. It was just a laundry basket full of clothes, stacked even higher with a rolled-up sleeping bag and a backpack. *Phew.*

I tried to close the door quietly, but these were old doors *and* old hinges, which refused to cooperate.

As the door clicked shut, I held my breath while Scott's eyelids fluttered open. I was sure my gasp at the imaginary *shadow monster* hadn't helped matters. After a couple of loud breaths, he sat up while holding onto his left side and then rubbed his eyes.

"Hey, babe. How did your day go? I need to look at your

schedule," he said as he stretched his arms out over his head, his left side less than the right. "I'd like to get together with you more during the day if I'm not in class. I can walk you to some of your classes, or we can hang out together in between." Scott rose to his feet and released a lengthy yawn. "After my leadership class, I went to your dorm, but no one answered the suite door."

I yawned, too, by contagion. "Oh. That must've been when I went to the Student Union Building to clear something up with Registration. Sorry. How's your side?"

Judging by his droopy eyelids and the near-constant stream of yawns, I wasn't sure the nap had helped much. Sometimes naps worked that way; they could almost make you feel worse. If I had waited longer, maybe he could've slept more. I longed for some rest myself.

"It's fine." Scott remained there blinking softly, and all I wanted to do was run over and wrap my arms around his huggable waist.

I took off my coat and draped it over the back of his desk chair, then sat to remove my boots. While I worked, Scott approached me from behind. He bent down and kissed the top of my head.

"So, how did *your* day go?" He rested his cheek on my head, his breath fluffing my hair.

"Fine." I stood, forcing Scott to lift his head and back away. "Before we talk about anything else, we need to change your bandage." I walked to the bathroom, hoping he'd follow.

A few minutes later, I had patched his wound with some fresh dressing and inspected it thoroughly, all while trying not to salivate over his impressive abdomen. Playing nurse allowed me to touch him, which I enjoyed immensely.

I strolled around his room, not sure what to do with myself.

It was like we had just met all over again and I was in his room for the first time. Yup, I'd come full circle, all right.

"I've got a lot of work to catch up on," I said as I reminisced about making love to Scott not so long ago. It was beyond anything I had ever experienced. What weighed heavily on my heart now was the idea that I may never get to enjoy those feelings again.

Scott ran his fingers through his hair and nodded. "Yeah, me, too." He let his arm fall as though it was too heavy, his hand slapping against his thigh.

He strolled over to his futon, where he sat and patted the seat next to him. "Come sit with me."

I took the seat next to him, pulling my feet up under my butt. I leaned back as Scott scooted forward and turned to face me, his elbows rested on his thighs.

"So how are you *really* doing?" He took my hand and looked deeply into my eyes, his support reaching out with invisible arms.

Staring into those vibrant blue orbs, I tried not to swoon. His thumb caressed the top of my hand, adding to the lure. Something else was happening that I wasn't quite sure about—a spark of arousal flickering in my cells, which was odd, given my circumstance. Scott was unquestionably the most beautiful man I had ever seen. If it were possible, he could make a rock lust after him.

He inched his head closer and spoke softly. "You can tell me anything. Was today rough?" His musky scent had me leaning in for more.

From the moment I'd met him, Scott had always made me feel safe—and understood. I let my mind drink up his kindness and compassion, allowing his sexiness to settle where it chose. The fact that my body was feeling this way was a good sign, right?

"It was fine. I'm just a little tired. It's been a long day," I said. "Nothing bad, just long." I didn't want him to worry, so I decided not to mention Henry.

I imagined any man behaving hostile toward me like Henry had done earlier would cause Scott to go ballistic, to say the least. Given his recent encounter with the law, I wasn't going there.

"Yeah?" He peered even deeper, as if he could see the truth hiding behind my pupils. I feared he would realize how dirty and sleazy I felt for being a part of a sexual encounter that was still threatening to pull me apart, piece by piece.

He lifted his hand to brush a few strands of hair away from my face, and I stopped myself from flinching. As attracted as I was, my body instinctively wanted to self-protect.

"You know how brave you are, don't you?" he said.

Brave? How brave was a person who didn't have the courage to show her gorgeous boyfriend how hot he really was? All I wanted to do was brush my fingers through his caramel hair or caress the sides of his strong jawline.

His torso flexed as he turned toward the corner of his room. "As you can see. I've got some of my things all packed up. I just need to work on my books and clothes."

With his head turned away, I visually took in every inch of his back, his shoulders, and his arms. I wanted to paste my face against his back and listen to the sound of his heartbeat and his lungs. Enjoy the smell of his skin. He was all I ever wanted, and more. All I had to do was allow myself to *feel*.

When I didn't respond, Scott turned to look at me.

I nodded while remembering all the wonderful moments we had shared.

"I may have a new place lined up."

As I watched his soft lips moving, I thought about our first kiss on that beautiful mountain top. He could have had anyone, but Scott loved me. Even after everything I had been through—*we* had been through—those same butterflies were reminding me to live again. Another good sign, and I was taking mental notes.

"That's nice," I said while half-remembering what we were talking about.

Scott sat back and reached his hand out to touch my shoulder. He started rubbing but then stopped, his body frozen in place.

I hated that we felt the need to be so careful with each other.

"It's okay, you can touch me. I won't break." *I may flinch, but I won't break.* I forced a smile.

Scott exhaled, his hand resuming a rather welcoming back rub. "Are you hungry? We can go get a bite somewhere."

The warmth from his fingers worked like magic, softening my tough outer crust. I closed my eyes. I relaxed my muscles. I heard moaning and realized it was coming from me. My legs came out from under me, my head tipping back.

Slowly, Scott repositioned himself, allowing both of his hands full access to the concrete wall that used to be my back.

"What did you say?" His touch felt so good, I could barely focus.

I pried my eyes open to catch the corner of Scott's mouth twitching upward.

"I asked if you were hungry. But that's okay. I'm happy to stay right here." He moved his fingers to my neck and then my head. How I was staying upright was beyond me. Underneath that tough outer crust, my insides flowed like hot lava.

Even my mind took a vacation, traveling to another time and place where Scott's fingers were stroking my breasts, his other hand reaching between my legs. A generous lover, Scott had always excelled at pleasing me. And he took that responsibility seriously. The first time we made love, I almost lost my mind. The memory made blood throb throughout my body, forging a new sense of urgency and sexual thirst.

"Mmmm. Don't stop," I said.

Scott moved closer, his mouth nearing my ear. "I love you so much, babe. I can't tell you how much I've missed you." His breathing heavy, Scott's hands brushed up and down my back in gentle waves

I could feel his need for me, his lips hovering close to my skin. Outside, the world seemed hostile, but not in here. Not with him. The only thing that Scott had ever made me feel was safe, happy, and incredibly horny. Depriving myself from him was like swearing off water. I couldn't live without water, and I couldn't live without him. As long as we had each other, we could fix anything.

I opened my eyes and turned toward him. Enough waiting. My fingers ran through his silky curls, ready to indulge. Was I going to let some psycho decide my fate? I loved Scott, and he loved me. My palms caressed his jaw and his neck. His blond whiskers bristled against the tips of my fingers. Once again, I filled my lungs with his signature scent—my aphrodisiac.

Scott closed his eyes but didn't move, allowing me to explore him without interruption.

Feeling confident, I sent my mouth to graze at the edge of his perfect nose, and then I went for his lips.

Scott wrapped his arms around my body while I savored the taste of his succulent mouth.

I pulled away and appraised him. "Are you sure this won't hurt your side?"

"Are you kidding? Screw my side. I'll live." He pushed his lips back onto mine.

Our tongues explored, hungrily.

My body tingled and then tingled some more. Everything

was working as it should. More importantly, I wasn't freaking out.

I wanted to straddle him, open his pants and feel him inside of me—pulsing as I moved my hips up and down until the top of my head was ready to explode. If only I could forget for just a moment, allow myself to be caught up in that pleasure, something only Scott could give me. I wanted *that* feeling back, and I wanted it from him. His hand grazed over my chest and my nipples hardened, longing for his attention.

He stopped, his head drawing back. "I didn't mean to ..."

"Don't stop." I breathed the words onto his skin, blood and desire moistening my body from within. Only one thing could satisfy me now.

Scott hesitated, his eyes wide and curious, his smile wavering as if not sure what to do.

I needed this—*we* needed this.

"It's okay. I've missed you just as much. *Please* don't stop." I moved my hand to his fly and stroked the bulge that fought to break free.

Scott tilted his head back. "Are you sure?" His voice grew soft and throaty.

After a few seconds, he leaned forward, returning his hand to the back of my head.

I don't need a counselor; I just need to feel again. ... I needed *this*.

He pulled away again, only this time he stared adoringly. "God, I love you. You are the most beautiful human being I've ever known." He captured my lips again, transporting me out of tragedy and into physical attraction and lust.

My breasts flattened against the muscles in his chest, calling out to him. *Touch me, stroke me, bring me back to life.*

"I thought I was going to die without you." He kissed my

cheek as he spoke, his lips waltzing down my neck. "You taste so fucking good."

I found his zipper again and opened his fly. His erection burst forth ready to give me what I wanted.

He moved his hips upward, allowing me to pull his pants lower and then his boxers. I was careful of the wound but determined to get a hold of him, and I was close.

As Scott unbuttoned my blouse, flashes of Rick's face shot through my brain like a bullet.

I jolted but mostly on the inside. *You aren't welcome here. Go away.*

With a new sense of urgency, I yanked on my blouse, the fabric ripping and the buttons popping.

An excited spark captured Scott's beautiful blue irises. He held his side and moved closer, his hands cupping my bra-covered breasts.

"I only gave you half. I want you to remember this experience."

What?! Instinct took over, and I drew back as if Scott had shoved me. "What did you just say?" The contents of my stomach curdled like a carton of spoiled milk.

Scott flinched, his body as stiff as a board. He clutched his side. "I didn't say anything, babe." And then he winced.

Horrible images came at me like a murder of crows ready to peck my brain to death. Rick had taken my mind hostage, and he wasn't letting go. *Please. No more.* The last so-called human who had touched my body was still violating me again and again.

I thought the rape was bad, but somehow, this felt worse. This was the lowest of lows for me.

When Scott reached his hand out to embrace my shoulder, I flew off the futon like a rocket, landing sideways on the floor.

Pain shot through my hip. My back, pierced by the corner of the coffee table, throbbed.

"Are you all right?" Trying to get his pants back up, Scott jumped to my aid, pulling me off the floor and gently guiding me to the futon. Droplets of blood seeped through his shirt, his face pale and strained with pain and alarm.

What have I done?

Scott continued to console me, his hands caressing my arms. "I'm sorry, babe. I didn't mean to ..." Scott grabbed at his side again, making a grunting noise in his throat.

This wasn't *his* fault. He was injured, for God's sake. Yet, I still had an overwhelming urge to hit him. Hit someone.

I'm ruined, Scott. Just leave me alone and find someone else.

"I can't talk right now. I need a minute." I bolted into the bathroom and stood with my face plastered up against the door. What I really wanted to do was disappear ... forever. Needing some form of relief, I bent over the sink and splashed water onto my face, my tattered shirt flapping by my sides. Droplets of water ran down my chest, saturating my bra and adding to the unpleasantness.

A few seconds later, Scott came in the room. He placed a hand on my back, and I wanted to wiggle it away. His touch had become a constant reminder of how damaged I really was.

"I'm sorry, Sara. I ..." He stopped, unable to finish.

I continued to splash water onto my cheeks, hoping to camouflage the tears that stung my eyes. Finally, I couldn't take it anymore.

When I straightened up, Scott had a towel ready, which I used to bury my face in. "It's not your fault. It's me. I'm so sorry. I don't want to put you through this."

Scott bent his head closer to my face. "You have nothing to be sorry for. We were overeager. There is no need to rush things. We love each other, and we have our whole lives to make love. You just need time to heal." When I looked up, he smiled a sad smile. "I may need a few *thousand* cold showers to get me through, but on the bright side, you'll have one clean boyfriend." He touched the side of my head, his smile amazingly still intact. "I'm not going anywhere. I would wait forever for you if I had to."

He felt that way now, but how long would his patience run? Forever was a long time.

It took me years to grapple with the accident that had ripped my parents from my life. The outer wounds had healed, the inner turmoil was still raw. The PTSD. The guilt. The trauma altered who I was and why I had become such a cautious person. What would happen to me now? I wanted to shut down and isolate. That was all I knew. Trying to function and be in a relationship in this condition was an impossible task. It was a bridge too far, and I wasn't sure I could pull it off.

I looked into Scott's soothing eyes and forced a smile. He was everything to me.

For him, I would try.

Chapter Seven

I changed into a school sweatshirt, and then I spent the next several minutes re-bandaging Scott's wound. Luckily the sutures were intact. Only one area had lost some blood, which I cleaned up and taped as best I could. He had a doctor's appointment the next day, which was reassuring.

Scott stood and grabbed our coats. "Let's get you something to eat." He took my hand.

Together, we walked with heavy footsteps toward the cafeteria for some dinner—or maybe it was just my feet that were dragging against the ground like a bag of trash, my limbs weighed down with sorrow and anger. Once we filled our trays, we found a remote table in the back, where I kept my head bowed, too upset to speak or eat.

Sitting right beside me, I could feel Scott watching my every move. "You need to eat, babe," he said several times. He kept moving my tray closer. Pretty soon, it would be on my lap.

I stuffed a few bites of the worst turkey sandwich I had ever eaten into my mouth to satisfy him. Then again, food had lost all flavor. Maybe my tongue didn't work right, either. Maybe Rick's drugs had ruined that, too. Nothing would surprise me.

My inner voice tried her best to comfort me. *It will be okay. It has to be.*

Scott's phone flashed an incoming call on mute. Then a text message caught his attention.

"Who is it?" I asked.

Scott read the small screen. "It's Jason. He said his car broke down, and he's getting it towed to the local dealership. He wants to know if I can pick him up there." Another text message flashed in front of him. "He can't reach Heather. He thinks she's in class."

"That's too bad. You should go. I mean, of course." This new turn of events gave me the possibility of some breathing room. Something I really needed right now.

That was until Scott glanced up from his phone with puppy dog eyes. "Come with me?"

I chewed on my lower lip. *What can I say here?* "Amy sent me a text a little while ago. She said she really needs to talk to me about something." I was lying of course, mainly to avoid hurting Scott's feelings.

Scott raised one eyebrow. "Amy wants to talk to *you?* Are you sure it's not the other way around?" His brow lowered in support of his inquisitive mind.

I stared at my plate, my hands knotted, trying to come up with my next lie. "I think she wants to talk to me about lining up a counselor." I *did* plan to talk to Amy about that very topic. I figured she'd have some good insight.

I also knew Scott would support me on this.

Scott placed his one large hand over my two. "It may not be as bad as you think," he said with a tilt of his head. "Counselors are trained to handle trauma. They know what to do."

As I looked at his supportive face, I wanted—more like

needed to believe him. If anyone could convince me things would be okay, it was Scott. I took out my phone and sent a text to Amy, asking where she was. I hoped she wasn't off campus with Luke or at work. If she were, I'd have to fudge another reason to stay on campus.

"On my way back to school," Amy texted. "Why?"

I explained where I was and asked if she had any plans.

The same question came back: "Why?"

Scott stood and carried his tray, along with mine to the return bin.

"I wondered if you wanted to hang out," I texted back.

Amy returned fire with an all caps "YES." She even offered to meet me outside of the cafeteria. She said she was parking her car nearby. A lucky break.

Scott returned a moment later.

"Amy is coming to meet me." I patted his lower back as he stood next to me. "I'll text you later, okay?"

Scott bent over and kissed me, his face lingering. "Take your time, and good luck." He touched the end of my nose with his finger. "Listen to Amy, she knows what she's talking about. Text me when you want company, okay?"

I nodded.

After he was gone, I packed up the remaining trash from my meal and headed for the door.

* * *

"Thanks for meeting me," I said, as I walked with Amy toward our dorm.

The snow had stopped, and the sky had cleared. It was still chilly out, but somehow a full moon shining above made it feel less so, even though I knew from my Vermonter upbringing that clouds provided a blanket for the winter sky. Cloudy nights meant warmer nights. The air had also calmed, which helped immensely. A few stars even poked out, ready to bedazzle the night sky.

Amy swung her rose quartz keychain from her finger. She always claimed it had healing powers, but I hadn't seen any evidence of it. If I had, I'd own a dozen by now.

"No problem. So why isn't Scott with you? Is he in a night class or something?" Amy applied some lip balm as she spoke.

I could feel my teeth mashing together while I contemplated my answer. "No. I guess I just needed a little time ... alone." I glanced over at her, sheepish. "Things didn't go so well in Scott's room, earlier."

Amy stopped abruptly, her face in full-outrage mode. "Don't tell me he's already tried something with you."

When I nodded, she let out a venomous huff, lifted her hands up around her head, and rolled her eyes. "What an asshole. Doesn't he realize what you've just been through?" She thrust her lip balm into her pants pocket and clenched her fists by her side. For a moment, I thought she was going to hunt Scott down and give him an earful, or worse.

I raised my palm. "No. Wait. I didn't say that right. It's not what you think. Actually, it was *me* who made the first move."

She crossed her arms and stared at me with unwavering resolve, her jaw working the problem back and forth.

I couldn't let Scott take the rap for something *I* had caused. "Just a couple of days ago, we thought we were never going to see each other again, and I guess I just wanted to be close to him. I missed him so much. He's my world, Amy." I crossed my arms, too, casting my own dirty looks. Why did I have to justify myself? Wasn't it bad enough that I couldn't make love to the only man I had ever loved? Scott's words, "We have our whole lives to make love. You just need time to heal," rang in my ears. I hoped and prayed that he was right. This wasn't a sprained ankle or a broken arm—it was much more serious than that—an invisible wound that controlled everything: my heart, my body, my mind.

Amy's brow eased up a bit, her shoulders lowering. "I understand that, Sara, but *he* should have known better. What you've been through." She shook her head and spoke slowly. "This isn't something that's easy to recover from. You need—"

"I know, I know ... time to heal." I said it harshly because that's how I felt: harsh and angry. Not at Amy, at life.

We started walking again while Amy continued to reprimand me—at least that's what it felt like.

"You can't take this lightly. I told you about my aunt who counsels women who have ..."

Just say it, Amy. Women who were raped and ravaged and groped in ways that made them want to rip their skin off.

"This is serious shit, and you need help." She paused as though waiting for me to concede.

Did she actually think I didn't know that? Did she actually think I had forgotten? Every second of every minute, of every hour, of every day—I thought of nothing else. If one more person reminded me of my *situation* ... "I know! It's only been a few days ... I'm still trying to get my head on straight." I was stumbling, tripping over my own words. I knew I needed help, but that first step felt gargantuan.

"Of course you are, but the sooner you get help, the faster you will recover."

Before I had time to stop myself, the words came thundering out. "I get it. Do you think I want to talk to some stranger about what that psycho did to me? Do you have any idea ..." I choked back the screaming that was booming between my ears.

Amy took a step closer. "Sara." She sounded so condescending, and I hated that, too.

"I'm sick of being the girl with all the problems. Why can't I just be—" I shook my head.

"What?" Amy stood rigid, her hands fanning out. "Spit it out."

I stomped my foot. "Why can't I just be normal? Sara the orphan girl. Sara the rape victim. Sara the pathetic loser."

I sped off feeling the anguish rising in my chest. First my parents and now this? Was I destined for a life of suffering? Was I cursed?

"Sara, wait."

Amy's voice didn't stop me. My legs refused to listen.

I just wanted to get away from it all. To run and never stop. As I sprinted toward our dorm, I wondered why Rick had chosen *me* to prey on. Why couldn't he have at least drugged me enough to spare me from these horrible memories? I slapped at my head, trying to knock them out.

"Sara, look out!" Amy's warning came a moment too late.

I slammed into a man who reeked of cigarettes and alcohol. The slippery pathway didn't offer any resistance as the both of us plummeted toward the ground.

"Goddamn it," the stranger said in a gravelly voice.

I practically gasped when I realized it was Henry propping himself up on his elbow, trying to return to his feet. *Oh, great.*

He rose up and brushed the snow from his dark-green work pants, not offering any assistance to me. Although, I felt badly when I noticed his bare hands covered in snow. At least, *I* had gloves on.

"I'm so sorry." I stood and brushed myself off as well, trying to get my bearings. "I wasn't watching where I was going."

"Isn't that typical of you entitled college brats. You never watch where you're going." He flailed a hand. "You just plow on through." His cheeks reddened against the chilled air. "This is the second time you've harassed me." He pointed. "You've been warned."

Amy sprinted up from behind me. "Jesus, have a cow why don't you? It was an accident." She took my arm and turned me toward her. "Are you okay?" She inspected me, her hands brushing the snow off my coat.

I nodded still feeling an unpleasant burning sensation in my spine from the last fall I took in Scott's room. The way my life had been going, maybe a deadly fall was next for me. Would I break my neck?

"None of you spoiled brats ever answer for your actions. And I'm sick of it."

Amy glared as she spun on her heels to face Henry. "What did you say, shithead? Listen, she didn't see you, but maybe you needed a jolt—" Using her knuckles, Amy knocked against her head, "knock some sense into that thick skull of yours."

I grabbed Amy's arm, but she snatched it away.

Henry glowered at her, while I released an exasperated breath.

"Yeah, maybe *you* need some sense knocked back into *your* head." Henry's voice was low and pitted with anger as he pointed his arthritic fist at Amy.

As I watched the heated exchange, my heart threatened to pound through my ribcage.

When Amy took a step forward, I grabbed her arm—hard this time. "Just let it go." I turned to face Henry. "I'm sorry, Henry. I wasn't watching where I was going."

Amy stared at me, her brow reaching toward her hairline. "You know this asshole?"

"Who are you calling asshole?" Henry's rage made me consider Ethel. Was he ever mean to her, too?

Amy pointed. "You—asshole."

My entire body quaked. I tried to speak but my voice came

out weak. "No. She didn't mean that." The acids in my stomach burned, threatening to bubble up and melt my chest and throat.

"The hell I didn't." Amy kept her eyes locked on the old man.

I snapped my head around, sending a muscle spasm all the way into my temples. "What is the matter with you? Why are you making things worse?" The pitch of my voice was alarmingly high. "It wasn't his fault—it was mine." When I turned to face Henry, he was walking away, sputtering under his breath.

"Heading home to beat your wife?" Amy's words brought Henry's work boots to a screeching halt. With shoulders extending toward the sky, he turned around and blasted her with a dark stare that made my stomach lurch again.

My esophagus charred to a crisp, a terrible whooshing noise came rushing through my ears like water through a fire hose. I shut my eyes and covered my ears, trying to stop the internal storm from approaching.

Amy grabbed my shoulders causing me to open my eyes, her face inches away from mine. "You don't look so good."

When I didn't respond, she gave me a slight rattle. "Sara."

My racing heart made it difficult to breathe, much less speak. All I wanted to do was go back to my room, climb into bed, and cover my head with my comforter. "Why couldn't you just leave it alone?" I pushed her hands away and ran as fast as my legs would carry me. When I reached my dorm entrance, I swiped my key card just in time for Amy to catch up.

"Wait a minute." She tried to grab my arm again, but I whipped it away, accidentally slapping her across the cheek.

Unable to deal with the fact that I just hit my best friend in the face, I dashed inside and past the reception counter where a female volunteer's head sprang up, her gaze fixated on Amy and me. Her mouth gaped open in a what's-going-on sort of way.

I didn't care. Nor did I care about the other students who had stopped talking to watch me dash through the lobby, Amy trailing on my heels.

She caught up to me in the stairwell, grabbing me again and pinning me against the cinder block wall. At that same moment, a group of students entered the stairwell from the floor above. As they jogged past us, they gave us double takes before giggling amongst themselves. Once they were safely past, Amy eased up on her grip.

I thought she was going to light into me, but she didn't.

"I'm sorry. He was being so rude to you, and I guess—" She shook her head and spoke in a much lower tone, the frustration easing away. "I'm sick of assholes abusing you." She exhaled and took a step back. "I don't know how you're keeping it together." Her shoulders fell. "If it were me, I'd go fucking nuts."

I laughed without any humor in my voice. "I'm *not* keeping it together ... clearly." I set my backpack down for a moment and grabbed a water bottle to help wash away the remnants from the acid explosion in my throat and chest. The whooshing had subsided, but I was far from well.

"I'm afraid for you. And shit doesn't scare me easily." Amy took several deep breaths. "This kind of stress can break people, and I don't want to lose my friend." She stared down at her feet. When she looked up at me, a faint smile spread across her face. "You may be a dork, but you're *my* dork." She nudged me.

I thought back to when Amy and I had first connected as friends. Even then, she was on my side. I was her dork, and she was my take-no-prisoners friend. We were opposites who balanced each other out.

She blinked. Behind her guarded eyes, spiky black hair, and attitude, the inner Amy emerged. The one who got scared just like the rest of us and the one who had a heart of gold. On impulse, I wrapped my arms around her and held on tight, a gesture I knew she hated, but one I couldn't stop myself from doing. My water bottle crinkled against her back.

To my surprise, Amy hugged me back.

"I know, and I'm sorry. I don't mean to worry you. I'll get help." I pulled back. "I promise." I examined her face for red marks. "Is your cheek okay?"

"What?" And then she registered what I meant. "You didn't hit me *that* hard. No biggie." She waved me off.

Once our firestorm had been extinguished and we could both breathe again, we trudged up the stairs to our suite.

"Let me drop off my crap, and I'll come to your room." Amy keyed her door.

"Sounds good."

Once inside my room, I sat at my desk thinking about what had just happened with Henry. Knowing a man like that wandered the campus gave me the creeps. Both times I encountered him, he acted unhinged. It also brought another subject to mind: Carrie Stevens. Could Henry have something to do with her disappearance?

I pried my laptop from my backpack, powered it up, and typed the words, "Carrie Stevens, Commonwealth University." Within seconds, several article headlines flashed onto the screen along with some random pictures below them. None of the women in the photos looked anything like Carrie, so I clicked on an Instagram link instead, where I found a treasure trove of images. The first thing I noticed was Carrie's short, blue hair and thick makeup. This girl wasn't the all-American-poster girl I had seen at the press conference at the Student Union Building earlier, although there were similarities: her eye color was the same and her facial structure. I scrolled through a picture of Carrie kissing a guy with greasy, long black hair—a wild party exploding in the background. I found another pic of Carrie holding a shot glass in the air, her eyes bloodshot. The last one I saw included Carrie smoking a tightly wrapped cigarette. I peered closer, maybe not a cigarette.

At that moment, Amy entered through the door. When I didn't look up, she stopped short.

"What are you doing?" She leaned over my shoulder.

"That's Carrie Stevens." I glanced at Amy. "She looks much different, doesn't she?"

Amy furrowed her brow. "Who? Oh, you mean the girl who went missing? The one from the press conference?"

I nodded. "Yeah, weird, huh?" I pointed haphazardly over the screen. "It looks like she's changed a lot since her high school graduation photo was taken. She could be your sister, Amy."

"Why, because she dyed her hair and put on some make-up?" Amy shrugged before crossing my room and plopping down on my bed. "She looks better if you ask me."

"Well ... yeah. It's not a bad look. It's just different. Do you think they questioned Henry—you know, when Carrie went missing?" I turned to look at her.

Amy squinted at me. "Who?"

Oh my God, Amy, how could you forget HIM?

I raised both hands in the air, exasperated. "You know. Henry—the man you were just screaming at."

Amy's face opened, showing clarity. She nodded. "Oooooh, you mean, Norman Bates. Yes, I'm sure they did. Why?"

I turned back to my laptop and clicked on one of many articles about Carrie's disappearance. The first story I chose didn't offer anything more than I had already known. Last January, Carrie was leaving her French class, which ended at eight o'clock at night. They never found her belongings, and there were no witnesses who claimed they had seen her—at least not at the time that this article was published. Once I finished reading that story, I moved onto another.

"Sara!"

I put my finger up. "Just give me a sec." I scanned over another story until I found something new. "I guess Carrie had a boyfriend." I kept reading. "It says they questioned him but eventually cleared him of any wrongdoing."

Amy rose from my bed and walked back over to stand next to me.

"It also says Sheriff Murphy led the investigation and ran background checks on all the staff members at the college."

Amy bent down until her face was right next to mine, the scent of sandalwood wafting off her clothes and skin. "What exactly are you looking for?"

"I was just wondering if they questioned Henry."

Amy looked at me, a crooked smile widening her charcoal-colored lips. "You think Norman Bates is the person who kidnapped Carrie?" She covered her mouth with her hand, her eyes sparkling with amusement. "I thought you thought it was Rick."

I cringed at the sound of that name. "I still think it could be, but I also found out a little more about Henry than you know," I said in a defiant voice.

Amy returned to the edge of my bed and sat. "Okay. I'll bite. What are you talking about?" She motioned with her hand for me to continue.

I spun around in my chair. "Well, I met his wife, Ethel, when I was at the hospital the other day. You know, when I was waiting for Scott to be released into police custody." I swallowed, trying to block out another bad memory. "Anyway, she was wheeled out by a volunteer and waited with me until Henry came to pick her up."

"Why was she there? Did Norman Bates beat her up or

something?" Amy continued to grin at me, her feet dangling restlessly over the edge of my bed.

"No, she was hit by a car when she was walking her dog a couple of years ago—right near campus."

Amy jiggled her head while lifting her hands up as if to say *so?*

"I guess she was pretty banged up and had some long-term injuries from the accident. Professor Adams told me about it when we walked to class earlier today. Well, he didn't exactly say she had long-term injuries, I gathered that from the condition she was in."

Amy scrunched her face. "Wait. So, why were you and Professor Adams talking about Norm—I mean this Henry dude?"

"Because I saw Henry working in the library just before that and went over to talk to him."

Amy dropped her head and then looked up at me as if thinking I had lost my mind. "I'm sure that went over well. Why the hell would you say anything to that shriveled-up prick?"

"When I saw him at the hospital, he seemed so loving toward Ethel, so I thought he was a nice old man."

Amy's voice boomed: "Well, you couldn't have been more wrong on that one."

I felt like sinking into my chair and then the earth. "Yeah, I know. I guess I'm not very good at judging people's character, am I?" I ground my teeth as the words seeped through.

"Come on. That's not true." Amy shook her head.

I knew she hated my self-deprecating attitude. I did, too, but I wasn't able to stop myself.

"So, why are you telling me this? We need to talk about other, more important, things." The edge in her voice hinted that her patience was wearing thin.

Little did she know that this topic was much easier for me to discuss. "I forgot to mention that it was a hit and run."

Amy twisted her lips to one side, her eyes starting to roll.

Just give me a minute, Amy. "Professor Adams said that Henry had told the police he swore he saw a woman driving the car with a college parking pass stuck to her back window." I stared back at Amy while expecting a light bulb to go off over her head.

Instead, her eyes went blank.

No light bulb.

"So, what are you getting at?" She fiddled with a stud in her earlobe.

Argh. "What I'm saying is that you need to be careful who you're yelling at, Amy." My motherly tone made me think of Abigail, which I was sure Amy didn't appreciate. "What if Henry thought Carrie Stevens was the girl who hit his wife?"

Amy stood and returned to my desk. She picked up my laptop and examined the screen. "It says here that Carrie was a freshman when she went missing." She looked down at me. "Didn't you say that Henry's wife was hit two years ago?"

I nodded. "That's what Professor Adams had said."

"Okay. I'm gonna check." She set my laptop on the desk, the screen facing her, and then got down on her knees. Using my laptop mouse, she searched for what I assumed was another story about the accident. It didn't take her long to find the article with the information she must've been searching for.

"Here it is." I watched her irises ping-ponging back and forth. "Yeah, it happened a couple of years ago." Amy's gaze slid from the screen over to me. "Carrie wasn't even going to school here when Ethel was hit."

I suspected she was now waiting for *my* light bulb to go off. The one that told me this was ridiculous.

It was starting to work. I thought about all the struggles that

Henry *and* especially Ethel had to deal with. Who was I to accuse him of something so horrible? "I guess I'm letting my imagination go a little wild. Sorry."

Amy slid the laptop toward me. "It's okay. You just need to focus on yourself right now." She stood. "Is Scott coming over here?"

"Yeah, but not until I text him."

Amy placed a hand on her hip. "Do you want to talk about what happened, or are you going to continue stall tactics?"

She knew me so well. I shook my head but knew she wouldn't give up.

"Sara. If you don't open up to someone, you're going to go bonkers." She put a finger gun to her head. "Sorry, but it's the truth."

"Okay, okay." I took a breath. "When I was sitting next to Scott in his room, and he was rubbing my back, I started remembering how good he used to make me feel. I wanted to experience that again." I motioned with my hands. "You know, *really* touch him." I dropped my chin. "I thought it might help." Looking back, it *was* a rash move. What was I thinking?

Amy exhaled through her nose as she loomed over me. "I understand. And sex can be a great way to forget your problems and focus on something else." She scratched her forehead. "The problem is, Sara, sex is what caused the trauma. Sex from a fucking, lowlife, scumbag, pig that doesn't deserve to live." She bared her teeth and then straightened her expression. "I don't mean to keep bringing up my aunt, but you have to redefine what sex means to you. There are steps you can take that will help you dismantle one bad memory while allowing new, fresh memories to take their place."

Who are you, and what have you done with my best friend, Amy?

"That's what I heard my aunt say over the phone to someone once. But what the fuck do I know?"

That explained it.

Fine. You win.

I let the pain in. It coursed through my veins like a bad virus, ready to destroy me whole. "Rick is still with me, everywhere I go. He won't leave me alone. How can I make love to anyone when it all seems so dirty now?" I lowered my forehead onto my desk.

"It's not as bad as you think." Amy sighed and patted my shoulder. "You need someone who's qualified and can help you. There are a lot of women *and* men who have been sexually abused in this world, and I gotta believe they work through it. I think you'd be surprised how many people go through this."

I knew she was right. Although I had to wonder if I could ever look at Scott or sex the same way again. I doubted it. A more disturbing question loitered at the edge of my brain: Did Scott deserve to be shackled to a woman who may never be right in the head? Had he escaped one life sentence for another?

Chapter Eight

I awoke to my second day of second-semester classes. It was Thursday, and the weekend awaited. I was ready for an academic break. Scott had already left this morning. I vaguely remembered the touch of his soft lips against my forehead. His words "Have a good morning, babe," still rolling around in my subconscious.

No nightmares to report, thankfully, and Scott's wound was healing up nicely. We were back to sleeping on a pallet on my dorm room floor. I asked Scott if he minded, and he said it was fine by him. By his quick response and rapid packing, I sensed he was just as eager to be rid of the Kappa house as I was. His musky cologne clung to the pillow next to mine. I leaned over and inhaled, like a coffee connoisseur would do with a can of fresh beans.

Scott hated early-morning classes, although he'd made an exception for one that began at nine. Regardless, it wasn't school that had gotten him out of bed at such an early hour. He had a lead on two apartments in town and didn't want to miss his chance at seeing them before they were gone. From what he'd said, apartments didn't last long, especially those near campus. With the new semester already underway, the pickings were slim. I liked the idea of having a place to "get away." I used to envy Amy for having that luxury with Luke.

I jumped into the shower to get ready for my math class at 9:00 a.m. While I had committed myself to a teaching degree, I wasn't quite sure what subject I wanted to teach, so my guidance counselor had suggested I try a few subjects to see which one I would connect with. My history class from last semester didn't do much for me, nor did Environmental Science from yesterday. My opinion could change on that one. And then there was my next class: Elementary Math. I wasn't optimistic. Math was never my subject. English however, had always intrigued me. Or it did until I took Professor Baker's creative writing class from last term, which also included Mindy and Charlene. So far, I hadn't seen any sign of them around campus. If they did turn up, especially in one of my classes, I had already decided I wouldn't hesitate to drop it. Maybe they left school or dropped out. A girl could dream. I hadn't seen much of the Queen of Hearts, otherwise known as Rachael, either. Man, that girl was mean, unlike Mindy and Charlene who just wanted male attention, especially from Scott. Rachael held grudges.

Move on, Sara, my inner voice ordered.

What I really wanted to do was teach special needs kids like my mom had. My Child Development class was my first step in *that* direction. All bases covered. After my math class, I planned to stop by the counselor's office to sign up to do more tutoring. Maybe they would assign me to Gwen again, the girl I had tutored last semester. Gwen's mother had sent me a card over break, which included a watercolor picture Gwen had painted of the two of us, a heart drawn around it. "Miss you, Miss Sara," it read. I put the picture on my dorm room wall and stared at it often, a smile always lifting my heart. Gwen may have been special needs, but she was leaps and bounds kinder than most of the people I knew.

Once I was out of the shower, I checked my phone and discovered a text from Scott: "Found a place. One-bedroom duplex, utilities included. Not too far off campus."

I texted back: "That's great. I can't wait to see it."

"I paid the deposit and plan to move in this weekend. Wanna help me?"

I grinned. "Of course, silly." Then I noticed the time. "I've got a class at 9. I'll call you when I get out. Love you." It felt so good to say those two words again and equally rewarding to read them in a reply text from Scott. "Love you, too, babe."

After I had blow-dried my hair, I grabbed my favorite camel-colored cashmere sweater and a pair of skinny jeans to wear to class. The sweater was a Christmas gift from Abigail. It always wrapped my body in just the right amount of warmth and softness. I thought of it as my Abigail-hug sweater. As though she could feel me thinking about her, my phone rang, Abigail's name illuminating on the display.

"Hello?"

"Hi, Sara. I haven't heard from you since you've been back. I was worried. How are your classes going?" She paused. "Are you feeling any better about things ... you know, about that Scott person?"

That Scott person? I swallowed a heavy dose of apprehension.

How was I going to deal with this? What could I say to set the record straight? If I told Abigail I was back together with Scott, she'd want to know why. A simple explanation wouldn't do. Not after I had told her during winter break about Scott cheating on me more than once—and how on one occasion, I had seen it with my own eyes. I really made him sound awful, even describing the pictures with Mindy and Charlene. Rick was a magician who flashed his magic wand and made people believe things that weren't true. *Why did I fall for it?*

"Sara? Are you still there?" she asked.

"Yes, sorry. I've got a class in half an hour, and I wanted time to grab a quick bite." I chewed on my lower lip, preparing for my next lie, something I'd been doing a lot lately. "I'm doing well. Sorry I haven't called. You know how it is, I had to get unpacked and catch up with Amy and Der..." *Derek's gone.* Everywhere I ventured—a roadblock. "And I needed supplies for one of my classes. It's just been busy." My pits were sweating, the cashmere more a hindrance than a help. "How are you feeling? Has Mel been kicking a lot? You're almost there, just a few more months."

Abigail giggled over the phone. "Oh yeah. And Mel likes to kick a lot in the night, sending my bladder into spasm. She'll be a night owl, I can see that already. I wake up Joel every time I make my mad dash for the bathroom. Poor man always thinks something's wrong."

Joel grunted an "uh-huh" in the background.

I laughed, too, but in a nervous sort of way. "That's too bad. I hope she lets up on you."

Abigail paused again, and I imagined her face going slack. "I don't want you to worry about things," she said. "I know how you tend to fret."

Fret? She had no idea. I laughed again, only this time to myself.

"If those girls start bothering you again, I want you to tell me about it. What were their names? Mindy and—"

"Charlene and Rachael," I said, helping her finish.

"We can go to the dean if we have to. You shouldn't have to put up with people bullying you, and if that *Scott* tries to contact you, stand your ground. You deserve much better than someone like him."

The defiance in her tone was front and center, and I appreciated her support. I wanted so much to defend Scott and tell her what a hero he truly was—how he was willing to give up his entire future for me—that he never did cheat on me, not once. His heart never faltered. What stopped me was the aftermath of what would happen if I told her the truth—especially about the rape. The woman, who I had adopted as my mother, would be frantic. I had to lie, but only for her safety. If her health suffered, I would never forgive myself. Once Mel was born, I'd come clean about it all. By then, I'd have a better handle on things. *It's only a few months.*

"I know. Listen. Can I call you later? I've really got to run," I said.

"Okay." She exhaled. "I just wanted to make sure you were okay. I love you."

"Love you, too. Oh, and tell baby Mel I love her. Hugs to Joel, too. Bye."

Feeling like a total loser for lying to the woman, who like Amy, had been there for me during some of my darkest days, I threw on my coat, gloves, and boots, grabbed my backpack, and headed outside. The sky was a vibrant shade of blue, a few horsetail clouds whinnying off in the distance. The temperature had improved as well, allowing me to pull off my gloves and stuff them in my backpack.

After my parents died, I had wasted so many years feeling alone and detached from the world around me. I finally realized I wasn't alone at all. I had Abigail. A woman who trudged to The Bauer School for Girls in Pennsylvania every chance she got. And when she wasn't visiting me, she was calling, texting, or sending me care packages. She had done her best to provide the support I needed, and I had to do everything in my power to protect her now. It was a lie of omission, no doubt, but it was necessary.

On my way to math class, I stopped by the cafeteria and bought a breakfast sandwich to eat on the fly. Scott called as I took my last bite and threw the wrapper into a trash can. I stopped for a moment in the courtyard to enjoy the sun beaming down on my face and to listen to what he had to say.

I used my special nickname for him this time. "Hey, handsome. So you found a place. That's awesome."

Scott's tone sprang to life. "Yes! It's only four miles away. It's a two-story duplex. It's old, but it'll work ..." His voice pumped with excitement. "I also found a place that sells used furniture. After my next class, I'm gonna check it out," he said. "The apartment smells like a chain-smoker lived there, and the walls look like they were painted in the seventies, except for a few, but the price is right ..."

When I was younger, there were moments when I could literally feel someone staring at me. It didn't happen often and was mostly due to my parents checking on me. Listening to Scott, a strange sensation crept over me—like a lizard that had crawled under my skin and was darting up my spine—a foreboding, if I could call it that. It couldn't be coming from Rick. He was still in the hospital with his jaw wired shut. So, what was causing this weird sensation now? Were my nerves getting the better of me? Was I getting sick? Or was someone watching me?

"I figured you can help me dress up the place." Scott chuckled. "Give it your womanly touch." There was an urgency in his tone. "Hey, babe, I've gotta run. I'm pulling into the parking lot now and have to grab my stuff for class." I heard shuffling, a plunk, and then, "Shit. Fuck." Scott returned to the phone a moment later. "Sorry, dropped the phone. Okay, love you, bye."

I chuckled. "Love you, too. Bye."

I stuffed my phone in my pocket and surveyed the area for the person who was sending me the heebie-jeebies vibe. No one was paying any attention to me. And I really looked. There was always the possibility that I was losing my mind. Amy had feared this would happen.

A small cluster of tiny birds flew by and landed on the second-floor ledge of the library. Back in Vermont, birds were scarce during the winter months, but not in Virginia. Warm days invited the brave feathered friends to come out and forage for food. As one bird pecked at the library's ledge, a pair of eyes emerged from behind the windowpane. Although the reflection against the glass distorted the clarity of the image, the face was unmistakable. It was Rachael. Reminding me of a ghost haunting her victims from above, she stood there, her eyes unwavering.

I glared back at her, hands clenched into fists.

A staring contest went on for about fifteen seconds before a twisted smile spread across her arrogant face and she stepped out of view. The fact that she had tried so hard to split Scott and me up was apparently not enough for her. She'd lost, and from what I could see, she was still angry about it. Too bad for her. After what I had been through, Rachael, Mindy, and Charlene were no match for the seething anger that smoldered in my veins. The harassing, the lies, the pitting me against Scott. There were moments when I entertained thoughts of confronting them, sometimes knocking out one of their perfect teeth. I'd never been a violent person or impulsive, but when faced with life-or-death situations, people changed, and I had. In their own ways, they had helped Rick nearly destroy me *and* Scott. Forever.

I looked at my cell phone for the time. "Crap." I shook off my anger and sprinted toward class.

* * *

My math teacher gave a pop quiz I was sure I'd failed, which didn't help my sour mood any.

After class, I checked my phone to find another text from Scott: "I'd like to take you to the apartment and see what you think. I can come by your room at 10:45 to pick you up. You should be out by 10:30, right? That's when mine gets out, too."

I typed, "Yes, I'm running to the counselor's office real quick. I want to do another semester of tutoring. I'm hoping they assign me to Gwen again. I'll be there very soon. Hopefully, someone will let you in so you can wait for me in my room."

"10-4," he texted back

After he had gotten locked out yesterday, I gave him a spare key to my room. Even though most of my life was a chaotic nightmare, I enjoyed knowing he had a key to my room just like he had to my heart. Kind of like a class ring, it was a sign that our relationship was getting back on track. Well, spiritually. The physical stuff was on hold, hopefully temporarily.

Not wanting to make him wait, I speed-walked to the counselor's office, where I waited for a pudgy, middle-aged woman with short curly black hair at the reception desk to finish her phone call. She kept adjusting her dark-rimmed glasses as she spoke on the phone. Once she was free, she told me all of the counselors were in a meeting for the next few hours. "You can leave a note in one of their mailboxes if you'd like," she said.

I wrote a quick note to Candice, the counselor who was accountable for Gwen and whom I had worked for last semester, letting her know I was available. I also requested a meeting, writing down my cell number, and then stuffed the note into her mailbox.

As I was walking out, I passed by the bulletin board, where

a flyer for a woman's self-defense class with the heading "Physical Force" caught my attention. I stopped and gave the leaflet a quick perusal, eventually taking one for myself. In the slot next to it sat brochures for a place called the Revive Treatment Center. According to the advertisement, it specialized in trauma, anxiety disorders, depression, grief, and loss. I pinged all five. A picture of a brown-haired woman with a sleek bob stood smiling next to a caption that read, "You are not just a patient here, you are family." I grabbed one of those as well.

Proud of myself for taking a step in the right direction, I gave myself a mental pat on the shoulder, hoping Scott and Amy would be psyched when I told them.

And then I remembered Scott was waiting for me.

I practically ran toward my dorm. The more I thought about this move for Scott, the more I loved it. I also wondered if being away from campus would help relieve some of the awkwardness between us. It was hard for me to let my guard down here. If only I could transfer somewhere … anywhere. I'd already rationalized why that couldn't work, so I let the idea go with so many others that had no way of coming to fruition.

I dashed up the stairs of my dorm and opened the door to the hallway of my suite. A set of voices echoed down the walls —loud, angry voices. As I approached my suite door, I realized who they belonged to.

"What the hell is wrong with you?" Amy said. "Are you trying to push her over the edge?"

My entire body froze, my breathing hitched.

"No. Jesus, Amy. Calm the fuck down!" Scott said. "I would never—"

"Bullshit. You would, and you did. Sara told me what happened." Amy's voice was loud and hostile.

I wished I had never told her. *Crap.*

"Look, I don't have to—"

"No, *you* look," Amy said, cutting Scott off.

I imagined Amy standing there in attack mode. "You have no idea what that sorry excuse for a human being did to her." Her voice bellowed. "She was his play thing for hours. You ever been marathon raped by a sadistic prick?"

How could you, Amy?

Who else could hear her? Were my other suitemates there? I was humiliated. My insides went hollow as if a simple touch could disintegrate me into a pile of dust.

"I know what that piece of garbage did to her. Why do you think I tried to end him?"

End him? I was growing sicker by the minute, the last few days flashing through my mind right along with the struggle to free Scott. I was beyond terrified I'd lose him either by knife wound or by jail sentence.

"Oh, so now you're going to tell me how you defended her honor? I'm calling bullshit on that one, too."

Amy, stop, please. What are you doing?

I had to get in there and fast. I inserted my key and reached for the knob, but it wouldn't turn. Someone was holding it back. Scott?

"Maybe you should have thought about what Sara needed for once. I'll tell you what she didn't need—was you going off half-cocked like some fucking Neanderthal."

No response came from Scott, or nothing that I could hear. I pushed on the knob, but whoever was holding it wasn't budging. "Let me in." My words were lost in Amy's rant behind the door.

"Did you ever think that if you hadn't beat that asshole up, Sara could have pressed charges? No. You only thought about what you wanted—what made *you* feel better."

"All I thought about was ripping that fucker apart." Scott's words sent a tremor throughout my entire body. I felt like a human piñata, their words battering me like a baseball bat.

I braced my hand on the door to stabilize.

"She's just been raped and then she has to save your sorry ass. I had to let that one go for Sara's sake, but I refuse ..." Her voice dripped with emotion. "*Refuse* to let you make her feel any more damaged because she can't fuck your brains out whenever you want it." Amy paused, giving me a chance to be heard.

"Let me in," I said as loud as I could. I jiggled the handle and pounded the door for emphasis.

All at once, Scott opened the door, and I stumbled toward him, his cheeks on fire and his eyes blazing.

He looked at me and then at Amy. "I would never do anything that would hurt her. And accusing me of caring more about myself is over the line, even for you."

My gaze shot to Amy who had cheeks just as red as Scott's, her arms crossed tight over her chest. "Why don't you just jerk yourself off and stop expecting other people to do it for you."

"Amy, that's enough," I said flabbergasted that she was behaving this way. "You have no right to say that to him. And why don't you just broadcast my problems to the campus on a loudspeaker."

Amy uncrossed her arms and made a humph sound. "There's no one here."

What about in the hall?

Scott looked at her and said, "You know what, Amy? One of these days that mouth of yours is going to get you into trouble."

Amy sneered at him. "Yeah? Well, that temper of yours has already gotten you ... and *her* into trouble." She paused and looked at me and then back at Scott. "Excuse me if I don't take advice from a meathead."

With lips mashed together and his eyebrows bearing down like two storm clouds, Scott turned and walked out the door, his fists swinging tight at his sides.

I ran after him. "I'm so sorry, Scott. She's just worried about me. She didn't mean it. "

"The fuck she didn't." Scott stopped and spun around, pointing at the door. "What exactly did you tell her?" He was practically spitting the words at me. "I would *never* push sex on you." His body went rigid, every muscle clenched.

I reached out to touch him, but he moved his arm away. "I know, and I told her that." I stared at him, my heart filled with sorrow. "I love you, and I trust you with my life. I'll speak to her."

It was as if Scott had turned to stone; he didn't even blink. "I'm done with her. I mean it, Sara. You're going to have to choose between her and me." With a blood vessel protruding from his forehead, he stomped his way toward the stairwell.

An ultimatum? Was he serious? I set my jaw. "Amy was out of line, but you have no right to dictate to me who my friends are. You don't have to like her, but you do have to understand that Amy was there for me when no one else was."

Scott stopped, took a breath, and said, "No one else was ...," his voice packed with appalled disappointment.

Oh no. "I didn't mean it that way. Of course, you were there." I was stumbling over my tongue. "I want to go with you." I pulled my backpack off my shoulder. "Can you just wait for me to drop off my stuff?" Once we got out of here, I could talk to him more freely.

Scott paused but only for a millisecond. "I've got some furniture to move. Jason said he'd help me." He pushed the door to the stairwell open, slamming it against the cinder block wall. It sounded like a bomb going off. "We're done talking."

Now we were both lying. Scott didn't have any furniture to

move, not yet, anyway. He just wanted to be away from me—away from Amy.

When I entered the suite, Amy was sitting on the couch. She stood and took a step forward.

"How dare you say that to him? Scott's not the enemy here." I patted my chest for emphasis. "I told you *I* initiated what happened. And he didn't pressure me. He's just as upset about what happened as I am."

She opened her mouth to speak, but I raised my palm, letting her know I didn't want to hear it.

"I told you about what happened because I was hoping you'd understand. I guess no one can really understand, can they?" I glared. "Not even you. I really didn't need this right now, Amy. I'm tired, and I'm going to my room. Don't follow me."

I expected her to say something more, but she didn't. Either she regretted her actions, or she still felt justified. I wasn't sure it would make any difference to Scott, regardless. My best friend and my boyfriend were now enemies.

Things just kept getting better and better.

Chapter Nine

On Saturday morning, I stood in Scott's new duplex, wiping a layer of sweat from my brow. We'd just spent the past couple of hours picking up a rental truck, loading up his things, and then unloading it all into his new place. Jason had already helped with the heavy furniture, and Scott had appointed me with unloading the smaller boxes.

Once Jason was finished, he dashed off to meet his girl-friend, Heather. From the edgy looks that Scott and I kept exchanging, I figured Jason was relieved to be rid of us. I also wondered if Scott had told him what had happened between him and Amy.

I hadn't seen Scott since Thursday, so I was relieved when he had texted and asked me to help. Although, I didn't take it as a good sign when he said he'd meet me in the parking lot. Amy was at Luke's place, so it wouldn't have mattered.

I didn't push it.

I soon discovered that Scott had found some good deals at a place called the Renew Store, sponsored by Habitat for Humanity, which included new and gently used furniture.

They supplied Scott with a floor lamp, a slightly used dinette set for his modest-sized dining room, a dresser, and an area rug, which he used to cover some of the faded and scratched-up imitation parquet flooring in the living room. Scott already had his TV, futon, coffee table, and a bookcase from his room at the Kappa house. He also bought a box of plates, utensils, mugs, and glasses that were a mismatch of styles but were on clearance. He even found a queen-size bed on closeout at a mattress store in town. He'd been busy and, needless to say, we had a lot to unpack.

I took a breath and grabbed a rather heavy box from the stack near the door. "Okay, where does this box go?"

Scott gave me a backhanded wave, his tone clipped. "Just set it anywhere. I'll deal with it later." He didn't even look at the box—or me when he spoke. Instead, he used his knee to finish lining up the sofa with the wall behind it. He'd been dismissing me like that all morning. He scoffed every time I was in his way, which today was often, and even rolled his eyes when I stumbled once, nearly dropping a lamp. (I was a klutz, but I didn't need him to make me feel bad about it.)

"Well, if you know what's in it, I can bring it to the right room." The box was heavy, and I didn't want to lug it upstairs if I didn't need to. Plus, he had numbered each box, so I assumed he had a system. I thought of another idea. "Never mind. I'll just open it. Where are your scissors?"

With rosy cheeks and few patches of sweat stains peeking through his gray T-shirt, Scott turned and let out a huff. "Christ, I don't know." He scowled. "I. Said. I'll check it later." His tone was sharp, his expression like barbed wire. Then a "sheesh" flew from his lips as if to say, "Can you be any more of a pain in the neck."

This was ridiculous. *Why did you even call me?* The temperature shot up my neck like a thermometer in a pot of boiling water. "Fine." I approached the coffee table and let the box drop. The contents rattled, and for a second, I almost hoped that whatever was inside had broken. "Maybe you'd rather do this alone. I have better things to do than put up with your *nasty* attitude." I made quick steps toward the door, grabbing my purse from the floor along the way. Yes, Amy was out of line, but I had enough to contend with right now.

I had just snatched my coat when Scott caught up to me. He hooked my arm, just as I had stepped one foot out the door. A winter blast flew in, soothing my steaming temperament.

"I'm sorry, babe." He tugged me back inside and took one of my hands in his. "I'm just tired. I stayed up way too late getting this stuff all packed up. I really do appreciate you helping me." He looked around the room and then back at me. "It's cool, though, right? We'll get it done ... together." He rested his forehead against mine and stayed there for a moment. The sweat from his brow made for a moist embrace.

I refused to make eye contact. It was a trap, and I was sure he knew it. What woman could refuse *those* eyes? I preferred to stay mad for a bit longer, although I had to remember that Scott had been through a lot as well. Facing a life in prison must've been terrifying. Maybe his nerves were frayed just like mine were—and even Amy's.

"Please, don't be mad at me. I didn't mean to be such a dick." The purr of his voice brought my defenses down.

He pulled away and smirked. "Feel free to smack me if you want to." He tapped his chin with his forefinger. "Give it to me right here."

I fought against a smile, which I assumed was his intention. Darn it. He was so frustrating. I made a fist and pretended like I was going to do it. "I just might."

That was when he grabbed me and hugged me tight. His voice poked fun. "You have my permission. I deserve it."

I closed my eyes and drank in his aura. Even platonically, Scott was the most tantalizing human being I'd ever known. If I had to, I could live on sight and smell alone, although I wasn't sure he could do the same for me.

I pulled my head away and grinned. "Okay, partner, let's get back to work." I slapped his rock of a bicep. "Never mind punching you, if you don't treat your help better, I'll just quit." If I had said those playful words to him months ago, he would have chased me around the apartment, only to whisk me up in his arms and make mad, passionate love to me. I thought of our escapade in the old, abandoned house last fall—the one that hosted the Halloween party. The thought of what we did together brought a wave of moisture between my legs. Although, the feeling didn't last long, thanks to Rick who was always there to ruin my life.

Discouraged, I went back to work.

* * *

The next day, I offered to get breakfast from a place in town that made the best egg sandwiches on onion bagels I'd ever tasted. Barely awake, Scott just nodded and closed his eyes again, his head dropping back onto the pillow like it was dead weight.

I stopped in Charlottesville and picked up some groceries along the way. The apartment was still in shambles, but it was starting to take form. I thought I'd make dinner for Scott and spent the early morning dreaming up a recipe in my head. My favorite dish was lasagna, so that would be on the menu for this evening. I grabbed the pasta, the various cheeses, the sauce, a loaf of garlic bread, and the mixings for a salad. The grocery store in town was more like a small mall, with a huge prepared food section and even a home essentials department. Scott had the basics, but what he lacked was a lasagna pan, which I grabbed, a pot for boiling pasta and heating up the sauce, and some mixing bowls. I also grabbed a cookie sheet, a colander, and parchment paper for the bread. Walking up and down the aisles, I found dried garlic, onion powder, and basil to enhance the sauce. With napkins, paper towels, laundry detergent, cleaning supplies, and a cart full of other stuff, I made my way to the checkout line. I had often envisioned what it would be like living with Scott, cuddling on the couch, enjoying late mornings in bed. Somehow the reality didn't quite match the dream. Baby steps. *We'll get there.*

My car loaded down with bags, I drove to the bagel place next.

Just the smell of those almost-burnt onions made my stomach cheer as I walked through the door. I planned to order one sandwich for me and three for Scott, knowing how ravenous his appetite could be.

"Next," said the guy behind the counter with a head full of tousled black hair and a thick mustache. He wiped his hands on his soiled and not-so-white apron.

I ordered my food, a large coffee, and an equally large tea.

While I waited, I skimmed over a newspaper left behind on one of the vacant tables. As I read over the headlines for the day, I thought about Carrie Stevens again. Maybe it was a diversion from my own problems, or maybe I was just curious, but I couldn't stop thinking about her. After Amy had left my room the other day, I double-checked Carrie's Instagram posts, correlating the dates with her disappearance. I clicked on each photo, from long ago to more recent, noticing her appearance had done a one-eighty. Her blonde hair had turned blue, cut short around her face, heavy emo makeup surrounding her eyes, and her outfits changed from classic to grunge. Amy wore similar makeup and clothing, and I loved that look on her. That wasn't the point. From her start at Commonwealth until her disappearance, this young college student had changed her look dramatically right before she disappeared and never resurfaced. Did she run away with someone? Or was her fate much worse than that? Rick was still on my list as a possible suspect, but appearances seemed very important to him—that and his reputation. I couldn't see him spending time with someone like Carrie, especially after the way he had treated Amy. Still, he certainly did have the evil gene, so anything was possible.

"Number twenty-six." I brought my number to the counter, collected my food, and headed out.

During the drive back to Scott's place, my mouth watered from the aromas teasing me from inside of my car. Scott was barely awake when I had left, and in case he had dozed back off, I made sure to walk with light footing up the wooden steps to his front door. My parents used to say I was a ghost, the way I would wander the house without detection. A few times, I made them jump. That always made me laugh, except for the one time when I had startled them in bed. They didn't seem at all amused and ordered me out of the room. Now I knew why, but back then I didn't have a clue. Parents having sex was a cringeworthy concept at any age.

Two trips back and forth from the car later, I had brought all the groceries inside the apartment and had placed the takeout on the counter. Since I didn't hear any noise coming from the second floor, I tiptoed up the stairs and put my ear to the door. As I stood there, an odd sound came from Scott's room that I couldn't quite identify at first. It was a rustling sound. *Was that a moan?* I pushed my ear harder against the door, which caused it to open and me to stumble into the room, center stage. *Crap.*

The tent that Scott had pitched at his hips told me all I needed to know. I wanted to run, but it was too late to get out of there, not without him noticing me, which he did a second later when his eyes bulged out of his head and his body went into full spasm.

"Jesus. Fucking. Christ. Sara. You scared the shit out of me." Scott sprang up, panting, his cheeks crimson. He bunched the sheet up around his waist, probably to hide the erection that he was trying to appease a moment earlier. "W-what's going on?" He wiped his forehead. "Uh. Did you get breakfast? I didn't hear you come in." He looked away, his chest expanding and retracting.

"I'm so sorry. I didn't want to wake you." I took a *very* long step backward and closed the door. I wasn't sure who was more humiliated from the experience, him or me.

As I flew down the steps, sounds of rapid movement came from the bedroom. I imagined Scott scrambling to find his clothes.

I sat on the couch, my arms hugging my waist. This situation was a first for me, but something told me it wouldn't be my last.

A moment later, Scott came sailing down the steps; his feet missing the last two, where he almost lost his balance and fell on his butt. Luckily, he grabbed the railing in time, saving his fall. He approached me in the living room, his gait accelerating with each step. "Sara, I didn't know you were—"

"It's okay." I rose from the couch and walked toward him. "I understand. You have needs." I swallowed, trying to figure out what I could say that would make this scenario less awkward. So far, nothing came to mind, so I improvised. "I got you some breakfast." I hurried toward the kitchen, where I pulled out two plates.

Scott followed me in but didn't say much. Neither did I.

Our quiet breakfast set the pace for the remainder of the day. Unpacking, homework, and a soccer game on TV allowed us to coexist without much interaction. I wasn't mad about what had happened. In fact, I understood. But what was I supposed to say to him? "I'm sorry I can't help you with that." Just yesterday, Amy was accusing him of being selfish for *not* jerking himself off. What a hot mess.

We had just finished a quiet dinner when Scott's cell phone rang. Most of the time, he'd hesitate to answer it, especially when we were together. Sometimes he ignored it entirely. This time, however, he answered it on the first ring. "Hello? ..." Scott listened for about fifteen seconds before he made a face, telling me the call probably wasn't good news. "No. I already told Mom about it. I don't want to get into it again." He stood and walked out of the room, but his voice carried. "That's right. What's the big deal?" He released a loud huff and then jogged up the stairs.

He was unaware that the walls in the apartment were like paper, which did nothing to hide his conversation. Maybe if he was whispering, which he wasn't—not even close.

"Why do you care so much about where I live, Dad?"

I figured it wasn't his sister. From Scott's reaction, I gathered his father had found out about Scott's sudden move off campus.

"I'll pay you back ... yes, really ... I have enough money."

I could feel the tension seeping through the floor above me. It hadn't occurred to me that Scott's scholarship probably included housing. How would that work now?

"What in the hell is *that* supposed to mean?" He paused, and I imagined his chest swelling, his arms bulging like The Incredible Hulk. "It's not like that. She's not just some girl, Dad."

My throat constricted. Did his father blame me for the move? It sounded like he did.

"Yeah. Well, I've got my own money to pay for it ... that's

right ... Where do you think? I've been working for you since I was a kid." Scott's feet padded across the floor, back and forth. "That's *my* money. I earned it."

I found myself staring at the ceiling, my attention riveted

"Why can't you just be happy I found someone?" His voice rose to an even higher pitch. "That wasn't her fault ... I was tired of that fraternity." More pacing. "Well maybe I will ... that's right ... I don't have time for that shit, anyway." Scott's voice grew distant, and I wondered if he'd gone into the bathroom.

Unable to stop myself, I crept up the stairs and planted my ear against the bedroom door. I made sure *not* to lean against it this time.

"Fine. I'll use Grandpa's inheritance to pay for my tuition."

Wait, what? His next words left nothing to the imagination.

"That's right. I'm quitting the team ... oh, you go right ahead ... good. Then maybe I'll just drop out." Something hit against the door, and I nearly jumped out of my skin. It was probably his cell phone since he had stopped talking. Another loud bang followed, only this one caused the floor to shake. It sounded like a bull was loose in there. As I listened, my skin bristled with fear.

I flew down the stairs, my heart racing. When I reached the dining room, I grabbed our plates and bolted for the sink, where I turned on the water and started scrubbing, my hands working nervously.

Ten minutes passed before Scott entered the room. By then, I had the dishes washed and was wiping down the table. I wanted to act as if I didn't hear anything, but I knew he wouldn't believe me.

"Is everything okay?" I brushed all the crumbs into my hand with a wet cloth and carried them to the sink.

Scott didn't answer right away. He stood watching me, yet not seeing me at the same time.

"Scott?"

He shifted his posture and said, "Everything's fine," his voice firm.

Fine. That all-encompassing word. How do I look, honey? *Fine.* How was your day, sweetie? *Fine.* Whenever I used that word, I was never even close, and my guess was Scott wasn't either.

When I returned to Scott's bedroom that evening, leaving him sleeping on the couch, I found his bookcase tipped over, the books strewn about the floor. That explained the mini earthquake. Given the age of the house, we were lucky it all didn't crash through the ceiling and into the dining room below, where I had sat eavesdropping. His cell phone flashed from the floor near the door, so I picked it up. The screen looked like a window that been shattered by a rock. I found some clear packing tape and covered the display to prevent more damage while I thought about Scott's temper. I also considered what Amy had said to him during their argument. It was wrong of her to blame him for what he had done to Rick. Even if I *were* able to file charges, who could predict whether I'd win. The senator probably had high-powered lawyers on speed dial. In fact, if I had filed charges, they may have tried to ruin my reputation *and* my future. I'd seen it play out a hundred times on the news. At least Rick had suffered, maybe not in the same way I was suffering, but he'd been held accountable. I understood why Scott did what he did, but at the same time, his behavior alarmed me—just like his cracked cell phone screen and the books scattering the floor were alarming me now. Scott had a temper, and I wondered if he'd ever turn that anger on me. I loved him with all my heart, but I would never put up with a man abusing me. Never again.

"What are you doing?"

I screamed and then jolted—my hand flying to my chest. "You scared the crap out of me." I chuckled, hoping he'd see the humor in it.

Nope. Scott stood there like a building, his voice frigid.

I took a breath. "Nothing. Just trying to fix your phone." I tore off the last piece of tape, wrapped it over the screen, and then handed it over to him. "I think you might need to get a new one."

Scott took the phone and stuffed it into the front pocket of his sweatpants. "I don't have the money for that. It's fine."

There was that word.

"Do you want to talk about the phone call with your—"

"No!" Scott bent down and pulled the bookcase back against the wall. A few more books tumbled to the floor.

I watched him put the books away, not sure what to say. I didn't want to talk about the rape, so who was I to insist that Scott open up about his father?

I knelt down and helped shelve some books. "Okay. If you decide you want to talk, I'm here to listen."

Scott provided no response as he stuffed a few books into the shelf, some with more thrust than required.

Later, I tallied the day up in my head: my morning was beyond embarrassing, dinnertime was hostile, and bedtime was even worse. I tossed and turned all night, and so did Scott. Every time I sighed, Scott would sigh a moment later. I wanted so badly to roll over and wrap my leg over his hip, my arm over his waist, and hold him close. Given what happened the last time I attempted physical contact, I decided against it. Our bodies were inches apart, but our souls, never more distant.

I stared at the ceiling fan that twirled slowly around and around in the darkness. I had to wonder if this was the beginning of the end for us. I hoped not. Scott was my whole world, my center, but a barrier was lifting between us, and I wasn't sure what to do about it. I couldn't even comfort him. Not the way I used to.

As I lay there watching the clock, all I could think about was how Monday couldn't come soon enough. I used to hate Mondays.

The next morning, I made an appointment at Revive Treatment Center.

It was time.

Chapter Ten

I sat with Amy in our 2D design class. She repositioned her black vintage fedora, played with her phone, and adjusted her overalls strap, before devoting her attention to her macramé bracelet. I knew why. When she was distressed or nervous, Amy fiddled.

Professor Adams stood at the front of the room chatting with one of his male students. From what I could hear, the discussion was more about a recent basketball game than his curriculum.

Amy drew in a deep breath. "I know you're pissed off at me, but he needed to hear those things."

I took off my fleece coat, draped it over my chair, and turned to face her. "No. He didn't. You really upset him. Everyone is already raw."

She wrinkled her nose. "He's a big boy. I'm sure he'll get over it."

I clenched my jaw. "I'm not so sure he will. Do you have any idea how difficult you've made this situation for me?"

Amy's eyes went blank. "Huh?" Then she leaned back and patted her chest. "Look, *I'm* not the one who—"

"You've got it wrong. I'm not talking about what Scott did. I'm talking about the fact that my best friend and my boyfriend can't coexist in the same room anymore."

Amy huffed. "That's bullshit. I never said I can't be in the same room with him."

I tilted my head and lifted one eyebrow, freezing my face that way.

"Oh." Amy made a snide smirk. "You're not talking about *me*."

I shook my head. "No."

"Nice hat." Mr. Adams bent down and flipped Amy's brim a notch. "I can't get over the outfits you wear." His gaze traveled over her flannel shirt, overalls, and lace-up boots. He lifted her hat a few inches off her head and then placed it back at a slight angle, which she straightened immediately.

"Leave my hat alone, or I'll tell your class you're addicted to *Sister Wives*."

Professor Adams smirked as he straightened a poster on an easel next to him. "Well, you watched it with me." He squared his shoulders while scratching his beard. "That makes you an accomplice, doesn't it?"

It took a moment, but Amy finally smiled at him. "Be careful, I know your other weakness."

My gaze volleyed back over to Dr. Adams, who said, "My weakness?"

Amy grinned, her canines showing. "If I shoved you into an elevator, would you remember, then?"

The professor's cheeks flashed red from the edge of his beard all the way to his forehead. "Oh." His posture shrunk a degree or two. "Yeah, well. Touché." He wiped a finger over his mustache and walked to the center of the room. "Good afternoon, class. Go ahead and take out your visual journals."

"When do you watch TV shows like *Sister Wives* with Dr. Adams?" I asked.

Amy chuckled. "He was joking. I stopped by his office the other day, and he was watching it. It was after hours." Amy shook her head. "I can't imagine being married to a man with a bunch of wives." She gave me a sideways glance. "That's fucked up."

"Hand your journal to the person on your left." Dr. Adams strolled around the art room. "If you don't have anyone on your left, give it to the person in the row directly in front of you." He stopped by a girl with flaming red hair. "I'll take yours, Cindy, since you don't have anyone on your left or in front of *you*." He patted her shoulder.

I handed my journal to Amy, who handed hers to the long-haired guy sitting next to her. A student with thick-rimmed glasses gave me hers.

"Journaling is great for self-discipline and a way to document your artistic skills as they improve over the length of this course. It can also pinpoint trouble spots or areas that need improvement. We will be creating most of our artwork on the computer, but I wanted to begin with the basics." As Dr. Adams strolled, he stroked his beard. "In our last class, I asked you to draw something that inspires you or has an impact in your life, good or bad. I told you to look around you for inspiration: at the sky, nature, friends, relationships, family, or whatever gives you that spark or ire." Mr. Adams placed a hand on the back of a student's chair. "Visual journals can be a great way to organize your thoughts, plan for the future, or push yourself to alter your perception. What inspires you today may be completely different tomorrow or months from now." He raised his index finger. "Which we'll find out when we do this assignment again at the end of the year."

The journal in front of me had a picture of a sun, tucked between two mountain ranges, a small stream running down the center where the ranges overlapped. The coloring was brilliant with the canary sun falling low on the horizon. Shades of salmon and peach helped to illuminate the paper sky. It was nice. Peaceful.

"On the adjacent page of the journal, write down your observations of the drawing and add your initials," Dr. Adams said. "What does the picture make you think of? Does it evoke any feelings or memories? This is all good feedback for the artist." He paused. "Look at color schemes, creativity, image clarity, proportions. Remember to be kind with your comments. We don't want to discourage creativity. We want to inspire." He nodded at a male student. "Right?"

The male student nodded back.

I glanced over at Amy who stared down at my piece: also a picture of some mountains—the Green Mountains of Vermont, actually. My drawing wasn't as pretty as the one in front of me. My mountains were a bit rough, the color schemes, muddled. I tried to make large, round hay bales, but the result looked more like tan smudges. I wondered if Amy noticed the most significant aspect of the drawing: the small figure on one side of the range and the three other, slightly larger figures, on the other side—a world away. I also wondered if she noticed the vast number of trees, which looked more like small, dark clouds with sticks, cluttering up "my" side of the mountain, while the other side, the one closer to the sun, was open ... free. The larger figures, who inspired me, were Scott, Amy, and Abigail. As much as I wanted to embrace the people in my life, a small part of me would always feel separate, different—especially now. Losing my parents at such a young age, my mind couldn't help but wonder if everyone else in my world was on borrowed time. I hated that aspect of myself—the second-guessing—the insecurity—but it was a part of me, whether I liked it or not.

Amy never said anything, and when I looked at her comments later on, she offered a few revealing words: "Portrait reminds me of loneliness and isolation."

Amy always got me.

* * *

After class, she and I walked back to our dorm. We talked a little but mostly about superficial stuff like the bipolar weather and Luke's band. As a guitar player, Luke had been playing in small clubs for a couple of years now. According to Amy, his music leaned toward classic rock, but he had a few new tunes that blended into the metal-grunge category. In fact, she said his new stuff reminded her of the band Alice in Chains. I'd never heard of them.

"Sky wants me to watch him practice tomorrow afternoon," she said as she opened the door to our dorm. "Are you down? It's at a bar in town called 'What Ales You.'"

We jogged up the stairs to our floor while I thought about my Tuesday afternoon schedule. Time felt so fluid lately. I wasn't sure whether I'd be on campus or at Scott's place. Then again, I hadn't heard much from Scott since I'd left him that morning.

"Sure. I'd love to go. I'm not twenty-one. And neither are you. How are we going to get in? You said it's a bar, right?"

"Yeah, but it's not open to the public during practice hours. Plus, Sky knows the owner. He's chill." She poked me with her elbow. "I've gotcha covered."

"Okay. I guess. What time?"

Amy checked her phone's calendar. "Four. You can ride with me."

"That works. I have class until three, so I'll come right back to my room." I thought for a moment. "I'll tell Scott I have plans, so he isn't around." I bit down on my lower lip, realizing the slip.

Amy gave me a look. "Yeah, make sure that *bad* Amy doesn't cross paths with the big guy." She made a halting gesture with her palms. "We wouldn't want that."

Time to change the subject.

I pulled the counseling leaflet from the front pocket of my backpack. "I was thinking of trying this place out." I handed her the brochure just as we entered our suite.

Amy's entire face brightened. "Awesome, Al. When are you going?"

"I have an appointment on Wednesday after our art class." I pointed to a section at the bottom of the page that included office hours. "See, it says their hours are from Monday through Thursday from ten to eleven and five to six." I pulled my hand back. "I can only make the five o'clock session work with my schedule, so I called and set up an appointment."

She handed back the brochure and nudged me. "Don't worry. You got this."

I sure hoped so. In addition to the rape, I wasn't sure what fissures were lurking inside of me, ready to burst open, releasing years of poisonous memories from my past.

* * *

What Ales You was located on the east end of Charlottesville, over by a set of railroad tracks, two breweries, and a winery. The two-story building stood alone on the street, its brick faded and its windows wide and blackened out. A large red awning spanned the front entrance with "What Ales You" inscribed in large white lettering.

Amy parked out back by a dumpster and led me in through the back door, which was left slightly open by a block of wood.

Once inside, we trudged over a set of rubber mats, our shoes squeaking from the friction, then through a vacant kitchen that smelled of old grease, and past the restrooms until we finally reached a large but dark, open area. The stage anchored the left side of the room, facing a generous dance floor. Surrounding the dance floor were a string of booths that lined all three walls (the stage taking the fourth). Three steps led off to the right where I assumed the bar was located since there wasn't one in sight.

A few guys emerged from backstage talking. One guy with dark, curly shoulder-length hair, was smoking a cigarette. Tattoo ink decorated his arms running all the way down to his wrists. The guy with slicked-back brown hair and aviator sunglasses was rather handsome, in a rock star sort of way. His black T-shirt and jeans, just tight enough to look good, added to his attractive image. The third man was our dirty-blond friend whose lanky body soared over his friends. That was Luke, or as Amy referred to him, Sky.

"There's my wildcat," he said, accelerating across the stage and down the steps toward Amy. He grabbed her hand and looked at me with a compassionate smile. "Hey, Sara. How ya holding up?" He touched my arm. "You doin' okay?" He stared for a moment longer.

"Yeah. I'm ... okay." Considering Luke had been with us at the hospital when we were waiting to hear about Scott's knife wound, I was sure he knew exactly what had happened to me.

Luke nodded as he swiped his chin. "Glad to hear it. Just, uh, keep on truckin' and things should turn around." He coughed, looking down, his body squirming.

Yup, he knew.

Of course he did. He was Amy's boyfriend.

He lowered his head and crouched to meet Amy's lips, his long arms coiling around her waist.

Amy reached around his waist, too, and pulled him closer, their bodies rammed up against each other. They kissed for a good two minutes, which felt like two hours. I stared at the ceiling, the floor, the walls, my head moving around like one of those Bobblehead dolls.

Finally, Luke pried himself away from Amy. He guided us up to the stage, where his other two friends remained. Sunglass guy was sitting at the drums, and tattoo guy was playing some chords on his bass guitar.

"Hey, guys, this is Sara. You already know my wildcat."

Amy smiled, her gaze sliding over them. "Yeah. I know these losers." She grinned.

Both men smirked back.

Luke turned toward his friends, pointing in their direction as he introduced them. "Sara, that's Danny over there on the bass."

Danny touched his brow with two fingers and gave me a Boy Scout-type salute.

"And Andy is the one banging on the drums."

Andy nodded but continued his percussion.

Luke turned back to me. "Our singer, Corey, is running late. He just got off work at Chipotle, and he's on his way." Luke looked at Amy and bent down for an additional kiss. His eyes sparkled with what I knew were amorous thoughts, which made me uncomfortable and immediately jealous.

After several more rounds of smooching and me standing there trying to look at anything *but* them, Amy finally pushed Luke away. "Go play with your boys." She licked her lips. "Get lost, loser."

Luke walked backwards toward his band, his eyes smiling. Then he turned and bent down to grab his guitar. The three band members started working together in unison on a tune.

Amy faced me. "Let's get some drinks."

"Okay," I said, glad to have my friend back.

She led me up the same three steps I had noticed before and into another section of the building where, my theory correct, the bar *was* located. A man with a long dark-brown beard and hair of the same color, shaped handsomely around his face, stood behind the bar.

"Hey, Amy," he said as he finished unloading a large container of ice cubes into a floor cooler.

"What's up, Chuck," Amy said with a flair in her voice.

The bartender, apparently Chuck, exhaled and shook his head. He carried the now-empty ice container through a pair of saloon-style doors toward the back.

"That's the owner," Amy said to me.

I nodded. "No nickname for him?" I smirked. "Or is *that* his nickname?"

"Nah, no nickname. That's his real name. I'm having too much fun with Chuck to change it." Amy leaned over the bar and called out to him. "Mind if we grab a club soda?"

"Help yourself," came a voice from beyond.

"Cool." Amy walked to the left side of the bar and flipped up a section secured by hinges. She grabbed two glasses off an upper rack and then a beverage tap, which she used to fill our drinks. The scent of lime wafted through the air as the liquid bubbled and fizzed in our glasses. As Amy continued pouring, a door opened on the right side of the room, flooding the airspace with a wide beam of intense sunlight that ricocheted off the lime-green, cobalt-blue, and amber liquor bottles standing guard against the back wall behind Amy.

I squinted, realizing the stark difference between the outer world and my dark surroundings.

A silhouetted figure came forward as the door swung shut, bringing definition to his skinny frame, extremely tight black jeans, leather jacket, and black stringy, shoulder-length hair. A chain connected his front belt loop to his back pocket, and a necklace, which looked like rosary beads, hung from his neck, along with a pendant of a large marijuana leaf.

Once the door closed, the room returned to darkness, save for the small lamps that stood along the bar, some Christmas lights that outlined the liquor bottle shelves, and a few hanging lights over the bar itself, casting small spotlights onto the honey-colored wood surface.

"Hey," the guy said. "Where's Big C?" he asked Amy.

Amy pushed the glasses over to where I was standing and rounded the bar. We both took a stool next to each other, Amy on my right.

"Out back," Amy said, taking a sip from her glass.

The guy came closer, standing next to her and not me, which I was happy about. He made me uneasy from the moment he'd walked in.

"You're Luke's chick, right?" He stared at Amy with his dark-gray eyes.

Amy continued to sip her drink, her gaze forward. "Yup."

The guy glanced over at me and then back to Amy. "I don't think I've had the pleasure. I'm Axl, or you can call me The Ax-Man. I've seen your guy play a few times." He drummed his fingers on the shiny wood bar. "Sick tunes." He continued to play with his finger drumsticks while Amy looked over at me and rolled her eyes. "If you want to score some weed, I just got some impressive buds."

That got Amy's attention. She turned her head. "Oh yeah? Whaddaya got?"

Axl pulled a bag out from his black leather coat.

A noise from the back room caused him to flinch, stuffing the bag back into his pocket. When the moment passed, and Chuck didn't materialize, Axl pulled the bag back out again.

From our previous conversations about weed, Amy had assured me it wasn't a gateway drug as I had suspected. In fact, she almost convinced me to try it once. I trusted her, which was why I had even considered it. She wouldn't push me to do something that would harm me. From the secondhand smoke I'd inhaled at the Kappa house, I had probably tried it already. Still, I feared what would happen to me if I did inhale a full dose. Would I lose control? According to her, it would mellow me or make me laugh or hungry. I told her I'd consider it another time.

Amy took the bag from Axl's hand and opened it. She inhaled and then examined the contents closer, touching the large clumps of dark grass with her fingers from outside of the baggie. "Okay." She reached into her pocket and pulled out a small change purse, which she opened to retrieve some dollar bills. Considering it was dark and her back blocked my view, I wasn't sure of the amount.

I took a sip of my club soda, which tasted more like Sprite, trying to convince myself that things weren't as bad as they appeared. Axl's aura had my haunches up. His size didn't intimidate—he couldn't have been more than five foot ten and skinny as a rail. I sensed a forebodingness behind his dark-gray eyes. Or his one eye, since the other one was covered with uneven black bangs that reached just past his nose. I felt the same vibe from Rick when we'd met. Although Rick had *pretended* he was sincere and kind, Axl didn't strike me as someone who would bother. He was who he was. At least that was my assessment. Needless to say, I paid a lot more attention to these things than I used to.

He took the money and looked at it with the same scrutiny that Amy had the marijuana, minus the smelling of course. Then he pulled out a wallet from his back pocket and paused.

I was amazed a wallet could fit in jeans so tight.

"You know." He flapped the wallet in the air subtly. "I'd be happy to front you this bag if you'd be willing to sell a few ounces for me." He smiled, a gold tooth twinkling from his bottom row. "In fact, I'd be willing to split the profits with you."

Okay, now I was *really* uncomfortable. Not only were they conducting a drug deal, but Axl was recruiting Amy to *sell* for him? Could I handle my best friend being a drug dealer?

Amy glanced over at me. "Nah. I'm good."

Axl leaned into Amy, his pointy Addams-Family chin closing in on her ear. "Come on. You look like a chick who could slay me some serious sales." He smirked. "In fact, you look like a woman who could do a lot of things. Why don't we journey over to my place? I can show you my stash." He leaned back and peered over at me. "You can bring your cute sidekick with you."

Amy laughed through her nose with a snort. "Not interested." She slid off the barstool and grabbed her drink.

I took it as a cue to take *my* drink, which I did and stood next to her. The glass felt cool and the condensation wet, against my hand. I took another sip, allowing the bubbles to dance their way down my throat.

"Look, we gotta bounce." She held up the baggie. "Thanks for the dope." With that, she led the way back toward the stage.

As we walked away, Axl said, "Don't forget where it came from ... or my offer." He ran up to us and handed Amy a small piece of paper with a phone number inscribed on it. After that, he darted off, probably to get a drink himself.

Given that the bar wasn't even open, he must've known the

owner, although not enough to reveal his secret career, judging by the way he'd flinched earlier.

We continued walking.

"You're not going to sell for him, are you?" I couldn't help but ask.

Amy stuffed the bag of pot into her coat pocket. "Chill out, Al. It's no big deal. But no, I don't have any plans to sell for that douchebag."

"Who is he, anyway?" I asked. "I mean, why is he here?"

We descended the steps toward the dance floor.

"How the hell should I know? It was good timing, though. I was out of weed."

When we reached the stage, the guys were taking a break from playing, although it didn't seem like they had been playing for very long. Then again, they could have been practicing a lot longer before Amy and I had arrived.

Luke sat on a large speaker while the bass player, Danny, perched himself on an oversized black suitcase with silver latches. The guy wearing sunglasses, Andy, sat on the floor, his back against Luke's speaker.

I took notice of a new guy with blond, messy hair who had joined the group. A Kurt Cobain look-alike, who stood off to the side. My guess was it was Corey, back from his shift at Chipotle.

Luke motioned for Amy to come closer. He grabbed a beer from a nearby cooler and handed her one.

She placed her club soda on a moving box and took the beer, downing a long sip. "When are you boys going to start playing?" Amy sat on Luke's lap, taking another swig of her beer.

Every time Amy paired off with Luke, I felt out of place and awkward. I never used to. This was something new. I felt like I was on my own private island of misfit toys. Maybe I should have stayed home.

The guy with the messy blond hair stood. "I don't think we've met." He approached me with his hand extended. "I'm Corey." He smiled. "If you have an overwhelming craving to eat burritos it's because—"

"I know, you work at Chipotle," I said cutting in.

I shook his hand. "I'm Sara."

"Would you like a beer?" he asked. "Since my rude friend didn't offer you one." He looked at Luke with a jutting chin.

"Oh, no thanks. I don't really drink much."

My answer prompted Luke to raise his beer in the air. "And that's why I didn't offer her one. I already knew that."

Corey nodded, his mouth pursed. "That's cool. To each his own." He returned to the box he was sitting on. "Good to meet you, Sara. I hope you like our tunes." He rubbed his nose and smiled. "We're not used to having such hot ladies at our rehearsals."

Amy choked on her beer. "Since I'm sure you're *not* talking about me, I'll warn you right away. Don't bother, lover boy. She's got a boyfriend." Amy's voice carried an edge to it.

No one spoke for a few seconds.

I wanted to plunge my head in my glass of club soda to refresh my flaming cheeks.

"Hey, want to take a few puffs before we start?" Luke said. "We'd have to go out back. Anyone got any weed?" His gaze roamed over his friend's faces.

Amy reached into her pocket and pulled out the infamous baggie. "I just scored some from a strange dude up front." She jiggled the bag in the air.

Luke set his beer down and took the baggie from Amy's hands. "What weird dude?" His brow lowered a notch.

Amy lifted her shoulders up and down and said, "I don't know, some guy named Axl who came into the bar."

Aviator man, aka Andy the drummer, peeled at his beer label from across the stage. "That dude is baaaad news." He took a pull from his beer. "I mean, seriously bad news."

Corey nodded, as did Luke and the bass player, Danny.

I was intrigued. "What do you mean?"

Andy sat up straighter. "He's known for getting chicks to sell drugs for him."

Amy and I exchanged a look.

"He used to date this chick who sold for him, until she either took off or went missing last year."

What? Amy and I looked at each other again, only this time with wide eyes.

"Are you talking about Carrie ... as in Carrie Stevens?" I asked. "Was *she* his girlfriend? The girl who went missing from campus last January?"

"Yup, that's her," Andy said with a nod.

Luke pointed with the hand holding the bag of weed. "Oh, yeah. That's right. I remember now. Didn't she sell meth to some kid who OD'd? Docs revived him, though." He snapped his fingers. "What was his name?" He looked upward as if the answer would rain down on him. "I worked with him at Oak Hollow Pizza last year. His sister goes to school here, too." I could tell he was forming the details in his head. "Zach something. Wait ... Zach Moore," he said with a snap of his fingers. "He was a cool kid. Used to deliver the pizzas. Kind of shy."

Amy stared at Luke. "Don't leave us hanging ... what happened?"

Luke took one last sip from his amber bottle and belched. "Not sure. Zach didn't come back to work after that. I heard he dropped out of school." His eyes lit up. "You should've seen Zach's sister when she confronted Axl and especially, Carrie.

They were having pizza during my shift when Zach's sister walked in. Holy shit, was she pissed." He laughed. "Serious cat fight, I mean epic. The owner almost called the cops."

Corey, Danny, and Andy chuckled as though the story was funny. I didn't see any humor in it.

"Do you think Zach's sister had anything to do with Carrie's disappearance?"

The instant my question hit Amy's ears, she made a grumbling noise in her throat. "You have to excuse her. She's obsessed with this chick's disappearance."

My cheeks flared again as everyone glanced my way.

Luke picked up his guitar. "You never know. Crazier shit has happened." He looked over at me again. "From the sound of it, I wouldn't count out Axl, either."

"Why's that?" I was practically leaning in now.

Amy tried to cover Luke's mouth. "Don't encourage her."

Luke managed a few more words, despite Amy's efforts to muzzle him, his guitar almost sliding out of his hand.

"Axl has a reputation for knocking chicks around. I knew a girl who dated him once."

Amy stared him down. "A girl, huh?"

Luke leaned his guitar against his leg and kissed her long and hard. "Yeah. No one special."

A tight grin spread across Amy's face. "I guess you two hooked up, then?"

This struck me as one of those times when Amy was trying to burrow under Luke's skin like a tick, just for the fun of it.

"What makes you say that?" Luke asked with a slight stammer.

While they bantered about a possible love interest from Luke's past—not that I believed Amy *really* cared all that much about it—my mind sifted through this new information.

Three suspects were now on my list: Rick, Henry, and Axl.

Zach's sister was also a possibility. That made four. The trouble was, I had no idea who Zach's sister was.

Curious, I decided that there was no time like the present to find out.

Chapter Eleven

On Wednesday, I awoke from a restless night's sleep with what felt like a stomach full of thumbtacks. At breakfast, my yogurt didn't help much. I was on my cycle, but that wasn't the problem. I had an appointment at Revive Treatment Center at five o'clock, and my gut wasn't letting me forget it. My therapist's name was Dr. Zeller, and from the bright smile she wore in the picture on her website page, I assumed she was a nice person. I mean, she'd have to be, right? She was a therapist, after all.

While Scott slept in, I spent my time forgetting to rinse out the conditioner in my hair, putting on two different colored socks (which I noticed in my first class), and taking three wrong turns from Scott's place on my way toward campus. I also forgot a book I needed.

During 2D Art, Amy kept asking me if I was feeling okay. When I reminded her of my appointment, she did her best to reassure me it would go fine. At 2:30 p.m., I returned to Scott's place, knowing he had classes all afternoon. That left me with two hours to watch the clock until it was time to leave for my dreaded appointment. I managed to choke down a chicken salad sandwich, hoping the bread would settle my stomach, which hadn't improved much. It provided me with some relief, but not enough. It reminded me of the time I was in second grade and had to sing "Silent Night" for our Christmas concert. I was a nervous wreck and couldn't sleep for two nights prior.

This felt ten times worse. Back then, I had an entire class to hide behind. Not only did I have to go to this session alone, I also had to rehash topics that were extremely personal *and* terrifying "like tear you apart from the inside out" terrifying. My mind was riddled with trip wires.

Unable to concentrate on my uninteresting homework, I chose a more intriguing topic to focus on: Carrie Steven's disappearance. In the living room, I sat on the couch with my laptop, trying to remember Zach's last name—the kid Luke had said OD'd from the drugs that Carrie had sold him. If I couldn't remember Zach's last name, how was I supposed to find out who his angry sister was? Monroe kept flashing into my mind, which was Jason's last name. That couldn't be right. Instagram wouldn't include names, so I found a link to Carrie's Facebook page. I checked her friend's list for anyone named Monroe or Zach but found nothing. I couldn't find Axl, either. I was surprised her parents hadn't closed her social media accounts. Then again, maybe they were hoping someone would reach out or private message them with a new lead.

I should've written down Zach's last name or typed it into my phone, but I figured I'd remember it. I made a mental note to ask Luke when I saw him next. All in all, the only thing my unsuccessful searches were good for was burning time.

At 4:30 p.m., and after returning a text to Scott who had wished me luck, I drove across town, my hands visibly shaking. Was I even going to be able to speak? My throat thickened at the thought of it.

I parked and walked into a brick municipal-looking building, adorned with lots of windows, and found a sign on the first floor for Dr. Zeller, Suite 100, which was just down the hall. Once inside, a note welcomed me from the top of a side table: "Make yourself comfortable, and your therapist will be right out." Next to the sign, sat a small radio where light music played. The room smelled of rosemary with a hint of mint—all props meant to relax nervous patients, I was sure.

No one was there, so I took one of four chairs available and flipped through various magazines, my mind elsewhere.

Within no time, a squeak in the carpeted floor alerted me that Dr. Zeller was approaching. The same woman whom I had seen on the website, reached her hand out and smiled. "You must be Sara."

With sweaty palms, I rose to my feet, shaking her hand and trying my best to steady my lower lip from vibrating. In fact, my entire body was trembling. I hoped she didn't notice.

"I'm Dr. Zeller." She swept one arm toward an open door, ten feet away. "We're right in here."

I followed her in, my gaze traveling past a dark-maroon wingback chair with a table at its side, a spider plant by the only window with its blinds drawn, and over a lamp that cast a soft glow into the room. A floral loveseat sat facing the chair, which I lowered myself into right away.

Dr. Zeller took the wingback chair. Crossing her legs, she talked about the weather and a few superficial things before she took a breath and said the words I'd been dreading all day: "Why don't you tell me about yourself and what brought you in here today."

That was when my pulse thumped into my ears. Before I knew what was happening, the floodgates had burst open and a torrent of emotional rambling gushed out of me. Was I even making sense? I had no idea. I just rambled—and then the tears. A tsunami.

As she listened, Dr. Zeller reached over to the table next to her and offered me a box of tissues. I hoped she had a membership to Costco because I was going to need a lot of them.

* * *

And so it went. Dredging up old memories with Dr. Zeller every Wednesday had me nothing short of a basket case. In fact, since my first session three weeks prior, I'd been so distracted, I'd forgotten to tell Scott on two separate occasions that I was staying in my room and not at his place, causing him to worry that I was breaking up with him. Missing several phone calls and texts hadn't helped matters, either. I assured him that I wasn't going anywhere. I had laundry and cleaning to do and tests to study for. I also explained that with all the anxiety I was experiencing, brought on by pent-up emotions and years of suppressed guilt, I was struggling to remember to brush my teeth in the morning, much less make it to my classes and keep up with my schoolwork.

Scott smiled, hugged me, and said he supported whatever I needed to do. In fact, even though we hadn't spent a whole lot of time together of late, he was growing quite attentive when we *did* see each other. He made me dinner a few times (spaghetti, grilled cheese with tomato soup, and some sort of noodle-and-hamburger dish that came from a box), started leaving love notes in my notebook (something he used to do when we had first started dating), and was ready to provide a back rub or a shoulder to cry on whenever I needed it.

One night, I awoke from an anxiety attack—the kind I used to get after my parents had died. Feeling disoriented and scared, I focused on my breathing, hoping the disturbance would pass. My body felt like I'd just sprinted ten miles.

With his eyes half-mast and while releasing a yawn, Scott sat up and rubbed my back, his tone soothing. "It's okay. I'm here. It will pass in a minute. You've been dealing with a lot of shit lately." He positioned himself behind me and insisted I rest my body up against him, his strong legs providing great armrests. All at once his tone changed. "You know what I was thinking about today?"

"What?" I asked, trying not to pant. *Inhale ... exhale.*

"Remember the Tortoise Inn? The place we stayed at last fall?"

"Of course. How could I forget?" It was one of the most romantic weekends of my life. The charming hotel nestled at the base of the Blue Ridge Mountains, hikes through the picturesque landscape, fall leaves the color of candy corn blanketing the ground, the food, the lovemaking, and the beautiful necklace Scott had given me. *Where was that necklace now?*

"Man, we caught the foliage right at peak season. We really lucked out ... I keep thinking about that awesome dinner we had."

"Which one?" I sorted through the menu in my mind.

"The steak dinner. That filet was so tender I could cut it with my fork. I haven't had a meal that good since then." He brought his head around. "We'll have to go there again this spring. What was that dessert you ordered? The one you gave me a bite of?"

"Tiramisu, I think." I remembered the creamy custard filling, the ladyfingers saturated in espresso, and my favorite part: cocoa that covered the cake *and* plate in a blanket of chocolatey decadence. My mouth began to water.

"Oh yeah ... And remember that bed and how friggin'

comfortable it was? My back felt great." Scott's voice was as smooth as butter.

"I do. I think it was made locally." I tried to remember the brochure the mattress company had left on the nightstand.

Before I knew what was happening, my thoughts had shifted from my internal organs seizing up and my heart stopping to something more pleasant. As the muscles in my body relaxed, it wasn't long before my eyes grew heavy. More than that, I was downright exhausted, as if I *had* really run those ten miles, and this was the aftermath.

I drifted off to sleep, wrapped in Scott's arms. I wasn't sure how much sleep *he* got that night, but I certainly slept soundly. In fact, it was one of the best night's sleep I'd had in weeks.

A couple of days later, I took a selfie when I was wearing nothing but my bra and panties and sent it to him with a text: "The next time you feel the need to release some sexual tension, consider this photo my contribution. I'd rather you think of me than of a swimsuit model. Lol."

I figured it was safe enough, my underwear was no different than a bathing suit, although my brilliant idea didn't come without a boatload of worry attached, thanks to Rick and that camera of his. I shook the thought, and him, out of my mind, something I was getting better at.

Scott responded with his own text: "Wow. Thanks, babe. Don't worry, NO ONE else gets me hard like you do."

* * *

And here I was, back at Dr. Zeller's office once again. Looking back, I thought about what a hot mess I had been during that first session. When I had finally stopped rambling about too many subjects all at once, I was able to discuss my childhood. At first, I sped through it all with rapid recounts, until Dr.

Zeller urged me to slow down. When I did as she asked, the memories caught up—I wasn't able to verbally outrun them anymore. More tears flowed, enough that I used an entire box of her tissues.

After that, I discussed the rape and Scott's near incarceration. During all our meetings, Dr. Zeller made notes, nodded, and asked very limited questions. She listened more than she spoke.

Man, did time fly. Would I actually get through this one without blubbering? I sure hoped so. I couldn't imagine what the woman thought of me. Per usual, my palms were sweaty and my pulse rampant. My body's baseline.

Dr. Zeller cleared her throat. "In our previous sessions, you did an outstanding job of bringing me up to speed with your history." From the perch of her dark-maroon wingback chair, she stared at me through her soft brown eyes. Wearing a gray suit and tailored white shirt, she tapped her pencil against her legal pad, her dark hair tied tight in a bun. "There is one aspect of your memories that stands out to me." She uncrossed her legs and sat slightly forward.

Her comment made the already small room feel like the size of a dollhouse, as if the walls were closing in—or maybe I was shrinking. I lifted my collar out an inch to steal some cooler air. "What's that?" I said, even though I wasn't sure I wanted the answer.

"You've told me so much about your parents and Scott. You discussed the very traumatic rape." She paused, raising a palm. "Don't worry, as I said, you have patient-doctor confidentiality."

I had asked her that question twice now.

"I'm not sure if you realize this, but when you talk about Scott or your parents, or even your assailant, you do so as though what happened was *your* fault." She repositioned her legal pad on her lap. "I sense that you feel responsible for what has happened to your loved ones and to you. My question is, why?"

While I thought about her astute observation, I focused on the diplomas and awards that hung proudly from Dr. Zeller's walls. An undergrad degree, two master's degrees, and a PhD. Yup, this woman knew what she was talking about. I was safe here. And if I let her, she might actually be able to help me.

"Because it *was* my fault. All of it. The accident. The rape." There went my lower lip again.

"What part was your fault? Can you elaborate?" She recrossed her legs and sat back as though ready to take it all in. "Let's start with the accident."

"They didn't want to go out that night!"

"Who? Your parents?"

I nodded. "It had snowed that day, which was nothing new. In Vermont during the winter, it always snows. One year it even snowed on Memorial Day weekend. The winters up there are like a persistent cough that never seems to end," I said. "In fact, as a child, it seemed like I was always sick with one virus or another."

You're getting off track!

Dr. Zeller nodded, her gaze fixed on me.

"Anyway, I had a bad case of cabin fever that day, and I wanted to get out. You see, there's this really cool city called Burlington about an hour north of Middlebury, where I grew up. I used to love to visit Church Street where, even in the winter, you'd find people from all walks of life." I smiled at the memory. "In the summer, we'd walk the pedestrian-only street and watch performers while we'd eat Ben and Jerry's ice cream." I could almost hear the children laughing, amateur music filling the air, the sweet smell of ambrosia from the honey-locust trees. "The crowds weren't quite as thick in the winter, but the vibrancy and the energy always made me feel excited and rejuvenated. Burlington was also where my favorite restaurant was located, which was a Tex-Mex place called Coyotes. My favorite dish there was the chicken fajita burrito." As I spoke, I could almost taste the savory goodness on my tongue: the melted cheese, the marinated chicken, the sautéed peppers and onions. *Yum*.

"I've actually been to Burlington, so I know what you are talking about. I haven't been to Coyotes, but I'll have to try it next time I'm in town."

My voice lowered a decibel. "Unfortunately, they're closed now. I went home for winter break, and it wasn't there anymore. There are lots of other good places, though."

We both paused for a moment.

Dr. Zeller cleared her throat. "So, you had cabin fever ..."

"Yes. And my parents didn't want to make the trip, but I harassed them all afternoon until they agreed." The gravity of my words seeped into my chest like an oil spill. "If I hadn't made them go ..." I couldn't finish. I couldn't think about the "what-ifs" any longer. I'd spent so much of my life regretting that day.

Dr. Zeller put her pen and pad of paper on the side table.

"I see. And how was the rape your fault?" Her tone was even, unthreatening.

"I should've known that he was a bad person. If I hadn't gone with him or even become friends with him, then I wouldn't have been ... you know, and Scott wouldn't have beat him up and been arrested. I've really made a mess out of things."

She nodded, but not definitively—more like an acknowledgment of my words. "Are you aware that sexual assault is one of the most underreported crimes?"

"My friend Amy has told me stuff like that before. Her aunt counsels women who are victims of domestic violence."

"Did you also know that the reason it's underreported is because the victims feel the rape was their fault in some way? Or they fear others will think it was their fault? The victims already feel embarrassed, shameful, and dirty, but they also carry the burden of responsibility." She tipped her head a notch, her lips pursed. "I should've known he was dangerous, I may have given him the wrong idea, I shouldn't have worn that outfit, I shouldn't have drank too much." She regarded me. "Does any of that sound familiar?"

That was exactly how I felt. For some of it, anyway.

"It's a stigma. Some victims don't even acknowledge that it happened to them. There is a myth about rape that it involves a stranger in an alley or some remote place. Most sexual assaults don't happen that way, and we are trying to change the narrative so victims don't wait years to come forward, if they do at all." She blinked her kind eyes. "You said Rick drugged you? Do you feel guilty that you didn't fight back?"

I nodded. My limbs felt heavy, my mind clouded with unhealthy thoughts.

"In most cases, the victim doesn't fight back because they are unconscious or terrified. More times than not, the attacker doesn't fit a person's normal profile of what they believe a rapist should be. For example, if there wasn't any physical violence, a victim won't believe they *were* raped." She took a breath. "What I'm getting at, Sara, is that your feelings of self-doubt are more common than you realize."

My chin yo-yoed up and down again, the burden I'd been carrying, trying to lift itself off my shoulders. Although my guilt-ridden heart wasn't having it.

She laced her fingers together. "Those self-destructive feelings are barriers that stand in the way of your recovery. The truth of the matter is that none of those things are true. With your parents, they were adults that made the decision to take you to dinner. On any given day, that same accident could've happened when you weren't in the car. As you said, the winters were long. If you knew what was about to happen, would you have still gone?"

"Of course not. I would never." My jaw tightened—my spine stiff.

"How can you blame yourself for something you didn't know was going to happen?"

I shrugged, unsure.

"On another note, a predator took advantage of your trust and abused you in a horrible way. What he did was about *him*. Not you. In most cases, it's not even about sex. It's about control. People from all walks of life are abused every day who don't deserve it. That doesn't change who you are as a human being. It changes how you feel and perceive things. You are still the same person you were before this happened. I'm not saying that it doesn't affect you. Of course it does. You may feel a loss of control in your life. For that, you need to find ways to regain that control. You may need some coping mechanisms such as meditation, biofeedback, or yoga to help control the anxiety and the PTSD. There are lots of possibilities here, even medications, although I like to exhaust other avenues first. To be so young and to have not one but two major traumatic events is a lot for anyone. The fact that you are getting out of bed in the morning is more than most people could manage. At the very least, give yourself some credit for that. And on top of it all, you're still taking classes and managing your everyday life?"

"Yes." My insides went all fuzzy with a new, more alien feeling. *Pride?* Was I not the coward I had convinced myself I was?

Dr. Zeller sat straighter in her seat and placed her hands on her lap.

"I want to give you an exercise to do. Close your eyes," she said.

I did as she asked, not sure what was about to happen next.

"Now I want you to imagine a little girl that is a younger version of yourself. This child is about twelve years old, the same age you were when your parents died. I want you to picture this child vividly. She is you."

I pictured a small Sara with long gangly legs, curly hair, and blue eyes too big for her face.

"Okay, now I want you to imagine that this child has just lost her parents. She's alone and has no one to turn to," she said. "Really look at that younger you and try to imagine how she feels. Because you know how she feels, don't you?"

Eyes still closed, I acknowledged her question, my throat going all tight again.

"Next, I want you to imagine that you are walking by this child. She is crying, but you ignore her. When you stop ignoring her, you tell this younger you that what happened was all her fault. She was eager to get out of the house during a long winter and enjoy a fun dinner with her parents. This little girl has lost everything and continues to cry. Once again, you tell her that it was all *her* fault. This child is devastated, and you are the only one who can help her but you choose not to."

I saw little Sara standing there, her hands clasped in front of her waist. She was looking for someone, anyone, to come to her aid. No one came. She was alone. I burst into tears and lowered my head. This was awful, why was she putting me through this?

"Okay now take a deep breath, Sara. Breathe in." Dr. Zeller inhaled loudly.

I inhaled with her.

"Now exhaaaaaale." She blew out the words with her breath.

I followed her breathing.

After she repeated this exercise a few times, she said, "Okay. Now I want you to open your eyes and look at me." Her voice was practically a whisper.

I lifted my head and focused on the calmness of her eyes, the angle of her mouth.

"How did you feel about that child?"

"I felt protective. I couldn't say those things to her." I choked the words out between sobs. "I couldn't do it." My hand shook as I raised a tissue to my eyes.

"So, you couldn't say those cruel things to an innocent child, even when that child was you?" she asked.

I shook my head no.

"But you *are* doing that, Sara. You are doing that every day. Whenever you think of your parents, remember, deep inside you are telling that little girl that she deserved what she got and that you and she were responsible for all those bad things that happened. As far as the rape goes, would you blame a friend who had been through the same thing you had? Would you think *she* deserved it?"

Again, I shook my head.

"You are being harder on yourself than you would anyone else." She handed me *another* full box of tissues.

I grabbed one and used it to wipe my face clean, the small trash can next to me filling up.

"Every time you want to blame yourself for what happened to your parents, I want you to take a moment, close your eyes, and imagine that little girl again. When you tell yourself that you are dirty or should be ashamed, imagine telling that to your best friend or even a stranger. It's much harder to cast judgment on an innocent child or another person, isn't it?"

She was confronting me with a new perspective that challenged my destructive habits.

"Yet, you have no trouble tearing yourself apart for the same nonsensical reasons."

She was right. I was putting myself through hell for things I didn't deserve. Why was I so hard on myself? If Rick had done that to another woman, I would *never* have considered blaming her. So why was I blaming myself?

"We have a lot more work to do here, Sara." Dr. Zeller leaned over her lap. "But seeing how strong you are already—and without my help—I can honestly say, that *with* my help, things are going to get much better for you."

* * *

During my ride back to campus, my mind and body felt lighter somehow, the air a little friendlier, less static. The internal clenching that I had been doing for years was starting to ease and with it the hope for more healing. I was feeling confident, something I hadn't experienced in a very long time. I wasn't weak. I was strong—brave even. *I'll try to do better by you, little Sara.* If I wasn't able to stand up for myself, how could I expect anyone else to do it for me? My new perspective was unlatching the gates to what I hoped would be more change and growth.

Waiting on the passenger seat of my car sat a flyer I had been ignoring. In bold letters, the words yelled out at me: "Self-Defense Classes at Physical Force. Every night at 7:30 p.m. (except Sundays). Walk-ins welcome. First class is free."

Okay, okay. It was time for that, too.

When I returned to school, Amy sent me a text saying she was at the snack bar if I wanted to join her. I noticed the time was 6:20 p.m. I had just over an hour to meet her, grab some dinner, and make that self-defense class in time. I was pumped and didn't want to lose my momentum.

I sent a quick text to Scott, letting him know I would see him later that evening. "My session went well. Can't wait to share."

After changing into some workout clothes, I headed out to meet my friend, trying not to skip along the way. That would be lame. I did the skipping on the inside, instead.

Amy and Dr. Adams were sitting at a round table near the back wall when I walked into the snack bar. Those two were spending a lot of time together. This was another change from high school. In college, we were all adults.

They both looked up as I approached their table.

"Hi, Dr. Adams." I looked over at Amy. "Hey, Amy."

Amy was on her phone but raised her hand in a half wave.

"Hello, Sara. How is your day going?" Dr. Adams moved a chair out next to him. "Have a seat, young lady." He smiled.

He was such a nice man.

I took the seat he'd offered and smiled back. "Thank you. My day has been good, actually. How about yours?" My voice sounded perky, almost giddy. Not my normal droll.

"I can't complain, I guess." He moved closer, tapping his shoulder against mine. "No one would listen if I did."

We both chuckled.

"I think I may go grab an iced tea and a sandwich. Can I get you anything?" I asked as I stood.

"No. Thank you. I have my trusty caffeine boost right here." He wrapped his hands around his stainless-steel travel mug.

I looked over at Amy, who shook her head. She wasn't saying much on her phone, just listening. Judging by her furrowed brow and tight lips, I sensed the call wasn't a pleasant one.

While I darted up to the food counter to grab a drink and a sandwich, Dr. Adams continued reading from a textbook in front of him, and Amy, now turned away from the table, kept her phone pressed to her ear.

When I returned, not much had changed by way of activity. Not until Amy slammed her cell phone down on the table. "I'm so sick of this."

"Who was *that?*" I asked as Dr. Adams's whole face widened.

Amy turned to face us both. "My mother. It looks like my annoying little sister got into my mint collection of record albums and broke one in half. How the fuck do you break a record album unless you're trying to?" Amy's cheeks fumed red, her pupils dilated. "This is the last straw. She's been taking my things since I left for school. If my mother doesn't handle it, I will."

Dr. Adams made a cringey face. "Yikes. I wouldn't want to be on *your* bad side." He took a sip from his travel mug.

Amy leaned back and stared into space. "Yeah, well. Maybe I'll just make her eat a can of dog food like I did when she was younger."

Professor Adams broke out in a coughing fit. At first, I thought he was laughing until his face turned as red as a barn and his eyes watered.

I patted his back. "Oh my God, Professor, are you choking?"

He shook his head but continued to cough with such velocity I thought he was going to vomit or pass out. With Amy and me staring at him, he finally gathered his breath and sighed. "I've gotta run." His voice squeaked like a windpipe blocked of oxygen.

Coughing and gagging, he thrust his book into his bag, grabbed his things, and sped off like a race car, his hacks backfiring behind him.

Several people stopped and stared.

"What the hell just happened?" Amy asked as if I'd know the answer.

"I don't know. He must've swallowed wrong. I've done that many times. It's scary." I stared at the door he had just flown through. "I hope he's okay." I glanced over at my friend. "You're not *really* going to make your sister eat dog food, are you?"

Amy smirked. "Nah. I was only fucking around. She's annoying, but I'll find another way to keep her out of my room. I'll get my brother, Griffin, to help me out. She used to pull the same shit with him. Honestly, I don't know what's the matter with her. If she doesn't stop stealing people's stuff, she's going to find herself in jail one day." Amy's brow softened. "I'm really concerned about it. I'm thinking about going home next weekend to talk to her." She scoffed. "If I can do that without strangling her first."

I took a sip of my tea, feeling almost guilty for my good mood. Then I thought a little good news might be good for Amy, too. "Well, I just had a great session with Dr. Zeller ... "

* * *

That night, I started my first self-defense class. I'd spent enough time tearing myself down. It was time to fight my way back onto that horse called life.

Dressed in my workout clothes, I sat on a red floor mat that covered the room at Physical Force, a gym not far off campus. The room was rather large with recessed lighting and royal blue padded chairs along most of the walls. The color scheme was vibrant, the walls clad in posters of people doing karate kicks and self-defense moves. In one corner stood a crowd of human-dummy punching statues, along with other devices.

Wearing a dark tank top and workout pants that molded perfectly to her petite and muscular frame, my instructor spoke.

"Welcome class. I see some familiar faces tonight, but for the newcomers, my name is Sheila. Congratulations on taking charge of your own protection. I can't tell you how important it is. Next week, we'll have some of Charlottesville's finest here to share statistics about crimes against women—especially college students who are often walking around campus at night. I'm sure you heard about the girl who went missing from Commonwealth University last year."

That piqued my interest. Being in touch with the cops, Sheila might know more about the case.

"We're going to look at several self-defense moves that don't require strength since often the victim may be at a disadvantage physically against their attacker." She turned toward a man standing behind her who was at least a foot taller than she was, her long brown braid swinging along her back. "This is my colleague and co-owner, Tristan. As you can see, Tristan is much bigger and stronger than I am. He will be part of my demonstrations." She pivoted her body toward the entrance and motioned with her hand. "Before I forget, we have a sale going on right now that includes pepper spray, rape whistles, keychain flashlights, and some training pads and videos that you can use to practice with at home or in your dorm room."

With short-clipped dark hair and muscular arms and legs, Tristan stepped forward wearing a tank top and gym shorts. He had a hot body for sure. "Welcome class." He clapped his hands, the size of baseball mitts, together with a thud. "I want to take a minute and congratulate each and every one of you women for coming here. Women can feel helpless because they don't know what to do when they are in danger. We are going to show you some techniques that anyone can do—and I mean anyone." Tristan glanced at Sheila. "Even if I tried, I couldn't overpower this five-foot-three-inch female standing right next to me." He looked her up and down. "And believe me, ladies, I've tried."

A few chuckles drifted through the class of females as I attempted to imagine a muscle-bound guy fighting against a petite woman. A bull and its toreador.

A predator such as Rick used a different technique. He was a snake who would sneak up and bite you when you least expected it.

Sheila patted Tristan's beefy arm, her hand looking miniature by comparison. "That's right. Tristan is going to be the attacker, and I will be the victim. You'll learn what you can do with the *right* moves, regardless of your strength level. The first technique we are going to show you is used when someone grabs your arm. ..."

By the time class was over, I had several exercises to practice. Maybe Scott could help me, which I mentioned when I texted him later as I left. The thought of physical contact with Scott made my heart flutter. I also told him a little bit about my session with Dr. Zeller. I felt invigorated as I drove out of the parking lot. This class was going to be a weekly habit until I felt confident enough that I could handle myself in battle—hoping it would never come to that. Full of positive energy, I actually hummed all the way to Scott's place.

When I pulled into his apartment complex, excited and ready to share my day, an unfamiliar car had taken my parking space. Scott had two spaces for his unit—his jeep took up one spot, and someone else had taken up the other, forcing me to park along the street. The Pennsylvania license plate and the "Williams and Son, Chrysler, Dodge, Jeep" sticker in the back window told me who the owner of the other vehicle was.

What was Scott's father doing here?

Chapter Twelve

I inserted my key into the lock and opened the door with trepidation. No one was in the living room, but the TV was on, some commentators discussing last weekend's Super Bowl.

"Is that you, babe?" Scott's voice rang out from the kitchen just as my nose picked up the scent of coffee brewing. A few gurgles from the coffee maker, told me it was almost ready.

"Yup, it's me."

A moment later, Scott appeared from the tiny dining room. He rushed over, kissed me, and peeled my coat from my shoulders. "From your text, I'm eager to hear about your day." He opened the closet door under the stairs and hung my coat on a hanger while I removed my boots and set them on a shoe tray next to the door. Then he quickly closed the gap between us. "My dad's here, and he's not too happy," he whispered.

Between the living room and the dining room was the half-bath, where another person emerged, a man who was strikingly handsome for his middle-aged years. Not blond or brown but more of a hot toffee color, Mr. William's hair was cut short, his sideburns accented by slivers of gray. Scott's striking blue eyes and left dimple came from his mother, but his dad had provided everything else: facial structure, height, broad shoulders, and strong jawline. What diminished his handsome appearance was a distinctive wrinkle forged across his forehead—that and his near frowning lips. His pale-blue eyes, not nearly as vibrant as Scott's, narrowed in a scrutinizing sort of way, his crow's feet pronounced and *not* from smiling.

"Who's this?" he asked with an edge.

Scott turned and draped one arm over my shoulders. "This is Sara. I've told you about her many times."

Mr. Williams looked at me, his expression deadpan. "I was hoping we could talk alone, son. We have some *matters* to discuss. And I don't need an audience."

If I could judge how this visit was going to go on my first impression, I would say, *not* good.

I looked up at Scott. "I can go back to my dorm. You two should have some time to talk alone."

"No. That's okay." Scott's brow tensed. "Please stay." He said it in a don't-you-dare-leave-me sort of way. Then his gaze slid over to his dad. "We can talk in front of Sara."

From the phone call I had overheard the other day, I wondered if Scott was worried to be alone with his dad. I hoped he was going to tell him that he was *not* leaving school, even though he had said he was over the phone. That would be a good place to start.

Mr. Williams exhaled, pinching the bridge of his nose. "Look, son. She doesn't want to be here for this."

Scott tightened his grip on my shoulder. "What's the big deal? She's fine."

I tried to wiggle free. "No, really, Scott. If he wants to—"

"This is my place. And I want you here." He stared his

father down. "Anything you want to say to me, you can say in front of Sara."

Scott's father shook his head. "I don't know what's happened to you, but I'm assuming it has something to do with *her*."

Me? How am I at fault?

Mr. Williams crossed his arms. "I don't like what I'm hearing from you lately."

A sudden heatwave flared in my chest like a torch. "Mr. Williams, I can assure you—"

"I'm. Talking. To. My. Son." He uncrossed his arms. "Who is she to you, anyway? Your girlfriend? Your fiancé? She better not be your wife." Mr. Williams lifted his brow, his gaze aimed at Scott. "She's not pregnant, is she?" He looked right at my stomach.

Whoa. "Excuse me? I don't appreciate what you're imply-ing." I wanted to backtrack right out the door and return to my room on campus. I removed Scott's arm. He was making me feel pinned.

Scott whispered something under his breath that sounded liked "Jesus Christ," before he said, "You've been here ten minutes and you're already starting in?" He looked at me briefly. "Who should I tell her *you* are, my father?" Scott inched his face forward, his hands braced on his hips.

This was going nowhere fast.

Mr. Williams pointed, his voice husky. "Watch it, son. You're already on thin ice."

Scott scoffed.

Before Mr. Williams could say anything more, I stepped forward and reached my hand out. "Look. We've gotten off on the wrong foot here. Let's start over. I'm Sara. Scott's non-preg-nant girlfriend." If I was willing to make light of his insult, I hoped he was, too.

Scott's father didn't shake my hand or soften in any noticeable way. Quite the opposite. "Is that supposed to be funny?" he said. "My son's life is in complete disarray and you're making jokes?"

I pulled my hand back and shrunk a little. "No. Of course not. I was just trying to ... things aren't as bad as you—"

"Don't talk to her like that!"

"Oh, don't lose your cool, son. I was only joking with Sierra."

"It's Sara, actually," I said, my cheeks starting to smolder.

"So, tell me, *Sara,* why is my son acting like a total lunatic?" As if he was throwing mental darts, he pinpointed Scott and then me. "He has opportunities that any other person with a working brain would die for. And if he's not careful, he's going to blow all of them. In the short time he's been back at school, I have to ask myself, what's changed to cause all this impulsive behavior?" He stared right through me, punctuating his accusation.

I felt like I was in a lineup at a police station. My first time meeting Scott's father was a total disaster. Did he know about the arrest? I hoped not.

Scott regained his grip on my shoulder.

Even though he was far from an attacker, I mentally thought about what I'd do if he was.

"As I told you already, Dad. Sara had nothing to do with *my* decisions."

I tried to intervene. "Scott, tell him that you're not—"

"Excuse me, son, I'm having a hard time understanding your actions lately." Mr. Williams widened his stance. "What happened to Mr. Independent? Where's the kid who said no girl would ever control him? Last year, you were dodging women who you said were stalking you, and this year ..."

Stalking him?

With red cheeks, he fanned one hand in my direction. "Now you're moving off campus, abandoning your teammates, dropping out of school. I can already see the problems *this* one is causing. Does she live here with you?" His gaze scoured the room, where my books, my shoes, and my "stuff" sat in full view of his critical assumptions. "You two playing house, are you?"

Scott removed his arm from my shoulder, thank God.

"So what if we are? What business is that of yours? Sara's special to me. She's not like the others. Why can't you see that?"

Scott's wavering tone traveled back in time. He sounded like a child trying to convince his father of something that was important to him. At least it sounded that way to me. I was flattered he was defending me but equally sad for him.

"All I know is that you were doing fine until you met some girl, and now, suddenly you're turning your life upside down. You better think twice about what you're planning to do. If you haven't done it already."

I could feel the heat radiating off Scott's body. As far as school went, Scott hadn't missed one class since that hostile phone call with his father. It was obvious to me he was just bluffing or saying things he didn't mean. I was hoping he'd share that with him, but it wasn't looking that way.

Why not clear this up?

"You're not going to do this to me again. It's my life. I'll do what I want with it. And I find your interest in my soccer career, my fraternity, and my schooling—another thing you've never had anything to do with—a load of bullshit." He flung both hands up. "This is so typical of you. You only show up when there's a problem—and even then, you're three weeks late."

Scott's father rubbed his jaw, his neck corded, and his lips tight.

"It's just like all those years Kelsey and I were in school. You never came to anything we did then, either. But boy, if you heard one of us had done something wrong—or what *you* thought was wrong—you were right up our ass about it." Scott's eyes brewed with resentment, his voice drenched with frustration and disappointment.

Mr. Williams shook his head as he flailed one hand or the other to help him make his point. "What do you know? You were just a snot-nosed teenager. You're lucky I was there to straighten you out. Somebody had to do it."

"That wasn't straightening me out. It was bullying, and you know it."

Scott's father barked his response. "I never bullied anyone; ask your sister."

"No. You just neglected *her*. I could take it, but Kelsey ... she tried everything: sports, plays, debate teams—but you never gave her the kind of attention she needed. Remember that science project she did for you, Dad? The one she spent three months on, hoping you'd be proud of her."

The muscles in Mr. Williams' jaw flexed. "That's just about enough—"

"She even picked a project that related to your dealership— that solution that would melt ice faster off car windshields. She was so excited. Hoping to make you proud. Just so you'd notice her or acknowledge that she had done something you approved of." Scott turned to me. "Do you know what my father did on the day of her science fair?"

I gulped, dreading his answer.

"He went golfing with a couple of his loser business-owner friends who also neglected their families." Scott's eyes were wild, his face angry-red.

I didn't know what to say. What he described was awful,

but I didn't dare speak. The last thing I wanted to do was make matters worse.

Face contorted, Mr. Williams looked like a volcano that was about to erupt. He shook his fist. "Those *losers*, as you put it, are the pillars of our community. When we had the recession not too long ago, it was those *losers* who stood by me. They brought me extra business, they even fronted me some cash when I needed it. But I guess you wouldn't bother to know that, would you. You're too busy being self-righteous. If I made any mistakes, it was being too easy on you. I should've made you work harder."

Scott mashed his lips together as if he was preparing to spit venom. "I'm self-righteous?" He slapped his hand against his chest with a hollow thud.

It sounded painful.

"I'M SELF-RIGHTEOUS? Hoooly shit. The only conversation you ever want to have is about yourself. You could give a shit about anyone else. Thank God we had Mom. We'd be nowhere without her. And as far as making me work harder, I've been working at your dealership since I was ten, cleaning cars and shitty bathrooms. You wouldn't even pay me until I was fifteen." His shoulders spiked higher like boulders thrusting through the earth's crust. "I was there weekends, holidays, summers, and whenever you needed me. While my friends were off having fun, I was working full-time-plus hours for you ... everything we did ... was all for you."

My heart was hammering in my chest. *How bad is this going to get?* I'd never seen a father and son quarrel like this. Any arguments I'd had with my parents were mild by comparison. We bickered. This was a three-alarm fire.

Mr. Williams moved slowly until he was nose-to-nose with Scott. "Let me tell you something, you spoiled little brat." He poked his finger in Scott's chest, his words laced with invisible razor blades. "I've worked my tail off so you and your sister—and your mother I might add—didn't have to want for anything. I busted my ass for this family."

Scott shook his head and exhaled. "Keep telling yourself that, *Dad*." He said the word *dad* with such disdain in his voice.

I wanted to touch Scott's arm to calm him, but I wondered if he'd feel it. Nostrils flaring and fists dangling, both men looked like two bulls ready to lock horns. I was terrified of what might happen next. The only question was, who would advance first?

Mr. Williams took the lead, shoving his son and causing Scott to stumble backward and me to gasp. "You think you're man enough to stand up to me?"

Scott gained his footing and stepped forward. He was ready to blow, I could see the pressure building in his chest. "Don't. Touch. Me. I'm not a little kid anymore. You don't scare me."

I sensed Scott *was* scared. Terrified, even. So was I.

"I don't know who you think you're talking to." Mr. Williams glared at me next. "I can see what a *great* influence you have on my son."

My guard went up through the roof. "I didn't tell him to quit school or the soccer team," I said, incredulous. "In fact, I was trying to—"

"You're a looker, that's for sure." Mr. Williams surveyed me from head to toe and then back again. "He's always had good-lookin' girls in his life. What I can't figure out is, what's so different about *you* that he's willing to flush his entire life down the shitter?"

"He's not leaving school," I said, since Scott wasn't going to.

No reaction came from Scott's dad. It was if he couldn't hear me anymore. The shields were up; the two-way communication, shut down. Something in his unrelenting actions made me wonder if he didn't want to listen. He just wanted to be heard *and* obeyed. Scott's childhood flashed before me, and his poor sister, who obviously never got the love or attention she so longed for.

"Since you obviously don't care what I think, maybe you ought to consider what this will do to your mother. You almost killed her once. You gonna finish the job this time?"

What does that mean?

The levies had crested, and anger pulsed through the veins in Scott's forehead and neck. He lunged forward and shoved his father, who stumbled backward hitting the wall behind him and knocking over a lamp, which shattered against the floor.

I screamed. "Oh my God. Are you okay?"

Scott snapped his head in my direction. "Is *he* okay?"

I stopped, speechless.

Mr. Williams steadied himself. "That's just fine, son." He caught his breath and headed for the door, rubbing the back of his head along the way. "You've gone too far, and now you're going to be held accountable. You're cut off. No more money from me. You can make your own way from now on." He reached for the knob. "You want to throw your life away for some skirt? You can do it without my help."

Skirt? The insults were stacking up. Obviously, I had no clout here. I was guilty by association. "What is the matter with you? He's not quitting school or the—"

"Good. I have Grandpa's inheritance and my own money," Scott said cutting me off.

Scott's father pulled the door open and turned to face him. "No, you don't. Not anymore. When I said you are cut off. I mean, you are CUT OFF."

Scott's body went rigid, his neck muscles tight and threatening. "So, you're going to steal my money now?"

Mr. Williams didn't bother to answer; he stormed out the door like an agitated grizzly.

Scott followed him out, screaming. "You can't take what isn't yours. That's my money. I earned it. You touch my money, and I'll call Mr. Pinker and have him sue your ass for theft." He returned a moment later, slamming the door so hard, the wall shook. Then he walked by the coffee table, and using one arm, swept everything—books, papers, remotes, and cups—to the floor.

"Scott, you need to calm down."

He walked over to the wall, made a fist, and pulled his hand back like an arrow about to shoot from its bow. More damage followed: a new fist-sized hole in the sheetrock.

My stomach filled with acid. I had never seen Scott so unhinged.

"Look. Destroying our apartment isn't going to solve anything." I approached him, trying to take his hand, now swollen and red.

Scott yanked it away. "How the fuck am I going to pay for this place?" He wiped his forehead and started pacing like a tiger in a cage. "I need to get a job. I'm going to have to quit school."

I stood in front of him, taking hold of his arms. "No, you aren't. If that's truly your money, he can't take it. My parents left me money, and that's mine. It's in my account. Unless your dad has a joint account with you, he can't legally withdraw it."

Leaving my grip, Scott plunked down on the couch, his head in his hands.

I sat next to him, rubbing his back. "Let's not jump off a building just yet. Your dad was upset, and I'm sure he regrets what he said to you ... or I hope he does."

Scott looked at me, making a *pfft* sound with his lips. "You don't know my dad."

"That's true. He's intense. But why didn't you just tell him that you weren't quitting school?"

"He wouldn't have believed me, just like he didn't believe you. I've been through this with him before. He gets his mind set and no one can convince him otherwise."

"What do you mean?"

Scott swiveled toward me, the anguish written all over his face. "I *mean* that he doesn't listen. When I was in high school, I asked him if I could take a summer off from soccer and cut back on my hours at the dealership. I just needed a break—one goddamn summer. My dad heard some scouts were coming to the club games and summer practices, and he went ballistic— said I was ruining my life and even threatened to kick me out if I was going to become some bum on the streets. He came at me, just like he always did whenever I did something that made him angry. This time, I fought back until my mother suffered a panic attack, which at the time I thought was her heart. She literally collapsed. It really freaked me out. If something worse had happened to her, I would've blamed myself. I had to let it go, even though I was eating antacids like they were candy. For years, he wouldn't let me live that down. Said I was throwing my life away... sound familiar?" He stared at the floor and released a loud breath. "It's all such bullshit."

"That's what your dad was talking about?"

He nodded, but it was subtle.

"He was really horrible to you. I'm so sorry. I'm sure your mother doesn't blame you for what happened." I continued a one-handed back rub, which seemed to steady his breathing as he continued to stare at the floor. His shirt was sweaty, his body odor stronger than when he had just finished soccer practice. This was a lot for anybody to take.

We'd only talked about him leaving the frat. Assuming he didn't mean what he'd said to his father about quitting school, I was trying to give him his space. Maybe that was the wrong move.

"I understand why you are leaving the fraternity, but why are you quitting the soccer team? And you are *not* leaving school, right?"

Scott stared up at the TV. "I need to get a job, and I won't have a lot of extra time." He grabbed the remote from the floor and muted the sound, then tossed it back onto the coffee table. "Plus." He turned to me, his voice softening. "I want to be here for you."

I rested my head on his shoulder. "You *are* here for me. And I've got classes, my therapy sessions, my new self-defense class. Plus, I want to tutor again—if I'm not too late for that. You don't have a lot of outlets right now, and soccer would be a great way to keep in shape and let out some of that aggression on the field. I know what a great player you are. You love it. Have you even talked to the coach?"

Scott shook his head.

I slid my arm around his waist and pulled him a little closer. "Maybe you should go talk to the coach and see what he thinks. I'll go with you if you want. Don't make any hasty decisions until you do that at least. Okay?"

Scott paused.

"Okay?" I shook his body for emphasis.

"I guess I could do that."

Progress. I took a breath and slapped my hands against my thighs. "Okay, let's get some ice on that hand." I stood and went into the kitchen, where I filled a sandwich baggie with ice. I covered the baggie with a dish towel and handed it over to Scott, who had followed me in.

We sat at the dining room table.

"Try moving your fingers," I said. "And make a flexing motion." I was worried he'd broken something.

Scott flexed his hand, making a noise in his throat as he did so. "It's fine."

"If it's not better in a couple of days, you may need to get it X-rayed."

Scott smirked. "Sara. It's fine. I've broken my hand before. It's just a little swollen." Seeing Scott smile was beyond reassuring. My sweetie was returning from the dark side.

While Scott continued to ice his hand, I thought about his father. "Man, your dad has issues."

Scott pulled the ice away from his knuckles, which looked slightly worse for wear. "Tell me about it. I used to be terrified of him when I was younger."

"I can see why," I said, hoping he felt my support. My heart broke for him.

Scott had spoken about his father, but nothing had prepared me for this. There was no excuse for his father's actions, but there was also no excuse for Scott's *reactions* either —and he was more important to me. This wasn't the first or even the second time Scott had lost his temper in front of me.

"Just because someone jumps off a bridge doesn't mean you have to," was something my mother used to say. She'd use this phrase when I had done something wrong, like neglect my homework or complain that I couldn't go to a movie that was beyond my age level. I'd often argue that if other kids were awarded these freedoms, why wasn't I? After reciting the above catchphrase, she'd go on to explain that she didn't care what other kids did or what their parents allowed them to do. She cared about *me*. "I'm raising you to be a responsible and respectful young woman." Somehow, her argument always made me feel special—as though she cared for me more than the other parents did for their own kids. That was how I felt about the situation with Scott. Even though his father had acted horribly, that didn't mean Scott had the right to do the same. When dealing with parents, even angry ones, there had to be some decorum. Scott had every right to defend himself, but that didn't excuse what he did to our apartment afterward or to his room a few weeks ago. I didn't like seeing him lose it that way.

I took a breath. "I love you, but we need to talk about what happened here." I kept my tone soft.

"My father is an asshole. End of discussion."

You don't get to decide that, Scott.

"I agree, but I'm not talking about him. I'm talking about what happened after he left." I pointed at the abused wall, a nervous twitch crawling up my spine.

Scott stood, looking down at me from what felt like Mount Olympus. "It's not a big deal. I'll fix it." His eyes went cold, his voice gruff. "Now, drop it, Sara, I'm not in the mood."

The way he towered over me, leaning in as if to intimidate, for a moment, I wasn't sure who I was talking to, Scott or his father.

"You're not addressing the real problem here," I said with a slight stammer.

His pupils dilated, not an ounce of compassion in sight. "If you have something to say, say it."

Be strong. "Fine, I will. You need to control your temper. It scares me sometimes."

"I scare you?" Scott continued to loom, his posture less than friendly.

Like father like son. That was a legacy he would have to shed if he wanted to be with me. I thought of my recent session with Dr. Zeller and let that memory fill me with strength.

"Yeah. Sometimes. You knocked over your bookcase a few weeks ago and ... you broke your phone ..." I paused.

"What?" His question came shooting out at me like a rocket —and almost as loud.

I startled, jumping to my feet. "What do you mean, what? You just punched a hole in the wall and ransacked our living room. You shoved your father, and look what you did to Ri—"

Scott wiped his mouth, a low but eerie laugh escaping from his lips. "Are you seriously going to sit there and defend *Rick?*"

His words shot right through me like nails from a nail gun. It was as if my feelings didn't matter. Just a moment ago, he was professing his desire to be there for me.

"You know who you sound like? Amy."

I'd reached my limit. He was *not* going to bully me. "No. I am not defending that disgusting excuse for a human being, and how dare you accuse me of such a thing. I just—"

"I've heard enough. I thought you were on *my* side." Scott thrust his palms up, shutting me down.

This stubborn side of him was his least attractive attribute. He was downright unnerving. "I am, but we need to be able to talk about—"

"If you're so afraid of me, then maybe you should go." He threw the bag of ice into the kitchen sink and then walked to the stairs, ascending the steps two at a time.

"Fine with me," I yelled as loud as I could.

Then I released a heavy sigh. "Well, that went well," I said to myself. Now he was mad at *me*. At least the feeling was mutual. I walked into the living room, trying to decide what to do next. I considered cleaning up the glass or picking up the mess on the floor—I even contemplated going upstairs to try and reason with Scott, but I was too bothered to try. It had been a long day of emotional ups and downs. I wanted to celebrate the day, not fight about it.

I had to remind myself that whatever was going on between father and son had nothing to do with me. *It's not your fault.* That's what Dr. Zeller would say. I wasn't responsible for this recent upheaval in Scott's life; it had been going on for years.

The progress I had made in my session earlier made me want to do what was best for *me* for a change. At that moment, what I wanted was to be alone, where there was no tension and no stress. I needed to meditate as Dr. Zeller had suggested. She was teaching me some techniques to decompress and clear my mind. I thought about the last exercise in which she instructed me to close my eyes, focus on my breathing, and think about my body, looking for spots of tension and anxiety. I realized most of my tension hid in my neck and shoulders. I rolled them back as a reflex. This was the perfect situation for an exercise such as this one. Listening to my "little Sara," I grabbed my keys, put on my boots and coat, and walked out the door.

Little Sara and I needed a mental time-out.

After my last class the next day, I darted over to the counseling office to see if I could get a tutoring job. It was now four weeks into the term, so I suspected my chances were slim. I hadn't heard from Scott all day, but I also knew he had a full course load on Thursdays, so I chose not to worry about it. If I didn't hear from him by the time I finished studying later, I'd worry. Until then, I figured he needed a cooling-off period. So did I.

Inside the Student Union Building, I dashed up the wide marble steps, turned right, and walked down a hallway toward a door marked "Counseling Office."

The same dark-haired receptionist who was there on my last visit greeted me. This time, I noticed her name tag read "Wendy."

"Is Candice in?" I asked, hoping to catch her this time.

"Yes, she is," Wendy said. "Let me see if she is available."

A few minutes later, I was standing in Candice's office, the sunlight beaming in through her office window and off her shiny auburn hair. "Hi, Sara. Long time no see. Did you have a nice break?"

She was wielding some serious energy as she swiveled in her office chair, picking up stacks of paper and shuffling them around.

Candice knew nothing about my situation, and I wanted to keep it that way.

"It was good. How about yours?"

Candice bent over and pulled a messenger bag stuffed with folders out from beneath her desk. "Ouch." She shoved her index finger into her mouth and sucked on it. "Paper cut." She pulled her finger out and grimaced. "What did you say?" She tipped her head back and closed her eyes. Then she took a breath.

"I said my break was good. Yikes. That looks painful," I said cringing.

"It is." She straightened up in her chair. "My son is home sick, and my husband has to leave for a business trip." She picked up a few papers and then dropped them in the same place, like someone would do who was flustered. "I've got to call a parent and then distribute some flyers in the staff mailboxes for an upcoming job fair before I go." She sighed. "There just aren't enough hours in the day."

"I've come at a bad time. I'll go."

"It's okay. It's good to see you. Maybe we can catch up next week?" She raised her brow and paused.

"Yes. That would be great. I'd like to talk to you about tutoring again this semester."

Candice pulled out a file from her drawer. "Sounds good. We're already scheduled for this semester, but since you are still currently an employee, I could use you for back up. We can discuss it later. Because now," she picked up the handset for her landline phone. "I've got to make this call before my husband kills me for being late."

On her desk sat a stack of flyers with the words "Spring Career Fair" printed across the top. "Do you have to distribute those flyers in the staff mailboxes here?" I pointed a thumb over my shoulder, "out by the reception area, or do they have to go all over campus?"

"Just here. I've already distributed the others."

Her long breath told me Candice was overwhelmed.

"Would you like *me* to distribute the flyers for you on my way out?"

With phone in hand, Candice stared at the wall as if considering my offer. "You know, that would be a huge help." She grabbed the sheets and handed them over to me. "If you don't mind."

I took the flyers. "It's no problem."

She slouched. "I'm so sorry I didn't get back to you yet, Sara. I've just been slammed with work. I promise to call you for a meeting next week, okay?" Her phone made that howler noise that happens when it's been off the hook for too long. Candice pushed the hook button to stop the obnoxious whining.

"No worries. And I hope your son feels better." I stepped away to give her some privacy to make her call.

When I reached the mailbox area, I let Wendy know what I was doing and got busy. I was just about finished shoving each sheet into every nook I could find when a name popped out at me: Carrie Stevens. *What?* It was under one of the lower mail slots but crossed out. I crouched, squinted, and looked closer. Yup, it was definitely her name.

I brought the leftover sheets out to Wendy. "Could you give these handouts back to Candice? She had to make a call, and I don't want to interrupt her."

Wendy smiled and reached her hand out. "Sure thing."

I turned to go, but then stopped. "I couldn't help but notice the name 'Carrie Stevens' on one of the mail slots. I heard about her disappearance. Did she work here? I thought she was a student."

Wendy's smile faded. "She worked in this department for a year before she started school full-time." With a sad face, she shook her head. "Isn't it just awful what happened to her?" She caught herself. "Well, I guess we don't really know *what* happened, do we?"

With my feet nailed to the floor, my mind raced like a car in the Indy 500 trying to absorb this new, rather crucial, development. Amy was wrong. Carrie Stevens *did* work here the year before she went missing. That meant, she was also here when Ethel was hit by that mysterious car.

Chapter Thirteen

I pushed through the doors of the Student Union Building, eager to get back to my room to tell Amy what I'd discovered, when an alarming sight halted me in my tracks.

Raking leaves and staring at a small cluster of girls who were talking amongst themselves, was Henry. I walked a good distance away from him, monitoring. He paused his work a few times and stood there gawking at them while leaning against his rake.

Was he taking a break or listening? Either way, the girls gave no indication that they even noticed this hostile man lurking nearby.

The sky was clear, the air still. Temperatures had risen into the fifties, a nice change. Cars passed by on the main road just off campus. Squirrels shot up and down thick trees with lightning speed. Voices spattered through the air as they would on any other normal day. Where was Carrie during all of this? Was she in a place where she could see the trees or the sky? Could she even breathe anymore?

I suddenly felt very cold inside.

When I was back in my room, I unloaded my things and sat at my desk, ready to dive into "Carrie land." I was about to power up my laptop, when a loud noise came filtering through the wall from Amy's room. *What was that? Did something fall against the wall?*

I flew to her door and knocked.

No one answered.

I knocked again before some rather loud laughter erupted from within her room. Was Luke in there with her? Knowing Amy, I imagined them both naked doing all sorts of kinky things. I pulled my hand back and took a step away, hoping they didn't hear me. A loud thud struck the door from the other side, just before the knob turned and Amy appeared, fully clothed.

"Hey, Al. How's it hangin'?" She covered her mouth and laughed like she couldn't help herself.

Something about her eyes wasn't right. Her pupils dilated. "Is Luke in there with you?"

"Nope. Skywalker isn't here. Practicing in his band, he is." More laughter ensued. Amy let the smile melt away for a moment. "Up here pleasing his wildcat, he should be." After finishing her impersonation of Yoda, she bent over and cracked up some more. It was weird to see this side of her. Amy was *never* giddy.

Are you drunk?

"Okay, let's get you inside." I helped her straighten up and escorted her back into her room, wondering what she may have consumed.

SueAnne and Mia, our other two suitemates who I hardly ever saw, came strolling down the hall, glancing over at us with their customary curling lips and disapproving stares. After they had made it clear last fall that neither of them had any interest in being friends with Amy, who they assumed was out of control, the four of us managed to coexist in our suite without interacting much. They were nice, but just not on our wavelength. Seeing Amy in this condition probably only confirmed their suspicions about her. As long as they didn't report her, I didn't care what they thought.

I closed the door behind me and walked Amy over to her bed. I expected to smell alcohol on her breath but there was none. Once on her bed, Amy rolled around and waved her arms as if she was playing an invisible harp. What the heck was going on?

"Amy, what did you take?" I asked.

She sat up and stared at me.

Her eyes weren't her own, her pupils dominating her distinctive green irises.

"Smoked some weed, I did."

Oh great, more Yoda impressions.

"Did you also take some pills?" I had no idea what to ask. Drugs were way out of my wheelhouse.

"No pills, did I take." She angled her head and stared at something on her desk.

I looked, too, but saw nothing unusual there, at least nothing interesting enough to cause Amy's head to lean forward, her gaze fixed, her hand reaching out. Given her obvious interest, I wondered if she was seeing a tiny dragon or some other mythical creature. Maybe it was Yoda himself.

Someone knocked, but not on Amy's door. It was farther away than that. Was it our suitemates? Did they hear her? I didn't want Amy to get written up for this.

I opened her door and peered out at Scott standing ten feet away.

He turned his head. "Oh. Hi, babe. I was wondering if we

could talk." His voice was low and somber and his eyes uneasy. I knew that remorseful look. I'd seen it before.

Amy sprang from her bed and tried to move around me on her way out the door.

There was no way I was letting her go anywhere in her condition. I used my body to block her attempts to spring free.

"Look. It's the big guy. It's. The. Big. Guy. Come to visit, he has."

I pushed Amy back. "Go sit on your bed. I need to talk to him."

Scott's brow lowered, his lips slightly parted.

"No way, man. I wanna talk to Scottie. Scottie tissues. I should've called him Scottie tissues." Amy roared with laughter.

Scott took a step closer, a grin forming.

"Have you two been drinking?"

"Not me." I shoved Amy back again. "I don't think she's been drinking, either. I just came back half an hour ago and found her this way."

"Is she tripping?" Scott asked.

"Tripping? What does that mean?" I asked as Amy wrapped her arm around my neck from behind and leaned into me. My self-defense class came to mind again. "Amy, stop." I walked her back into her room and forced her to sit on her bed. "Look at that." I pointed to her desk, which caused her to stare, barely blinking.

While she was occupied with the invisible *something*, I hustled back to her doorway. "Phew." I wiped my forehead. "What is tripping?" I asked Scott again.

"Did she tell you what she took?" He leaned his hand against the jamb, peering around me.

"No, in Yoda-speak she said she smoked some weed."

"Sold me some special weed, Axl did." Amy rolled off her bed and onto her floor, cackling away.

Even Scott chuckled, but then wiped the smile away when he looked at me.

"I'm worried. Do you think she could OD like that Zach kid did?" Funny I could remember his first name but not his last.

"Who?" Scott squinched his face up, trying to fill in the blanks.

It was too much information to share right now. "Never mind. Do you think I should take her to the hospital?"

Scott shook his head. "Nah. She'll be fine. Maybe get her to drink some fluids. If she smoked some weed, it might've been laced with something."

"Sold me some kick-ass weed, Axl did."

"Who is Axl?" Scott asked. "Did she and Luke break up or something? Did he finally get tired of being ordered around?"

Not now, Scott.

"No. Axl's some guy that we met when we went to watch Luke practice with his band at a bar a few weeks ago. The guy gave me the creeps."

That brought Scott's haunches up. Big time. "Did he make a move on you?" Scott grabbed my arm but not hard. "Because if he did—"

"No, no. Of course not. It was nothing like that."

Scott stared at me for a moment as if to see if I'd say more, then his shoulders released.

Unfortunately, Amy had returned. "What did you say about my Luke Skywalker?"

I held Amy back. She was like a human-sized puppy, bursting with energy and mischief. "Listen, can I call you later? I can't leave her like this. I'm going to do some research on overdosing, and I want to call Luke." I chewed on my lower lip, worried that Scott wouldn't understand. Given the events of the past twenty-four hours, things were tense between us, to say the least.

"You talkin' shit about me, Scottie tissues?" Amy squinted and pointed with a floating index finger. "You better not be. You better not lay a hand on Sky, either. I'll massacre you with my lightsaber." She moved the same finger up and down making humming noises that I assumed resembled the futuristic weapon.

"She doesn't know what she's saying." I pushed Amy back again. "Go lay down. I'll be right there."

Luckily, she listened this time, waving her hand at me.

Scott rubbed his chin. "Can't we just talk for a few minutes? I'm sure she'll be fine."

"I can't, Scott. Not right now."

"She's not an infant, Sara." He motioned with his hand to my room. "We'll be right next door." When I didn't budge, he drew in a deep breath and held it for a second before speaking again. "Why don't you just come to my place when you're done *babysitting?*"

He said babysitting with an edge that I didn't appreciate. I was about to tell him to get lost, when he took a step away and then stopped. He palmed the back of his neck and exhaled. "Christ. I didn't mean it that way. This is not how I wanted this visit to go. I came here to apologize, that's all. I'm sorry I acted the way I did. Come to my apartment when you're done here, and I'll try to do a better job of explaining myself. I'd stay and help, but something tells me it may make matters worse." He approached me, dropped a kiss on my forehead, and then said, "You're a good friend, babe, and I love you for it."

"Okay, I love you, too," I said as he walked away, I zoned in on his butt. A girl could look.

That was when Amy started howling from her room. *Are you a werewolf now?*

It was going to be a long night.

$$* * *$$

I chose not to take Amy to the hospital since she didn't show any signs of an overdose, other than possible hallucinations and dilated pupils. I also knew that if a doctor diagnosed her with an overdose, it could hurt her standing at the college. I decided I would only take her to the emergency room if she got worse, which she didn't. I kept checking her body temperature, skin color, and heart rate, and I wouldn't let her sleep, not until she was somewhat coherent. By that point, Luke had shown up. I wanted to call his cell phone earlier that evening, but I didn't know his number, and Amy's drug-induced brain couldn't seem to come up with the password to *her* cell, so I gave up. When his jam session ended, and he finally arrived, Luke snickered about her condition and handed Amy his coffee as if that would cure all her woes. By then, the crisis was mostly over. Amy still acted strangely but not quite as animated, and she could form complete sentences instead of *Star Wars* babbling.

"She won't come down from her trip for a few more hours," Luke informed me, his voice even, indicating no sign of alarm.

The only time Luke's brow had tugged downward was when I told him that Amy had purchased the laced weed from Axl.

"She needs to steer clear of him. He's a strange dude," he said. "I was out of weed this afternoon, and I think she wanted some. But I just got a new stash, so I'll hook her up from now on."

From her bed, Amy grew sleepy. "Let's smoke some," she said in a faint voice.

I pointed at Luke. "Don't you dare!"

He assured me he wouldn't.

When I left, Amy was sprawled out over her comforter while Luke was lying next to her, staring at his phone.

I was dog tired. So tired in fact, that on my drive to Scott's apartment, I called Abigail to keep me awake, even though the drive wasn't that far. I'd been busy lately and had missed hearing her voice. Her groggy hello told me I had probably woken her up, and then I looked at the time on my dashboard, which flashed 11:30 p.m. *Dummy.*

"I'm so sorry. I'll call you tomorrow," I said.

"No, that's okay. How's it going? Where are you? Why are you out this late?"

I guessed she had picked up on the sound of my left turn signal and the noise of the car. "Oh, I went to a movie with Amy. She decided to stay at Luke's place. He's her boyfriend. I just dropped her off." Thank God she couldn't see my bad poker face.

"Oh. How's Amy doing?"

"She's good," I said. *Other than her near drug overdose, that is.*

"What movie did you two see?"

Crap. I thought of a recent title and ran with it, which seemed to satisfy Abigail's curiosity.

"How are your classes going? Do you like your teachers?"

What was it about moms? They had more questions than anyone I'd ever met.

"I do. I think I told you Amy and I took another art class together. I also like my child development class. The teacher is kind of a granola-type, but I like that about her. She has a special needs child and relates a lot of her lessons to her own experiences." I yawned.

"You sound tired. Are you close to school?" Motherly tone, activated.

I smiled. "Yup. I'm almost there." I turned right onto Pinewood Drive, which was Scott's street.

"Have you met any new boys there?" For the first time in our conversation, her voice carried a lift.

While I thought about my answer, Joel asked her who it was on the phone. "It's Sara," she said to him.

"This late?" he said.

"Shhhh. I'm trying to hear," Abigail reprimanded.

I pulled into Scott's place and parked. "Nope. I haven't had time to meet anyone." I turned off the engine and now realized I had to finish this call in the car.

"Don't let Scott jade you. There are a lot of nice young men out there. I am glad that you aren't rushing into anything, though," she said, yawning herself.

"Well, I'm at school, so I'll let you get back to sleep."

Just then, Scott's front door opened. He emerged in his T-shirt and sweatpants, his hands plunged deep into his front pockets and his arms tight against his body. Wearing boat shoes and no socks, he jogged down the steps, advancing on my car. Man was he sexy ... and a little too close for comfort.

My heart began to pump a few beats faster.

"Okay. We were thinking of making a trip down there at the end of the month. Joel heard about this nice bed-and-breakfast not too far away. He loves Bold Rock cider and wants to go there. Plus ..."

As Abigail droned on, Scott closed in on me. He stood outside of my window, his breath fogging up the air. After a second, he knocked on the glass, his face inching closer, curiosity abundant. Then he made a gesture as if to say, "Why aren't you opening your door?"

"Abigail," I said, interrupting her mid-sentence.

"Yeah?"

"Can I call you tomorrow?"

Scott opened my car door. "Hey."

I glanced up at him and raised my index finger up for him to wait. "I've got someone here who wants to talk to me."

"This late? Is it someone you know?"

"Yes, it's a friend." I could feel Scott's brain trying to process what was happening in front of him.

"Sure, but make sure you call me, so we can discuss our visit," Abigail said through another yawn.

"I will. Loveyoubye." I opened my door.

"Who was that?" Scott stood close, opening the car door wider.

Tired of lying, I said, "Abigail." I took a moment to grab my backpack and a tote bag with a change of clothes from the back seat. I had already stocked enough shampoos and toiletries in both locations. Clothing was a bit trickier.

Scott took my backpack from my hands. "You told Abigail I was a *friend?*"

"I guess I'm tired. It's been a long night."

Scott's head inched back just enough, his eyes narrowing.

He was confused, and I wasn't sure how to explain my way out of this.

I closed all my doors and used the remote to lock them. "Uh. Well, she was going on about something, and I didn't want to lengthen the call any longer." I headed for his front stairs. "It's cold out tonight." I bounded the steps and practically sprinted to his front door, a new surge of nervous energy propelling me.

Once inside, a clean and straightened-up living room and a fresh coat of spackle over the hole in the sheetrock sent me a comforting message. No more broken glass. Scott helped me out of my coat and hung it up as I removed my boots. I set my bag by the stairs as Scott sat on the couch next to a floor lamp I hadn't noticed before. I did, however, notice the empty box from Target out by the dumpster but wasn't sure which apartment it went to. Now, I knew: it was our new lamp.

I crossed the room and took a seat next to him, hoping that more drama wasn't ahead of me.

Scott smiled, sort of, and then placed his hand on my knee. "I'm sorry about last night," he said. "You're right about my temper. I do have to control myself. And I'm sorry that I scare you."

"You don't—"

"Wait. Let me finish. The last thing that I want to be ..." He paused, his mouth gripped tight. "... is like my father. I'm glad you shared how you felt. I should never have told you to leave, and I hope you will forgive me. Whenever I act like a complete shithead like I did last night, I try to remember the stuff you're dealing with and what you've *had* to deal with your entire life." He let his head drop. "Not only are you a better person than I am, but you are stronger than me as well. I told you last fall that I was used to being the one in control, but since I've met you, that's the last thing I am. I worry that I'm going to lose you and that someone like Amy is going to come between us."

"She won't. I promise."

"I've seen it happen before. The best friend hates the boyfriend, and soon the boyfriend is old news."

I grabbed hold of his hand. "I promise you that no one will come between us. I will work on Amy. She's just protective, but she doesn't hate you like you think she does." I swallowed. "And even if she did, I'd never let her come between us. You are the love of my life."

Scott's entire body seemed to settle with his last breath. "All I want to do is wrap you up in my arms and hold you there ... forever. I hate thinking that you lost your parents when you were so young and what happened to you here at school. The thought of it just makes me nuts." He tightened his grip on my hand. "I promise to try and step back from my own juvenile feelings and learn from your example. If *you* can hold it together, I sure as hell should be able do the same." He bent his head closer, resting his forehead against mine.

I loved it when he did that.

"My dad was right about one thing: you are the first girl who has ever had this much influence on me." He pulled his head back and stared into my eyes. "In fact, you're the first girl I've ever really loved."

Flattery encouraged a comforting sigh from my lungs. "Really? You've never loved anyone before?"

He squinted, his inner glow returning. "I think I thought I was in love once or twice ... until I met you. It's been different with you from the very beginning."

Feeling tingly and overly modest, I shrugged.

Scott brought his face so close I could practically taste him. His musky scent teased me to linger. "I'd really like to kiss you right now."

Oh, please do. "Go ahead, handsome."

It was as if we were on that mountain again and I was anticipating my first kiss.

He touched his lips on mine, his hand lacing through my hair at the nape of my neck. He moved his lips slowly and softly while I closed my eyes and drifted into the warmth of his alluring mouth. He felt like spring water against my skin, every taste and smell, so familiar.

I touched his jawline, strong and determined, then let my fingers trace over his gorgeous face. It felt so good to be this close to him again.

He planted several little pecks around my mouth, his breath drawing me in.

When I couldn't take any more softness, I reached my hand behind his head and pushed his mouth harder onto mine. My lips seemed to part on their own, my tongue dying to taste more of him. To mingle with his.

Scott pulled away and stared at me. "Let's not push things too far." He moved away and started to stand, leaving me disappointed on the couch.

I reached up and grabbed him, pulling him back to me. "Please. I know that sex is too much for me right now, but can we just kiss a little more?"

Scott lowered himself onto the couch. "I can't think of anything I'd rather do." He wiggled his head a little, his eyes rolling upward. "Well, I can think of *one* thing I'd rather do."

I giggled. "I know. Me, too."

His face got all serious. "That wasn't meant to make you feel pressured. I'm okay waiting. There will come a day when you have this awful shit behind you. And I'll wait patiently until then." He tapped the end of my nose with his finger. "But when that day does come, babe, you may not get out alive."

My inner thighs trembled, my insides jittering with so many wants and needs. If only I was ready to embrace those feelings. But I wasn't ready. Not yet. I moved my lips over his. "Until then."

Chapter Fourteen

The sun came streaming in through the blinds, welcoming me to another Friday. I rolled over in bed and wrapped my arm around Scott's shoulders, my face planted up against his back. I inhaled his alluring aroma. "Good morning, handsome."

After a few deep awakening breaths, he rolled over, kissing my forehead. "Mornin', babe." He cupped my cheek in his hand. "Thank you for sharing your therapy session with me last night." He pulled me closer for a hug. "Just thinking about 'little Sara' rips my heart out. You know, maybe someday we'll have a little girl of our own, and you can experience all those moments you missed with your parents." He held me strong.

Goose bumps traveled up the back of my neck, carrying a message of excitement and hope. "What a nice way to think about it." I longed for the day that I would share a family with this man.

"I'm so glad you're going to see that therapist. She sounds like she knows her shit." He pulled back and smirked. "And I have to say I'm impressed with those self-defense moves you showed me. I want a rematch."

Our so-called practice moves didn't really amount to much, other than Scott keeping hold of me as much as possible. I did manage to pin him once, but I suspected he let me do it. It was too much fun to take seriously, which was therapy in itself.

"Oh, yeah? Don't forget, I had you once." If only I could *have* him for real. *Be patient.*

Scott sprang up. He pulled me into a headlock and gave me a soft noogie, along with several kisses to the top of my head.

I fought him off and laughed.

Last night was bonding for us both. It was light and fun like fresh air and sunshine. Before I met Scott, I'd grown used to mental droughts of loneliness.

Breakfast brought more enjoyable moments, both of us dancing around each other in the kitchen like performance artists as we toasted our bread, poured our cereal, and brewed our coffee and tea. Scott kept running into me, his hands roaming over my waist. He bounced a few kisses off me when our faces were in close proximity. It was what I had always imagined living with him would be like.

We sat across from each other, flirting with our eyes.

"I met with Coach Sumner yesterday."

I took another bite of cereal, trying not to jump for joy. I hated the idea of Scott losing all aspects of his previous life. The fraternity wasn't nearly as important as Scott's soccer scholarship or his academic career.

"I guess I'll stay on the team. If I need money, Coach said he may be able to set me up with some new construction work with a buddy of his. Stuff like painting and finish work." He took a sip of his coffee. "I may not need the job after all because I also called my bank, and you were right. My dad can't take money out of my account." He set his mug down. "My mom called after she found out what happened." His nostrils flared a little. "Of course, my father told her a *completely* different story —said I was disrespectful and confrontational." He scooped some cereal and milk into his spoon and tipped it back into the bowl. "Honestly, I was hoping he had come here on a peace mission. I should've known better."

My heart frowned for him. I truly hoped his father would one day see what a wonderful son he'd raised—or according to Scott, his mother had raised.

"Sounds like a lot happened yesterday. I'm glad you were able to talk with the coach and your mom." I reached my hand across the table to take his. "Your dad will come around. He was probably just scared that you were going to quit school. No parent wants to hear those words." I tugged on his hand. "Abigail would kill me if I even considered it."

Scott took a few more bites of toast and then carried his plate and empty bowl of cereal to the counter. "I've got practice Saturday and Sunday. I've missed a couple already and Coach wants me to condition."

"That's fine. I've got a test in Environmental Science that I need to study for. Since you're busy, I'll go to the library tomorrow."

"I meant to ask you, what did your dad mean about girls stalking you? Was that true? Did someone actually stalk you?"

"I have no idea what he was talking about. He spouts weird stuff all the time." Scott returned to the table and bent down for another smooch. His breath smelled and tasted like toasted bread and coffee. Yum.

* * *

When I walked into art class, I scanned the room for Amy, hoping she'd be there, but she wasn't—not yet, anyway. I had already texted her earlier to make sure she was okay. She texted back that she felt like crap but would survive. That was a relief. She had been pretty out of it.

I found our usual table and set my backpack down to unload my classwork.

Dr. Adams looked over and waved. I waved back. He stood in front of a whiteboard, where he wrote down some class assignments. Scrawled across the corner of the board was a classic quote from his favorite movie *The Big Lebowski*. Every week he replaced it with a different one, probably to keep us guessing. This week he delighted us with the movie phrases about being called a "Dude" or "His Dudeness."

Amy and I had watched *The Big Lebowski* last fall. I found it very funny, even with all the F-bombs. I used to tell Amy she was being very un-dude when she got upset—another fun habit I hoped to revisit again soon. Things were moving slowly, but I was getting there.

A few minutes later, Amy dragged her feet through the door, her untied army boots scraping against the industrial-grade linoleum. Her eyes were red and puffy, her normally unique outfit drabbed down to black yoga pants and a not-so-white T-shirt with a stain on the front. Carrying a large to-go cup, she plunked her laptop on the table and then sunk into her chair.

"How are you feeling?"

Her head flopped sideways in my direction. "Like dog shit. No. Like dog shit that's been eaten and digested first, and then—"

"I get it."

She blew out her lips and placed her forehead on the table. "Sorry. I've puked three times this morning, and I missed all my earlier classes." She lifted her head, grabbing hold of her cup like a woman who had traveled the desert without water. "This ginger ale is the only thing that's keeping me alive."

Ginger ale was a wise choice. That always helped me when I was sick.

"Welcome, class," Dr. Adams said from the front of the room. "I've written down some resources that I want you to look up on your laptops. Your assignment for class today is to examine these pieces of art and their design based on the materials, the artistic processes, and the inspiration to create them. Each piece of art has a history that you will need to research. You won't have time to finish today, so this will be your homework assignment for the weekend." Dr. Adams tapped the cell phone of a student who was texting during class. Sitting in the front row, the girl wasn't even hiding it. When the professor's eyes lingered on her, she put it away. "Later, you will create works of art that your classmates will interpret, so this will help prepare you for what to look for. Instructions on how to do this properly are included in chapter six of your textbooks."

Amy groaned.

* * *

After class, I walked with Amy along a pedestrian rotary lined with brick pavers that encircled a life-size statue of Thomas Jefferson on the way to our dorm. Winter greenery brightened up the gray granite that supported this powerful bronze figure. The campus had statues all over the place of famous figures, but Thomas Jefferson was a favorite since he had lived nearby.

Amy had been quiet during class. Not that I could blame her. She wasn't the only one who had to endure a drug hangover, so I could relate. I thought of Rick and his date-rape drug, but before I could go down *that* rabbit hole, Dr. Zeller's voice pushed its way through my unpleasant thoughts: "Breathe slowly and deeply. Focus on your surroundings. ..." Within a few seconds, I was feeling much better. It also helped that I had some questions for Amy about what had happened, some more serious than others. My mind was busy, leaving little room for counterproductive thoughts.

I contemplated my best approach, when she spoke first.

"I vaguely remember you helping me out last night." Amy made a fist, which she used to softly punch my arm. "Thanks, Al. I owe you one."

I shook my head. "You owe me nothing." I hesitated for a moment. "Seeing you so out of it, I worried that maybe this Axl guy took advantage of you." My stomach tightened at the thought. "Did he?"

Amy took a quick sip of her drink. "Nope. I didn't even smoke until I was close to campus. That scumbag must've put something in the weed, though. What an asshole." She sucked on her drink until her straw sputtered with air. "I'm going to his shithole of an apartment right now to return his crap weed." She passed a trash can where she tossed her empty cup.

"Alone? Is Luke going with you?"

She wiped her mouth with her hand. "He can't. Right after Sky gets out of class, he's heading to Roanoke with a buddy to look at a used amp he wants to buy."

"Why don't you just flush it down the toilet? There is no reason for you to go there."

Amy looked at me sideways. "What if I'd been driving when that shit had kicked in? I probably would've driven into a tree or worse, another car. I've smoked pot since I was fourteen, and I've never had a reaction like that. I'm returning it to him ... personally."

"Then, *I'm* going with you. You can't go there alone." I wanted to suggest Scott come, too, but I figured it wouldn't go over well.

One side of Amy's lip curled. "Look, I went to buy his crap weed by myself. I can handle it." She burped. "Oh that felt good. Ginger ale is kicking in."

"I didn't realize you went to his place." I stopped and took her arm. "I *am* going with you. No argument. I won't even get out of the car, but I'm going."

"Fine." Amy burped again.

This time, I could smell the ginger. Yuck.

When we returned to the dorm, we dropped off our stuff and headed out to the parking lot, where the Amy-mobile sat waiting. She munched on a box of crackers along the way. When Rick had drugged me, it took days before I could eat normal food again. I remembered how Amy had brought me ginger ale and toast. At the time, it felt like my last meal. I was on the edge.

Snap out of it. This isn't about you.

As her old box of a car rattled down the road, I cranked her heater up, which rewarded me with an icy blast of air through the vents. The midday sun provided a sliver of warmth through the windows but not enough for my liking. When had I become such a lightweight? Growing up in Vermont, a forty-plus degree day encouraged residents to celebrate in their shorts and T-shirts, me included. Back then, I couldn't wait for the temperatures to rise so I could wear lighter clothing. I always knew spring was coming when I was able to open my bedroom window, allowing the sounds of the cars on the street, the birds in the trees, and even the wind to reacquaint with my ears. Since I'd moved south, it was amazing how quickly my blood had thinned.

* * *

Amy turned into an apartment complex on the eastern edge of Charlottesville, not far from the bar we had visited the other day. White vinyl siding covered in green mold, piles of old furniture and trash, and a few old cars in the lot made the complex feel sad, as though it had seen better days. Whenever I saw buildings crumbling or homes in disrepair, I tried to envision what they looked like in their heyday. For this place, that heyday must've been quite some time ago.

Amy pulled into a space between a silver car with duct tape on the fender and a telephone pole before she cut the engine. "Okay. You stay here. I'll be right back." She grabbed a brown paper bag sitting next to her and climbed out of her Volvo.

I jumped out, too, and stared at her over the roof of the car. "Are you sure? I don't mind going in. It may help your case if you aren't alone."

Amy's expression hardened. "What case? The asshole is going to give me my money back, or I'm going kick his nuts into his throat." She made haste toward a door with most of its dark-green paint missing.

"Be careful, and stay by the door. I'll get in the driver's seat in case you need to go quickly."

Amy looked back at me and rolled her eyes. "What the hell? We're not robbing a bank, Al."

Ignoring her comment, I crossed the front of the car and slid into the driver's seat, anyway. As I waited, I put my mind to work to avoid worrying. The one time I had seen Axl, he made me uneasy. Anyone who sold drugs for a living was capable of anything in my book, even kidnapping or murder. I thought about Carrie Stevens again. She had sold drugs for him. A dangerous trade. And Luke had mentioned Axl was abusive. Ever since he had said that, I kept wondering if Axl had anything to do with Carrie's disappearance. The news article I had read said the police had questioned her boyfriend. I should've looked for his name. With all the articles listed, it must've been included in one of them. Henry came to mind. I'd have to research Ethel's accident to find out more about it. Maybe Henry made a statement about the make or the model of the car he had claimed he saw speeding away. Since Carrie had worked in the Counseling Department, I wondered if Candice would have more information about her, like what kind of car she drove. Rick never left my list of suspects, either, although with these new candidates, he was becoming less probable. While I worked that all out in my mind, Axl's apartment door flung open and Amy emerged, slamming it behind her.

I jumped out of the driver's seat and returned to my side of the car.

As she approached, I was about to ask her how it went, when she shook her head, her eyes stern. The message was clear: not here.

On the ride back to campus, she finally offered more. "That asshole wouldn't give me my money back. I threw the shit weed at him and he refused." She laughed with no humor. "He actually tried to get me to sell drugs for him again and said he'd not only pay me back, but he'd get me anything I wanted."

"You came back so fast, I assumed he wasn't home."

We stopped at a traffic light, her crystal keychain swaying.

I sat sideways in my seat, facing her. "What did you say?"

Amy slammed on her horn. "Move it, dipshit," she said to a car that hadn't moved even though the light had turned green. "I told him to forget it." She looked over at me and heaved a heavy sigh.

"What's wrong?"

She shrugged one shoulder. "Nothing ... much. Maybe I shouldn't have come. Sky was right, that guy is bad news. I'm staying the hell away from him." She removed one hand from the steering wheel and pointed at me. "You thought that Norman Bates dude had kidnapped Carrie, but I wouldn't be surprised if this douchebag did it. She probably stiffed him on some drugs, and he beat the shit out of her." She returned her free hand to the wheel. "I'm just spitballing."

"I haven't been able to tell you this, but Carrie worked at the college the year before she went missing."

As though on cue, the college rose up in the distance, gold domes and cupolas flashing their hats for the cars that passed by them on the road out front.

"So?"

Frustrated, I crossed my arms as Amy found a parking space. "So ... she could've been the one who hit Ethel with her car. Dr. Adams said that Henry swore—"

"I know. I know. You already told me all this." Amy shifted into park and turned in her seat. "You know what? Maybe Norman Bates *and* Axl kidnapped her." She started acting all animated for effect. "Maybe Axl is Norman Bate's son and together they—" She smiled and pushed on my arm. "I'm just fucking with you. I can see you've been thinking a lot about this." She paused and looked out the windshield. "It's possible that any one of those dirtbags could've done something. Whoever did it, I hope they get caught."

"Me, too." Somehow, I would make the connection to Carrie. I just wasn't sure what it was. Yet.

* * *

That Saturday, I found an open table at the library and pulled out my Environmental Science textbook to prepare for my test. Since Scott had committed himself to the soccer team, he seemed happier, his mood a bit lighter. He went out jogging last night with Jason and then on his own first thing this morning before he headed out for practice. When he was putting on his soccer attire, I walked into the bedroom just in time to catch sight of his impressive body stark naked. He made a move to cover himself until I told him not to.

"Give me something to think about while you're away."

Everything from his sculpted abdomen to his mammoth arms and legs was a sight to see. His manly parts were even sexier, especially since I knew how much they loved to please me. Scott turned around and bent over to climb into some compression shorts, allowing me a perfect view of his backside. I wanted to reach my hand out and squeeze.

"Are you all right, babe?" Scott stood in front of me forcing his head through the neck of his T-shirt.

I snapped my brain into focus. "Just admiring the view."

Scott made a funny noise in his throat. "I'll show you mine if you'll show me yours." He caught himself. "Sorry. I couldn't help myself. We'll get there."

I opened my textbook and sighed as I thought about it all. "Soon," I said to no one in particular. When would I know the time was right? I was anxious to ask Dr. Zeller about that in my session on Wednesday. In fact, that would be the first thing I planned to bring up.

* * *

Ninety minutes later, I was contemplating a jaunt to the coffee counter for a caffeine fix of tea when a leopard print designer backpack dropped on my table, a cloud of perfume, strong and pungent, surrounding me in noxious gas.

I looked up at Rachael and scowled. What was *she* doing here? "What do you want? And I have about zero patience for whatever it is."

Rachael stood there staring at me, like she did in the window not too long ago.

What was she, a psycho?

Finally, she said, "I had you pegged all wrong."

The heaviness in her voice told me she didn't mean that as a compliment.

"You come off like some poor little orphan girl, but you're not at all what people think, are you?"

I rose. "I don't know what your warped mind is cooking up, but—"

"Does Scott know you're selling drugs on the side?" She glared, her hand braced on her left hip. "Oh yeah, I know all about that." She wobbled her head as though it was too riled up to stay still.

I shook my own head at the absurdity. "Are you completely insane?" I was being rhetorical.

Rachael leaned closer from across the table, her hands flat on the surface, her perfume nauseating. "I saw you and your psycho friend, and I know what you were doing." She pointed. "You may have fooled Scott for now but wait until he hears the truth about you."

I batted her hand away, adrenaline shooting through my veins like a geyser. "Don't you dare point at me. After what you did last semester, you've got some nerve." I grabbed my book and stuffed it into my pack. If Rachael kept this up, there was no telling what I would do. My body quaked with anger.

"I saw you there yesterday." She grabbed her backpack and slid it closer to her. As she did so, my eyes zoned in on the monogram adorning the front pocket: Rachael Moore.

"I don't know what you are talking about."

Moore. Why did that name sound familiar? My mind went into processing mode.

"Sure you don't. Liar." Rachael slung her backpack over her

shoulder just as the name made a connection in my memory banks.

Zach Moore. That's why Jason's last name had popped into my head at first. Monroe was close to Moore.

I almost gasped at the revelation. Zach, the kid who OD'd, had to be Rachael's brother, the one who Luke had said dropped out of school. The name fit. That meant Rachael was the person who stormed into the pizza joint where Luke had worked and screamed at Carrie. Luke said she practically chewed Carrie's head off. He also said the owner almost called the police. It sounded just like something Rachael would do. Carrie had sold the drugs to Zach, and Rachael had blamed her for it. Knowing how Axl had laced Amy's weed with something, who knew what concoction Zach had ingested. Did he suffer permanent damage? At a loss for words, I just stood there, trying to prevent my mouth from hanging open.

"If you think you're going to get away with it, you're dead wrong. If it were up to me, I'd wipe all you druggies off the face of the earth. You're nothing but parasites."

"I don't do drugs, Rachael."

"Yeah, right. And don't bother telling me that emo friend of yours isn't selling. She's just like ..." Rachael clamped her mouth shut and made a hmph sound just before she stormed off.

Was she going to say Carrie? My mind was whirling with motives.

A new suspect had emerged, a person who enjoyed being mean and spiteful and had already shown her hand at blackmail. Was she capable of kidnapping or murder? Her last statement echoed back at me. "If you think you're going to get away with it, you're dead wrong." Was she being dramatic or literal? With her, it was anyone's guess.

Chapter Fifteen

I took a few moments in my room to pull up Zach Moore on Facebook before I went to see Scott at soccer practice. When the page came up, an image of a young man with thick brown hair and a full beard, stood in front of the Commonwealth University Admission's Building, a smile stretched across his face. Not a bad-looking guy, Zach's slanted gray eyes were the same shape as his sister Rachael's, who was plastered all over his feed with him. It made me wonder if Rachael was always mean or if what happened to her brother had changed her.

I scanned through images of Zach sitting at a restaurant overlooking a large river with his father, mother, and sister all wearing sunglasses and bright smiles—Zach sitting outside of a baseball game, Rachael raising a set of two-finger-bunny ears behind his adolescent head—Zach as a youngster, standing on his front stoop, Rachael towering over him, both of them dressed formally as one would do for a special occasion or holiday. What I didn't see were any recent photos—at least nothing over the past year. I wondered what he looked like now.

A knock on my door pulled my eyes off the screen. Was Scott here already? Practice canceled?

It was Amy. The scent of fried food wafted off her clothing as she entered my room. "Hey, what's the big guy doing today? Sky is practicing with his band, and I just got off work. Wanna hang?"

Two thirty-four flashed on my clock. "Scott's at practice for another couple of hours. I was thinking of going to watch for a bit. Want to come with me? We can grab some drinks on the way."

Amy's lips twisted their disapproval.

"I'll buy." I grinned dramatically.

"Fine."

* * *

We sat on the bleachers while I sipped a hot tea and Amy, her coffee. I told Amy all about my encounter with Rachael.

She wrinkled her face up when I was done. "What the hell is wrong with that chick? And how did she know we were at Axl's place? Was she following us? We were only there for what, ten minutes tops?"

I nodded. "I know. Weird." I wanted so badly to let Amy in on my theories about Rachael and Carrie Stevens but wasn't in the mood for more jeering.

Amy's cell phone dinged with a text. She looked down at her screen and started typing. While she did so, I watched my gorgeous boyfriend kick the soccer ball to one of his teammates. Scott was outfitted in a royal-blue mesh pinny along with several other players. Another group wore yellow. His thighs bulged beneath his athletic shorts as his champagne curls moistened from exertion. Even sweaty he was sexy—probably more so. How I was managing to stay celibate was beyond me. Living with him was like sitting in front of a buffet full of my favorite foods, none of which I could eat. And I was starving. I enjoyed the view, the smell, and the taste of his lips, but I couldn't yet indulge. "When that day does come, babe, you may not get out alive," he'd said last night. I smirked to myself. "We'll see who doesn't get out alive."

We *had* successfully cuddled a few times and even made out, and I hadn't had a nightmare since that first one. Nothing as dramatic, anyway. I still suffered flashbacks and a few panicked moments, but they were diminishing as my mind worked to heal itself. What I didn't want to do was take a leap that would set me back further than I was before. I was counting the days till my next session with Dr. Zeller.

Hands on his hips and chest moving with each breath, Scott looked over at me and winked. I blew him a kiss.

The sun crept out from behind a fluffy cloud fringed with darker edges, showering the field in a warm glow and casting bright reflections off the bleachers. The skin on my arms and neck tingled as a flash of warmth shoved away the chill. All day, the sky had a funny look about it. The clouds hurrying much faster than normal, almost like a time-lapse. A bold gust of wind told me why. A front was moving in, a cold one, despite the sun trying its best to fight against it.

"Hey, Sara." Jason approached. "What's up?" He took the bench next to me.

"Hey, Jason. Not much." I looked around him. "Where's Heather?"

"She's busy with some friends."

"Oh. I haven't seen her much this semester. I'll have to text her for a lunch date."

Jason nodded. "I'm sure she'd love that." He stared at the field and then back at me. "Scott told me about his dad during our run last night." He zipped his jacket up a few inches.

"Those two have been fighting since I met Scott in middle school." He widened his legs and leaned back against the bench behind him, his arms providing an easel for his body. "They've never seen eye to eye on much of anything."

A few grunts and commands came floating off the field as the scrimmage descended upon a goal. Scott stood off to one side, jogging around while keeping his eye on the ball.

"Well, I hope they work it out." The wind blew a few strands of hair over my face. I wiped them away, hooking them behind my ear. "It wasn't the best time to meet Mr. Williams."

Jason sat forward and leaned his shoulder into mine. "Don't worry about it. He's always had an attitude about Scott. I'm not sure what it's all about." He glanced over with those soft brown eyes of his. "Their arguments were going on long before now." Jason clapped and then whistled with two fingers at the field.

I appreciated him confirming what I had already known, but it somehow didn't make me feel any better. I wanted to make a good impression with Scott's parents, hoping they'd be my future in-laws. What did Scott's father tell his mother about me? I couldn't even imagine. To him, I was a lowlife, who laughed about serious issues and was steering his son into a ditch. I just hoped I'd get the chance to set the record straight someday.

I sighed.

Amy, Jason, and I watched the scrimmage for another thirty minutes as the afternoon sun edged its way below the horizon. The wind picked up, whipping my hair in my face every chance it got. Scott scored a goal, then looked over at me and smiled, his hair dancing in the wind. He reminded me of a proud peacock spreading his feathers.

After I took my last sip of tepid tea, I crumpled my cup and stuffed it under my leg so it wouldn't blow away.

Amy's phone rang. She listened for a few seconds before

saying, "That sucks. Hard to sing when your throat hurts. I'm at the soccer field with Sara." She paused. "Yes, the soccer field. Come and get me, and I'll ride with you back to your place." She paused again. "Who? Come get me, first. It's getting fucking brutal out. We can drop him off on the way." Amy made a shuddering motion as she ended her call.

Jason chuckled. "Hey, I'm gonna split. Tell Scott I'll go for a run with him tomorrow if he wants the company." When Jason stood and walked off, Scott glanced over at him and tipped his head. Jason returned the greeting with a short wave of his hand.

I loved that they were such close friends. Like Amy and me. Somehow, I had to find a way to thaw the tension between Scott and Amy. Just like with Scott's parents and me, I wanted us all to get along.

Wearing a plaid, earth-tone flannel shirt and a knit winter hat with side flaps, Luke came walking up with Andy, who was donning his signature aviator sunglasses and slicked-back hair. Luke sat next to Amy and Andy perched himself next to me.

The wind carried the smell of leather off his jacket. "What a nice surprise to see you here." His teeth perfectly straight, his jawline covered in just the right length of stubble, Andy smiled like a pop star at a photo shoot. "I was hoping you'd come watch us practice again soon."

I glanced over at Amy expecting her normal "get lost, she's taken" warning, but she was too busy talking with Luke about their plans later.

"Yeah, we'll have to do that."

A gust of air drove through the bleachers, rattling every loose nut and bolt.

Andy put his arm around me and shimmied closer. "Man that wind bites. You'll have to keep me warm."

I detected a citrus flavor in his cologne as I laughed nervously and wiggled out of his embrace.

Andy backed off without much resistance telling me his flirtation was harmless.

"Sorry. I didn't mean to—"

"It's fine. No worries."

"Who do you know on the team? "He stared at the field, his gaze scanning.

Finished with her conversation with Luke, Amy decided to answer for me. "See that blond, the six-foot-plus Thor out there in the blue pinny? The one who's glaring at you right now?"

She wasn't kidding; Scott's jaw clenched, his shoulders rising, and his eyes fierce.

"That's her boyfriend and who we came to see." Before the next blast could knock her over, Amy practically jumped to her feet. "I gotta bounce. You want to walk back to the dorm with us?"

My legs were freezing, my hair was starting to feel like it was caught in the spinning heads of a cotton-candy machine and, on top of that, my butt was getting sore. If I walked back with Amy, I could watch TV and veg until Scott finished practice. "Sure. I'll go back with you." I got up, too.

"You're welcome to hang with us later," Andy said standing.

Amy smirked. "Give it up, Romeo."

We moved toward the exit, when someone calling "Sara" hit my eardrums.

I turned as Scott came jogging over.

"Now you've stepped in it." Amy nudged Andy who ran his hand through his hair a few times, his cheeks the color of bubblegum. "Not so chill now, are you?" Amy giggled as the three of them walked away until they reached the ticket box, where they stopped and waited.

I pulled my hair out of my face from the last slap of wind and pushed up on my toes for a kiss.

Scott kissed me back, but his eyes were *not* pleased. "Who the fuck is that dude? Is Amy trying to replace me already?"

I shook my head, surprised at how quickly he had come to that absurd conclusion. "No. Silly. It's Andy, a friend of Luke's. They're headed downtown, and I didn't want to sit here alone. I'm going back to my room until you're done. Just come get me or send me a text when you're leaving, and I'll meet you down at your place." I touched his firm abdomen, enjoying the rock wall of muscle for a moment. "You look great out there. You haven't missed a beat."

Scott bent down for another, much longer kiss, only to have his teammates ridicule him.

"Come on, dude, get your ass back in the game."

"See you later," he said as he took a step away. "And tell Andy to keep his hands to himself."

Back at Scott's place, I ordered pizza, then sat on his couch in my flannels watching the movie *When Harry Met Sally*, one of my mom's favorites, while Scott showered and changed. A strong scent of paint reeked from the spot on the wall where a hole used to be. Scott had watched a YouTube video about how to cover the area, and he'd done a good job with it. One more coat of paint, and it would be seamless. Thankfully, that wall was white, unlike many other walls in the apartment that were adorned in brown, orange, and even one in turquoise. That was in the upstairs bathroom.

Wearing sweatpants and a pale-yellow T-shirt, Scott came jogging down the stairs a few minutes later, his hair wet, his fresh scent competing with the pungent paint odor.

"I ordered the pizza and got out some paper plates."

"Cool." Scott went into the kitchen and came back with a cold beer in his hand and a glass of water. He took a sip of his beer and sat next to me. "Here you go, babe. I saw you didn't have a drink." He handed me the glass of water and stared at the TV. "What's on?"

"Thank you. It's *When Harry Met Sally*, but you can change it." I grabbed the TV remote from next to me and handed it to him before I took a sip of water.

"Nah. It's fine." He sat back and took another swig of his beer. His eyebrows furrowed and then relaxed a few times as if he was working something out in his head. Finally, he took another drink and put the near-empty bottle down on the coffee table. "So, who was that guy at the scrimmage again?"

I knew it. He hadn't gotten over the harmless "arm around my shoulders" from earlier. I rolled my eyes and placed my glass down next to his beer. "Come on, Scott. He's a friend of Luke's."

Scott turned his entire body, ready to confront. "Well, you must know him well enough that he's comfortable putting his arm around you." His eyes probed.

"For God's sake, he was just joking around. And I've only met him once."

Scott grabbed his beer off the table. "When was *that*?"

"I already told you. When I went with Amy to see Luke practice a month ago." I took the remote and muted the sound of Billy Crystal arguing with Meg Ryan. We didn't need two arguments competing with each other in one room.

Scott finished what was left of his beer and smacked the bottle down on the table, adding another small nick to an already blemished surface. "Amy again."

I scratched my head, trying to remain calm. "You are the

only one who has a problem here. Amy hasn't said one bad thing about you."

Scott made a rumbling noise in his throat. "Other than accusing me of putting my own feelings over yours and ruining your chances of arresting rapists who deserve to fucking die. Or warning me that if I laid a hand on her boyfriend that she'd cut me in two with her lightsaber."

A laugh shot out from my throat. "What? Are you kidding me? She was on drugs, Scott. You can't hold her responsible for—"

"Then she takes you to bars where drug dealers and friends of Luke's want nothing more than to get you in the sack. I saw the way that guy looked at you." His cheeks fired up, right along with his eyes.

I opened *my* eyes as wide as they'd go. "Well, that must've been quite a trick because he was wearing sunglasses. You know, Scott, I spent all last fall worried that you were cheating on *me*. I had to endure your nasty ex-girlfriends and people like Rachael, who are far more dangerous than Andy is. She's still harassing me, you know. I'm sorry if Andy bothered you, but what this really comes down to is you not trusting me. And I have never given you a reason not to."

Scott's brow relaxed, his eyes softening. "I know. You're right." His voice dipped lower. "When he put his arm around you, I just wanted to run off that field and beat the shit out of him. Seeing the four of you together was like watching what my life be would be like without you." The warmth from his hand found my shoulder. "A guy went fucking bonkers over you last semester, and ... I don't know." He shook his head and dropped his chin for a moment. "I don't have any excuse. Other than, I'm terrified I'm going to lose you again."

How can you think that? "You are *not* going to lose me. After everything we've been through, we still came back to each other. You're right. I did have a lunatic who obsessed over me last semester, although I suspect it had more to do with being told *no* than anything else, but you had a whole population of women who were crushing *big time* on you. I'm sure they still are."

I know Rachael is. Mindy and Charlene were still MIA. By now, I was convinced they must've dropped out or transferred somewhere.

Scott moved closer to me. He used his gentle voice. "You're really going to think I'm a selfish bastard when I say this, but what do I have to offer you right now?"

I tilted my head, confused. "What are you talking about? You have *yourself* to offer me."

"Yeah, but there's not much I can *do* for you anymore." He raised his brows and then lowered them, staring at me as if I should know what he meant.

An invisible bonk to the head, and it dawned on me. "You think because we're not having sex right now that you are less appealing to me?"

Scott nodded subtly. "Maybe."

"What?" I grabbed his face with my hands. "You're crazy. Just being with you is enough for me—more than enough. Your back rubs, your late-night talks off the ledge, your listening ear, not to mention, your fun-loving personality and kind heart." My eyes drifted upward as I reeled off the list. "Your soft lips, your gorgeous body that I get to enjoy regardless, your fun meals—"

"Okay, okay. I get it." Scott put his hands over mine still framing his face.

Just then, the doorbell rang, followed by a knock.

"That must be the pizza." I got up and grabbed the money that I had already laid out on the dining room table.

I understood his insecure feelings. I did. I had promised

him not too long ago—the night he had given me that necklace —that I'd never leave him. But those were different circumstances, and I was never going to fall for something like that again. If anyone said anything about Scott in the future, I'd talk to him first, let him explain.

Scott walked over to the door and opened it while I crossed the room, handing him the money. Pepperoni, hot melted cheese, and baked crust had my mouth watering with anticipation.

Once we refreshed our drinks and had our plates loaded down with pizza, we sat in the living room to continue our movie. I turned the volume back up and took an enormous bite of my slice, the cheese stretching like taffy.

Twenty minutes later, we both sat back with full bellies. Scott was on my right, and I used his body as a backrest. I loved feeling him close to me, his subtle movements, his lungs taking in oxygen, his manly scent. It always brought me comfort.

"Did you say Rachael was still harassing you?" Scott asked from behind my head.

I scooted forward and turned around. "Yeah, she came to the library yesterday and said that she knew I was selling drugs because she'd seen me do it. She also said that I wasn't going to get away with it." I wobbled my head. "I'm paraphrasing."

Scott rattled his own head. "You've lost me. Why would Rachael think you were selling drugs? That's nuts ... even for her."

I swallowed. *Be honest.* "Well ... remember how out of it Amy was the other day?" I hadn't talked much about Amy lately. It was a touchy subject.

Scott nodded, his eyes too narrow to read.

"I guess that Axl guy had laced her pot with something, and she was really sick the next day. You should've seen her when she came to class. I'm surprised that she even made it there. She had been throwing up all that morning, and she was really pale—"

"Sara." Scott raised one palm. "Can you get back to how this relates to you and Rachael?"

I wrung my hands. "Luke was out of town and Amy was really upset about what Axl had done to her. She was going to his place to return the weed and demand her money back." I placed my hand on Scott's knee, my eyes pleading for his understanding. "I couldn't let her go alone."

Scott tipped his head back and exhaled as though the situation was becoming clear to him, before he moved to the edge of his seat. "Don't fucking tell me you went to this Axl person's house?" His eyes glared, demanding an answer.

I remained silent, which told him all he needed to know.

"You went to a drug dealer's house? Are you insane?" He grabbed my forearm, his grip tighter than normal. "Do you know how dangerous that was? I can't believe you would do that." After he released a huff of disapproval, he sprang to his feet and paced the room.

"She was going, and I couldn't stop her." I rose to my feet, hoping to make my point. "I didn't even go in. I waited in the car."

Scott rubbed his jaw, his eyes searching the air for answers. "What if he had done something to Amy? Then what were you going to do?"

"I would've called 911 or *you*." I wiped my sweaty palms on my flannels, which were starting to feel too warm for the moment. The pizza wasn't sitting well, either.

He faced me, his hands waving their outrage in the air. "And what was I supposed to do? I have no clue where this scumbag lives. Would you be able to tell me or a 911 operator where to find the place? And how far away was it? Plus, he could've had other addicts there with him. You have no clue what danger you put yourself in." He set his jaw and shook his head. "And once again, Amy was at the center of the trouble."

Which is why I didn't tell you, Scott.

I stepped forward. "She didn't ask me to go. This wasn't her fault. And nothing happened." I walked a little closer. "Amy came out a few minutes later and said he wouldn't give her the money back. We left right away."

Scott lowered his voice to an alarming level. "Sara, you can't keep this kind of stuff from me. How am I supposed to keep you safe if you keep running around town going to shit bars and drug dens?" He rubbed his forehead like my dad used to do when he was flustered.

"It's nice that you worry about me, but I'm not a child."

"And how did Rachael know about it? Have you been there before?" Scott's tone was sharp and unforgiving.

"No. I think she followed us. I'm not sure."

"Why would she do that?"

Oh good, a reason to change the subject. "Do you remember that girl who went missing last year?"

By the time I had Scott fully up to speed with my suspicions and he had finished another beer, I wasn't sure by the look on his face if he thought I needed a tranquilizer or straitjacket. We had returned to the couch, but I wasn't sure how long Scott was going to remain there.

He squeezed his eyes shut. "Let me see if I get this straight. You think that this janitor, Henry, may have kidnapped some girl you know nothing about because she may have hit his wife with her car two years ago? But then you also think this Axl loser could've done it—the drug dealer, whose house you just went to without any thought for your own safety? And now you also think that Rachael could've done something to her, seeking revenge because Axl and Carrie sold drugs to her younger brother who OD'd? Does that cover it?"

He opened his eyes and waited, his eyebrows slanted with impatience.

"Um." I hugged my arms around my waist for support.

"Sara. You don't know anything about this Carrie chick. She could've been a nutcase for all you know. She could've even done something to herself."

"Why? You think she killed herself?"

"You don't know that she's even dead. If she was into drugs, you don't know what happened."

Hating that he might be right, I hissed like a little girl whose parent had just told her she couldn't have another piece of candy. "I was just trying to—"

"You need to let this go." Scott leaned closer to make his point known. "Let the police do their jobs. You are not in any position to be sneaking around digging up dirt on people. He placed both hands on my shoulders.

"But—"

"Sara." His voice was firm and parental. How had Scott become my dad? "If you don't stop this, I'm going to call Abigail."

I was outraged, my lower lip quivering. "What? No. You can't do that. She's pregnant, Scott."

His gaze remained steady. "You need to reign this in. I can't have you behaving like an amateur vigilante for some whacked-out girl who probably caused her own problems."

My mouth hinged open. "How can you say that? You don't know what happened to her any more than I do."

Scott palmed the back of his neck. "I'm just sayin'."

I flew to my feet. "Wow. That's harsh."

Scott stood and grabbed me around the waist. "I'm sorry. I didn't mean it that way. Of course I want them to find her. From what you just said, it sounded like she was dealing drugs.

Weird shit can go down when you choose that line of work. Weird shit."

I wrestled out of his arms but stood near.

Scott sighed. "I've seen it happen before. We had a kid in high school who dealt drugs, and one day, the cops found him next to a mud puddle, drowned. His face was battered so badly they had to use his fingerprints to identify him." He kissed my forehead, his tone soothing. "Police are trained to take risks." He looked into my eyes and smirked. "And even though you are becoming quite the badass in your self-defense class, let the appropriate people handle this."

I gazed up at him, my lower lip quivering. "Promise me you won't call Abigail."

Scott tugged me closer, allowing my head to rest under his chin. "I won't. But you have to promise *me* something, too." He pulled back and gripped my arms. "I can't tell you not to look into this, but *promise* me that you won't go back to Axl's place, or to Rachael's dorm, or even to this Henry guy's place snooping around."

I nodded. How did he know that I was contemplating every one of those things?

Chapter Sixteen

After my Tuesday classes, I arrived at Scott's place tired from a long day of running around campus. I made one trip to the library to study for an Elementary Math quiz that I was confident about and then returned a couple of hours later to finish a mock lesson plan for my Child Development class. My professors liked to load on the work.

When I drove in, Scott's parking space was empty, exciting me with the prospect of some free time to myself. I was ready for flannel pj's, a cup of hot tea, and a catnap on the couch before I had to gear up and make dinner.

I let myself into the apartment, removed my boots and coat, and approached the stairs, where a small wastebasket from the upstairs bathroom sat empty next to the steps, a new bag lining the can. Carrying the trash can with me, I jogged upstairs to put it back and change into some comfortable clothes.

I washed my face and reached for a towel, when a small red smudge called out to me from the edge of the sink. I bent closer to examine the stain further, my eyes following the cabinet down to another blot on the linoleum floor. Memories of Scott's bathroom at the fraternity house from last semester strobed through my mind—his sink splattered in blood, the toilet, and the floor. The soiled T-shirt. My chest became a hive for a colony of invisible bees, all stinging my insides at the same time.

Calm down, Sara. This is not a crime scene.

Scott probably cut himself shaving. I sat on the edge of the tub and performed my breathing exercises, until I was convinced everything was okay. Was this going to happen to me every time I saw blood? A vision of my future son standing in front of me with a scraped knee, while I curled into the fetal position on the floor came to mind.

As I shook that thought away, I rinsed down the sink and wiped up the blot on the floor before going about my end-of-the-day routine.

I practiced my self-defense moves for about thirty minutes before I rewarded myself with a nap on the couch, my body nestled under a plush throw. Before I knew it, my eyes fluttered open as a TV commercial tried to sell me fabric softener. I yawned and looked at the clock on the cable box, which flashed 5:35 p.m.

I let my mind rouse to full consciousness and then pried myself off the cushions to start dinner. By 6:30 p.m., I was just finishing a chicken-and-pasta recipe I had found online, when a text chimed in from Scott: "Running late. Don't wait to eat dinner."

I sat at the table, eating my one-pot dish and enjoying the flavors of parmesan and tomato tastiness while baked garlic bread lent the room a tantalizing aroma.

Once I had my fill, I put the casserole dish in the oven to keep warm for Scott, along with the remnants of the garlic bread, and cleaned up my mess.

I pulled out my books and started on a paper for my Environmental Science class. My topic was deep-sea mining, a subject I knew nothing about.

An hour later, I texted Amy, hoping for a nice long chat to break up the monotony: "What are you up to tonight?"

I stared at my phone for several minutes, willing it to respond. No dots. No nothing. She was probably with Luke.

I grumbled to myself and continued my boring research.

* * *

The front door opened, causing a wintery blast to stir me like an alarm clock as I sat slumped over the dining room table.

"Hello, sleepyhead." Scott came in the door and removed his coat and shoes. He traveled with a tailwind of cool air over to me and bent down to kiss the top of my head. His body smelled like the outdoors, with a shot of locker room perspiration. Times ten. He rarely smelled bad, although he did tonight. Just like he did on the night he fought with his dad. I tried not to plug my nose or make a nasty face about it.

"Sorry I'm so late." He walked over to the hall closet to hang up his coat.

I looked at the clock on my laptop: 11:06 p.m.

"Wow." I yawned. "You *are* late. How come?"

Scott continued past me and into the kitchen, where he poured himself a glass of water.

"After practice, I went to the gym to do some strength training." He sat at the table and took a long swig of his water.

"I didn't realize the gym was open that late," I said.

Scott rolled his head back and exhaled, his eyes closing.

"Are you hungry? I've got—"

"Not really." He moved his head back into position and took another drink, emptying the glass.

"Have you eaten?"

I forced myself off the chair and approached the oven, where I pulled out the now-cooled casserole dish and set it on the counter. "It was really good. I've also got garlic bread." I was used to him coming back famished, especially after a practice or workout.

Scott shook his head, his mouth forming a distinct frown.

I took a minute to cover the dish with foil as well as the bread and put it all in the fridge. When I returned to the table, Scott sat staring out the window into the darkness.

"Did you grab dinner on campus?"

When he looked at me his right eye drooped lower than the left, almost as if he was winking, but not quite. "What happened to your eye?"

Scott sat forward and gripped his empty glass, which shattered in his hand like someone had shot it with a gun. A drizzle of blood flowed down from his palm, creating a small puddle on the table.

My knees went weak, my throat filling with bile.

"Oh my God." I ran into the kitchen and grabbed a wad of paper towels, which I moistened before I returned to Scott.

"What happened?" I opened his hand and pulled out a chunk of glass, inviting more blood to spill.

My stomach lurched, my anxiety storm from earlier returning with the strength of a typhoon. While I coached myself that nothing was *really* wrong, Scott didn't move, his eyes vacant.

Hold it together. You can handle this.

"Doesn't it hurt?" I dabbed the blood away to reveal a cut that was smaller than I had expected. *Phew.* Once I had the wound patted clean, I grabbed his other hand. "Here hold this in place. I'll get some Band-Aids."

I was taking control, and it felt good for a change.

Scott nodded but didn't otherwise react. "My hand spasmed," was all he said.

I darted into the other room and fished through my purse for a small first-aid kit, contemplating the bigger one I carried in my car. After the accident with my parents, I never left home without one—or two or three in my possession. I found what I needed and returned to Scott, who was staring down at the wound.

His right hand, the dominant one, was taking quite a beating lately between punching holes in walls and crushing glasses. I didn't think it was possible to crush a glass like that. Maybe it was cheaply made?

"Come on. Let's wash that off in the sink." I tapped Scott's shoulder to snap him out of his trance. If he was this tired, why didn't he come home sooner? I hated the thought of him driving in this condition.

"It's nothing." He followed me into the kitchen, where I turned on the water and gave his hand a light rinse. After I dried the area again, I bandaged it and then took a few minutes to clean the glass off the table. When I was finished, I walked Scott, who was still standing at the sink, into the dining room and sat him down. What was going on with my zombie boyfriend? Had he pushed himself too far physically? Was he sick?

"Okay. Wound is clean. Now, what is wrong? What caused the glass to shatter like that?"

Scott kept his head down. "I must've lifted too much weight in the gym. That's all. It happens." His voice sagged right along with his posture.

I lifted his chin, but his eyes remained downcast. "What happened to your eye then?"

"I got beaned in the head with a soccer ball at practice."

I cringed outwardly. "Oh. That sounds painful." I touched

the side of his face. "I noticed there was some blood on the sink upstairs. Was that also from you?" It was a stupid question. We were the only two people living here, but I wanted to get him talking.

Scott rubbed at his nose. "Yeah. I got a bloody nose earlier. I get them in the winter, sometimes."

I kissed his forehead and hugged him. "Boy, you've had a rough day, haven't you?" From his body language, I was making a vast understatement.

I examined him further. "Are you sure you're okay? Is something else wrong?" My mind wrestled with what I was witnessing.

Scott shook his head and stood. "No. I already told you what happened. I'm just fucking beat. Jesus, can't a guy be tired?"

Why so defensive? I was only asking.

He walked with limp legs over to the stairs. "I'm going to take a quick shower and rack out."

Rack out? Was that guy talk for go to bed? I didn't dare ask.

"Okay. I'll see you up there." I stood and walked around the apartment turning off all the lights. Normally Scott helped me with these things.

As I shut down my laptop, I couldn't help but worry. Triggers were going off in my head like a bunch of snap firecrackers. Scott's despondent behavior reminded me of how he had acted after that Halloween party from hell. His swollen eye, brought up a memory of Derek and *his* injuries—the ones Rick had caused after Derek had stollen the evidence. The bloody bathroom. *The secrets.* Was Scott being honest with me about what was going on now? I wanted to believe he was, but how could I, after everything I'd just been through. Rick was gone. Scott and I were together again. He never cheated, and in fact, risked his life to hold Rick accountable. The reason Scott was lying before was because he was being victimized and blackmailed. Was that what was happening here? Did he confront Axl and didn't want to tell me about it?

My inner critic kept needling. *Something isn't right here.*

* * *

After a terrible night's sleep, I walked into 2D Art to find Amy's regular chair empty. I really wanted to talk with her about Scott and a nightmare I had that was too bizarre to make any sense out of. In the dream, I was trying to find Scott in all these strange places but couldn't. At one point, I was digging a hole in the ground. Maybe I was trying to uncover the truth, but I was no expert when it came to the subconscious.

As class started, I kept glancing over at the doorway, hoping she'd show up. I hadn't seen Amy since Monday when we had our last class together. We hung out for a few minutes afterward in our dorm. She texted me on Tuesday morning about an assignment for this class, but I hadn't heard from her since then. It was unusual for us to go so long without communicating with each other. I sent her a quick text asking if she was sick or something.

Halfway through class and while the other students were all doing their assignments on their laptops, Dr. Adams sauntered by. "Where's your second half?" he asked, which I understood this time. "She looked a little pale last Friday, so I was wondering if she'd even be here on Monday." He sneezed and pulled out a handkerchief to wipe his nose. "Sorry. Allergies. Did she have a relapse or something?"

"I don't know, actually. I texted her but haven't heard back. I hope she's not sick. She stays down at her boyfriend's place a lot, so I don't see her every day." When it came to Amy, I wasn't used to being out of the loop.

Dr. Adams stuffed his handkerchief back into his blazer pocket. "Tell her I hope she feels better. I trust you can give her the class assignment? It's also online."

I nodded. "Sure."

After class, I dodged over to my dorm room and knocked on Amy's door.

No answer and no sound came from her room. Two more texts and two hours later, I still hadn't heard anything. Weird. I wished I had Luke's number or even knew where he lived.

* * *

"Do you think you are ready for such big a step?" Dr. Zeller sat in the same dark-maroon chair, while I remained on the same floral love seat across from her. I had just asked her about having sex with Scott again.

"Sometimes I think I am. But ..." I paused, assembling my thoughts.

"Have you been doing your breathing exercises and meditation?" she asked, tapping a pencil on her lower lip, a pad of paper cradled on her lap, ready to take notes.

"Yes, I do the breathing often and meditate before I go to sleep at night. It seems to help me clear my head."

Just not last night.

"Have you had any more nightmares or flashbacks?" she asked.

Do I want to get into this? Last night wasn't a nightmare per se, and it definitely wasn't a flashback.

"Not nightmares, just some bizarre dreams. And the flashbacks aren't as bad as they used to be." Time seemed to be helping them fade but not completely.

"Do you want to talk about the bizarre dream?"

"Not really. Let me think it through some more. It wasn't

scary. Just strange. And it had nothing to do with Rick or my parents."

The dream could wait. I wanted to talk more about being physical with Scott again, and I only had forty-five minutes to cover it. I was ready to pick her brain clean like a vulture on *that* subject.

Dr. Zeller shifted in her chair. "Are you feeling pressure from Scott to be intimate?" Her brow lowered a tad, and she stopped tapping her pencil on her lip.

I shook my head. "No. Not at all. It's me who wants to be with *him*. He's been very patient." I crossed and then uncrossed my legs, my hands fidgety.

She grabbed a small yellow stress ball with a happy face on it from the table next to her and handed it over to me.

I started squeezing.

"When recovering from a sexual assault, there is no right or wrong answer as to when a victim is ready for intimacy. Some bounce back quickly; but others can take years."

My body slumped. *Years?* More squeezing. "I'm not sure I can wait years. Just looking at him when he's changing is difficult enough. Sometimes I just want to reach out and touch him."

Her face brightened. She crossed her legs and leaned forward. "That's a good sign. Desire is important. Some victims who have experienced a sexual assault don't even make the connection between the trauma and their problems with intimacy. I've had clients who came in here about sexual problems that we later discovered stemmed from a prior sexual assault." She took a breath. "We know what happened to you, so you have a full understanding of why you feel the way you do."

I searched her eyes, hoping she'd give me a magic pill or conjure a spell that would rewrite history for me. I wanted to take that next step ... so badly. This was the real world, however.

"I don't want to tell you what to do, but I would suggest taking things slowly."

As I expected, she was not saying what I wanted to hear.

"You have a lot working in your favor. Your partner knows what happened to you, so you can be honest with him about your feelings. It sounds like he's not pressuring you, which is also good. You want to separate being intimate with Scott from the rape. What we want to do is change your negative feelings about sex to feelings of nurturing and empowerment. You can start small. Try touching each other non-sexually and see how that makes you feel. When you get to a point where you become uncomfortable, stop and try again another time. The trauma is still very new, and it may take some time for you to be fully comfortable with intimacy."

"We *have* cuddled and kissed," I said.

Her eyebrows shot up. "Oh? And how did that go?"

"Good. I didn't have any problem with it." I smirked. "I actually liked it."

"Did you feel aroused in any way?"

I chuckled and rolled my eyes. "Oh yeah. You should see my boyfriend. He could arouse a nun. I haven't been able to undress in front of him yet, but I want to."

Dr. Zeller smiled, compassion evident in her eyes. "That's good news. Keep moving forward. It's healthy. Just be prepared for some bad feelings that may surface. If that happens, use those relaxation techniques I taught you. It will pass. You're testing the waters as you go. Remember, you've made some substantial progress already, so take comfort in that." She reached forward and touched my knee. "Be patient with yourself."

* * *

Before my self-defense class started and while trying to process the rest of my session with Dr. Zeller, I met up with Heather at a coffee shop on campus for a quick visit. I hadn't seen much of Heather since the turmoil began at the beginning of the semester, and I was eager to see her. I didn't have a lot of friends, and I was hoping Heather and I could get to know each other better, especially since Scott and Jason were best buds. I envisioned family cookouts with the four of us and vacations.

I walked in the door, allowing the fresh aroma of coffee grounds to greet my nostrils. I'd always loved the smell of coffee—the beans of varied flavors, the grounds and the brewing—but never the taste, which always landed bitter on my tongue.

Wearing a light-pink cardigan layered over a white V-neck top, Heather sat near a window, waving me over. Recessed lighting brightened her long walnut-colored hair. All that was missing from her near-perfect smile and her chocolate pudding eyes was a flowery lei around her neck, and Heather could be a poster girl for suntan ads in the tropics. She was striking to say the least.

She stood when I approached.

"Hey, stranger," I said leaning in for a hug.

"I know. It's been a while." Heather returned to her chair.

I glanced up at the drink counter as I removed my coat and draped it over a chair. No customers were in line. "Let me go grab a drink, and I'll be right back."

A few minutes later, I had my chai-tea latte and was ready to catch up with my friend. Cinnamon whirled around the steam floating off the lid of my cup. "I saw Jason the other day at Scott's practice."

Heather finished chewing on a biscotti she must've ordered before I had arrived. "Yeah, he told me." She brushed the crumbs from her fingers. "I'm so glad you texted me. I'd been meaning to get in touch with you, anyway." She blinked her long lustrous lashes and tipped her head slightly. "How are you doing?"

I looked at my cell phone for the time, which was limited. At least I had changed into my workout clothes already, buying me an extra minute or two. "I've been going to counseling, and that's been a huge help."

Heather rested her arms on the table, her eyes thoughtful. "That's awesome. I'm happy you found someone who can help. I heard that Scott has his own apartment now. Jason said it's a pretty cool place. I feel badly that I haven't been down to see it." She shrugged. "Been a busy semester so far."

I waved her off. "Ah. No worries. We've all been busy." I took a quick sip of tea, the cardamom complimenting the cinnamon as it slid down my throat.

"Are you and Scott adjusting okay? I know it must be weird after all the crap you two went through." Her eyes dipped. "Especially for you."

I snuggled my cup with my palms. "Yeah. For the most part." I took another sip of tea. "Scott wasn't happy with me the other day, though. He's been acting a little strange lately. It didn't help when I told him that I'd been doing a tiny bit of research on that Carrie Stevens person who went missing last year. She's the college student that—"

"I know who Carrie is." Heather's expression changed, her voice carrying an edge.

"Oh yeah. I forgot you were here when she disappeared."

Were they friends?

"Why were you researching about *her*?" I could almost see the question marks in Heather's eyes.

I needed to explain myself. "I saw the press conference with her parents last month, and I guess it kind of stuck with me. At first, I thought Rick might have had something to do with it, but then I found out some things about a few *other* people around here. I told Scott about it, and he got upset. He practically ordered me *not* to go looking for trouble. He said he was afraid I would put myself in danger."

Heather seemed to be thinking hard about this. Her normally bright face had dimmed. "Hmm. Did Scott mention how strange she was? I mean like bat shit. I feel bad that she's missing, but something wasn't right about her."

So not friends. And what did she mean by "Did Scott mention?" I thought he didn't know her. I sat up straighter, my mind starting to reel. "What kind of strange? Did you know her?"

Heather palmed her coffee mug, exhaling. "I didn't really *know* her. I saw her in action, and she was just ... I don't know. I'm surprised Scott hasn't told you about what happened."

Something happened?

She'd mentioned Scott twice now in relation to Carrie. This wasn't sounding good.

"You should ask him. I probably shouldn't say anything more. Talk to Scott about it."

"Scott knew her? He specifically told me that he didn't know her." *What is happening?* Had Scott lied to me? Did he actually know this girl? I felt like I was walking through a thunderstorm with metal rods attached to my head.

I swallowed another sip of tea to remain calm, a fresh case of heartburn getting worse by the second. "It's okay to tell me, Heather. I'm sure Scott will tell me, anyway." I was pouring it on, hoping she'd open up.

She hesitated. "*He* didn't do anything wrong. It wasn't like that." She stuttered a little.

He was involved with her? I felt sick, breathless. "Then

what *was* it like?" I grabbed her arm from across the table to jolt her. "Heather. What's going on?"

"Just ask Scott about it. I'm sure he'll tell you." She glanced down at her cell phone as she pulled her arm away. "Oh, shit, I've gotta run." Within seconds, Heather was up, had her coat on, and was on her way out the door, the words, "Let's try to do this again soon," in her tailwind.

I couldn't even acknowledge her. All I could do was concentrate on *not* spontaneously combusting. This felt so much like last semester. The lies, the deception. But it wasn't Scott's fault back then. I couldn't think straight. More triggers. More anxiety.

I skipped my self-defense class and went straight to Scott's place. I had vowed I'd confront him if something else came up and that was exactly what I was going to do. I'd give him a chance to explain. I owed him that.

On the way there, my cell phone rang with a number I didn't recognize. "Hello?"

"Hey, Sara. It's Luke. Is Amy with you?" he asked.

"No. I haven't seen Amy since Monday. I figured she was with you." My brain reminded me it was Wednesday.

"I haven't seen her since yesterday afternoon." His voice was elevated—tense—so unlike "easygoing" Luke.

"I'll head back to campus. Maybe she's in her room."

"I'm in her room right now."

"Maybe she's working. I could—"

"I just left there. Was she in her room last night?" he asked, with a briskness I wasn't used to hearing from him.

"I don't know. I stayed at Scott's apartment. But she didn't come to art class today."

Don't panic. This was Amy, the girl who could take on the world.

Luke exhaled over the phone. "Where the fuck is she? I've been calling and texting her since last night."

I pulled into a McDonald's parking lot and shifted into park. "I texted her several times earlier, too, but she didn't get back to me, either. Come to think of it, she didn't text me back last night." My stomach tensed. "Do you think she's in trouble?" My heart ramped up for another catastrophe I wasn't prepared for. They were piling up like snowbanks around my nervous system.

No answer. Then Luke exhaled again. "Nah. I'm sure she's just at the store or something. Her car is gone. It's not the first time she hasn't gotten back to me right away, and I was busy last night with the band, so she probably stayed in her room. I'll hang here until she comes back."

"I'll come stay with you."

"No. Don't worry about it. As soon as she comes in, I'll text you."

"But—"

"Seriously, don't sweat it. It's cool. She'll show up."

"She hasn't bought any more weed from Axl has she?"

Luke chuckled. "Nope. I gave her some of mine and made her promise she wouldn't do it again. I've got a call coming in. I'll let you know when she shows up."

As soon as the call ended, I tried Amy's cell phone. It went right to voicemail. Was her phone off? I sent her another text: "Amy, where are you? Luke is worried and so am I. CALL ME." At least I had Luke's number now, which I planned to keep using until Amy showed up.

I drove out of McDonalds and right over to Scott's place, not planning to stay long, unless Luke called me back with some better news.

Scott was sitting on the couch when I walked in, elbows rested on his thighs, head down. The TV was off. Very atypical.

He paused and then said, "I have some things I need to talk to you about."

My first thought came rolling out of my mouth. "Did you talk to Heather?"

Posture crumbling, he nodded in a subtle way. "Yes, but I wanted to talk to you, anyway." He got up and approached me, his hands reaching out to take my coat.

Am I in the Twilight Zone?

I thwarted his efforts and did it myself, annoyed. Why was he so secretive?

After I hung my coat up, I followed Scott over to the couch and plunked myself down.

"This is about Carrie Stevens, then?" I tried not to snarl.

"Yes."

"So, you *did* know her?" My heart was barely hanging on. "You lied to me about it, then?"

He shook his head. "No. Not really." He raised his palm. "Let me explain."

I crossed my arms and waited. *Breathe.*

"At the beginning of last year, I went to an off-campus party, and she was there. I drank too much, and we ended up back at my room."

The thought of Carrie and Scott together made the bile in the back of my throat thicken and my stomach churn. Who hadn't Scott slept with? This wasn't his finest hour.

"I didn't sleep with her." He joined his eyes with mine. "We messed around, but we were both too drunk to do much else." He swallowed hard. "Anyway, she kept coming by, but I told her I wasn't interested." Edginess cut through his voice as though defending an argument I hadn't made. "I didn't lead her on. She just wouldn't take a hint. She started coming to my soccer games and practices. Then over winter break last year, she showed up at my dad's dealership to buy a car. It was fucking nuts."

I pictured the troubling scene in my head as he spoke. "So, what happened?"

"Nothing. I told her that if she didn't back off I was going to get a restraining order."

I huffed. "So, when your dad said you had girls stalking you last year, that's what he meant?"

With a bowed spine and sagging shoulders, Scott nodded as though it was killing him to admit this. "That's all the contact I've had with her. I didn't see her after that." He palmed the back of his neck. "I swear."

I lowered my chin to let all the possibilities sink in, none of them good. "You didn't see her because she went missing."

Scott shook his head vehemently. "No. I didn't see her long before that."

"Did the police question you?"

A new rut plowed across Scott's forehead. "Why would they question *me*?"

I uncrossed my arms, not sure about the accusations my mind was drawing up. "Because she was harassing you."

"So?" His eyes narrowed, staring me down.

I took a breath. What was I saying? This was Scott, after all, the love of my life—the man who fought dragons for me. Still, my mind struggled. "Putting all that aside, you lied to me on several occasions about this. I asked you when we first met if you knew her. You said no." My eyes widened. "I asked you what your dad was referring to about the stalker comment and you brushed it off. Then the other day, I asked you once again about it, and you still claimed you didn't know her." My wheels were turning right off a cliff, my stomach doing several flip-flops.

Scott tried to take my hand, but I refused to let him.

"You're right, I did. What was I supposed to say to you when we first met? 'Hey, this girl went missing last year and, oh by the way, she was a stalker that wouldn't leave me alone.' With my dad and the other day, I should have come clean. I wanted to tell you the other night but lost my nerve."

"Why? What were you afraid of?" I glared, my mind filled with skepticism.

"Losing you. It's such a fucked-up situation, and I wasn't sure how you'd take it."

"But you were so mean about her—like you didn't even care that she was gone." My voice plunged lower. "Like she deserved what she got."

Scott huffed. "I wasn't mean about her. Of course I care, but I was trying to make you understand that she may have brought whatever happened on herself." He fanned a hand out. "She wasn't right in the head."

I couldn't sit any longer. "After everything we've been through, how could you lie to me?" I headed for the closet and retrieved my coat, slamming my arms into the sleeves.

Scott followed me over. "Where are you going?"

"I need some time to think. I'm not sure about any of this."

Scott stood back. "What? Come on, Sara. I'm not the only one who's not being honest here." He drew a deep breath. "Abigail doesn't know we're back together, does she?"

I stared at his protruding eyes.

"You haven't even told her what happened to you."

I grabbed my keys from inside of my coat pocket. "She's pregnant, Scott. I didn't want to—"

"Upset her?" His tone mocked.

"It's not the same thing. I was protecting her."

Scott made a sweeping gesture with his hand, shaking his

head. "Bullshit. It *is* the same thing. You just don't want to admit it. This was an awkward situation for me. I didn't even know you were curious about Carrie until the other day. It's not as if we haven't had a shit show going on since we got back from break. When was I supposed to bring it up? In jail?" He approached, his voice calmer. "I'm sorry I didn't tell you about Carrie. But there was nothing to tell." He blinked, his eyes going all wounded puppy on me. "Please don't go."

My cell phone dinged from my other pocket. I took it out and stared at a text from Luke: "Any word from Amy, yet?" I felt sick and equally frustrated.

I texted him back: "No. I'm on my way."

"Look. Luke hasn't seen Amy since yesterday, and he's worried. I'm worried, too. She didn't show up for class today. I'm going back to campus to help him look for her."

Scott's eyes froze over. "Amy can take care of herself. Right now, *I* need you here." He pointed his index finger toward the floor as though demanding I obey.

I gazed up at him, galled by his attitude toward my friend. "Amy is my best friend, Scott. She was there for me when I needed her." *How can you not see that?*

"And I wasn't?" He glared. "You are always choosing *her* over me."

"That's not true. This is important, Scott. What if she's missing?"

He puffed out a breath as though amused and rubbed his forehead. "Don't you think you may be jumping to conclusions? Here you go again with your conspiracy theories. I'm sure she's fine."

His apathy coiled inside of me like a rusty screw. "Just like Carrie was fine?" My mind screamed with the wrong possibilities. "Funny how eager you are to brush this off."

"What's that supposed to mean?" Scott thrust his hands on his hips.

My head swirled with images of bloody sinks, puffy eyes, exploding glass, Scott punching a hole in the wall, and finally, Rick's bludgeoned face. "You hated Carrie and you hate Amy, too." My voice fell to a whimper, my body quivering. "Please tell me you didn't do anything to my friend."

Scott's mouth fell open, his head jerking back. "You think." He touched his chest, his voice weak. "I would do something to hurt Carrie *and* Amy? You think I'm capable of that?"

The mistrust slammed between us like a concrete wall.

"I'm sorry. I'm just—"

"When did I lose your trust, Sara?" He wiped his mouth with his hand, his expression dour. "You know what? You *should* go find Amy, so you can realize how ridiculous you sound." He exhaled, shaking his head. "I can't believe this." He paced, his eyes distant.

I couldn't reassure him because I didn't know—not for sure—my mind swam with doubt.

Finally, Scott made a humph sound so light I almost missed it. It was as if he'd worked something out in his head before he trudged over to the door. "I think it's best if you leave before you say something *else* you might regret." He opened the door and stood there, allowing a cold chill to claw at my heart.

I walked past him, my body bristling with sorrow, fear, and love. If I was right, Scott was a monster who I would never forgive or stop punishing. If I was wrong, *I* was the monster, and *he* would never forgive me. I'd obliterated our lives, our futures, and our hearts in this one defining moment.

Scott closed the door without even looking back at me.

He was different.

I was different.

What was I doing? I'd lost the ability to distinguish the good from the bad. Down was up, inside was out. My equilibrium swayed like a ship on turbulent waters. My balance was off and so was my perspective. I couldn't find my bearings. Just like *Alice in Wonderland*.

I drove out of Scott's parking lot feeling hollow and alone—a place I knew very well.

* * *

When I reached my suite, Amy's door sat open making my heart spring with hope for just a moment—until I discovered Luke sitting on her bed.

"No word?" I walked into her room, appreciating all the signature scents and decorations with a little more fervor—the sandalwood that permeated into her bedding and clothing from the incense sticks she liked to burn, the dreamcatchers and bohemian wall hangings that brought a feeling of sanctuary, even the peace-sign mug that captured stains from her dark lipstick. Her Kurt Cobain poster. It was all there, but not Amy.

Staring down at his cell phone, Luke shook his head. "Nope."

"Why don't you go to your apartment, and I'll stay here. That way, we've got both locations covered." Luke agreed and dragged his slender frame out the door.

After he left, I called the local hospitals and even the Police Department, who offered nothing. I was tempted to file a missing person's report but kept hoping Amy would come walking through the door and I wouldn't have to. I also wasn't sure how long you had to wait to file a missing person's report. I had an inkling that twenty-four hours was the normal wait time. I wanted to text Scott but my fingers refused to comply.

For the next several hours, I sat on Amy's bed, my back

against the wall, worrying and texting back and forth with Luke, until somehow my eyes refused to stay open.

As the sun burst through the horizon, shedding light on the earth and the situation, I awoke to the realization that my best friend in the whole world was gone.

Chapter Seventeen

Thursday morning.

Phones ringing, dispatchers calling out instructions, paper shuffling, and squeaky chairs rolling across the tiled floor, the police precinct was buzzing with activity. I remembered the high counter from my last visit, where today a man in a uniform stood, cycling people through. Luke and I waited in line behind a man in a mechanic's uniform, his hands dark from working in oil, his clothing reeking of it. Once the man finished asking the officer about an encroaching neighbor, we moved forward.

After running a hand through his short, thinning hair—more salt than pepper—the officer's brown eyes found me. "Can I help you?"

"Yes, we'd like to file a missing person's report. We're past the twenty-four-hour waiting period."

"There is no waiting period to file a missing person's report in the state of Virginia."

I looked at Luke, scolding myself internally for not coming in sooner.

"Let's begin with your names." His badge gleaming off the fluorescent lights, the officer bent down to pull out some paperwork from a shelf below. He placed a form on the counter and pulled out a pen from behind his ear.

"My name is Sara Browne, and this is Luke ..." I paused realizing I didn't know the rest.

"Luke Henshaw," he said, staring down at the form.

"I'm Officer Thorpe. What is your friend's name, and how long has he or she been missing?"

Luke leaned closer placing a hand on the edge of the counter. "She. And her name is Amy Pearce. I haven't seen her since Tuesday afternoon."

The officer's gaze rode over Luke's wrinkled T-shirt, unbuttoned flannel shirt, and scrambled dirty-blond hair. "And who are you in relation to the missing person?"

"I'm her boyfriend." Luke coughed and drove his hands into his pockets, his arms lining his slender body. I sensed he wasn't comfortable here. Neither was I.

"Did you check your cell phone?"

I piped in. "Yes, neither one of us has heard from her since Tuesday. I checked the hospitals around town and the police stations."

Luke's eyes thanked me from a foot away.

"Could she have gotten into an accident and we don't know about it?" I asked.

The officer peered down at me. "I'll check the accident reports, but I don't recall seeing anything about a young woman since Tuesday. I assume you've checked her residence?" His eyes lowered to his form.

"She's a college student." I glanced at Luke. "We're all college students, but Luke lives off campus."

Luke nodded. "Yeah, I was busy Tuesday night, so I don't know if she stayed on campus or not. All I know is she hasn't answered any of my calls or returned any of my texts since Tuesday afternoon. Her car isn't at my house or anywhere on campus. I checked all the parking lots."

"Good thinking, Luke." This time *my* eyes thanked *him*.

The officer checked his watch and wrote more information down. "So you're not sure when exactly she went missing, but it could be approximately thirty-six hours?"

We both nodded.

"And you said she's a student at Commonwealth here in town?"

"Yes." I found myself wiggling in my shoes, wishing he would stop asking questions and do something like send out a S.W.A.T team.

Officer Thorpe took his paper and came around the front of the counter. "Follow me." He motioned with his hand. "I'm going to send you back to speak to one of our officers, who will get a full description from you and any photos you might have on your phone. Try to remember important things like what she was wearing last, any tattoos or markings on her body that can be identified."

Identified? As in *"the body was identified by ..."* The thought of Amy being identified in some cold morgue had me teetering. This couldn't be happening. But it *was* happening, just like the accident that killed my parents happened, and just like Rick happened, and just like Scott ...

Dr. Zeller would tell me to breathe. Turn inward, focus on my body ...

"Is she on any medication?" Officer Thorpe startled me as he addressed Luke.

My nerves were like a roller coaster with no rails.

"No," Luke said.

"Does she have any impairments that we need to know about?"

Again, Luke answered no.

We followed the officer farther into the precinct and up to an office, where a woman, also in uniform, had just hung up her phone. Officer Thorpe explained the situation to her in front of us. The female officer pulled out another set of forms and told us to take a seat, which I was happy to do considering my legs had turned to rubber, my mind a firework display of morbid thoughts and fears, shooting off at the same time.

Two hours later, we had answered every question about Amy that was asked of us. It was hard because I hadn't seen her in two days. I couldn't say for sure what she was wearing last, only what types of clothing she would often wear. Luke said she had on her black skinny jeans, a black T-shirt with the words "Get Lost" on the front, and her typical green army jacket, the last time *he* saw her.

When the inquiry was over, two police officers followed Luke and me back to school, while another squad car went to the University Police Building to notify them of the situation and to get Amy's contact information. They wanted to notify her family. I rode in Luke's van, my muscles taut with fear. How had this happened? Amy seemed like the last person who would go missing. She was strong, but she was also impulsive, and I knew that about her. Could there be a connection with Carrie Stevens? Had she gone to Axl's place alone even though Luke had told her not to? And then I thought about Scott. My sorrow deepened on so many levels. If Scott had any part in this, I was done—done with love, done with trusting people, done with school ... done with everything.

"I cleaned out all of Amy's ... *paraphernalia* last night, just in case," Luke said, returning me to the moment. "Her room is clean now." He let one shoulder rise and fall. "Not clean but ... you know what I mean."

"Yes. That was good thinking."

His hand gripping the steering wheel, Luke's eyes accommodated the same dark rings that mine did. "I know people think she's a hard-ass, but deep down, she's not like that."

I touched Luke's arm. "Of course. I know that." I thought of the times—and not so long ago—when Amy had been my *only* lifeline through a forest of despair. She brought me food, guidance, and hope when I was unable to fend for myself. I fed off her strength until I could function again. What she did for me was beyond normal friendship, and I wouldn't let her down now. "We'll find her, Luke."

I flipped the visor down to shield my tired eyes from the morning sun, bringing a photo of Amy and Luke into view, held on by a large clip. Sitting on what I assumed was Luke's couch, Amy had her legs across his lap, her tongue pointed at his ear. Luke had his eyes scrunched tight, his mouth cringing. Normally, the amusing photograph would have made me laugh. Not today. It just made me miss her more.

"I know you already said she didn't, but do you think Amy could've gone to Axl's place?"

Luke shook his head. "I drove over there last night on my way back to my place. I asked Axl about having any weed and then acted as though I had forgotten my wallet. He didn't seem off in any way." He glanced over and quirked his face. "No more than usual. He even offered to front me some weed, but I turned him down. I have a buddy who knows him. He said he'll keep an eye out." Luke stopped at an intersection to wait for a school bus to pass through. My cell phone flashed 8:30 a.m., but it felt more like 5:00 p.m. already.

"Has Scott seen her? Or does Amy have any other friends that I don't know about?" Luke asked.

"No. Scott said he hasn't seen her, either." I swallowed a billowing mass of uncertainty that was clogging my throat like a tumor.

A battle was going on inside of my head. There were moments when the thought of Scott hurting Amy, much less Carrie, was nothing short of insane. And then *other* facts would chip at my brain like an ice pick. The dabs of blood on the sink cabinet, for starters. Was Scott's bloody nose the reason the upstairs bathroom trash can was at the bottom of the stairs with a new bag in it? Had he filled it up with soiled tissues and decided to change it out, or maybe blood got on the bag itself? Everything about Scott was off Tuesday night: the swollen eye, the way he shattered a glass in his hand, his lack of appetite, the late-night workout, his somber mood. Was he upset about lying to me? Or was there another, more-serious reason for those things? I rubbed my forehead hoping a new revelation would come to me. I knew Scott, but then again, I *thought* I knew Rick. The stakes were too high for me to brush off my suspicions. Amy was missing, and there was no denying that.

Luke glanced over. "No other friends you can think to ask, then?"

"She used to get together with one of our professors once in a while, but I saw him yesterday, and he was asking me why Amy had missed his class, so I know he hasn't seen her. I don't know about her job, though. She may have friends there."

"I checked with the people at her job, and no one mentioned anything."

I was impressed with how on top of things Luke had been.

Putting my doubts about Scott aside, I considered suspects like Henry and Rachael. Henry had argued with Amy, and Rachael hated everyone. Not only that, but she thought Amy *and I* were drug dealers. Before I mentioned them to Luke, I had to do a little more digging. I doubted that Rachael with her dainty frame could overpower someone like Amy, but the custodian, Henry, could. *So could Scott.* While Luke's two-tone van (one part white and one part rust) ambled down the road, I shoved the image of Scott hurting my friend out of my head. It was like closing a door against a strong wind. If my worst-case scenario was in fact true, I feared what it would do to me. I barely survived losing Scott the first time. This was different. My mental seesaw switched sides, and now my rational mind was screaming, "Of course he wouldn't do that, and shame on you for thinking it." If only I knew for sure.

* * *

Back at school, I stood on the outskirts of Amy's room while one police officer wearing gloves pulled hair from Amy's brush and put it in a bag marked "Evidence." Another female officer worked in the bathroom, coming out several minutes later with a toothbrush in a similar-looking bag. They dusted for prints and then left with her laptop.

None of us could find her cell phone. And the police said it wasn't pinging a location.

I spent all day hopping from Amy's room to mine, unable to go to class. I couldn't leave. Just in case. Luke stayed with me, until he decided to drive around town searching. I offered to go with him, but he suggested I stay behind in case Amy showed up, although his defeated tone told me he didn't think that was likely. By nightfall, I couldn't stand being inside anymore. My stomach was ravenous and the oatmeal bars I'd been snacking on weren't cutting it. I needed air and sustenance to keep my mind sharp.

I hadn't heard a word from Scott.

Still wearing the same workout clothes from the day before, I ventured outside where several news crews were setting up near the Welcome Center by the dorms—probably to interview students as they walked past. Luckily, they weren't quite ready as I strolled by. At least the disappearance had hit the airways. That was a good thing. The more exposure the better. What was Amy's family doing? Were they on their way here? I remembered how frustrated Amy had been with her little sister for stealing from her.

A glowing ring encircled the moon like a halo, and I suspected the reason. I checked a weather app on my phone, which informed me three-to-six inches of snow was expected to fall within the next twenty-four hours. In Vermont, we'd call that a dusting. In Virginia, however, the locals considered it a significant storm. I hoped it wouldn't compromise the search for Amy.

I took a breath.

Somehow, the upcoming weather event helped me to take stock of my life. My optimistic side hoped Amy would show up and everything would be okay again—or as okay as it was, anyway. Deep down I knew that wasn't possible. Even if Amy did show up, it would be really hard for Scott to forgive me, and who could blame him? Would I forgive *him* for suspecting something so heinous about me? I was driving myself crazy about it. On top of that, I missed them both terribly.

I looked up realizing I had passed the Student Union Building and was approaching the library. I was halfway across campus with no memory of how I got there. It was as if I were sleepwalking with my eyes wide open and my brain asleep. Out of the corner of my eye, a dark figure dusted the walkways with salt. Hunched over and scowling, he looked up as several girls walked past him unaware, his breath producing puffs of steam like an old locomotive. How did this nasty man go unnoticed? One last sweep of salt and Henry crumpled up his bag and walked away.

My feet started moving before my mind had even contemplated a plan. I put my hand in my coat pocket to feel the container of pepper spray I had purchased at Physical Force. Wait. Why did it feel so thin? I pulled out a highlighter and scoffed. Had I managed to grab a highlighter off my desk instead of my pepper spray? Boy, I really was out of it. All I had now was my keychain with the LED flashlight, which dangled from my fingers, and the defense moves I had learned from my self-defense class.

Or you can turn back.

I couldn't. I had to explore this. Amy was missing, and if Henry was the man responsible, I had to find out.

I stayed far enough behind him that he hopefully wouldn't hear my footfalls or notice I was tailing him. He walked along with a slight limp that I hadn't noticed before. Was that a recent injury? Laughter and voices floated through the air when two girls burst through the doors of Campus Creations on my left. Derek's old haunt. My stomach yelled for me to stop and eat, but my mind refused to listen.

Stuffing his empty bag under his arm, Henry pulled a small package out of his coat pocket and shook it before taking out a cigarette and placing it into his mouth. He cupped his hands around his face until a spark ignited. As he continued walking, his cigarette smoke trailed behind him like exhaust from a car. A moment or two after each puff, my nose caught the remnants of his unhealthy habit.

"Evening, Henry. Headed home?" Wearing baggy work pants and a thick coat, a dark-skinned man stood near a trash can pulling out a large bag filled to capacity and beyond. A few items spilled over and onto the ground. Cigarette in his mouth, Henry bent over to pick up a few pieces of trash, which he handed over to his friend along with his empty bag of salt.

I stopped walking and stood near a large oak tree, where I

examined my cell phone with artificial interest, keeping the two men in my sight. Cars drove past on the road just ahead drowning out their voices along with all the students who strolled along the walkways. A horn blared in the distance.

I watched until, finally the man patted Henry on the back and carried his large bag of trash to a wheelbarrow-type contraption, where several other full bags of refuse sat waiting.

I took a step forward anticipating Henry doing the same, but he didn't. Instead, he stopped and peered over his shoulder. I froze, my breath halted, my heart racing. Not sure what to do, I coughed and used my hand to cover my mouth. Was he watching me? I didn't dare to look.

A group of students walked past me toward the crosswalk about a hundred feet ahead. When I was confident they were providing me with enough cover, I glanced up just as Henry stepped off the curb and onto the street. On the move again, I crossed the road about twenty seconds later, worried I'd doubled the distance between us. A car drove past, forcing me to wait longer than I was comfortable. I picked up my pace just as the car turned into a residential housing complex.

Henry proceeded through a wide alleyway wedged between two apartment complexes while I stayed half a minute behind him. We were in a less populated part of campus, devoid of streetlights and people. When Henry walked behind the corner of a building, I was sure I had lost him. The sound of a metal door opening caused my feet to pick up the pace. I rounded the corner just as the door to the Grounds/Mainte-nance Building (according to the sign) closed tight. *Crap.* What was I going to do now? From the far edge of the parking lot and next to a trash and recycling enclosure, stood Henry's rusted-out old truck. I remembered it from when he had picked Ethel up at the hospital.

Grabbing my LED keychain, I approached the vehicle with caution. As I drew near, a dog barked from a neighboring lawn, sending my nerves into spasm. Once I caught my breath, I inched closer, casting my LED light onto the exterior of the truck but not certain why I was doing so. I mean, what was I hoping to find? The light from my flashlight reflected off the frost and grime attached to the driver's-side window.

I heard a noise and looked toward the door Henry had just entered, fearing he was coming back outside. Thankfully, there were no windows on this side of the building, only two large garage doors for loading bays. Were there cameras? I saw one off to the side. But could it see *me*? Seconds ticked away as I waited to see if the source of the noise would produce a human being.

When nothing happened, I moved closer to the truck. The light cast from my flashlight punctured the smudged windows and fell onto a bench seat decorated with several upholstery tears and a mallet. I tried the door. Locked. I shed my light over the surface of the mallet for any signs of blood but saw none. On the passenger-side floor sat a half-open toolbox full of screwdrivers, a hammer, some paintbrushes, and a large wrench. No knives that I could see or weapons. I threw more light onto the dashboard full of dust and one Hawaiian Bobble doll wearing a bikini. Squinting my eyes for a better view, I continued to scan the interior of the truck looking for anything suspicious until I gave up and headed toward the truck's bed.

Just as I rounded the back of the truck, the sound of metal hinges squawked through the air like an angry pterodactyl. I crouched down by the back bumper, wondering where I could run or hide if anyone approached the truck. I concentrated, doing my best to listen for footsteps or voices.

All at once, a presence came up from behind me. My neck stiffened, my breath petrified in my throat. Had Henry seen me earlier? Was he waiting for me? The same baritone dog continued to bark, cutting the air with tension and danger.

I rose slowly, trying to gain stable footing. My body trembled with adrenaline and fear, my breathing so rapid my brain struggled to focus. Feeling a loss of blood sugar, I regretted not eating earlier, my knees agreeing as they weakened beneath me. It was too late now. A hand came down on my shoulder. The moment had come, the one my self-defense instructors had prepared me for. Time moved in slow motion as I grabbed the strange hand off my shoulder and twisted my body around. Before I could process what was happening, I had my attacker's arm behind his back. Everything went as my instructor, Sheila, had said it would.

Until I heard something I didn't expect.

"Sara, what are you doing?"

The voice wasn't gruff or angry, and there was no stench of cigarette smoke in the air. I adjusted my eyes to take in the full head of dark hair in front of me.

"Professor Adams?"

At that moment, the metal door flung open and Henry stepped out into the night air.

I had grabbed the wrong person.

"I'm so sorry." I released my teacher at once and stood back. My face and body twitched with uncertainty and remorse.

Professor Adams rubbed his shoulder. "I didn't mean to startle you. I saw you crouched down and thought you were hurt or something." He removed his hand from his shoulder and straightened his blazer. "What were you doing?"

Henry moved closer, his eyes mere slits. "What are you doing near my truck?" His voice blended in well with the dog that continued to wail, refusing to rest its voice.

"Nothing." I took several steps away from his vehicle. "I was just—"

"We were just talking," Dr. Adams said providing some credibility to my lack of explanation.

Keeping his face angry, Henry unlocked the door to his truck and jumped in. He started his engine and revved it like a NASCAR driver, before speeding off with a squeal of his tires. Amy had nicknamed him Norman Bates, but he seemed more like Argus Filch from *Harry Potter* to me, only with shorter hair.

I put my hands to my temples to gather my thoughts and decompress from the embarrassing situation. What just happened was crazy. "I'm so sorry, Dr. Adams. I'm a little upset right now about Amy." I tried to hold it together. "Did you hear that she's missing?"

His fingers went to his mouth as it fell open. "I heard talk of a student who went missing, but I didn't know the name." He lowered his chin. "Oh no. Is that why she wasn't in class on Wednesday?"

My lower lip trembled. Considering Luke was beyond worried and Scott was MIA, Dr. Adams was the only person I could talk to about this horrible situation. My emotions swirled at the sound of his compassionate voice. "I think so. We don't know exactly how long she's been gone. I haven't been able to reach her cell phone." Tears bit at my eyes.

The dog continued its rant in the distance, until finally, it stopped. Had the owners taken it in for the night? I hoped so.

Dr. Adams came closer, his hand once again finding my shoulder, only this time, I didn't turn into the Black Widow on him. "That's terrible, Sara. I know how close you two are." He bent his head closer. "I'm sure they are out looking for her right now. Is there anything I can do to help?" He reached into his blazer pocket and pulled out a handkerchief, handing it over to me.

I wiped my eyes and sniffed a few times, trying to stop the

dam from coming completely loose. I was hanging on by a thread. "No. I appreciate you asking, though. I should get back." I handed him over his handkerchief and looked around. "I'm glad you were here. Are you parked nearby?"

Dr. Adams turned his head toward a dark-blue sedan parked under the only lamppost in the parking lot. "Yeah. I stopped here to ask maintenance to take a look at the heater in my office before heading home. It feels like one hundred degrees in there. I have to keep my window open." He took a step toward his car. "How far away is your dorm? I'd be happy to give you a lift back."

The sound of claws scraping against pavement hit my ears followed by a croaky moan that wasn't human. All at once, a dark creature lunged at Dr. Adams knocking him off his feet. Metal jingled onto the pavement.

I screamed as the large dog mauled my teacher. "Oh my God. Get off!" I flitted around them, trying to figure out what to do, my arms flailing, and my nerves in full spasm.

The black dog and Dr. Adams rolled on the ground, screams of terror erupting from my teacher's lungs. The dog scratched his neck and then bit his arm.

I stepped forward and kicked the animal as hard as I could. The enormous beast skidded backward, its claws scraping against the pavement. Not wasting any time, my teacher sprang to his feet and ran to his car as the dog set his eyes on me.

When I was a child, a neighbor of mine kept his dog tied up, regardless of the weather or the time of day. Whenever I passed their house, that same dog with the dirty white fur would growl and bark, saliva dripping from his fangs. I was terrified of that dog until my dad told me once that the poor thing was just unhappy about being tied up all the time, watching the world pass it by. He said how you treat a dog had a lot to do with its behavior. Treat a dog well, and you'll have a cuddly companion that will follow you to the ends of the earth —treat a dog badly, and you'd have what I was staring at in this moment. My dad also told me what to do should I ever encounter an angry animal. Thinking fast, I ripped my coat off and wrapped it around my arm, just as the dog thrust its body forward, his fangs leading the way. It latched onto my arm but didn't puncture the skin, although I could feel its canines bearing down.

The dog gnawed at my arm with its powerful jaw causing me to stagger. If I fell to the ground, it was all over, and I would lose my advantage. But if I could land another kick to its ribs, it may buy me the time I needed to get away.

Just as I wondered where Dr. Adams had gone, a hand came out of nowhere, holding a small device and thrusting it into the animal's fur, emitting a blue light and a thrum of high voltage. *Stun gun?* The animal whimpered as it struggled to get away. Even though I was immensely grateful for the assistance, a part of me felt sorry for the poor creature. What had caused it to behave this way? Who was abusing it?

"Are you injured?" Dr. Adams kept his eye on the dog until it stumbled out of sight. He turned to me. "Did it break the skin?" He stared down at my arm, covered in my coat with several tears in the fabric.

I took a breath. "No. I think I'm okay." I unwrapped the coat and examined my arm. "It didn't reach my skin." My eyes homed in on the blood trickling down Professor Adams's neck. "It looks like you weren't so lucky." I stepped closer as he used his free hand to cover the wound.

"It's not that bad." He reached into his blazer a second time and used the same handkerchief to hold against the abrasion. "I'll clean it up when I get home." He breathed deep. "Wow. That was a close one." He blew out his breath. "We better get out of here in case it comes back."

He walked toward his car while I followed close behind. I acknowledged the irony of facing danger twice in one night—and within a few minutes of each incident.

"It's a good thing you had that stun gun." I stared down at the device still gripped in his hand, curious about why he had one in the first place.

When we reached his car, Dr. Adams stuffed the red-sodden handkerchief in one pocket then patted his others down. He looked around aimlessly. "My keys!"

I remembered the metal clanking against the pavement. "You dropped them, I think. I'll go check."

"No, that's okay."

Before he could argue, I ran to the spot of the attack and grabbed the heavy set of keys off the ground, returning a moment later. "Here you go." As I handed them over, a rose quartz crystal pendant glinted off the streetlamp from above.

I glanced down at the pendant and then back at Dr. Adams. I knew of only *one* person who had a pendant like that. Plus Amy had told me she had made it herself, so there couldn't be another. There had to be an explanation. I tried to make sense out of what I was seeing.

Dr. Adams exhaled, his shoulders falling. "I wish you hadn't seen that."

His words hit my eardrums a millisecond before an electrical shock ran down my chest and through my limbs. My body stiffened like a board, before a giant Charlie horse attacked all my muscles at once. Although my body was in full spasm, my mind was fully aware of what was happening to me. As I slowly lowered toward the ground, I hoped Dr. Adams would catch me. I was no longer in control.

Dr. Adams did catch me, sort of. He half carried, half dragged me to the other side of the car, where he opened the passenger door. He *shocked* me again and then leaned into the vehicle, but I wasn't able to see why. All I could think about was trying not to die as electricity threatened to stop my heart. When he pulled the device away, I had a moment of relief before a rag covered my mouth and nose, a sweet, pungent odor assaulting my airways.

A hard pinch in my arm and then everything went black.

Chapter Eighteen

The face of Dr. Adams danced in front of me like the reflection from a funhouse mirror. He was smiling then angry, twisted and scary. An enormous crystal pendant swung like a wrecking ball on a grandfather clock. Why was it important? Teeth from an animal hovered in the distance, growling and barking like claps of thunder. What did it all mean? Sleep. I needed sleep. All I could do was float, like a feather in the wind, as lightning flashed and threatened, its power able to destroy. Sleep was the only answer, my only way out.

"Wake up, Sara. You have to go now." I startled—my eyes wide. I was sitting in the back seat of my father's truck, the ghastly smell of burnt rubber and oil permeating the air, the windshield a gaping hole. I tried to move, but the crumpled truck forbid it. "Mom. Dad. Where are you?" I struggled until my body grew tired, my spirit shattered like the glass littering my chest and lap. *Why did you leave me?* An orb of light rose from the front of the broken vehicle, a silhouette approaching.

As my eyes struggled to fathom or focus, two beings blended into one.

"We never left you. We've been here all along."

Tears rolled down my cheeks, the back of my head throbbing. "No. You left me alone, and I've been alone all these years, fighting to live without you. I don't want to fight anymore."

The essence moved closer, a translucent hand caressing my face. "But that's not true. You were never alone." The spirit formed into my father, then my mother, the voice both his and hers. "They are waiting for you. You have to fight for *them*."

A scene appeared before me: A woman with auburn hair was kneeling on her living room floor and a baby running into her arms with new legs and bouncy red curls, a man crouching down to join them. I couldn't see their faces, but somehow I knew them. *Abigail ... Mel ... Joel.* My family. I reached out to touch them before they changed, transforming into something new.

My parents spoke again. "*He* needs you."

I was suddenly under an arch, the prettiest arch I'd ever seen. An abundance of fresh ferns, gardenias, and roses fluttered in the breeze paying homage. I could almost smell their sweet fragrance. The light around me shimmered with softness and comfort. A man appeared or maybe he was always there. Wearing a crisp white shirt, his broad shoulders and caramel curls were familiar. *Scott.* I wanted him to turn and face me, but he wouldn't. I wanted to reach out and touch him, but I couldn't. I loved this man, and he loved me. He was also my family. My future.

Everything grew hazy, shapes blending, forming into a cloud that dissipated before me, like a fog surrendering to the bright morning sun, taking my parents and everything I held dear, with it.

"Please. Don't go. I need you."

Their voices came in a whisper. "Find your strength, Sara."

I awoke to darkness so thick I blinked to confirm my eyes were open. When I tried to touch my face, wrist restraints fought against my efforts. What happened? And then I remembered Dr. Adams. All my theories about Axl, Rachael, Henry, and even Scott doing something horrible to Amy were wrong. It was Dr. Adams—the last person in the world I would've ever suspected. Did he also take Carrie? Was she here, too? And where was Amy?

A musty odor infused the air as my spine crunched against a hard surface. Cold bit at my fingers. Where was I? The stale air reminded me of my attic back home.

My mind processed, no answers coming.

I moved, allowing splinters to poke through my shirt and into my back like tiny swords. The wind blew without touching me, creaking the trees. A woodpecker jackhammered in the distance. What I didn't hear were cars or people.

Grunting from the effort, I attempted to stand, my head slamming hard into a very low ceiling. Maybe not an attic, after all. I pictured an enormous crate out in a forest somewhere desolate. Had Dr. Adams buried me alive? What did the world look like outside of this dismal space? How trapped was I? And then another deep-seeded fear crept over me like a poisonous spider. Would I die here?

I thought about Scott. Even though I had mistrusted him and accused him wrongly, none of that seemed to matter anymore. All that mattered was finding Amy and Carrie and fighting my way back to him. Even if I had to dig my way out, I had to try.

Keeping my head low, I pushed up on my knees, the splinters challenging my every move. Wrists clamped together, I reached out to feel for a wall and touched something cushiony, the surface almost like paper. As my hand glided sideways, I hit a board, which protruded several inches. On the other side of the board was more cushion. I knew what this was: insulation. A memory sparked from a time when I had helped my father insulate our attic back in Vermont. Being the only child, I provided both daughter and son support. I played baseball with my dad and learned recipes from my mom. And sometimes it was the opposite. My dad loved to cook. What I recalled most about the attic job with my dad was the itchy skin that persisted on my arms after we had finished working. "A good hot shower will rinse off those tiny pieces of fiberglass," my father had said. The recollection brought me comfort as I continued forward, my knees burning, the ceiling losing height. And then I butted up against something that stopped my heart.

It was soft, and it was human.

No sound came from the person, who I hoped was Amy. Was she dead? Terror burst through my chest as I whimpered. With my hands quivering and tears falling into the dark void, I felt along her body until I reached her face. The acidy scent of vomit along with another strong aroma tugged at my stomach. My fingers traced over her nose, her piercings, and her eyes. It *was* Amy, I was sure of it, and she was warm. I lowered my ear to what I assumed was her mouth and listened, my heart waiting to beat again. And then I heard something. Was it the wind or her breath, I couldn't tell. I traced my hand down her neck and her arm until I found both of her wrists restrained like mine. No way to check for a pulse there, I quickly found her neck again. It took several tries, but I felt it. A slight throbbing under the skin. It wasn't strong, but it *was* life.

I put my face closer again. "Amy, it's Sara. You need to wake up."

She didn't respond.

"Everything is going to be okay. We are going to get out of

here." I told her what I wished to be true and what I would fight with every fiber of my being to make happen. When she didn't move or make a sound, I rose to my knees and explored the area using my hands to graze the outer barrier. The insulation suggested an attic or a crawl space. So did the slanted ceiling. If that were true, there had to be a way out.

I was weak from hunger. I was tired. And I was terrified. Not a good combination. My stomach growled as footsteps reached my ears, rattling my body with panic. The footfalls grew louder until the wall beside me moved. Not sure what to do, I laid back down and closed my eyes, trying not to hyperventilate. Playing dead with my heart hammering against my ribcage was unbearable.

Light touched my eyelids, and I squinted them open but only a sliver. The narrow beam didn't reveal more than what I had already realized. This was either an attic or a crawl space, insulation covering the walls nearby. I couldn't distinguish more beyond that.

A hand came down on my wrists and dragged me out of the confined space, the splinters carving up my back.

"Please, Dr. Adams. Don't hurt me." As I drifted out of the room, my eyes found Amy lying on the floor. She was wearing a T-shirt with the words "Get Lost" scrolled across the front as Luke had remembered. I flailed my arms and legs to make the job more difficult for the Mr. Hyde who had abducted me.

He panted as he struggled against my efforts.

"If you stop fighting me, I won't hurt you."

He let out a grunt and yanked me one last time into the light and onto a wooden floor.

"I want you to listen to me, Sara. I need you to understand." He held a syringe up. "If you fight or try to escape, I will have to drug you." He allowed a few droplets to land on my arm for emphasis.

"No. Please. I won't fight," I said through quivering lips.

While Dr. Adams put the needle down on a nearby box, I sat slumped against a wooden knee wall that smelled of pine, and I forced my eyes to take in the scene before me.

Try to remember the details.

The irregular-sized room was small, housing several stacks of plastic storage bins, banker's boxes, folding chairs, and a portable rack of old clothing. The sloped ceiling accommodated two fixed skylights that cast natural light onto the floral vintage wallpaper that garnished all the walls except one—the one I was leaning against.

To my right stood a closed wooden door. I imagined getting up and running out that door toward my freedom. If only I could free my wrists, I might have a chance. Every time I tried, the zip tie's sharp edges threatened to sever.

The whoosh of a stiff breeze collided against the house.

Dr. Adams pulled a folding chair closer, where he opened it up and perched himself in front of me.

"I never intended to bring you here." My so-called favorite teacher wiped his brow. "It was my mistake to keep that pendant on my keychain. I should've known better. If it wasn't for that dog—" He clamped his mouth shut, shaking his head. "Some people deserve what they get, and others ..." The wrinkles at the edges of his brown eyes softened. "I'm sorry this happened to you. I truly am. I want you to know that it's not personal. I've always liked you, Sara."

"What about Amy?"

A dark shadow crept over his face, the muscles in his jaw flexing. "Amy is another story. There are people in this world who do nothing but hurt and take from others." His eyes grew distant. "I've known women like Amy before." He stared down at me and sighed. "I'm going to try to help you understand. You need to know the truth. I owe you that much." He straightened up as though to gather himself. "When I was a very young child —too young to remember, my mother died of cancer. Several years later, my father married a woman who had a teenage daughter. That daughter's name was *Angela*." He said the name with fire on his tongue.

All at once, a noise filtered in from another room. *Voices?*

His gaze lowered to the floor. "Angela prided herself on being *bad*. She called herself the 'Angel of Death', plastering her face with dark makeup and her body in grungy clothing. Her room was filled with merchandise she had stolen from the mall or wherever else she could find to pilfer. She'd hang out with her boyfriend, who shaved his head, his face a fishing lure of piercings. Tattoos of demons and carnage covered both of their arms and necks. They smelled like stale liquor, tobacco, and evil." His eyes found me. "My father and his new wife took a long honeymoon and left me alone with Angela, who promised to take care of me." He breathed deeply. "Oh, she took care of me, all right. With the help of her boyfriend, they locked me in a closet almost every day. You've seen firsthand the damage they've done to me, haven't you?"

I nodded, recalling the moments in the elevator when Dr. Adams was sweating profusely, his breathing labored. "It's been a problem for me since I was a kid," he'd said.

"The only food they allowed me to eat was dog food. I was only ten. What kind of people could do such a thing?" He clenched a fist. "For two weeks, I was their prisoner. After a few days, I refused to eat any more of their slop. I couldn't stomach it." He made a grimacing face. "They tried to force the food down my throat, until I vomited it all over them. Then they whipped me with a belt until my back bled." He adjusted his shoulders as though the pain was still very real.

My own back throbbed, forcing me to fully understand the experience.

"I still wouldn't eat. Starving to death was the only power I had left. I'll never forget what Angela said to me. 'You better start eating, or I'll do something to your father. I know dark magic, and I can make things happen.' I'd seen her using Ouija boards and Tarot cards in her room. She'd burn incense and chant late at night." His voice cracked. "I was only a kid. I didn't know any better. My father had been ill recently, and Angela used that experience to convince me that she had caused it." Dr. Adams sniffed. "I was terrified. I did as they asked. I ate the dog food. I sat in the closet. I only came out to use the bathroom and to clean myself. When my father returned, Angela told him I'd been sick. Once again, she threatened me, saying if I told him what they'd done to me, she'd kill him, and then I'd be stuck with her. Forever. There would be no one left to protect me."

I pitied him. I knew what it felt like to be alone. Then I thought of Amy lying on the floor in the prison behind me, and I realized that this man didn't deserve my sympathy.

"I endured years of her abuse until, on my fifteenth birthday, my father dropped dead of a heart attack in our kitchen. By then, I was bigger, and Angela was less of a threat. At his funeral, she whispered in my ear that my father had died because of me. She said he was so disappointed in his son that he died from heartbreak." A tear slid down his cheek. "When they lowered my father's casket into the ground, all I wanted to do was push Angela into that hole and cover it up. I hated her more than I had ever hated anyone in my life." He paused and stared up at the ceiling. "I put my anger to good use, researching plants that were toxic until I found one called water hemlock that I ground up and put in her tea. Angela was always experimenting with plants and herbs, so I knew no one would suspect anything deliberate." An eerie smile cracked from his lips, his eyes dancing with joy. "I stood over her, watching her gasping for every breath. She tried to yell at me and accuse me, but the poison had robbed her of her voice, just like she had robbed me of my childhood. All she could do was roll around on the floor, holding her throat. It was a magnificent sight."

My God. He had watched another human being die and enjoyed it. I was mortified.

"After she died, I called the police and played the doting stepbrother."

Just like the dog that had attacked us, Dr. Adams was tortured into becoming the very monster he had detested. Angela had bullied him beyond sanity.

He leaned over his lap, his arms rested on his thighs. "Over the years, I've met lots of Angelas. I made a point to get to know them. I was the person they confided in or made fun of. For some, I was their best friend."

I thought about how Amy had connected with this man. She detested most of her teachers, but not him. She trusted him.

"You know why I did that?" He stared down at me but didn't wait for an answer. "I needed to see their patterns, their weaknesses. That way, they would never suspect me, when their health deteriorated. They wouldn't have any idea they were being punished by someone who they thought was so safe."

I couldn't believe what I was hearing: the making of a serial killer. Professor Adams was never a nice middle-aged man who enjoyed movies like *The Big Lebowski* and connecting with his students. His interest in Amy was vengeful and wicked.

He leaned closer. "I'm not as heartless as you think I am. I never killed any of them ... not until Carrie. And I didn't set out to kill her, either. I meant to make her sick as I had all the others, slipping toxins in her drinks. The others eventually recovered, not knowing what had happened to them. They were punished. With Carrie, I played along with her lifestyle and convinced her to sell me drugs that I used against her. What happened to her was a mistake. I gave her too much." His eyes lit up again. "But when I witnessed her taking her last breath, I realized that I had saved the world from another Angela. I can't tell you how rewarding that was." A sardonic smile spread across his face. "When I met Amy at the beginning of the year, I knew I'd met another Angela, and I had to rid the world of her, too. And I will. After she is punished for her cruelty."

I shook my head as best I could. "No. You are wrong about Amy. She's not like that."

Dr. Adams looked at me as if for acknowledgment. "You were there, Sara, when she told us what she did to her little sister. You heard—"

"She was only kidding." I forced a laugh with no humor in my voice. "She never did anything to her sister." I thought about how he had choked on his coffee and darted off. At the time, I thought his behavior was random, like he'd swallowed wrong. But it wasn't random, he was reacting to something visceral. "She even said so after you were gone. She said how worried she was about her. She's not who you think she is."

Professor Adams stroked his beard. "I'm sorry that you got tangled up in this. I truly am. As I said, it's not personal. But I can't let you live now. I won't make you suffer, as I will Amy. It will be quick and painless."

His words crashed down on me like a tidal wave, drenching me in sweat and terror of what was coming next. *The syringe.* Was it toxic? And then I thought of Scott again. "He needs you," my parents had said. Was it a dream or were they really there? All I knew was that I had to survive—I had to see him one last time.

The wind continued to roar outside.

Professor Adams rose before me like a giant—one who could squash Amy and me with one step. "It's time for Amy's wake-up call." He pushed the chair back and walked toward the wall right next to me. A cupboard-style door sat open with two brackets flanking both sides—a thick piece of wood propped up against it. We were definitely locked in, and with reinforcements.

Dr. Adams unfastened his belt, his body looming and scary.

I swallowed a sob. "Please don't hurt Amy. You're wrong about her." What was he planning to do? I shuddered at the thought of it. Amy's pulse was weak, and I feared that another "punishment" may finish her off. I couldn't let her die, not like this.

More voices came from outside of the room. Who was out there? I gathered up all the oxygen my lungs would permit and unloaded. "Help. Please. I'm being held prisoner." My voice came out hollow and frail, but I persisted. "Help. Somebody. Help me."

Dr. Adams shook his head as he squatted next to me. "I can't let you cling to false hope. You are yelling at my police scanner." He crossed the room, and using a key, opened the door, amplifying the sound from the other room. A man was talking and then a woman, but I couldn't hear the specifics, static clouding their words.

My hopes slouched right along with my spine.

"I'm not stupid, Sara. I stay informed about what is going on. A couple of months ago, I knew they were looking for Carrie's backpack before the public did, just like I knew they weren't going to find it. I also know they just discovered that you may be missing, and they are searching the campus for you right now."

Was Scott part of that search party? If he was, he was probably sick with worry. I thought about Carrie's parents and then Amy's family and mine. If we didn't escape, they would never know what happened to us. They would never suspect Dr. Adams. He was our friend, the one teacher who Amy and I could relate to the most. I had raved about him to Scott on several occasions. Not only that, I had told Luke that I was sure Dr. Adams hadn't seen Amy since he was asking about her during our last class. I'd helped Dr. Adams without meaning to. If only I hadn't been wasting my time on people like Axl, Rachael, and Henry. *HENRY*. He saw Dr. Adams and me together. Would he tell anyone? Or would he *not bother* since he hated college girls, anyway? Maybe he thought we got what we deserved.

Silence filled the room as I sat there slouched against the wall like a rag doll. I worried about Amy and what to do. *Think, Sara, think.* And then an idea sprang to life as Dr. Adams bent down to enter the crawl space.

This wasn't going to be easy, but it was all I could muster.

I pushed myself up, forcing strength into muscles that didn't have any. "You are wrong about Amy, and if you kill us both, it will be *you* who is the monster. What happened to you was awful, but that doesn't excuse what you are doing now."

Not acknowledging me, the professor lowered to his knees and bent closer to the crawl space entrance.

"I lost my parents in a car accident when I was young. Close to the same age you were when Angela abused you."

The professor sat back on his hind legs. "It's too late for this—"

"I was alone, but I never blamed anyone for what happened ... except for myself. When I came back to school from break, a horrible man tricked me into going to a remote house, where he raped me. He was vile and heartless. Just like you. You justify your savagery with some insane notion that you are doing it for the world. It's all a lie. You are doing it for your own selfish reasons. All disturbed people say the same things to themselves."

Dr. Adams got to his feet, his belt clutched in his hand. "Stop talking, Sara. I'm warning you." His pupils were big and black as coal.

"I was angry. I wanted to hurt someone, too. But I didn't. You know what I did?" This time, I didn't wait for *him* to answer. "I sought counseling and took self-defense classes. What I didn't do was turn my anger into something ugly as you have. I didn't hurt innocent human beings who had nothing to do with what happened to me. You could've started a support group for victims of bullies. You could have done a lot of things that would have helped others. You decided that these individuals were evil. Do you think Carrie's parents would agree with you? Did you see them at the press conference? Do you know what you've done to them? Did they deserve to be punished, too?"

Beads of sweat dotted my teacher's forehead.

"You have become the very thing you hated. *You* are the Angela now. You decide who is good and who is bad. You play God over other people's lives. Only you're not God, you are the devil."

Dr. Adams stood rigid, his Adam's apple moving slowly. It was if he was choking down the truth I was forcing him to swallow. "I don't want to hurt you, Sara." He wiped his brow and exhaled.

I mocked laughter again. "You are going to kill me, anyway. I'm an innocent person who has done nothing to you. Angela was right about one thing."

He stared down at me, his face twisted with rage. I barely recognized him anymore. He was a stranger, and he always had been.

"Your father *would* be disappointed in the man you have become. Angela was mean and savage, but you are far worse. You can justify it any way you want, but the truth is, you are a sick man who gets joy from making people suffer. You. Are. Angela."

Dr. Adams flinched as though he'd been struck by his own stun gun. His cheeks fired up.

I looked directly into his smoldering eyes. "I know exactly what you are. A monster."

He let the length of the belt fall next to me, keeping the buckle in his grip. "I thought you were good, Sara. But I can see I was wrong about you." He bared his teeth just like the dog had done in the desolate parking lot.

Knowing what was coming next, I covered my face as best I could and braced. My only comfort was knowing that Amy was safe ... for now.

My captor pulled one arm back and whipped the belt down on me with a grunt, lashing at my hip and upper thigh like an attacking cobra. While my skin singed with pain, he pulled the leather weapon back and struck me again, this time wounding my side and shoulder. I groaned in agony, wondering how bad this would get. And then I cried, my body quaking. "Please, stop."

But he didn't stop. The belt battered my arms, my legs, my shoulders. Searing pain sliced through my ear. I let out a guttural scream. "Stop." I didn't want to die this way. He said it would be painless. He lied.

His hair a mess, his eyes filled with fury, he pulled back again and paused.

I peeled my arm away from my face and looked up. The bandage on his neck from the dog attack had sprung open, blood mixed in with sweat, drizzling down his neck. He examined the stain on his collar, catching his breath. It was as if he'd transformed into a character from a horror movie, no longer human, although the blood said that he was.

I once believed this man was the kindest most compassionate teacher I had ever met. Underneath his Jeff Bridges smile was a madman, waiting to destroy whoever triggered him.

He combed back his hair, closed his eyes, and took several deep breaths. As he laced his belt through the loops of his trousers, he regarded me as I lay there in a huddled mess on the floor.

"I'm sorry that happened. You should never have said those things. I am not a monster. You are."

He retrieved the syringe and bent down, taking hold of my arm in a gruff manner. Then he plunged the needle into my skin, sending a stinging sensation through my veins. I almost welcomed the fuzziness that followed. He may have poisoned me, but somehow, I didn't care. Fatigue pulled me under like quicksand, and I knew I didn't have much time left. Soon I would be lost. Possibly forever.

Dr. Adams dragged me back into the dark abyss. Before he closed the hole to our cave, a few haunting words flew from his impostor lips: "I don't have time for this right now. If you'll excuse me, I have to go join the search party for my two favorite students."

Chapter Nineteen

I awoke to the sound of a familiar voice calling out to me. "I know ... someone is ... in here. I can ... hear ... you breathing?" Amy sounded so withered; her voice tinny.

Grateful to be alive, I tried to sit up. My head felt like it was splitting in two, my skin like it had been put through a cheese shredder.

"My name is ... Amy. What's ... your ... name? Are ... you ... being ... held ... by Adams?" She paused, her breathing heavy.

My friend was okay. I wanted to cheer from the rooftops. Compromised or not, it was good to hear her voice again. I sobbed with silent tears of joy.

"Amy it's me, Sara. Yes, he captured me, too." One of my ears burned like the sun. It was as if I'd been rolled in hot coals and *then* put through a cheese shredder.

"What? ... Sara? Oh ... my ... God. How?"

My voice shook. "He's crazy, Amy. We have to get out of here. How badly are you hurt?" I forced my body off the floor, wincing with each movement. The drugs manipulated. The zip ties restrained with sharp precision. I was alive, though, and that had to be enough.

"I ... don't ... know. I'm ... so ... cccold."

Outside, the wind pounded the house, punctuating her words.

I crawled toward the sound of her voice until my arm brushed up against her form. She was sitting up. Another good sign.

"How ... did ... you ... get ... here?" Between sniffles, Amy spoke through audible shivers.

"I was following Henry. It's a long story. Right now, we need to focus on getting out of here." I reached out to touch her and she gasped.

I pulled my hand back, alarmed. "How badly are you hurt? Where is the pain coming from? Can you move?"

Amy didn't respond at first. She panted instead, the warmth from her rancid breath touching my face. "That lunatic messed up my shoulder ... I tried to fight him off ... he twisted it ... felt something pop." Her voice lowered to a whimper. "He keeps drugging me ... and ... his belt ... my back feels like hamburger." She yawned, her words frail.

I patiently waited, knowing how hard it was for her speak.

"Shit. I'm so tired and cold ... can't think straight ... my head ... don't know how long ... been here ... made me eat disgusting ... shit."

That explained the smell. It was most likely remnants of the dog food on her breath. I knew what he was doing and why. Did *she* know? "Did he say anything to you?" I felt bad for making her work so hard at answering, but I had to know.

"He said ... crazy shit I didn't ... understand ... I've been so out of it ...don't know ... what ... is going on." Her voice whined in pain. "I'm scared ... Sara ... thought ... never see ... you again." She cried.

I swallowed my tears. "Everything is going to be okay. You're alive. I'm alive. We are going to get out of here."

I leaned my head closer until it touched hers. "He is a sick man. But that doesn't matter right now, either." I paused. "Listen."

The wind continued to whistle, rustling something on the outside of the house.

"Can you hear the wind?" I realized it was louder in here than in the other room. That meant the walls were thinner, less finished. The fact that I was able to touch the insulation, supported my theory.

"Uh-huh ... how ... are we going to ... get out ... of here?" Amy asked. "I tried ... to kick the door ... but messed up ... my ankle ... I don't know ... what day it is ... wwhen ... is he cccoming ... back?"Panic fragmented her words.

"It's daytime, or it was. He pulled me out not too long ago and talked to me. When he left, he said he was joining the search party to help find us, so hopefully that will buy us some time. How bad does your ankle hurt?"

"Bad." Amy's voice shook some more. "Are ... *you* hurt?"

"Not too badly." My neck and several other body parts disagreed, and I feared he had torn part of my ear off. I wanted to put my head down and sob right along with Amy, but wallowing wasn't going to rescue us.

"He's ... a nutjob ... Sara ... I think he ... took Carrie ... too."

"I know," I said as I sat back on my butt to stretch my legs. My knees were sore, and I needed circulation through my muscles again. The nerves in my feet tingled as blood flow regained. "But people are looking for us. There are two girls missing now. That is going to get some attention. Luke and I went to the police station asking about you, so the search has already begun."

"Sky." Amy's sobs grew heavier. "I never thought I'd miss ...

that bonehead so much. They … will never … find us." She sniffed, her words flat and overcome. "Sorry … I'm trying to talk better." She paused again. "He. Asked. Me. For. Ride. Home. … said his car wasn't working … couldn't find my cell phone to tell Sky where I was … he asked me in." Her breath grew rapid as though she was either laughing or hyperventilating. "I thought he wanted to get laid." Another pause. "He claimed he had an art project that he wanted to do … asked for my opinion … the next thing I knew …" She took several more breaths before two final words hung between us. "Stun gun."

"He's a master manipulator. A sick man. He surprised me, too. Not like that, but—" I shook my head. "We have to focus." I taxed my brain with how we were going to escape this dark prison. "We are in some sort of attic space." I put my hands between my knees to keep warm. The wind continued to shriek, making me feel even colder than I already was. If only I could clear my mind. "There's insulation along the inner walls. I haven't checked the entire area, but I know that much. We could try to pull out the insulation and then kick the inner wall in. The problem with that plan is that the inner wall is made of thick paneling, so it won't be easy to kick through it. You already hurt your ankle with the door. Even if we do get inside the house, he locked the door in the adjacent room. There are no windows, except for some skylights. I didn't see any cranks or levers, so I'm guessing they don't open. We could try to stack some storage containers, but it would be difficult to break that glass."

Amy's shivering body kept touching me. "I'm so fucking cold." Her words trailed off.

She was fading.

I wrapped my arms around her and held on tight. "You have to stay with me, Amy."

The wind lashed outdoors, trying to tell me something—

something my mind hadn't grasped yet. Then it came to me. "There has to be a vent somewhere in here. Otherwise, the wind wouldn't be so loud. If there is one, I can kick it out and maybe we can escape to the outdoors. I don't know what the outside of the house looks like. I was unconscious when he brought me here, but you do. What do you remember? I'm assuming we are on a second floor, but I don't know that for sure. Are there drainage pipes, rain gutters, or small roofs that we could lower down onto?"

Amy's body moved against the floor, her breathing heavier.

Trying to avoid her wounded shoulder and ankle, I shook her. "Amy."

She jolted. "What?"

"I need your help. What does the outside of the house look like?"

"It's ... old farmhouse ... white ... chipped paint ... two floors, I think ... detached garage ... looks like a small barn." She paused. "... porch on the front ... covered in windows." Her voice grew raspier as she spoke. Finally, she coughed. "Jesus ... that stun gun hurt ... you have no idea."

I thought about the temporary paralysis I had endured from my own blast. "Yes, unfortunately, I do."

"Oh ... man." Amy's voice weakened again.

The wind flapped something on the other side of the room, supporting my vent theory. "You stay here. I'm going to see what's making that noise."

Amy's breath lowered to the floor as I imagined her body did. "Okay," she said so lightly I could barely hear her.

Deciding to fight that battle later, I crawled along the floor, using the flapping sound as my beacon. To my left the ceiling angled downward, so I went straight, keeping my hands out to avoid any barriers while realizing what life must be like for blind people. They lived in the dark all the time. My bound wrists made movement difficult and painful. The zip ties kept reminding me how sharp they were.

When I reached the source of the noise, I ran my hands along the wall. It took several tries, but I finally felt something different. It wasn't metal like a vent, but it had a texture unlike the other parts of the wall around it, which consisted of wood studs and insulation, or so I guessed. The surface was thick like heavy-duty construction paper only rougher. I ran my hand along it several more times trying to determine what it was, until it finally came to me. My father used to keep stacks of it in our garage whenever a strong storm loosened a roof tile. It was tar paper or something along those lines. Using my fingernails, I searched for the edge, where I peeled up the paper and yanked it away. Metal staples had reinforced it well, causing the paper to tear free in small sections. With a new surge of optimism, I continued to tear and rip until diffused light entered the room.

And then I could see.

It felt like a miracle. I glanced back at Amy lying in the fetal position in the center of the confined room. What I hadn't noticed before was a thick stain not ten feet from her body. Vomit. Cobwebs clung to the low ceiling above her head. Poor Amy. She was paying the price for things that had nothing to do with her. We had to get out of here. It couldn't end like this.

I turned my attention to the now-exposed metal vent. The tar paper not only kept out the light, it also provided a shield for the cold that was now torturing my fingers. The wind flew past the small vent, whistling like Old Man Winter. I felt around the edges of its triangular shape, realizing the space was far too small for a human body to pass through. I jimmied my fingernails deeper sending shooting pain into the nerve endings. I pried and pulled until one of my fingernails broke off. I shuddered. I sucked the finger to relieve the pain until I decided that it didn't matter. If Dr. Adams came back and saw what I'd done, a broken fingernail would be the least of my worries. The tar paper was in tatters now with no way to put it back in place.

I had to keep working, and so I did, wiggling each piece free. I wedged and pulled all around the vent's edge. It took what seemed like hours to get one corner of the vent to give way.

I glanced back at Amy's unconscious body once more.

The loose edge encouraged me to keep working as I tugged at the vent as best I could. Three broken fingernails later, I had hold of it, enough that I could get a full finger underneath. I pulled with all the strength I had, until the vent broke free.

Before I did anything else, I placed the vent vertically between my knees and used the rough metal edge to saw away at my zip tie until my hands sprung free. The wind outside shot through the opening, colliding with the sweat on my brow. Although the hole was too small for a person, I was able to stick my head out to see what awaited us outdoors.

The sun hit my retinas like the flash of a camera. I screwed up my eyes and panned my head back and forth at the white blanket covering the earth. In my distress, I had forgotten all about the snowstorm from the night before. A woodpecker, maybe the one from earlier, tapped on a tree nearby. There were no houses that I could see or roads, just woods and lots of it. I looked down at two stories of house before the structure met the ground. No porch as I had hoped for or eves that could provide footing. In fact, there was nothing on this end of the house, nothing but chipped white paint and forest. The snow on the ground wasn't deep, judging by the layers on the trees and the evergreens. Spots of earth were already poking through. If we jumped, there would be no cushion.

I combed my brain for another option but couldn't think of any. All my progress was for nothing. There *was* no escape, and now we were going to freeze to death. Maybe that was a better ending. If Professor Adams returned and saw my handiwork, I knew what would follow. I only hoped our families wouldn't suffer for too long. The *not knowing* that Carrie's parents had endured would spread through Scott, Luke, and both of our families like a cancer. It would take years for them to recover. I knew that because that's how long it would take me if the tables were turned. I sat back and covered my mouth to muffle the sniveling. I ruminated over how silly I'd behaved with Scott. I should've known he would never hurt my friend. How could I believe something so horrible? The last words I said to him came from fear, pain, and betrayal. I was so very wrong. But would he blame himself for this, anyway? I had blamed myself for something as random as icy roads for six years, so I knew the damage guilt could inflict.

If this was my end, I wanted to spend it with my friend, who was just as victimized as I was. Meeting Amy was one of the best things that had happened to me since I came to this school, just like meeting and falling in love with Scott was my other best thing. They were both gifts. I wasn't alone. And as my parents had reminded me recently, I never was.

I glanced over at Amy again, my eyes drawn to the opposite wall from across the crawl space. What I saw was hope in the form of another sheet of tar paper about the same size as the hole I was sitting in front of right now. Ignoring my bruised knees and throbbing fingertips, I grabbed the vent and sprinted on all fours toward my destination. I knew what to do and wasted no time working the vent free. Using the edge of the first vent as a wedge spared my fingers this time and produced a much faster result. By the time I had the opening cleared, I was in a cold sweat. I reached my head out this time and looked down on a roof just ten feet below.

I wanted to scream with joy or jump up and down, and I did on the inside. With freedom in my grasp, I worked to broaden the hole. I used my hands at first, then gave up and started kicking with my feet, making sure to stay within the two-by-fours, which I could now see. I kicked at Dr. Adams, I kicked at Rick, and I kicked at icy roads and Rachael. I kicked at everything that had caused me pain until my feet stung and the hole relented into a helpful size.

Inside our frozen locker, I shuffled over to Amy and shook her. She moaned a few times until her eyes fluttered open. Red welts, dried blood, and bruises dressed in shades of black, blue, and yellow covered her arms, neck, and face. Dried vomit and dog food caked her mouth. If that wasn't alarming enough, she had no shoes.

"Sara?" Eyes bulging, Amy looked around as if amazed that she could see me. "What's going on?" She sounded much better. The drugs were wearing off.

"I've found a way out." I propped her up. "Look." I pointed to the opening. "There is a porch just about ten feet below. I've cleared the hole. We can lower down onto the roof of the porch and then get to the ground. Where are your shoes?"

The wind drove through the small space like a hurricane, causing Amy to shiver. She was so pale. "When I tried to kick the door in, he took my shoes as punishment." Her eyes popped. "Jesus. You look like hell." She stared at my body and face, the same way I had just done with her.

Then we both snickered before I waved her off. "It doesn't matter." I didn't tell her what *she* looked like. What was the point? "Before we go, let's get your hands free."

I pushed her knees up, placed the vent between them, and went to work.

A tear ran down Amy's cheek, her eyes glistening. "Thank you." Deep emotion and gratitude laced her words.

When she was free, we descended upon the opening, my hopes high and my adrenaline shooting through the roof.

"I'll go first, so I can help you down," I said.

Amy rubbed her shoulder and nodded. "Okay. You've got this, Al." She always said those words to me when she knew I needed the boost. I also loved the way she sounded less like a victim and more like the Amy I had grown to love—the girl who could take on the world.

Moving feet first, I pushed through the opening, my stomach scraping along the rough edge beneath me. I had no coat, but thankfully, I still had my sneakers on, unlike Amy.

Inching my way fully out, my legs hung loose in the wind until finally my feet made contact with the roof below. I let myself fall the final inch until I was standing on the roof of the porch. I looked around for a vehicle but saw none, only tire marks that traveled along the dirt driveway and past the southern corner of the house, judging by the angle of the sun.

Our only source of light was trekking its way toward the horizon, but it wasn't gone yet. We had less than an hour before darkness descended. If Dr. Adams was in fact helping with the search, he'd hopefully be detained until sundown.

Timing was critical.

"Okay, Amy. Come down now. I'm ready for you."

Two bare feet poked through the wall. I caught her dangling legs and guided her body toward me. My hands beyond cold, I slowly steered her down until she was standing right next to me. Then I made a decision that was probably not smart, but I offered her my sneakers.

At first, Amy refused. "No. You'll need them."

"Just put them on. You're hurt and that will already slow us down. I grew up in Vermont. I can handle a little cold."

We sat on the roof, where I took my shoes off.

Every time Amy moved a certain way, she winced and grabbed her shoulder or favored her ankle.

Not a moment to waste, I took over and tied the shoes on

her feet. Her left ankle was swollen and blue. I couldn't tie the sneaker, so I stuffed the laces inside.

I stood and then helped Amy up. The roof was made of asphalt, which allowed for better footing than slate or metal. At least something was working in our favor. We baby stepped our way to the edge of the roof and looked down. My feet pulsated with cold.

A distressed picnic table stood off to the side while two trash cans kept each other company near a barren oak tree. The barn Amy had mentioned rose up from the ground near a spot where the driveway widened into a circle. An old tractor took refuge where the grass changed height near the back edge of the structure.

"Okay. I'm going to go down first again."

Amy took my arm. "No. You don't have any shoes on. Let me go first."

I sighed in an annoyed manner. "You can't with that hurt shoulder or ankle. I can go down there and push that picnic table over, so you have something to step onto."

Amy looked down and then up at me. "Fine. You take your shoes back, and then you can throw them up to me."

I shook my head, frustrated that this process was taking so long. Dr. Adams could arrive at any moment. Knowing the persistence of Amy, and to save time, I offered a compromise.

"I'll take one shoe. That will give me some traction." Before she could argue, I lowered down and untied the shoe holding her good ankle. I thought of just pulling it off but didn't want to hurt her. Amy held onto my head for support and balance.

She didn't fight me.

While enjoying the warmth of one foot, I followed the same sequence of events from the crawl space. I lowered my body down until my hands were clutching the edge of the roof. There was no rain gutter, which probably wouldn't hold my weight, anyway. When I let go and hit the ground, a stinging sensation shot up from my feet and into my legs that made me pause and take a breath.

"Are you okay?" Amy peered down at me, her eyes strained.

"Yes. Just need a minute." I ran to the picnic table, ignoring the discomfort from one very cold foot. At least on the ground, the wind wasn't as strong. Or maybe exertion gave me just the body heat I needed.

Feeling the resistance in the weight of the picnic table, I yanked as hard as I could, dragging it over to the porch, wet earth hitching a ride under its legs.

Amy was already on her stomach and lowering her legs when I got there. She groaned a few times until she finally hopped onto the table and lifted her hurt ankle, biting down on her lower lip.

"Son of a bitch. That smarts." In her elevated position, she peered into the porch and then did a double take. "You'll never guess what I'm looking at." Standing unsteadily on her good ankle, Amy brought her elbow back and slammed it into the window.

I jolted in place. "What are you doing?" *Are you insane?*

Amy crouched down and reaching into the broken window, pulled her hand back with a pair of boots attached. "Look. He's going to know we've escaped, anyway." After she brushed the loose glass off her arm, which thank God wasn't cut, she sat and pulled the unlaced sneaker off her compromised foot. "If we're going to make a run for it, we both need something on our feet. They were just sitting there on a table, right in front of me, asking me to take them."

She handed me back the sneaker and put the boots on while I sat on the table next to her. She was right, the tracks and loose earth I'd made from the picnic table across the lawn were enough to signal that something was amiss. The recent snowfall only highlighted the table's path. Then there was the hole in the wall above the porch. I pulled off my wet sock and did my best to wipe it clean of snow and dirt. Then I put it back on, followed by my sneaker immediately after. My mother had always told me never to wear sneakers without socks. "You'll get blisters," she'd said in a tone that spoke of experience. Having no concept of how far away civilization was, I needed two uninjured feet.

I helped Amy down from the picnic table. She staggered and stumbled a bit, but somehow, she made it work. I stood beside her, taking the arm from her good shoulder and wrapping it around my own. Together we hobbled across the muddy driveway, *Thelma and Louise* style, another movie Amy had made me watch.

"I think it's best if we follow the direction of the driveway but from the woods. If he comes driving down, he'll see us, so we need to stay out of sight."

Amy nodded, her mouth frowning with each step. She started breathing like a woman in labor. "I just hope I can make it. If memory serves, the road is a good distance away." She paused for a moment. "You know what, Al?"

"What?"

She paused.

"You are a real badass. You have a lot more balls than even I'd given you credit for." She smirked. "I won't underestimate your she-power again."

I smiled back.

Amy shook her head. "You saved my ass. There is no other way to put it."

"Does that mean I get a new nickname?" I had to ask, enjoying the upper hand fate had dealt me.

"Don't push it, *Al*."

The wind cracked the trees and deepened the cold that was already slowing down my muscles. I wished I had checked the porch for a coat. At least being this close to each other Amy and I shared our body heat.

We half walked, half stumbled through the thicket, over broken tree limbs and rocks. I looked back at our footprints wishing the sun would set and allow us more cover. The position of the sun told me night was arriving soon.

"If we get out of here, Al, I'm going to make that asshole pay for this." Amy grunted as she forged forward.

"*When* we get out of here, I'll help you. Now save your strength and focus on walking."

I helped her over a fallen log when the sound of a car hit my eardrums like a bomb going off. *Oh no.* I tried to convince myself it was from a road farther away until the engine growled closer, then a splash from a mud puddle made my heart skip a beat. We needed more time.

I looked at Amy and she looked at me. "We need to get farther into the woods," I said.

I longed for food and water and more importantly rest. On top of that, Amy was wounded far worse than I was. It didn't matter. We had to keep going. We were out of options.

Feeling my adrenaline fade, I pushed my muscles harder, pulling Amy along with me. My lungs labored, my knees weakened, my mind drifted. I kept going, deeper into the woods, away from the waning light and away from danger. Soon I couldn't hear the car any longer, but that didn't provide me with any comfort. We were a good distance away. For several minutes, we continued without incident. I started to feel confident that maybe it wasn't *his* car after all. The noise could be something else. My senses weren't exactly sharp, but Amy had heard it, too.

The snap of a branch had me sweating and freezing all at the same time.

Amy's face turned ashen.

My lower lip trembled along with every other muscle in my body. *Our footprints in the snow.* We had made the job so easy for him. We'd left a trail.

Twenty feet ahead, another partially downed tree held branches and organic matter that rose up, creating a natural tarp. I hobbled with Amy to the other side and set her down.

"What are you doing?" she said in a whisper.

I motioned with my hands toward a branch and mimicked grabbing it and stabbing someone. Then I pointed to a large tree and used my fingers to simulate walking.

She nodded and lowered her body to the ground.

Carefully and as quietly as I could, I tiptoed over to the branch and gripped it in my hand. I stood back and leaned against a living tree and waited, hoping the snap was an animal and not human. Another cracking branch and a footfall made my breath catch. Danger had found us. My pulse roaring, I tried not to breathe too heavily or panic. The wind worked against me, rustling loose limbs and debris nearby. It sounded like he was everywhere. Snow crunched under a shoe. I'd heard that sound many times in my childhood. There was no mistaking it. He was here.

Tears ran down my checks as I clutched at memories from my life. I thought about the moment when I had first met Scott, and how his big blue eyes had dazzled and comforted me. I reflected on our kiss on the mountain when I knew I'd fallen in love. The necklace he had given me with his love and devotion attached. Even the time when he ran down the police station steps and grabbed me in his arms, tugged at my heart. "I can breathe again," he'd said. If this was truly my end, I wouldn't die loveless. I would take all those memories with me to the next world. Professor Adams couldn't have them. They were mine.

When I looked over, Amy's tear-stained cheeks and the distant look in her eyes suggested she was also saying her own goodbyes. She grabbed a fallen branch and looked up at me. We both nodded. This was it. We would fight to the death.

My self-defense classes played out in my brain as I searched for the right moves. Stab hard and deep, I told myself. Aim for the chest. Claw at the eyes. Kick at the groin.

A steaming breath floated past me. He was close, only feet away.

With white knuckles and my weapon poised, I widened my stance and prepared myself for war. Just when I was about to launch my branch into whatever stood in front of me, a familiar voice rode the wind past my ears.

"Sara. Are you out here?" Everything in me seized. My body swayed, my mind racing, my heart leaping. I wasn't sure how to breathe or think. I grabbed the tree and held on. Could this be true? Was my mind playing tricks?

Staying tight against the bark, I peered around the tree to find the last person I ever expected to see. Standing there, unshaven and gorgeous, was my Scott.

His eyes locked with mine, his mouth hanging open. "Oh, thank God it's you. Are you injured?" Taking two long strides, he ripped his coat off and wrapped it around my shoulders, soothing me in his musky scent and the warmth I had missed desperately.

I thought my heart was going to burst. All the fear and horror I had endured rose up from my chest and exploded into a sob so deep, it rattled my bones. "Scott. It's you. It's really you. I never thought I'd see you again." I didn't just cry, I blubbered.

Keeping his arms outstretched, Scott took hold of my shoulders, his eyes examining my face and my body. "You're hurt. What did he do to you?" He took my hand and kissed my broken fingernails. His eyes welled over. He kissed my ear. "I thought I'd lost you." He held me so tight I feared my lungs would collapse. I didn't care.

He pulled back and held my face, his troubled eyes spilling with tears. We remained that way, staring at each other, absorbing where we were. There were no words. There was only love.

"Don't forget *me*, Big Guy."

Scott's face turned toward the raspy voice calling out to him.

"It's Amy. She's hurt," I said, wiping my cheeks.

Scott dashed over to her, bent down, and picked up her tattered body as if she were made of air. With his big strong arms, he cradled Amy like she was a child.

Her feet dangled in the air. "Where's Sky?" she asked.

"He's searching the house." Scott blinked, his eyes begging me closer.

I ran to him and held his arm, my body leaning in for support.

"How?" I asked, amazed at this turn of events.

"I'll explain later. Let's get you two out of here."

The three of us bound together as if by rope, trudged out of the woods and away from our close encounter with death.

Chapter Twenty

Inside an ambulance, I stretched out on a gurney while a female paramedic with friendly amber eyes and blonde hair pulled back into a ponytail dabbed antiseptic on my wounds. Amy was already on her way to the hospital.

Through an open door, two firetrucks, a fleet of police cars, a white van marked "Tactical Unit," and another van with the words "Forensic Unit" across its side, cluttered Dr. Adams's driveway, with more cars arriving by the second. A police officer walked past the ambulance with a German shepard in tow.

Wearing dark-gray cargo pants and a button-down top of the same color, the woman who introduced herself as Annemarie, had already asked me various questions about what happened, what drugs Dr. Adams had injected me with, and any medical history I could offer. I was able to provide a pretty good rendition with the exception of the drugs. I was clucless on that front—I only knew how they made me feel, which she listened to with professional candor and a nodding head. The inside of the ambulance resembled a small hospital with a neck brace hanging from a pole, a folded wheelchair, various monitors, bags of first-aid kits, nozzles, tubes, a ventilator, and other equipment I knew nothing about. How anyone could keep track of what went where was beyond me.

A warm hand caressed my shoulder. Scott sat across from the paramedic leaning over me like an eagle safeguarding his nest. He watched Annemarie's every move, his forehead wrinkled and his eyebrows drawing together.

When she asked about any possible sexual assault, Scott put a hand to his mouth. I could feel him holding his breath.

"None," I was happy to report, allowing Scott to exhale and the blood to return to his cheeks.

The paramedic did a cursory inspection of my limbs and neck and then covered me with a thick blanket before she took my temperature and blood pressure along with sugar readings.

"I'm not surprised at all that your blood pressure is slightly elevated and so is your temperature. Dehydration will cause that, but the IV will replenish those fluids and nutrients quickly."

I glanced down at the needle in the back of my hand tethered to a small bag on a hook.

"Did he use a stun gun on you?" Annemarie asked as she stared down at two sets of bite marks on my upper chest that looked like a vampire had sampled me for his lunch.

"Yes."

Scott took my hand; his lips pressed together, his eyes tense. "Motherfucker," he whispered.

After cleaning the exposed areas, Annemarie applied small bandages to some wounds while leaving others alone.

When she moved on to my ear, I winced at the burning sensation shooting through my head.

Scott cringed as though he was feeling the pain right along

with me. He tightened his grip on my hand. "You're doing great," he said with a nod and a tight smile.

Suddenly I had this image of being pregnant and ready to give birth and Scott sitting next to me just as he was now, saying those very same words. Strange how my mind worked and how random my thoughts could be. At least we still had a future together. I was thankful for that.

"Is it torn?" I asked apprehensive.

Annemarie shook her head. "No. It's just a cut. But I'm sure it stings a little. I'm almost done."

Once the initial sting subsided, I was okay with the rest.

She examined my back, using tweezers to extract a few splinters I was happy to be rid of.

"I've taken care of the exposed areas." Annemarie wadded up the soiled dressing, along with the trash from the bandages, and threw them away in a canister next to her. "At the hospital they will do a more thorough examination. Before I finish, are there any other areas that are causing you extreme pain right now?"

I shook my head. "Nothing extreme, but I ache all over."

"That's to be expected." Annemarie nodded and pulled off her rubber gloves just as Sheriff Murphy knocked on the opened door at the back of the ambulance.

He peered in. "How much longer before you're done?" he asked Annemarie.

"I'm pretty much done now. How much time do you need? I'd like to get her to the hospital. I've already called it in, and they are waiting for her."

Sheriff Murphy climbed into the ambulance and closed the door, his giant shoulders intimidating in the confined space. He removed his wide-brimmed hat and sat on a built-in bench behind the paramedic.

Scott sat up straighter and stared at him, his face hardening.

I understood why. Sheriff Murphy had arrested Scott not too long ago. What an awkward situation.

"I won't be long." His gray eyes found me next. "I'm sorry that I've seen you twice now under such dire circumstances." He glanced at Scott and then me again. "I'm sure glad that we found you in time. This is one of those days when it pays off to be a sheriff." He gave Scott another look. "You and I need to talk about your methods, young man, but that can wait."

Methods? Was there another reason for the tension I was feeling between them? You could cut it with a knife.

By the time Scott, Amy, and I had wandered out of the forest, the cavalry was already here. I hadn't had time to find out how Scott even knew where to find me. It appeared that we had a lot to talk about.

Scott squared his shoulders. "Given the circumstances, I didn't have time to dick around."

The sheriff raised a palm, his face stern. "We will discuss this later." His words were harsh this time. "And I understand the danger these girls were in. Dr. Adams wasn't on our radar ... yet."

"He wasn't on mine, either," I said. "He told me he took Carrie Stevens, too. I kept thinking it was an older man who works at the college or a student named Rachael."

"Yes, I am quite certain Dr. Adams was the perpetrator who also kidnapped Miss Stevens." Sheriff Murphy's eyes narrowed as his attention honed in. "Did you say, Rachael, as in Rachael Moore?"

"Yes."

The sheriff looked up at the ceiling for a moment and exhaled. "We are *aware* of Miss Moore." He scratched his head. "She's been—how should I put this—quite aggressive in surveilling a local drug dealer named Alexander Gallagher, even though, on numerous occasions, we've ordered her to desist."

My eyebrows went up and then down, understanding how "aggressive" Rachael could be. "Do you mean Axl?" I asked.

The sheriff nodded.

"She accused me of working with him." I suddenly feared that I was saying too much. "But I wasn't. I don't even do drugs or smoke pot. I barely drink." I started to sweat, ready to recite my entire history when Scott patted my arm and gave me a don't-worry-about-it look.

Sheriff Murphy raised a palm. "Relax, Miss Browne. We know. Let's get back to the matter at hand. I'd like to ask you a few questions before you go to the hospital. We get better results when the victim's memory is fresh." He eyed the paramedic. "If it's not too much trouble."

"I can give you a few minutes." Annemarie, who had been cleaning up, stood, folded up her stool, and moved to the front of the ambulance, where she grabbed a clipboard off a hook and started writing.

"Mr. Williams, would you mind leaving us alone for a moment?" With the stool out of his way, Sheriff Murphy slid down the bench closer to me.

"I'm not going anywhere." His back ramrod straight, Scott squared his eyes with the sheriff. "Wherever she goes, I go." He wasn't playing.

All I could think was *Please don't get into a fight.*

The sheriff pulled out a pad of paper and pencil from his coat pocket, all while shaking his head in a subtle way. "All right, young man. Can't say I blame you."

Annemarie spoke through a small window to the driver about timing, when the sheriff cleared his throat. "Let's start from the beginning. How did you get here?"

I had only covered about half of the bizarre story, when the door opened, another officer appearing. "Sheriff, we've found something. You need to come take a look."

I feared the worst. *Was it Carrie?* The professor's chilling words haunted me once again: "But when I witnessed her taking her last breath, I realized that I had saved the world from another 'Angela.' I can't tell you how rewarding that was." How could anyone feel good about ending another person's life? When I was younger, I'd read one of my father's favorite books: *All Quiet on the Western Front*, which didn't speak at all about satisfaction or revenge, only suffering. The soldier in that tale and in many real stories across history, took no pleasure in taking the lives of others. To enjoy such a thing, separated a man from the beast within.

Sheriff Murphy put his pad of paper and pencil back in his pocket. "I think you've given me enough for now. Once they've examined you and released you from the hospital, I'd like to take a full report." With that said, he rose like a polar bear and, hunched over, walked toward the door, where the other officer was standing by. The entire ambulance swayed from his weight. After he jumped down, the sheriff poked his head in one last time. "We contacted your mother, and she is on her way here. I spoke with her about an hour ago and assured her we had found you." He glanced over at Scott again.

Clearly, the sheriff and Scott had some unfinished business.

"She asked that you call her when you can. I was going to offer my phone, but—"

"She can use mine." Scott pulled his cell phone from his pants pocket.

The sheriff nodded and closed the door behind him with a clunk.

How much did Abigail know? And how was she taking it? *Oh God, the baby.*

As the ambulance started down the road, I dialed Abigail's number, my mind and my body restless.

When she answered, a low-pitched humming told me she was already on the road. Of course she was; this was Abigail.

"Hello?" Her pitch was high and unsteady.

"Mom. It's me."

"Oh, Sara." Abigail burst into tears, or maybe she'd already been crying. It was difficult to say. "I've been so worried about you. Are you okay? How did this happen? I'm putting you on speaker phone."

My throat clotted with emotion. "I'm okay. I really am. It's a long story. Are *you* okay? How's the baby?"

"What? Me? Yes, I'm fine. It's you I'm worried about. The sheriff told me what happened. You are leaving that school as soon as I get there. I'll help you pack your bags. First, you have to deal with bullying and now this." She took a quick breath. "My lord. I've never heard of anything like this. Teachers kidnapping girls." Her sobbing distorted her words, but I was able to make them out regardless. Her emotional state was crystal clear. "I can't think about what might have happened. How did you get out?"

I glanced at Scott's downcast expression.

"I was able to break out with Amy, and then Scott found us in the woods."

"Scott?" Abigail paused. "Do you mean—?"

"Yes, I do." I lifted Scott's chin as I spoke, forcing him to see me. "Scott never did cheat on me, Mom. I was wrong about him."

"But you said you saw—"

"I know what I said. We have a lot to discuss when you get here, but there is one thing I want you to know." My eyes burned with new tears. "Scott never betrayed me. I am 100 percent certain of that. In fact, he's done nothing but support and protect me."

Scott broke eye contact and lowered his head, as if the weight of my words were taking their toll.

I reached out and touched his cheek. "There was someone at school who was doing things behind the scenes, manipulating all of us. I was wrong about what I *thought* I saw."

"What?" Abigail's words were barely a whisper. "What is wrong with the people at that school?"

"I know. But everything is okay now."

The sounds of the road filled the air between her and me.

"We can talk about it when I get there. Can I use this phone number to call you when we arrive?" she asked.

"Yes. This is Scott's phone, and he'll be with me. What time are you expecting to get here?"

"I got on the road at noon. My navigator says I'll be there by ten o'clock tonight. Joel made a reservation at the Holiday Inn in town. I tried to find a flight, but none would get me there sooner."

"Glad you're okay, kiddo," Joel said from what I assumed was the driver's seat. "Your mom is pretty shaken up over this. I'm sure you are, too."

"Please take good care of her, Joel. I don't want anything to happen to her or the baby. And drive safe."

"Don't worry about that, and you know your mother, I can't tell her not to worry. Until she sees you for herself, she's not going to feel any better. We'll call you as soon as we get close."

"Okay, love you both."

"We love you, too," Abigail said before we ended the call.

Not five minutes later, sirens wailed through the air, lights flashing, as we drove up to the emergency room entrance.

Annemarie spoke on a two-way radio. "We are driving in now. ETA fifteen seconds."

As soon as the vehicle stopped, the back doors sprang open and a man wearing bluish-gray scrubs stood behind a wheelchair gripping the handles. A pole with a hook shot up from the side.

Scott tried to help me down, but Annemarie insisted she do it (hospital regulations). Holding the IV bag, she escorted me over to the wheelchair, where she placed the bag on a hook. Once Scott's hand rested on my shoulder, the male hospital worker wheeled me inside.

Two women sat behind a long counter as I rode past, both of them looking up. Several boxes rested on the counter, full of files. Which one was mine? I wondered. A digital clock on the wall flashed 6:10 p.m. The sterile smell, beeping monitors, and a loudspeaker paging staff members every five seconds felt familiar from my last visit when I had come here to see Scott.

It seemed police stations and hospitals were becoming my regular hangouts.

Chapter Twenty-One

Three hours later, the doctor in charge of me signed the form that released me from the hospital. I'd been poked and prodded, had bloodwork taken, and was questioned over and over about what had happened pertaining to my injuries. The drugs that Dr. Adams had forced into my system were mostly gone.

Scott hovered around the area like a lion would protect his pride. Whenever a nurse forced him to leave the room, he stood right outside the door. I knew that because every time the door opened, I could see the edge of his shoulder. I didn't want him to leave my side, even for a second. My entire body, including my head, throbbed like a toothache. The doctor offered me mild painkillers, but I refused them. My mind was clear, and I wanted to keep it that way, so I took an ibuprofen. I also drank a lot of water, which helped immensely. So did the IV from before.

I hobbled off the table and put Scott's coat back on, letting his masculine aroma comfort me.

"Let's go find Amy," I said taking his hand.

Scott walked slowly with his arm around me, guiding me by several rooms with sliding glass doors, equipment everywhere, until we came upon a counter where four women sat in medical garb. Two rolling carts flanked the counter with narrow drawers that resembled a tool chest. I asked one woman with prominent brown eyes for Amy's room number and she directed me to the lobby and the information counter.

"She's one of the girls who was kidnapped." Another nurse with curly black hair said to her counterpart.

All the women looked up at us.

The woman with brown eyes punched some keys on her terminal and then got up and led us to a set of elevators. "I'm sorry. I didn't recognize you at first. She's on the fifth floor, Room 503. Take this elevator, and it will get you there faster. I remember when the other student went missing last year." She placed her hand on my arm. "We were all so glad to hear that you and your friend are okay." She smiled and walked away.

We took the elevator up to the fifth floor where we weaved our way down several hallways, following signs that included ranges of numbers. Through a set of double doors, we passed another nurse's station before we came upon Room 503. Men and women in scrubs hustled past us carrying clipboards or pushing carts with computers on them. A man walked by with a bouquet of flowers clutched in his hand, a young girl at his side.

When I entered Amy's room, Luke was sitting at her bedside, staring at his phone. My eyes teared up and my lip quivered at the sight of my friend. It wasn't because she looked bad, she didn't. Her coloring was good as she slept peacefully on the hospital bed, an IV attached to the back of her hand. She and I had been through a terrifying experience. We almost died together. If I had felt close to Amy before this incident, my feelings had quadrupled.

I had to admit, they'd done a good job cleaning her up. Her left shoulder was slightly larger than the right one.

Scott touched my lower back, his eyes supportive.

As I walked closer, blue medical tape peeked out from under her gown, winding down her arm and up over her collarbone like an extra layer of muscle. What I assumed was a medical boot exaggerated the size of her left foot from under the blanket. The girl had been through a lot.

"Oh, hey." Luke set his phone on a rolling table, rose, and hugged me.

"How's she doing?" I asked wiping my eyes.

Luke nodded as he rubbed his chin. "She's doing great. They had to sedate her to set her shoulder. The doctor said her ankle has a hairline fracture, but they don't think she'll need surgery. They want her to stay a couple of days as a precaution." Luke buried his hands into the front pockets of his jeans, as he often did. "You know my little wildcat: nothing's going to keep her down for long. The nurse told me her mother called. They just got in and are on their way over here."

"Oh good." I thought about Abigail. I was expecting a call from her soon as well.

"Did you have trouble getting past all the reporters?" Luke removed his hands from his pockets.

"A nurse guided us through another way. Why? Are there a lot of them?"

Luke made a face. "It's like a mob down there."

"Wow. I guess I'm not surprised." I approached Amy's bed, while Luke gave Scott a bro handshake.

"Hey, man," he said. "Remind me never to piss you off, dude. That was some gnarly shit that went down." He pointed at Scott. "I owe you, bro. You need some good weed? I just scored some."

Scott glanced over at me. "Nah. I'm good for now."

I sat next to Amy while she slept, realizing that I still didn't know how they had found us. Too much had happened to ask about it. I took Amy's hand in mine. Her skin felt warm, no longer cold like when I had found her, and her face was cleaned up. "Okay. Now that we have a few minutes. Can you tell me what happened, Scott?"

Scott and Luke exchanged a look as they descended upon Amy's bed.

"Nothing. It was no big deal," Scott said staring down at our sedated patient.

Luke chuckled but then stopped, probably for my benefit. He kept running his fingers along his scruff.

I shook my head. "Listen. I'm going to find out, anyway, so you might as well tell me now. No more holding back, right?" He had to understand how important this was to me.

I waited. The reluctance in Scott's eyes indicated he didn't want to tell me what happened.

Scott exhaled and palmed the back of his neck. "Whatever you want, babe." He approached a small lime-green couch positioned under a window and sat, while Luke remained next to me. "I went to your dorm this morning to see if you had found Amy yet. When I got there, Luke was sitting on the floor outside of your suite."

"Yeah. Remember when I left to search for Amy?" Luke waited for my confirmation.

I nodded. "Yes."

"When I returned to your dorm, it was late ... or early since it was almost morning. I knocked a few times, but no one answered, and I didn't want to wake up your entire floor, so I planned to wait until sunrise." Luke moved his hands as he spoke. "I figured you were getting some rest. And it was only a couple of hours. At six o'clock, *this* dude showed up." He motioned toward Scott.

Scott piped in. "That's right. Luke told me that you hadn't found Amy, and he was about to wake you up to help with the search. He also filled me in on your trip to the police station." Scott lowered his eyes, guilt weighing down on his shoulders. "I had sent you a bunch of texts and a couple of voicemails, hoping to reach you." He looked at me and paused, emotion straining his face. "I'm so sorry, babe."

Luke's eyes registered confusion, but he remained silent.

"It's okay. We can talk about the other stuff later. Let's keep going."

Luke scratched his eyebrow. "Okay. Scott banged on the door until the tall chick answered and let us in. She was asking us about Amy, trying to find out what was going on."

"That was SueAnne," I said to help fill in the gap.

Scott swiped his jaw, a fresh crop of stubble blooming on his chin. "We told her what we knew and went right to your room. Your door was unlocked, so I went inside first, in case you were sleeping. We didn't want to startle you." Scott straightened up. "Your bed was still made, and the bathroom showed no signs that you'd been there recently. I sent you another text and even tried to call, but your phone kept going to voicemail."

Luke perked up. "I had already told Scott that Amy's cell was doing the same thing."

Scott widened his legs and leaned his elbows on his thighs as if he needed additional support to get this out.

Poor man. He must've been terrified. I would've been.

"When I heard that Luke hadn't seen you since last night, I uh." He rubbed the side of his nose. "I don't know. I kind of freaked out. I ... *we* started looking all over campus for you. I found your car in the parking lot, so I knew you hadn't left. We checked the library, the cafeteria, and all the snack bars and the coffee houses." Scott motioned toward Luke. "Luke checked the Panera across the street and the grocery store that's down the road. We basically checked everywhere within walking distance. It took us several hours to cover it all. I kept trying your cell phone and got no answer. You *always* answer, so it was odd."

It all reminded me of the time the tables were turned and *I* was the one trying to locate Scott. What a whirlwind our lives had become.

Luke nodded. "Yeah, especially since you and I had agreed to stay in contact with each other."

"I remember," I said.

"Sheriff Murphy had called me." Luke tapped my shoulder. "Remember, we gave our cell numbers to the cops?"

"Yes," I said, intrigued.

"He told me that they'd set up a command unit in the Welcome Center near the dorms and asked if we had heard from Amy. I said no and that I hadn't been able to find you, either, or reach you by phone." Luke moved a tray on wheels back and forth as he spoke.

Scott fanned his hands out. "I didn't have a fucking clue what to do. Luke and I wandered around campus. As the day wore on, I suddenly remembered you saying something about a janitor, so we headed over to the Maintenance Building. I asked for a guy named Henry, who also happened to be the dude I was talking to. I then asked him if he'd seen you. I pulled up a picture of you on my phone and showed it to him. He said no." Scott blew out a breath and shook his head. "I've always been pretty good at reading people. I sensed he was holding back or lying."

I thought of all the times Scott had known when *I* was lying or when something was wrong: the threatening letters, Abigail's trip to Newport News, lying to Abigail about Scott being back in my life. I was thankful for his keen observation skills.

"He looked at the picture again and said he thought he saw

you the night before talking with a teacher in the parking lot. I pressed him on who, but he said he couldn't remember ... at first. I asked him if my fist down his throat might jog his memory."

Luke pinched his lips and chuckled through his nose, as if he was still blown away by Scott's actions.

I was, too. Not surprised, though.

"Then he said he had his name because the guy, who turned out to be Adams, had filed a work order to repair the heater in his office. He gave me his office address. He showed me the sheet with his name on it and the date." Scott rubbed his hands together. "When I saw that, I thought we'd hit a dead end, since I knew Adams was a friend of yours. I asked him if he had any video footage to back up his story." Scott sat back. "Henry said that the cameras only covered the loading docks, but he showed them to me, anyway. He was right. They didn't reveal anything. Henry said that if you were missing, the cops weren't going to help. They were worthless. Then he started to rant about it. The guy was obviously an asshole, but I didn't think he was keeping anything else from us." Scott tipped his head back and forth in a that-was-just-my-opinion sort of way. "It was a gut feeling. So, with nothing else to go on, we decided to talk to Adams. I figured if Henry was lying, we'd be back, which I told him."

Luke leaned up against the wall, crossing his arms. He seemed just as engrossed as I was.

The paging system out in the hall called a doctor to the O.R. Shadowy footprints passed under the door from outside our room.

Scott sighed. "When I walked into his office, Adams was packing up his shit to leave for the night. He seemed put off by me at first, which I assumed was because he didn't know who I was. He grabbed a scarf from his coat rack and wound it around his neck but not before I saw the bandage there. Right away, I could tell something wasn't right with this dude."

"How could you tell?" I asked, imagining every detail.

"I don't know. He just seemed … off." Scott cleared his throat and sat forward again. He kept fidgeting, his face all red like he was flustered. "Anyway, I told him who we were and asked him if he'd seen you or Amy."

"What did he say?" I was on pins and needles.

"He said he saw Amy last Monday during class, which Luke had already told me on the way over there. But he also said he hadn't seen *you* since class on Wednesday. That wasn't what Henry had told us. Plus, I could tell he was lying. The dude was sweating, and his eyes were shifty." A light shined in Scott's eyes. "I decided to try something: I bluffed. I told him that we'd already been to the Maintenance Building, and we knew that he was there the night before. I told him the video footage showed him in the parking lot with you."

Luke nodded and smirked. "You should've seen his face. His eyes bugged out of his head like a friggin' toad. Knowing Amy, she'd probably call him toad man."

I glanced up at Luke. "Yeah, I'm sure she'll have an even better name for him when she wakes up."

Luke laughed and rubbed a hand across his mouth. "You got that right."

My eyes found Scott again as he continued.

"Seeing him so freaked out, I asked him what happened to his neck."

Luke uncrossed his arms and walked over by the window where Scott was seated. "The dude said some crap about being attacked by a dog."

A burst of laugher flew from my lips, from the irony. "He actually *did* get attacked by a dog. We both did. I already told the sheriff about it in the ambulance."

Scott offered a curt nod. "Yeah, but I didn't know that at the time. I thought he was lying again. After that, I forced him to tell me the truth and then we dragged his ass over to the Welcome Center and threw him on the ground in front of the sheriff."

I practically gasped. "That's unbelievable. What did the police say when you did that?"

Scott's shoulders lifted.

I could tell he was proud of what he'd done.

"They didn't say anything. I told them this was their guy, and I was going to go get my girlfriend back," Scott said with conviction.

Still holding Amy's hand, I moved to the edge of my seat. "How did you know where he lived?"

Luke and Scott exchanged another knowing glance as Luke held back a grin.

Something was up with these two.

"This fucking guy." Luke pointed a wagging finger at Scott. "Before we brought Adams to the sheriff, Scott told Adams that if he didn't tell us where you were, he was going to start breaking his fingers one by one." Luke made a "nasty" face. "Adams said he would never do anything to hurt either one of you."

Scott stared at the wall behind me. "That was when I broke his pinky finger."

Luke shuddered. "Yeah, that was gnarly, and the dude wouldn't stop screaming. I thought someone was going to come in at any moment."

Scott's face hardened, his cheeks firing up. "I asked him again where you were. He refused to tell me, so I broke his ring finger. I grabbed him while he was whimpering and said that if he didn't answer me, I was going to break the rest of his fingers next."

Luke's eyes found mine, his mouth turning downward. "You ever broken a finger?"

I shook my head. "No."

"It hurts like a son of a bitch. Much worse than breaking a toe."

My gaze bounced back to Scott. "What happened after that?" His story was so surreal, like he was talking about someone else. I was beyond engrossed.

Luke chuckled as if he couldn't believe it himself. "He started blubbering like a baby, and then he confessed. First, he said he didn't do it, and then he said he was messed up in the head from some shit that had happened to him a long time ago. He also said he didn't hurt either one of you—and you were safe. He rambled on about how he was going to release you, anyway."

My throat thickened, my stomach in full clench mode. "He was lying. He told me he was going to kill me." My lips trembled, tears welling from my eyes. I let go of Amy's hand and lowered my head, the reality too much to bear.

Scott jumped to his feet and rushed to my side. He knelt and took me in his arms. "We don't need to discuss this right now." He rubbed my back and kissed my head repeatedly.

You're alive. It's over. I had to remind myself of that. I inched away from Scott, ready to hear the rest. "It's okay. I want to hear about it. It helps."

"Are you sure?" Scott's eyes were clouded with worry and fear. He wiped my cheeks with his hand.

I imagined how scared he must've been.

I nodded and caressed his stubble, my forehead resting against his. Then I took a breath and straightened up. "I'm okay. So, what happened after he said he was going to release us?"

Scott rose but stayed close, his hand on my shoulder.

"When I heard that, I beat the asshole in the head a few times and then I held onto him as I searched his pants and blazer for his wallet. When I had the address, Luke and I dragged his ass over to the police. I told him that for his sake, you both better be okay. Because if you weren't, there wasn't a courtroom or a prison that could keep him safe from me. When we reached the Welcome Center, I tossed his wallet on top of him, said a few words to the cops, and then we left. I didn't want anyone stopping us or slowing us down. When we got to Adams's place, we saw the broken window and the footprints in the snow. I kicked the door in so Luke could check the house while I followed your tracks."

I stood and buried my head under Scott's chin. For several seconds no one spoke as I took refuge in the arms of my soulmate. How could I have thought he could possibly hurt Amy? The guilt was overwhelming. And yet, he was still here, still fighting. God, I loved this man.

"That is quite a fucking story, Big Guy. You may want to call Stephen King for a movie deal."

All our heads snapped in Amy's direction.

Her eyelids fighting to close, she smiled wide.

I let go of Scott and leaned closer to her. "How are you feeling?"

"Me? Oh, I'm fucking great." More relaxed then I'd ever seen her, Amy glanced over at Luke. "Sky, see if you can score me some more of these drugs. Also, can I use your phone for a sec? There's something I want to check." She wiggled her fingers at him.

Luke's face brightened. "Yeah, sure." He moved closer and handed her his cell phone.

Amy typed and swiped a few times until she smiled and handed the phone back to Luke. "To answer your question, Al, I do have a nickname for our sicko professor, and it's Barney."

Barney? I tried to make sense of the name. *She couldn't mean the friendly TV dinosaur who entertained toddlers, could she?* I remembered the show from when I was little.

"You know how dickhead liked to quote *The Big Lebowski?* I knew he was a Jeff Bridges fan." She brushed her hands down the length of her blanket, smoothing out some wrinkles. "Well, Jeff Bridges did another movie called *The Vanishing,* where he played a sick asshole who liked to kidnap women. Sound familiar? Maybe that's why Adams liked him so much. His character's name was Barney Cousins." Amy nodded once as if proud of herself.

Luke smiled his approval, right along with Scott and me. It made sense—as Amy usually did.

"So whenever we refer to that lowlife, we can call him Barney." With that settled, Amy looked over at Scott. "Hey, Big Guy?" she said.

Scott's brow shot up. "Yeah?"

Amy used her index finger motioning him forward. "Come here. There's something I gotta tell you."

Scott glanced over at me as he moved closer until he was standing over her bed. He probably thought she was going to tear into him as she had in the past. "Glad you're feeling better, Amy." Scott tried to smile.

I could tell he was leery.

Amy waved her hand out haphazardly. "Never mind that." She turned to look at him. "Come on, come closer. I'm not going to bite."

Scott looked at Luke, who quirked an eyebrow.

"You better do as she says," Luke said, his eyes tentative.

After rubbing the back of his neck, Scott bent over until he was right in front of Amy's face.

"Yeah?" he said, his tone unsteady.

And then Amy did something I never thought I'd ever see

her do in my lifetime: she cradled his cheeks in her hands and kissed him. It wasn't just a peck, either, it was a real kiss that lasted long enough that Luke and I slanted forward like two pine trees bent by the wind.

You better not use tongue, I thought comically. But ... seriously.

When Amy finally unlocked her lips, she stared into his eyes and said, "Remind me to never ... *ever* criticize your temper again. Now, I get it. Sometimes you just gotta kick some ass." She grinned and then glanced over at me. "The two of you are like superheroes for fuck's sake."

We all laughed, the tension dissipating in the room.

As Scott moved away from Amy, she mouthed the words "Thank you," at him.

I was glad I was present for such a warm moment.

Scott's eyes smiled down on her as if to say, "You're welcome," with a soft blink.

It seemed Scott and Amy weren't the only ones who had called a truce.

A few minutes later, Scott and I were exiting the side entrance when we saw Henry helping Ethel into his truck. As he rounded the front to get into the driver's seat, Henry spotted us. At first, he hesitated as if trying to decide what to do. From what Scott had told me about their heated exchange, I wasn't sure if he was going to yell at us, or worse.

Henry approached, frown lines dominating his weathered face, and old tobacco reeking off his skin and clothes. Something about him had changed. It was in his eyes—a softness that wasn't there before, or maybe it was compassion.

Scott stood firm at my side, his protective arm hooked around my waist.

Henry stroked his chin, his eyes downcast. "I, uh," he said, shuffling his work boots against the pavement. He took a breath and raised his chin. "Well, heck, I didn't mean to snap atcha like I did." His cheeks flared as he scratched what little hair remained on his head. He regarded Scott. "Your man did a fine job lookin' out for ya." He turned toward his truck where Ethel awaited. "Glad you and yer friend are all right." He took off, ready to end this awkward moment.

"Henry?" I said.

He paused but didn't face me.

"Thank you for helping Scott, and I'm sorry about what happened to Ethel. I hope they find out who did it."

He nodded and waved a hand in the air as he continued toward his truck.

Somehow I knew Henry had a warmer side to him. How else could he be married to someone as sweet as Ethel?

A phrase came to mind that my mother would often say whenever someone surprised her: "Wonders never cease."

Chapter Twenty-Two

Just as Scott and I were walking out of Amy's room, ready for some much-needed rest, a woman wearing a dark-blue skirt and a yellow blouse with a scalloped collar approached. With her long, black silky hair cascading down her back, she smiled and reached her hand out. "I'm Debra Parilli, one of the hospital media representatives." She shook my hand and then Scott's before giving each of us her business card.

"I'm Sara, and this is my boyfriend, Scott."

"Yes. I know, and it's nice to meet you both. I wondered if I could have a moment of your time."

Oh great. Was I ever going to get out of here?

Scott put the business card in his back pocket and rubbed the back of his neck. He looked at me with red eyes. I was just as tired as *he* looked.

As Debra started to speak, Sheriff Murphy walked up with his hat in his hands. "Miss Browne," he said to me and then he glanced at Scott. "Mr. Williams." His tone was a tad heavier, his eyes less forgiving.

It made me think of Scott's dad and how disapproving he was toward his son.

"Good evening, Sheriff Murphy. I'm Debra Parilli, the hospital's media representative." Wearing bright red lipstick, she smiled and regarded us all. "I was just about to tell Sara that the hospital has designated a conference room for the media." She focused on me again. "There is quite a crowd gathering. I wanted to check to see if you were up for a press conference or wanted to make a statement at this time. I also wanted to let you know that as long as you are a patient here, I am available to assist you with whatever you need." Her makeup perfect, Debra continued to flaunt her professional prowess.

"I don't really have a statement right now. Amy might when she's feeling better. She's still pretty out of it. I'm grateful for the offer and the help. The staff here has been very nice, but I'm not staying."

She nodded, her flowery perfume engulfing my nostrils. "I'm glad to hear the hospital has been treating you well. When you are ready to leave, I can escort you out and around the crowds."

"I can walk Miss Browne out. I know the way," Sheriff Murphy said as he turned his hat in his hands. "I need to speak with these two ladies for a moment, first." He tipped his chin toward Amy's room.

An ominous lump formed in my throat.

"Okay, then. You have my business card. Please call me when and if you need any other assistance. If it is acceptable to you, I will inform the press that you are all recovering nicely and taking some much-needed time to rest." Just as quickly as she had arrived, Debra was down the hallway and out of sight.

The sheriff walked into Amy's room, Scott and me on his heels. He motioned toward the same lime-green couch. "Why don't you have a seat. I would like to talk with you for a few minutes while I have you here. It won't take long."

Amy sat up straighter, her eyes narrowing. "What's going on?"

Sheriff Murphy centered himself in the room, his gaze finding each of us as he spoke. "It's nothing to worry about. I have some information I would like to share with you, that's all."

Scott and I sat on the couch, and Luke sat next to Amy on the edge of her bed.

"Several news stations have already broken the story, so you may already know this, but I wanted to deliver this information personally in case you do get confronted by the press. I figured it was best for you to hear it from me."

I gulped and looked at Scott, who wrapped his arm around my shoulder and pulled me close. "I'm right here, babe," he said in a whisper.

Thank God for that.

"We found a body on the property of Dr. Charles Adams today."

When I was in the ambulance earlier, I remembered an officer telling the sheriff that they'd found *something*. A feeling of dread festered in my gut. The news was dire after all. "Is it Carrie Stevens?"

The sheriff continued to pull on the brim of his hat, the same way I used Dr. Zeller's stress ball during some of my sessions. "We're not certain it's Carrie. They are running forensics on it now. We suspect it's her, though. The clothing checked out to be hers, and so did the backpack that was buried along with her."

Amy's eyes widened, her cheeks blanched. "Jesus Christ," she said. "Carrie's body was on his property?" Her shoulders shuddered, enough that I noticed.

She had narrowly escaped the same fate. So had I.

The sheriff nodded.

Scott pulled me closer, his eyes darkened with the possibilities of what could have happened. At least that was the way it looked to me.

Luke lowered his chin as if contemplating the same things we all were.

A moment of silence ensued.

Amy crossed her arms tight over her chest. "I'm not surprised. What was the deal with that asshole? Did he just hate girls or something?" Her voice wavered as Luke leaned over and held her.

I thought about Carrie's parents at the press conference. I wondered how they would take the news. Would it be a relief to finally receive some form of closure, or was this new information shattering their last hope?

"I suspect Dr. Adams carried preconceived beliefs about certain types of women," Sheriff Murphy said.

"What is that supposed to mean?" Amy asked, her eyes glistening with tears, her lip turning down.

Feeling my neck heating up and my eyes tearing, I said, "I'll tell you about it another time, Amy." I just couldn't go through it again. Not now.

Amy stared at me. I could see her brain working. "You mean to tell me, you know something I don't know?"

"Yes. As I told the sheriff earlier, I do have a good idea why he took *her* ... and *you*." My skin felt prickly, my heart overwrought. "I'll explain in more detail when you're up for it, but Dr. Adams had some issues that stemmed from his childhood. He grew up hating certain types of women."

Amy tilted her head. "What types of women?" She pulled away from Luke as if too upset to be comforted.

I could see the worry and the hurt in her eyes. Was she up

for this? Amy was a tough person, but she was also tired of being judged. How was I going to tell her that not only did Dr. Adams judge her, he pretended to be her friend and almost killed her for things that had nothing to do with her. Like me, she didn't make friends easily or trust. I glanced over at the sheriff, hoping he could provide some assistance.

He cleared his throat. "We have a lot of information to sift through before we can make a determination about Professor Adams. Preliminary information—provided mainly by Miss Browne here—suggests he may have seen certain females as a threat. That doesn't mean they *were* a threat. Our databases include all kinds of psychological profiles on serial killers and why they perceive their victims the way they do. Most of the time, it has nothing to do with reality."

"I wasn't a threat to that asshole. We were friends, for fucks sake." Amy slouched in her bed, her eyes working the situation.

Luke nodded his support.

She was probably going over every moment they had spent together, looking for signs of insanity. I was doing the same thing. I just hoped this wasn't going to cause her any long-term damage or PTSD, although, I knew it would.

"I promise to tell you everything, when you are feeling up to it."

"Is there anything else, Sheriff? Sara really wants to get out of here and get some rest." Scott stood and pulled me up to join him.

The sheriff hardened his eyes. "Not as far as *they're* concerned. But you and I need to talk down at the station, son. We have some unfinished business to discuss."

Amy perked up again. "Why? You aren't seriously going to press charges on him, are you?" Her eyes flared.

I loved hearing Amy defend Scott. It was like we were all a team again.

"Mr. Williams took matters into his own hands. He physically attacked the suspect, and if things hadn't worked in his favor—"

"I agree with Amy," I said, my muscles quivering, my pulse speeding. Was he going to arrest Scott for what he had done? *Again?* Why couldn't people just leave us alone?

Scott tried to take my hand. "Don't worry about it, babe."

"If it wasn't for Scott ..." My words had trouble squeezing past my anguish. Was this nightmare never going to end? I wouldn't let the sheriff take Scott. I couldn't. Adrenaline coursed, making me nauseous and wobbly. I was too tired for this.

Amy huffed from the other side of the room.

"Yeah, man. Scott did the right thing," Luke said from Amy's bedside.

"Scott and Luke ran down some leads until they discovered what was going on. Did Scott tell you that when he got to Professor Adams's office, he was getting ready to leave?" I asked indignant.

"I haven't spoken to Mr. Williams yet. That's why—"

"If Adams *had* returned home, he would've seen that we'd escaped from his house, and he would've come after us. There is a good chance that if Scott hadn't done what he did, we'd be dead right now." I was too wrung out to think straight, and I was rambling. "Thank God, he acted. And because he was brave enough to 'take matters into his own hands,' we are here talking with you now and not in a morgue with a tag on our big toes."

Scott touched my back. "Babe, it's okay. Try not to get so upset. He's just—"

"It's not okay. None of this is okay." I forced back the tears. Just the thought of Scott in another jail cell had me cracking like an egg on the inside.

The sheriff's eyebrows shot up. "I understand all of that, Miss Browne. And I didn't come here to upset you. I only wanted—"

"You should be giving him a medal for what he did." The volume of my voice rose with each exasperated breath. "Maybe if Carrie had had a Scott around, she wouldn't be in some cold lab where they are checking her DNA, just so they can tell her parents that their daughter will *never* come home again. Do you think that Carrie's parents care about," I made air quotes this time, "'taking matters into their own hands?'" A distress signal was festering in my chest: *panic attack ... ready to launch.*

The sheriff took a step toward me, one of his palms raised, then he shot me the same look my dad used to give me when I was acting irrationally. "Please calm down, Miss Browne. We are not going to press charges against Mr. Williams." He glanced over at Scott, his eyes softening. "I've spoken to the DA. I only need a statement from you and Mr. Henshaw." He motioned toward Luke. "Mr. Williams acted on his own behalf and without the consent of the department, so we are not responsible for his behavior, nor were we privy to it. It comes down to two men's word against one." He rubbed the gray stubble on his chin that I guessed wasn't there this morning. "I can't promise you won't get a lecture, but I need that statement. Take her home, get some rest, and come down to the station when you are ready, but don't take too long. We'll take care of it, then." He took a breath as if to reset himself. "I can't condone citizens going around taking the law into their own hands."

I was ready to argue when his furrowed brow told me he wasn't finished. Out of respect, I closed my mouth and waited.

"I understand the circumstances, and if it were my daughter out there, I'd be forever in Mr. William's and Mr. Henshaw's debt. Just between us, I'm glad he did what he did.

But if you tell anyone I said so, I will deny it. I am the sheriff of this county, and it is my job to maintain order." He squeezed his hat as he spoke. "I can't tell you how relieved we are to close this case. We've been working with various departments and running an ongoing investigation for a year now. I've had parents calling worried about their daughters going to school here. We are all relieved to put this matter to rest. We can finally close the book on this one." The sheriff reached his hand out to Scott, who shook it. "I wish Carrie was alive, but after enough time had passed, we didn't think that outcome was likely." Sheriff Murphy stared down at me, his voice fatherly. "I realize, Miss Browne, that Mr. and Mrs. Stevens have received some bad news today, but at least they will have some closure and can now move forward in the healing process."

Like a tire that had just run over a nail, my anger deflated, making me regret my rant. I was so protective of Scott and the people I loved. Especially now. But I had to remember that the sheriff was protective of *everyone*. "I'm sorry. I know. And thank you."

The sheriff turned to leave.

I thought of a question that had been nagging at me. "Can I ask one last thing?"

Sheriff Murphy peered over his shoulder.

"Did they have any other children? Carrie's parents?"

The sheriff nodded. "Yes. They have a younger daughter. And I am sure they will be keeping a close watch on her as she enters her teenage years."

I was relieved to hear that, but only a little. My heart ached for that family. Facing my own death, I understood what Carrie must've felt, and from the standpoint of losing my parents, I also understood the ache of loss. There were no winners in this scenario, only pain and suffering.

* * *

When we arrived at the Holiday Inn, Abigail was waiting in the lobby, her hazel eyes swollen and her arms hugging her round belly. Almost two months had passed since I'd seen her, and she was close to eight months along now. She looked ready to pop.

When Abigail spotted me, she ran over and hugged me almost as hard as Scott had earlier. Her lavender perfume embraced me a millisecond later. She looked up at Scott standing behind me, her eyes going frosty.

"Are you sure you're okay?" She pulled back and smoothed my hair around my face. "I've been sick with worry."

In the quiet lobby, a man wearing hotel garb stood behind the check-in counter observing. Due to the late hour, no customers were around to keep him busy.

"I know, and I'm so sorry." I laced my arm inside hers. "Let's talk in your room."

Together, we approached the elevator. When the doors sprang open, she glanced over at Scott again. "You are welcome to come if you want. But if you're too tired, Sara can stay with us tonight."

Maybe Abigail wanted time alone so we could really talk about what had happened over the past few months or maybe she didn't quite understand how Scott could be my enemy one minute and my hero the next.

Scott twisted his mouth to one side and scratched his temple. "Uh."

If anyone else had said that to him, Scott would have barked his response. He wasn't leaving me—not now, not ever.

"You're okay, right, hun?"

Scott nodded. "I'm good." He didn't argue with Abigail, but he didn't budge, either.

"I need him here." I stared into Abigail's bloodshot eyes until she relented and pushed the button for the fifth floor.

Once inside her room, I approached Joel and gave him a hug next. "Thank you for driving, Joel."

"No problem. We need to get you back to Vermont where it's safe." He smiled but not for long.

Scott's face twitched a bit. He stepped forward and reached his hand out to Joel. "Nice to see you, man. Wish it were under better circumstances."

Joel shook his hand and rolled his eyes in a flabbergasted sort of way. "Yeah. Me, too."

Abigail took hold of my arm and pulled me over to a small round table with two chairs. She sat in one chair, and I took the other.

Scott watched us. He palmed the back of his neck, his eyes wary.

Joel also watched us, until he slid his gaze over to Scott. "Hey, man. I thought I saw a bar off the lobby." He placed his hand on Scott's shoulder. "Let's go see if we can find ourselves a beer and let these ladies talk in private."

"Sure." Scott waited for Joel to grab his room key and a jacket.

"If they're closed, we may need to grab a six pack at the store."

The two of them walked out the door, Scott gazing back at me one last time.

I tried to smile but felt Abigail watching me. Smiling didn't feel appropriate even if it was just to reassure my honey that everything would be fine.

As soon as the door clicked shut, Abigail leaned across the table and clutched my arm. "How did this happen? Who was this sick man who kidnapped you? Why would he do something like that?"

I sucked in a breath, ready to unload. "I'll explain every-thing ..." This wasn't going to be easy for her—or for me. There was a lot to talk about, none of it pleasant.

I started with the girls who were harassing me before break, which she knew about, then moved on to Rick marking up my car, ruining my laptop, sending me those weird letters, and then drugging Scott—and finally, the nasty pictures that resulted from it. It was a mouthful.

"Was he the young man who picked you up over winter break and took you out to dinner?"

I nodded, remembering that she had met him—and how Rick had brought flowers and smiled that movie-star smile of his. At the time, Abigail was happy to see that I was getting out and moving on from Scott.

After I finished *that* story, I forced myself to explain the horror that took place in that remote house out in the woods. I danced around the subject until Abigail's eyes popped from their sockets.

"No. Please don't tell me he ..."

I kept my head down, the weight of the rape pressing hard on my heart like a cinder block. I wanted to sink into the floor.

A new wave of tears spilled from both of our eyes.

Abigail jumped up from her seat and came around to me. She knelt on the floor and hugged me as best she could around her pregnancy. I tried to pull her up, but she was sobbing too heavily. I was equally emotional.

"Please, Mom. Don't get so upset. The baby." I struggled to speak. "I didn't tell you because I was worried it would harm the baby. You have to think about your health right now. You have to think about Mel."

Abigail took a few breaths and found her seat, which she pulled closer to mine. "How can you say that? How can you not tell me these things? My heavens, Sara. You were raped?" She buried her head in her hands. "It's my job to take care of you and protect you. Your mother would be so disappointed in me."

Argh. I shook my head and grabbed Abigail's arm. "See, that's why I didn't tell you. I didn't want you blaming yourself for something that wasn't your fault. He was a manipulator and fooled a lot of people, even Amy. Please don't blame yourself. I couldn't stand it if you continued to do that."

Abigail pulled her hands away from her face and stared down at the table, tears puddling on the Formica. "I should've insisted you to go to school in Vermont." Her voice was feeble.

I grabbed her shoulders. "Listen to me, I've been going to counseling and taking self-defense classes. Plus, I have Scott here."

"What did Scott do when he found out that this Rick person had drugged him and ruined your relationship? When did he find out about the rape?"

And so the story continued, until Abigail stopped crying. Her hand flew to her chest and her mouth hung open. "I'm dumbfounded." She sat back in her seat. "Scott did *that?*"

I released a heavy breath. "He sure did. It wasn't easy getting the senator to agree, but he finally dropped all the charges."

Abigail stared off into space. "So you've been going to counseling? Is it helping?" She stared with earnest. "You seem so ... together about all of this. You're such a big girl." She ran her hand down my cheek. "How is that possible?"

I sighed. "To be honest, Scott has had a lot to do with that, too. And Amy. He's been there for me the entire time. He's helped me through some rough nights, and he's watched over me constantly."

Another distant look emitted from her eyes. She had a lot to think about. "Wow." Her brow wrinkled. "So how did this latest kidnapping take place?"

I sighed again. I needed the oxygen. "To be honest, I wasn't the target on this one. Amy was ..."

The more I spoke, the more bizarre my life felt—like a tall tale or a ghost story. As I talked about Amy and Professor Adams, a thought occurred to me.

"You know, Mom. When I found Amy, she was in pretty rough shape." My shoulders sagged under the burden of another revelation. "If I hadn't been in that parking lot, and he hadn't kidnapped me, I may never have found her. I don't know why the rape happened, but as far as the kidnapping, I am glad I was there. I don't know what I would've done if I had never been able to see my best friend again."

I pushed that alternate reality aside. I had to before it crushed me entirely.

Abigail took my hand and held it tight. "You are a very strong young woman." She smiled a little. "I'm so proud of you, Sara."

I closed my eyes and let those words shower over me. "Thank you, Mom. But Scott also had a hand in finding us."

She narrowed her eyes. "Really, how?"

Ten minutes later, I had recanted the entire sordid tale. Abigail asked a few more questions and then sat back again in silence.

"Maybe they'll make a movie about my life someday." I shook my head, blowing air through my lips. "A horror movie. It's crazy enough."

I guided her chin up. "Now do you see why I'm with Scott?"

"I do." A twinkle sparkled in her eyes. "And I've always said what a handsome young man he is." She winked.

"I remember." She'd said it enough times. "And I agree."

Abigail leaned in again. "If I promise you that I will take good care of my health no matter what, you have to promise *me* that you will never withhold any information again. I'm glad that Scott and Amy helped you after the attack. They sound like good people. And I'm glad that you managed to get away from this recent lunatic, but I can't leave you down here alone not knowing what is going on."

I looked her square in the eyes. "I promise." I almost raised my palm as if I were making a pledge—because I was.

Abigail refused to break eye contact. "I mean it, Sara. If you have anything else happen." She deflated her cheeks. "God forbid. You have to tell me right away. I hope its sunshine and roses from here on out, but regardless."

I patted her hand. "I know. I know. I get it. I will tell you everything from now on." Having that off my chest left me feeling weightless as if I was floating in a hot-air balloon. I took another refreshing breath. "Now that we've covered all my stuff, can we talk about you and the baby?"

Abigail regarded her belly, her hands roaming over the basketball. "She's been kicking a lot lately. One month to go. The doctor said when I have this strange urge to clean my house or feel a burst of sudden energy, I'll be close. He's an older man and a little old-fashioned."

We talked for another half hour and then we went to grab a cup of tea from the coffee station near the lobby. My throat was dry, and my mind wandered with fatigue.

Scott and Joel came out of the bar just as we headed back to the elevator.

When she saw him, Abigail ran over to Scott and embraced him. "I'm sorry I treated you so coldly before. I had no idea what was going on."

A slow smile spread across Scott's face, a relieved one. "I understand. It's been hard for me to believe, and I've been here during all of it."

Joel stood off to the side wearing a smile that said he was enjoying the peaceful moment.

Abigail stared up at Scott again, her eyes dewy. "Thank you for watching out for her. I feel so much better knowing that you are here to protect her."

Scott glanced over at me and then returned his gaze to Abigail. "I will always watch out for your daughter, Abigail, but something tells me she doesn't need me, anymore. She's stronger than you think."

I stood taller as he said those words. And thanks to my friends and help from a very good therapist, I believed him.

Abigail reached her hand out to take mine. "I'm starting to realize that."

Chapter Twenty-Three

We arrived back at Scott's place well after midnight. I wanted to talk with him some more but was so exhausted that I couldn't muster the energy. In fact, I kept dozing off on the way, my head leaning on Scott's shoulder. I was in dire need of a shower but feared it would only wake me up.

Before we had left the hospital to meet Abigail, Scott had bought me a ham and Swiss sandwich in the cafeteria. My stomach had stopped growling, and I was grateful for that.

As Scott opened the door to his place, I was relieved the reporters hadn't figured out where he lived ... yet. Droves of TV vans and trucks crowded the parking lot at the hospital, and I was sure they were also in full force on campus. For the time being, we had the place to ourselves, and I wanted to take advantage of the quiet while I could.

Abigail and I had made plans for dinner later, but I couldn't think about that right now.

I took off my sneakers and Scott's coat, which I'd been wearing (more like clinging to) since he'd found me, while he dropped his keys on a small table by the door and flipped the lights on.

"Can I get you something else to eat or drink?" he asked as he removed his shoes and then took the coat I was wearing to the closet to hang it up.

After I yawned so long I could hear my jaw crack, I was finally able to speak. "No. I'm so beat. I'm going to go wash my face, brush my teeth, and plop into bed." I started toward the stairs and then stopped. "Is that okay?"

Scott approached. "Of course." He kissed the top of my head and stroked my back.

Releasing a few grunts and groans, I ascended the stairs like a grandmother and found my way to the bathroom, where I washed my face and most of my body with a washcloth before scouring my mouth with toothpaste. The mirror told me I looked horrid, my skin a patchwork of raised-red welts, scrapes, and bruises of varying yellow, blue, and dark-purple shades. I found the softest pj's I owned and peeled off my dirty clothes and undergarments, blanketing myself in something clean and cozy. Just as I had turned down my side of the bed, Scott crept into the room. He went into the bathroom and turned on the sink for several minutes. When he returned, he grabbed a clean T-shirt from his bureau and a pair of compression shorts before he started for the door.

My brow bared down. "Where are you going?" I asked.

Scott stopped and grabbed the door casing with his free hand, his chin lowering. "I thought maybe you'd want to sleep in here alone." He turned his head toward the door and then back to me. "I was gonna sleep on the couch."

We really did have a lot to talk about. "What?" I bent over and flipped the blankets back from his side of the bed. "Don't be silly. I want you here with me."

Do you really think I don't want you here?

He took a breath as if relieved. Wearing a timid smile, he changed his clothes and climbed into bed.

The moon filtered just enough light through the blinds that I could make out his profile as he lay on his back, looking over at me a few times. Was he worried?

I nestled in close to him, prompting him to turn onto his side and drape his arm over me. At least he felt comfortable doing that.

"Let's talk tomorrow," I said, as my eyes refused to stay open.

Scott's breath warmed the nape of my neck. "You got it. I love you, babe."

"I love you, too." Those were our last words before my mind and body fell hard into a deep slumber, so hard, I caught myself snoring.

* * *

I awoke to the clanking of pans as footfalls paced back and forth from the floor below. I glanced over at the clock, which flashed 2:30 p.m. at me. I sat up and then winced from the pain. My body was still very sore, but somehow my muscles were relaxed —too relaxed, like my limbs were made of rubber. At least my mind was still relatively clear. I swung my feet over the side of the bed, careful to pamper those scrapes and bruises.

When I reached the bathroom, a sheet of notebook paper was taped to the mirror waiting for me, a heart drawn around the message: "Good morning, sunshine. Today is all about you. Come down whenever you are ready. I'll have breakfast waiting. I love you, babe, more than anything in this world, and I'm so grateful you're back."

I smiled as I took the note down and placed it in one of my notebooks for safe keeping. When I returned to my room on campus, I planned to store it in a box under my bed with all my other Scott memorabilia.

The hot water from the shower reminded me of every new abrasion my body had endured. With plenty of soap and water, I spent several minutes delicately extricating myself from Dr. Adams's house. Even though I looked like I'd been dragged behind a car, my spirit felt rejuvenated somehow. I was reminded of that session with Dr. Zeller and her exercise involving "little Sara." I also thought of Amy and how outspoken she was about my bravery. I had always looked up to Amy as someone to emulate. She was strong and confident. In this moment, the tables had turned, and I felt pretty good about being me. As Amy so eloquently put it: I was a badass.

When I emerged from the bathroom amidst a cloud of steam, the scent of bacon and onions lured my legs to the first floor. The kitchen was a world of savory goodness. Wearing my apron (a gift from Abigail), Scott shifted between flipping pancakes, stirring home fries, and turning bacon from a tray in the oven. He even had a cup of tea brewing on the counter near the stovetop.

He turned as I entered the kitchen. "Oh hey, babe. I heard you get up, so I finished breakfast." He leaned in for a kiss laced with coffee and love. "Well, brunch. How are you feeling? I didn't want to wake you. I figured you needed the rest."

I inhaled a serving of breakfast and smiled. "I slept well." My gaze traveled over the stove. "Where did you get all this food? And can I help?"

Scott reached for the tea that he'd covered with a small saucer. "No. I've got it taken care of. I went to the store early this morning. I figured you hadn't eaten anything decent in a couple of days. And that dried-up ham sandwich from the cafeteria last night wasn't going to last you long." He handed me the mug and steered me toward the dining room table, his hand on my lower back. "You just sit here and sip your tea." He darted to the fridge to pull out some almond milk (my favorite) and placed it in front of me. "I'll have breakfast ready in a few minutes." He pushed a small container of stevia closer to me and returned to the kitchen, but not before planting another kiss on my cheek, the scent of bacon clinging to his clothing.

I sat in my chair and sipped my tea while watching my handsome boyfriend labor over breakfast. He looked so adorable in my apron that I had a hard time controlling the urge to grab him and peel his T-shirt and sweatpants away. I realized he'd gone to so much effort, and I needed to be patient. After all, we'd need our strength for what was coming next, which was all I thought about as I watched him work, my eyes undressing him. I thought about Rick and all the angst I'd been feeling since the rape. I'd spent weeks going on months protecting myself from any additional hurt, but in doing so, I'd also closed myself off from any joy. Being inside Dr. Adams' house and feeling as though I may never leave, had forced me to think differently. Yes, Rick had violated me, and those memories would always be a part of my past, but they were also part of my survival. I had survived Rick, and I had survived Dr. Adams, saving my best friend in the process. I was brave, strong ... and incredibly horny.

Once he had the pancakes stacked on a plate, the home fries cooked, and the bacon draining on a paper towel, Scott placed a plate and silverware in front of me, along with a small glass.

He sighed. "Okay, go fill your plate, babe," he said as he poured me a glass of orange juice. "I don't have napkins, so grab a paper towel while you're over there."

I stood and kissed his dimple as it grinned at me. "I can't wait. I'm starving." *In more ways than one,* I wanted to say, but kept that part to myself.

Scott waited for me to fill my plate before he did the same. We met at the table, where we both dove in like starved animals —at least I did.

I took one last bite of pancakes and then wiped my mouth clean of the sugary maple syrup. That's right. Scott had bought the real stuff—what my parents used to call "liquid gold." No corn syrup with food coloring would satisfy a true Vermonter.

Scott had already finished his meal, which was no surprise as he sat there sipping his coffee.

I took his hand from across the table. "I want to apologize for accusing you of—"

"You don't need to." He put his mug down and shook his head.

I tugged on his hand. "I need to say this."

With timid eyes, he remained silent.

"I am so sorry for accusing you of doing something to Amy. I don't know what I was thinking. I should never have even considered those horrible thoughts."

Blood ran to Scott's cheeks, his shoulders drooping. The impact of what I had done was evident, and I felt horrible about it. I just hoped I could turn the tides and win his trust again.

"You have always been there for me, and when the chips were down, I abandoned you. I don't expect you to forgive me right away. I mean, if you accused me of the same thing, I'd need some time."

He angled his head. "There's nothing to forgive."

"Wait." I rubbed my thumb over his knuckles. "The truth is, I've had a hard time with trust since what happened with Rick. But it's not just that." I took a breath. "Seeing Dr. Zeller has helped me to understand how my parents' death has also affected me. Even though I wanted to open my heart to you and thought I had, I think I was always waiting for the next boot to drop or the ground to fall out. It's okay that you didn't tell me about Carrie." I smiled. "Who can blame a girl for going a bit crazy over *you*. I've done it myself. You have never faltered in your love or support for me, and I feel like I let you down."

Scott shook his head, his mouth opening.

I raised a palm. "Hold on. Just give me a sec. When I was held captive in that crawl space, I swear I saw my parents."

Scott's eyes widened, his face open and alert. "Really? Are you sure it wasn't a dream?"

"It may have been a dream or even the drugs, I'm not entirely sure. But I'd like to think they were communicating with me."

"What did they say?" Scott asked, fully engaged.

"They told me that I wasn't alone and that there were people here who loved and needed me." My eyes moistened. "I almost gave up, Scott. But what kept me going was ... you. I thought about all our special times together ... our kiss on the mountain, the necklace you gave me."

He reached his hand out to take mine, his lips pinched, his eyes brimming with emotion.

"I want you to know that I do believe in you, and I love you more than anything in this world. You are my future, and I promise." I pulled one hand back and placed it over my heart. "I will never question your character again. I would follow you to the depths of hell if you asked me to." I wiped a tear as it escaped from my eyelid, and then I paused to get myself together. I'd cried enough tears already.

Scott smiled. "Are you finished?"

I smirked and swallowed. "Yes."

He darted from the table, returning a minute later with his wallet in his hands. He opened the wallet and pulled out a small plastic bag that contained my beautiful necklace. The two delicate hearts wrapped in tiny diamonds glinted off the light pouring in from the window.

Scott moved his chair closer. "I had to wait for the clasp to be fixed." He draped the necklace around my neck and attached the new clasp. "I couldn't wait for an opportunity to give it back to you. I've only had it a couple of days." When he was finished, he took my hand and peered deep into my eyes. "About what you said, I *was* upset at first, and it tore me up inside. I'm not going to lie to you about that. In fact, I'm not going to lie to you about anything again. The lie was the reason I was so upset. I couldn't believe that after everything we'd been through—what *you'd* been through—that I would lie to you again about knowing Carrie. I was sick about it."

I remembered how badly he had looked on that night—disillusioned and crushed—and felt terrible about causing him such pain, which I wanted to say, but it was *my* turn to listen respectfully.

"When you left that night to go find Amy, I spent the better part of twenty-four hours stewing over it. Then, as the sun came up on the second day, I had to admit that it was *my* behavior that I was really angry about. Not yours. I thought about how I'd slammed the bookcase to the floor, about the fight with my dad, and the hole I punched in the wall, and even that lowlife, shit stain Rick and what I had done to him. I don't regret what I did, and I don't regret what I did to that sick teacher of yours, but those were different situations."

Since he was ready to open up, I was curious about one other evening not so long ago.

"What was wrong with you that night you came back so late from the gym? The night you shattered the glass in your hand?" I realized that it was *then* when I had started to doubt him.

He looked down and then up again. "Believe it or not, I was telling you the truth ... for the most part. I did overdo it in the gym, and I did get beaned in the head with a soccer ball. Truth be told, I was frustrated with myself for being in this situation, which was why I pushed myself so hard physically at the gym. And I guess I was avoiding you a bit until I could figure out how to come clean about Carrie." He released a heavy breath. "I gave you plenty of reasons to wonder about me. You even tried to tell me that my temper scared you, but I didn't listen, not really. I was too busy thinking about my own bullshit. I realize I've got some issues that I need to deal with, and I'm open to doing that now." His eyes shined with sincerity. "As I've said, I don't want to become my father. I want to be someone who doesn't come apart every time something stressful happens. I will seek counseling myself. Maybe Dr. Zeller can recommend someone. I'm doing this for you, but I'm also doing this for me." He moved his free hand to my knee. "I want to be someone that you'll be proud to have at your side."

It was all I could do to stay seated. "Look at us, Scott. We are both sitting here promising to do better for each other. You forgive me, and I believe in you. Let's stop berating ourselves for what we didn't or shouldn't have done, and let's just start fresh ... move forward." I paused. "I do have one last question."

Scott sat back and exhaled. "What's that?"

"Can we get back to being in love?"

His face lit up like a golden moon. "Yes! I like the sound of that."

"Okay, then." I stood and carried my plate to the sink, when Scott's cell phone rang from the living room. It reminded me that I needed to get a new one. Dr. Adams must've taken mine and Amy's. Maybe the cops had them by now.

It was Abigail.

As Scott cleared the rest of the table and did the dishes, I discussed dinner plans with her for later on. She wanted to come right over.

"I just woke up, Abigail, so if you could give me the afternoon, I really need it. I'll call you later, and we can make some plans for a late dinner. Or maybe we can just get pizza here."

She agreed, but her tone was less than enthused.

I understood her need to see me, but I had needs of my own.

The way Scott's butt moved and muscles flexed as he washed our dishes and wiped down the counter had my body calling out to him. It had been a while for us.

Something inside of me awakened, something familiar, like an old friend who had been standing by silently waiting ... for just this moment.

Once I ended the call with Abigail, I placed Scott's phone on the table. "I've just remembered something I wanted to show you. Come upstairs when you're finished."

With a dish towel over his shoulder, Scott turned his head. "Okay. Be right up."

My words weren't seductive, and there was a reason for that. I wanted a minute or two to survey my body again. Although, there wasn't much I could do about any blemishes now.

I dashed up the stairs and removed my clothes as fast as I could. Then I stood in front of the mirror. Reassessing my wounds, along with the bites from the stun-gun on my chest, I was less confident with my idea. I grabbed my clothes to cover myself up when Scott entered the room.

His words came out in a stutter, his eyes poking out at me. "What are you doing?"

The jig was up. No turning back now. Fully naked, I turned to face him. "I know I'm not exactly attractive right now."

Scott practically leapt toward me. "Are you fucking kidding me? You're smokin' hot, babe. Every time I look at you, it's all I can do to keep my dick from getting hard." The protrusion in his sweatpants practically nodded. "Are you saying what I think you're saying?" His eyes begged me to answer yes.

I stared at him through a veil of lust. "The way I see it, I didn't have sex with Rick. He had sex with me—not even me—my body. I want you to get in there and chase all those demons away. I need some new memories. I need YOU." I ran my fingers down his torso. "I seem to remember you saying that if I showed you mine, you'd show me yours." I pulled his T-shirt up and ran my tongue along his right nipple, my hands coursing over his six-pack. It felt so good to touch him this way.

Scott's breath grew heavy, his eyes glowing. Like a magician escaping his bonds, or maybe a male strip tease, Scott tore off his shirt and stepped out of his sweatpants as if they were secured with Velcro.

I wanted to giggle but wasn't sure he'd appreciate the humor in this moment. "Before we do this, let me look at you." I'd spent so much time missing him, and I couldn't wait any longer.

His pupils dilating, Scott drew in a deep breath.

"I won't take long." My words came out in a throaty gust of passion as I prepared myself for a field trip around Scott's gorgeous body. I started below his belly button, at his incredibly sexy V-line and inched my fingers upward, across his washboard stomach and pecs. Before long I had reached the summit of his mountainous shoulders. I ran both hands down his back, gripping both cheeks, my mouth kissing his back as I provided my light massage. He was a magnificent creature who deserved my appreciation—a work of art, really. When my fingers drifted over a small pink scar marking his left side, I bent down and kissed it, too. Even that was sexy.

I continued my tour until I had come full circle, where his erection stood waiting for my attention. Without hesitating, I took hold of him and stroked, enjoying the solidness and the size of him.

Scott closed his eyes and tipped his head back. "Jesus Christ, Sara. I might need a couple of tries to get this right. I hope you're done because I can't wait much longer." He placed his hand behind my neck and pushed my lips against his, his tongue roaming my mouth. Both of us claiming what we had missed. He tasted like syrup, more coffee, ... and desire.

My fires were stoked. I was ready.

He pulled his mouth away and walked his lips down my neck, his tongue finding my nipples, savoring them with warmth and softness. My nipples grew hard, longing for him to devour them as a dam of moisture broke free between my legs, my insides quivering and hungry.

My bones turned to liquid as Scott guided me back toward the bed, gently laying me down. With him hovering over me, I inched my body downward toward his erection, ready to devour every inch.

"Let me go first. I've been dying to taste you for so long." He mumbled the words, his eyes eager. When I didn't argue, he kissed his way slowly down my neck and chest, wandering over my stomach, and moving my legs out, he licked his way down my inner thigh. Finding his target, he caressed every inch of my soft tissue with his velvety tongue. My insides went crazy, yearning for more. While his mouth worked on one end, his fingers fondled my breasts and nipples, ramping up the sexual typhoon brewing inside of me. I grabbed the back of his head and held on for dear life.

The tingling sensation that I so longed for overtook me from within. Just when I couldn't take it anymore, I arched my back and screamed, "Oh, God," before an eruption of sensations too intense to describe consumed every inch of me.

Several panting breaths later, I stared up at Scott who beamed from ear to ear.

"There is nothing I like more than to make you feel that way."

I shimmied out from under him and tossed his body on to the mattress. It was like knocking over a Redwood. "Now it's your turn." Using my tongue as my guide, I trailed down his body until I reached his erection, where I used my mouth and my hands to stroke, caress, and suckle. Every groan that escaped from Scott's lips only encouraged me to work harder until he sat up and rolled me over like I was his wrestling partner.

"I want to be inside you when I cum," he said. "I want us to be *together*."

My legs quivered as he kissed my neck and chest, his erection touching the areas he had just excited with his tongue.

He looked down at me as if asking one last time for permission.

"Do it," I said with conviction. "I can't wait any longer."

When he entered me, my insides embraced him with a craving so strong I nearly lost my mind. He moved his hips back and forth, his powerful arms holding my body steady, his hypnotic blue eyes pinning me in place. That same tingling sensation resurged, ready to gush. Scott moved faster, tempting my inner tissue to reach higher peaks. I thought my head might explode, filling the air with a burst of colorful confetti. If it did, I didn't care. What a way to go.

I yelled for him, "Scott" as he continued to thrust his hips. Like strains of DNA, our bodies and our souls intertwined.

"Fuck. You feel good." He climaxed a second before I did— our grunts and moans creating their own heated conversations.

"Son of a bitch," he said with panting breath. "You're incredible."

Afterward, he cradled me in his arms and did something I never expected from him. He cried, but only for a second, like a cloudburst of emotion that cleared the way for the sun to reemerge. "All that shit that went down. I never thought I'd get this moment with you again." He kissed my forehead and then went into the bathroom where he ran the water for a few minutes. He returned a moment later, composed and smelling of mint toothpaste.

"No fair," I said. "Now, I've got to brush *my* teeth."

"As much as I want to keep the taste of you on my tongue, I figured *you* wouldn't, and I want more of those luscious lips of yours."

I pulled the covers back and swung my feet over the side of the bed.

Before I walked away, Scott took my hand and smiled, his radiant blue eyes ready for more nasty fun. "I'll give you a few minutes." He pulled me down for a succulent kiss. "Because we aren't done here."

I recalled his words from not long ago, "When that day does come, babe, you may not get out alive." *That* day had finally arrived, thank God, and I was ready for it. "Oh yeah." I pulled his lower lip back with my teeth. "I recall you saying I may not get out alive. We'll see who survives the day."

Scott chuckled and grabbed at me as I wrestled myself free to refresh my mouth. When I returned, he gave me a full-body massage, kissing every scrape and cut.

What we did next was more about playtime. We used our mouths and hands to excite and stimulate. Scott brought whipped cream into the mix, which added a fun twist. It wasn't long before my carnal urges had me mounting Scott where I controlled the rhythm and the pace.

"Don't move," I ordered.

"Yes, ma'am," Scott said, happy to comply.

I tipped my head back and savored the feeling of him inside of me, my hips moving up and down.

"You are sexy as hell," Scott said through panting breath. "I never want to forget this image of you—on top of me, using my dick for your pleasure. Ride it, babe."

And that was exactly what I did, uninhibited and mad for this man.

When our hearts settled down and while our impulses took a break, we did nothing but talk. We discussed the events of the past two days before we moved on to more pleasant things like where we'd spend the summer and how we'd handle living arrangements for the following year. I even mentioned Scott's father to see how he planned to handle that strained relationship.

Scott eased his head back and stared at me. "I'll talk to my dad. He can be a stubborn son of a bitch, but I'll give it my best shot."

When we made love again, I didn't climax quite the same, but I was glad for that. Once Scott had quenched my raging hormones, I was able to enjoy intimacy with him on another level. We both moved slowly and gently, our eyes fastened. When we orgasmed, it felt spiritual, like our souls were connecting in a way that went beyond physical attraction.

As the sun hid below the horizon, draping the frozen earth in a fresh layer of darkness, I lay in Scott's arms satisfied and relaxed.

"Do we *have* to go see Abigail?" Scott asked as he ran his fingers up and down my back.

I sighed. "Yeah. I can't get out of that one. But we can pick up where we left off when we get back."

"Mmmm." Scott purred in my ear. "I like the sound of that. I need to eat, though. You've drained all my energy, woman."

He looked into my eyes, his thumb caressing my cheek. "Are those ghosts gone? I did my best to chase them away."

"You did, handsome." I chewed my lower lip, a moment of doubt tugging on my confidence. "Rick may not be gone forever, and I still may see signs of him."

Scott rested his forehead against mine. "When and if that happens, I'll be here to run him off. Every time."

Letting that promise cleanse my soul, I took a deep breath and released it. Like the wind cresting over a mountain top, I felt free—free of guilt, free of shame, free of blame—just free. I still had work to do, but the shackles that were holding me back were off. No one controlled me anymore, no one except me.

Reviews ...

If you liked *Revive*, I'd be grateful if you would leave me a review on Amazon, Goodreads, or BookBub (no spoilers, please). For indie authors, reviews are immensely important.

About the Author

Since she was a little girl, award-winning author Tricia T. LaRochelle has been obsessed with tragic love stories. No rom-coms for her. Bring on the grit with a double side of turmoil. She likes to *feel* the character's anguish as they fight to overcome obstacles to be together. Growing up in central Vermont, she has seen her share of tragedy but remains a hopeful romantic. She now lives in central Virginia where she continues to foster the possibilities of how love can conquer all.

Revive is the second book in the *SARA BROWNE SERIES* and received an honorable mention for romance in the 2022 Incipere Awards, *Flickering Heart* winning first place in the same category.

Stay tuned for updates and announcements on Facebook, Instagram, and Twitter, or sign up for her newsletter at www. TriciaLaRochelle.com.

Also by Tricia T. LaRochelle

Sara Browne Series Romantic Suspense:

Flickering Heart - Book 1

Revive - Book 2

Handfast - Book 3

Bleeding Heart - A Holiday Romance - Book 4

Stand alone Contemporary Romances:

Sun in My Heart

Coming soon ... A Collision with Love

Acknowledgments

I never thought I'd get here. Somebody pinch me!

Both *Flickering Heart* and *Revive* waited years to emerge onto the literary stage. Once *Flickering Heart* launched, I knew *Revive* had to follow close behind. Both books support and complete a crucial journey for my main protagonist, Sara Browne, and both books need each other as much as Scott and Sara do.

And if you are looking for a stand-alone novel packed with emotion, *Sun in My Heart* is out, a contemporary romance with a twist.

Some of the same people who helped me with *Flickering Heart* returned to support *Revive*. My beta readers Olga Jackson and Melissa Shelton Harrison did a superb job pointing out any cracks in the plot's foundation as well as areas needing a little extra patchwork.

Debra Dynes was not only an excellent proofreader but also provided great observations about the storyline.

To my ARC proofers, Ryan LaRochelle, Hattie Firebaugh, Bob LaRochelle, Kim Catanzarite, and Cheri Gravett, I am forever grateful for your keen eye.

My cover designer, Anjanee, from 17 Studio Book Design, thank you for your patience and your ability to find the best images to represent both *Flickering Heart* and *Revive*.

Maddee James and her team at Xuni.com worked effortlessly on my website to support the growing needs of my writing and editing career.

Acclaimed actress Anne Tolpegin's performance in the Audible version of *Flickering Heart* and *Sun in My Heart* was beyond impressive. I am thrilled to announce she is back to portray Sara Browne once again in *Revive*. Look for the Audible version coming soon.

As I've said before, it takes a small village to pull something like this together. Hattie, Ryan, Sean, Cheri, and my husband, Bob, have offered continuous encouragement that literally kept me going when I doubted myself.

After the launch of *Flickering Heart*, so many people showed their support through social media and grassroots' efforts. Especially my sister Mary Tousginant, friends Cheri Gravett, Tammy Pariseau, and Kim Catanzarite, who went above and beyond for me. I will never forget it. To Craig Allen Heath, Noreen McCarten, Art Kerns, Liz Kracht, Chantal Bigras, Jeanne Pennington, Jeannie de Vries, Lee Adams, Terry Martin, Lisa Fincher, Callaghan Grant, and those fabulous book bloggers, I am also forever grateful.

My husband, Bob, has always had a front-row seat to the grueling and rather insane process of writing and publishing. He's never doubted my skills and always encouraged me to keep going, proving once again, I sure married the right guy.

www.ingramcontent.com/pod-product-compliance
Lightning Source LLC
Chambersburg PA
CBHW021212310726
48971CB00006B/1540